The Forsaken

Echoes from the Past

Book 4

by Irina Shapiro

Copyright

Contents

Prologue

She wasn't frightened at first. The twitches in her belly seemed insignificant, like the rumbling of distant thunder, and the shortness of breath and nausea had been her constant companions for several weeks. It wasn't until that first sharp pain that she began to worry, wondering if something might be truly wrong. She tried to sit up, desperate to pull apart the bed hangings and allow some light into the dim confines of the bed, but another pain sliced through her, forcing her back down and pinning her to the mattress. She rolled onto her side and brought her knees up to her chest, praying for the pain to stop, but it didn't. Waves of nausea and dizziness rolled over her as the spasms in her womb intensified, no longer rumbles of thunder, but sharp, jagged bolts of lightning. Her extremities began to numb, as her vision blurred and her hearing faded out. She tried to call for help, but her cry was like the whimper of a newborn kitten.

"Dear God, please, no," she prayed as hot, sticky blood began to flow between her legs, her womb mercilessly forcing the baby out. Somewhere deep inside she'd known that this could never be. She owed God a debt and He'd come to collect, with interest. He wouldn't allow a sinner like her to taste such joy. God was vengeful, and He was cruel, and in her time of need He had forsaken her.

She began to tremble violently as her breath came in short gasps, no longer seeing the darkness of her curtained world. What she saw were the faces of those she'd loved, floating before her like wispy clouds before the moon.

As she lay in a pool of her own blood, and life drained from her battered body, she had one final thought:

I've been murdered.

Chapter 1

July 2014

London, England

The morning had been beautiful, with abundant sunshine streaming through the uncurtained window, but by the afternoon, the sun had disappeared, giving way to ominous clouds and steady rain. Quinn came awake slowly, her mind returning from that other realm with difficulty. She listened intently, but heard nothing from the other room. Gabe and Emma must have gone out while she was sleeping.

Quinn burrowed deeper under the covers. There was no reason to get up—not yet. She still felt tired since the brief kip wasn't enough to make up for weeks of sleepless nights. She'd returned from New Orleans over two months ago, but still the nightmares persisted, the horror of those hours she'd spent locked in a tomb replaying in her mind with terrifying clarity. Once Quinn woke from the nightmares, shaking, sweating, and gasping for air, she could never go back to sleep, and wound up spending the wee hours of the morning watching television or reading—anything to get her mind off the images preying on her mind.

She felt safe here, in the London flat, but it wouldn't be theirs for much longer. As soon as Gabe found a job in Northumberland, they'd list the flat with an estate agent. The plan was to move to Berwick-upon-Tweed by the end of the summer, so that Emma could start school in their new neighborhood. Quinn had always assumed they would make their home in London once they were married, but life had its own plan, as usual. Gabe's father had passed away in May, leaving his elderly wife alone in the rambling mansion that had been in Gabe's family for generations. Phoebe Russell needed help managing the estate, but more than that, she needed company, or she would follow her husband sooner rather than later. Doing the church flowers and hosting book club meetings simply wasn't enough to keep her going in the face of grief and loneliness.

Quinn didn't relish the idea of moving to Berwick, but she could hardly refuse, especially since she genuinely liked Phoebe and wanted to help, and had accepted Gabe's decision with good grace. Her work commitments were finished for the moment. Quinn had submitted all her research files and footage to Rhys Morgan, but the third episode of *Echoes from the Past* had yet to be filmed. She was free to rest until Rhys presented her with the next mystery, and he was still on the hunt for a storyline that made for compelling television. The series had originally been contracted for three episodes, but the BBC had already commissioned a second series, confident that the program would be a success.

Quinn had yet to sign the new contract. She'd been dead set against agreeing to another series, but after what had happened in New Orleans, she was no longer sure she meant to refuse the offer. The truth was often painful, but it had to be told, especially since those whose lives had been affected were no longer in the position to tell their own stories. Quinn's ancestor, Madeline Besson, from whom Quinn had inherited her psychic gift, now rested in St. Louis No. 1 cemetery in New Orleans, interred next to her parents, Charles and Corinne Besson. Madeline had been erased from history by those who didn't want her true heritage to be revealed, but Quinn had been able to give Madeline a voice once more, and to add her name to the Besson family tree, but not without nearly paying a terrible price.

Quinn still experienced a stab of pain every time she allowed her thoughts to stray to Brett, the half-brother who'd fooled her so thoroughly into liking and trusting him. Brett was now serving a ten-year sentence in a Louisiana prison for the attempted murder of Dr. Quinn Allenby and her unborn child. Mercifully, Brett had accepted a plea bargain, making it unnecessary for Quinn to return to New Orleans to testify at his trial. Brett hadn't taken the deal to spare her, but to get a reduced sentence for himself, but Quinn was grateful nonetheless since she wished she could erase those few days from memory and going over them in court would have been incredibly painful.

She was also hesitant to see Seth again. Her biological father was irrevocably broken, as was his ex-wife Kathy. Their grief had brought them together, but no amount of emotional support could make up for what Brett had done to his pregnant sister in his desperation to bury the truth he couldn't bear to come to light. The Bessons were descended from a slave woman from Trinidad whose granddaughter had unwittingly married her white half-brother and produced Madeline, the beautiful girl with a psychic gift passed along from her mother's people.

Quinn exhaled loudly in irritation. She didn't want to think about Brett again. It was enough that he haunted her dreams; she wouldn't allow him to dominate her waking hours as well. She had her baby to think about. The high blood pressure, swelling of her extremities, and severe headaches that had plagued her in Louisiana had not improved upon returning home. If anything, they'd become worse. Quinn experienced shortness of breath, blurred vision, nausea and fatigue almost daily. She had been diagnosed with moderate to severe preeclampsia and had been prescribed blood pressure medication and advised plenty of rest. Quinn's obstetrician had strictly forbidden any physical activity, such as packing for their move, and stress was to be avoided as much as possible.

"Cup of tea?" Gabe asked, as he carefully opened the bedroom door. He held a steaming mug in his hand and set it carefully on the bedside table before giving Quinn a chaste kiss on the forehead.

"Where's Emma?" Quinn asked. "It's so quiet; I thought you two had gone out."

"She fell asleep on the sofa," Gabe replied. "We went to the park for an hour and then stopped by Bombay Palace to get a takeaway for dinner."

9

"Did you get me something totally bland and utterly tasteless?" Quinn joked.

"Of course. You know you're not allowed anything spicy or salty."

"Thank you. You're always looking out for me," Quinn said with a smile. She would love a curry, but she'd have to wait until after the baby was born to indulge. If she had it now, she'd have heartburn for hours and curse that damn curry the whole night, only to wake up to swollen ankles and a blinding headache. A nice, bland supper was just what the doctor ordered.

Quinn patted the space next to her, inviting Gabe to sit down. He got comfortable and rested his head against the headboard, closing his eyes. He looked tired and tense.

"Gabe, what's troubling you? And please, don't say 'nothing.' You've been short-tempered and withdrawn for days."

Gabe sighed. He seemed reluctant to talk, which wasn't like him. Normally, he was the one who wanted to talk things out and outline all possible solutions, but for the past few weeks he'd shied away from any serious conversations, changing the topic the moment anything stressful came up. He didn't want to distress her, she knew that, but whatever was on his mind wasn't going away and needed to be brought out into the open.

"Gabe, what's wrong?" Quinn asked again, determined to get an answer this time.

"Everything," Gabe replied, startling her with his vehemence.

"Surely not everything."

"No, not everything," he conceded with a guilty smile. "I just don't deal well with lack of control, is all."

"What is it you feel you can't control?" Quinn asked, although she suspected she already knew the answer.

10

"Quinn, we are due to move up north before the start of the fall term. That's less than two months from now. Truth is, every time I imagine myself back at the family home I suddenly feel as if I'm being buried alive. Sorry, I shouldn't have used that comparison, not after what you've been through."

Quinn reached over and took his hand in hers. "No, that's exactly the comparison you should have used, because now I'm in a unique position to understand what you're going through. Now, tell me why you feel so strongly about moving back."

"Quinn, I hate that house. I couldn't wait to leave for uni. I never went back, except to visit my parents. My life is in London, and has been for thirty years. And your life is here as well. I worry about you and the baby and I need to know that we have access to the best medical care England has to offer, and that's here, in London. And I worry about Emma as well. She's just beginning to settle into her new life. She's been happier these past few months, calmer. She's had fewer nightmares and has mentioned Jenna less often. She'll never fully recover from the death of her mother, but she's finally getting to a place where she can live with her loss. Uprooting her again might have repercussions. And then there's the financial cost of this move," Gabe added.

"We'll no longer have to pay two mortgages," Quinn said in an effort to make Gabe feel better.

"No, we won't, but we'll have to pay crippling death duties and spend a fortune on repairs. I had an inspector come out to the house last week. The roof needs replacing, there's dry rot, a large portion of the masonry is crumbling, and don't even get me started on the plumbing and electricity. Everything is in its original condition. I can hardly expect to address all these issues on a teacher's salary."

"What do you mean?"

"I've heard back from several schools up north. They're happy to have me, but only as an educator, and at a third of what I earn now."

Quinn studied Gabe's beloved face. He looked genuinely sad, and, for lack of a better word, evasive.

"What are you not telling me?" she asked.

"I've been offered the directorship of the institute," Gabe replied. "It comes with a hefty pay raise."

"That job is your dream come true," Quinn replied, finally understanding what had been eating at Gabe these past few days. He really would be sacrificing a lot to move back home to a place he had no desire to be. "Is there another option?"

Gabe shook his head. "Not that I can think of. My mother would never agree to leave her home. She's lived there for over fifty years, and I can't allow her to remain there on her own. It's too much for her."

"Gabe, there must be a solution. Surely your mother would understand, especially if you tell her about this opportunity."

"Yes, she would, which is why I can't tell her. She'll urge me to remain in London and do what's best for me, and I simply can't take her up on that with a clear conscience."

"Let me give this some thought," Quinn promised as Emma called out from the other room. "Emma is awake, and I'm starving."

"All right," Gabe agreed, but he still looked dejected.

Chapter 2

Quinn had just taken a forkful of her vegetable korma, which wasn't half bad, when Gabe's mobile began to vibrate. The rule was, no phones at the dinner table, but after Gabe glanced at the screen, he took the call, with an apologetic smile to Quinn. "It's my mother," he mouthed.

"Put her on speaker, I want to say hello," Quinn said. Putting Phoebe on speaker would ensure a much shorter conversation.

Gabe pressed the speaker button and Phoebe's voice flooded the kitchen.

"Hi, Mum. Are you all right?" Gabe asked. Phoebe rarely called in the evening. She called Gabe first thing in the morning when she woke up. She said it was her loneliest time, since every morning, for just a few moments, she forgot that her beloved Graham was gone, and turned to his side of the bed to say good morning. Each morning, she experienced her loss all over again, and needed to hear Gabe's voice to feel less alone in the world.

"No, I'm most definitely not all right."

"Are you ill?" Gabe demanded. "Do you need me to come?"

"I'm not ill, but I do need you to come," Phoebe replied. She sounded unusually jittery, her voice high and trembling with anxiety.

"Mum, what is it?"

"There's a body in the kitchen," Phoebe announced dramatically, as if she were in an Agatha Christie film.

"Whose body?" Gabe asked. "Is it Buster?" Buster was just a puppy, but he was the only other living creature in the house, and he might have had an accident.

"No!" Emma cried. She loved Buster and couldn't wait to claim him as her own once they moved.

"No, darling, Buster is fine," Phoebe reassured her. "Son, perhaps you should take me off speaker now. This conversation is not for Emma's ears."

"It's all right, Grandma Phoebe, I'm finished," Emma said and slid off her chair. "I'll go to my room."

Emma ran off, leaving Gabe and Quinn to stare at the phone.

"Mum?" Gabe prompted.

Phoebe took a shuddering breath. "The water in the kitchen sink wouldn't go down," she said. "I tried to pour that special liquid down the sink, but it didn't help. The water kept backing up, and it was brown and muddy."

"Go on," Gabe encouraged her. Phoebe had a habit of starting from afar. Very far.

"I called the plumber. Do you remember Peter Reed? Pamela's boy. You two went to primary school together."

"Yes, I remember Peter. Did he fix the sink?"

"Well, Peter said there was an obstruction, so he got this long metal rod and tried to push if through," Phoebe explained.

"Mum, is Peter lying on the kitchen floor as we speak?" Gabe asked.

"No, why would you think such a thing?"

"Because you said there's a body in the kitchen, and if it's not Buster, then who else can it be but Peter?" Gabe replied patiently.

"Now you're just being silly."

14

"Am I?"

"Of course. Peter left hours ago."

Gabe closed his eyes and took a deep breath, obviously praying for patience. "Mum, who is dead?"

"Well, I don't know, do I?"

"Well, I certainly don't," Gabe snapped.

"I would be happy to tell you if you'd stop interrupting me, Gabriel," Phoebe chastised him. "Where were we?"

"The long metal rod."

"Ah, yes. Well, Peter tried to clear the obstruction, but said it was much deeper than the rod could reach. He said that the pipe would need to be replaced. He had to break the kitchen floor to get to it." Phoebe exhaled loudly. "He made quite a hole. Much larger than was strictly necessary, if you ask me.".

"Did he find the problem?"

"Eventually. A tree root had grown through the pipe and caused a blockage. That's the tree just beyond the kitchen garden. It really is a lovely old thing," Phoebe went on. "I do love when it changes colors in the autumn. So beautiful. Your father loved that tree. Never wanted to prune the branches, not even when they started to bang against the window in the wind."

"Mum, the body," Gabe prompted gently.

"Right. Well, when Peter broke the floor and made the hole much wider than he should have, he saw it."

"Saw what?"

"The elbow."

"Whose elbow?"

"The body's elbow, Gabe. Pay attention."

Gabe looked like he was about to bang his head against the wall, but he took a steadying breath and summarized the situation in the most economical way possible. "So, Peter broke the kitchen floor and stumbled on a body. I'm assuming he called the police, who came and went, since if the burial was recent, they'd likely still be there, processing the crime scene. Given that the burial is not recent, these must be skeletal remains that you'd like me to excavate and remove from the kitchen. Am I correct?"

"Isn't that what I said?"

"Not quite."

"Well, it's what I meant. I refuse to use the kitchen until that thing has been removed. It's gruesome, son. The police unearthed enough of it to make coming into the kitchen simply out of the question."

"I'll leave tomorrow morning," Gabe promised. "Please don't disturb the grave any more than it has already been tampered with."

"I'm not touching anything. Haven't you heard me? I won't go into the kitchen."

"How will you manage?" Gabe asked, worried that his mother had declared a hunger strike, but Phoebe was too practical a woman for such nonsense.

"I'm going to stay with Cecily Creston-Jones for a few days."

"Mum, did Peter replace the pipe?"

"No, the police advised him not to touch anything until they've had a chance to examine the scene."

"Did he turn the water off in the entire house?" Gabe asked.

"No, just the kitchen. There's clean water in the upstairs bath."

"All right. Good."

"Why? What does it matter?" Phoebe asked.

"It matters because it takes time to excavate a burial site properly, and I will need water if I'm to stay at the house."

"You?" Quinn asked. "Don't you mean 'we'?"

Gabe's eyebrows rose unnaturally high in surprise, but he finished the phone call with his mother before addressing Quinn's comment. "If you think, for just one moment, that you will be working in the kitchen with me, you have another think coming, Mrs. Russell. You can come with me, if you wish, but you will march upstairs on arrival and rest, as per doctor's orders, while I deal with the situation in the kitchen."

"Like hell I will," Quinn retorted.

Gabe folded his arms and stared her down until Quinn conceded.

"All right, I will not do any physical excavating, but I will not be sent to my room like a child. I will assist you in spirit."

"Fine," Gabe agreed. "It was worth a try."

"What about Emma? Should we ask Sylvia to mind her for a few days?"

Gabe shook his head. "No, not after what happened last time."

"But it was a misunderstanding, and Emma loves spending time with Logan and Jude. Besides, she might be frightened by the skeleton."

"Quinn, with us as parents, she will have to deal with human remains soon enough. She's coming with us. We'll just keep her out of the kitchen."

"Deal," Quinn agreed and smiled broadly.

"You're excited about this, aren't you?" Gabe asked, grinning back at her.

"You know something, I really am. Nothing cheers me up as much as unearthing a skeleton."

"Me too," Gabe confessed. "This should be interesting."

"I'm just glad to know that I'm not the only one with skeletons in the cupboard," Quinn joked.

Chapter 3

July 2014

Berwick-upon-Tweed, Northumberland

Quinn had never particularly liked the manor house, but today, after only one day of standing vacant, it looked forbidding and sinister. Some might think her fanciful, but she knew that buildings, like people, had their own moods, and the manor wasn't pleased with having its secrets unearthed.

Gabe went in first, and when he opened the door with his key, the house seemed to almost suck in its breath. Gabe stopped on the threshold and stood still for a moment, as though he felt it too, but he would never say it aloud. Gabe wasn't one to give in to such superstitious nonsense.

"Come on in," Gabe called to Quinn and Emma, who were dawdling on the steps.

"Where's Buster?" Emma whined. She looked around as if she expected the puppy to come bounding toward her, but the place was clearly deserted.

"I expect Grandma Phoebe took Buster with her," Gabe explained. "She couldn't leave him here all alone."

"He would guard the place," Emma replied. "He's fierce."

Gabe tried to mask his chuckle with a cough. Buster was about as fierce as a newborn chick. "I'll call Mum and let her know we're here," he said as he carried their bags into the hall.

Quinn went up to the bedroom they'd stayed in when visiting her in-laws. She smiled as she passed Gabe's old room. Old posters hung on the walls, and every surface was covered with books, maps, and construction sets. The preserved teenager's room was a silent tribute to the boy Gabe had been, and a glimpse into Phoebe's nostalgia.

Gabe followed Quinn with the bags. He deposited Emma's case in the small bedroom next to theirs, where she'd slept before. The room must have been a dressing room at one time, but had been converted to a bedroom once such extravagances went out of fashion. Emma liked having her own room, but needed to know that Quinn and Gabe were next door and she could call out to them if she woke up during the night or wanted a cuddle in the morning.

Quinn opened Emma's case, extracted her pajamas and Mr. Rabbit, and put her toothbrush, hairbrush, and strawberry-scented shampoo in the bathroom. Emma stood in the doorway, looking disgruntled. She'd looked forward to seeing Buster, and was sorely disappointed.

"Hello," Phoebe called from downstairs. "Emma, darling, I'm back."

A happy bark followed, and Emma thudded down the stairs to say hello to Phoebe and her beloved pup. Quinn followed at a much slower pace.

"You are glowing," Phoebe said as she kissed Quinn on both cheeks. "How's my grandson?"

"It might be a granddaughter," Quinn answered with a grin. They'd had this conversation several times before, but Phoebe was sticking to her guns.

"It might be, but it isn't." Phoebe laid a hand on Quinn's rounded belly. "Ooh, I can feel his bum."

"How do you know it's his bum?" Quinn asked, curious. She frequently felt her stomach, but couldn't really tell what was what just yet.

"Because if it was his head, it'd be much harder. Russell men are notoriously hard-headed, or haven't you noticed?" Phoebe laughed.

"I heard that," Gabe called out from above.

Phoebe chuckled. "They have excellent hearing too, but only when it suits their purpose. Ask them to change a lightbulb or rake the leaves, and they go deaf in both ears."

"Have you come back to stay?" Quinn asked.

Phoebe shook her head. "No, dear. I can't remain in this house until that thing is removed. I know it's silly, but for some reason I find it very unsettling. And my friend Cecily has a very comfortable cottage with several guest bedrooms. Perhaps Emma should stay with me until you've finished."

"Yes, please," Emma said as she danced around Phoebe. "I want to be where Buster is."

"I think that's an excellent idea," Gabe said as he came down the stairs. "Cecily Creston-Jones is lovely, and I believe she has a puppy of her own—a Yorkie called Bertie. You'll be in dog heaven, Em."

"It's all right with me," Quinn agreed. Emma was too young to be present at an excavation of a skeleton, especially when it was in the kitchen.

"We'll make a start tomorrow," Gabe said. "Tonight, I'm taking everyone to dinner, including Cecily, to a restaurant of your choice. You decide amongst yourselves while I take a look at the 'lodger' in the kitchen."

"I want pizza," Emma exclaimed. "And ice cream."

"Of course you do, love," Phoebe said, smiling. "You always want pizza and ice cream."

"Don't you like pizza?" Emma asked her grandmother, as though suddenly realizing that not everyone might like what she likes.

"I do, but not as much as you do. How about dinner at the pub?" Phoebe asked Emma. "This way we can all get what we want."

"All right," Emma answered, shrugging. "Whatever." She enunciated the word, making it sound like an insult.

"Is that attitude I sense?" Phoebe asked Quinn as Emma ran after Buster.

Quinn sighed. "Some days I think she's already a teenager. By the way, Phoebe, Emma's birthday is in August, and we'd like to have a party for her. Perhaps we can do something really special, since it's her first birthday without her mum and she'll be feeling sad. I hope you'll come."

"That sounds like a good idea. I wouldn't miss it. If you need any help planning, count me in. I feel so restless since Graham died. I don't know what to do with my time."

"What did you do before?" Quinn asked.

"I made him breakfast, lunch, and tea. I bullied him into taking daily walks, and sometimes we watched television in the evenings. I didn't like the programs he enjoyed, but it was nice to spend time together—companionable. I'm busy enough during the day, but once it gets dark, the house feels so empty," Phoebe complained.

"It must be very difficult to lose your companion of so many years. My grandmother never got over my grandfather's death. She always spoke of him as if he were about to return. To her, he was still there, in the room, in her heart. Her Joe was looking after her, and she smiled as she died, knowing she would see him again."

"Do you think she did?" Phoebe asked.

"I'd like to think so, but the more logical part of my brain says that it's not very likely."

"I'd like to see Graham again, if only to give him a piece of my mind," Phoebe said. "How could he leave me like that?"

Quinn saw the tears and wrapped her arm about the older woman. "He didn't leave you, Phoebe. He was taken. He would have never left you. He adored you."

Phoebe sniffed loudly. "Would have been nice if he said so from time to time."

"He didn't need to. It was right there for everyone to see."

Phoebe nodded. "I know he did. I loved him too. I hadn't realized how much until he was gone. You and Gabe, don't ever take each other for granted. He adores you too, you know." Phoebe looked squarely at Quinn. "Don't ever hurt him, Quinn."

"I won't."

Phoebe nodded and walked away, going to see what Emma and Buster were up to. Quinn looked after her for a long moment. Why would Phoebe think she'd hurt Gabe?

Chapter 4

The following morning, with Emma safely out of the way, Gabe and Quinn made their way down to the kitchen, tools of their trade in hand. The hole in the floor wasn't as large as Quinn had expected, nor was it possible to see the complete skeleton. She supposed the coroner had seen enough to declare it a non-recent burial and left it at that. It would take several days to fully unearth the remains and label and bag all the bones and artefacts found with the body. Quinn settled herself in a kitchen chair with a cup of tea while Gabe went to work. He would use a trowel and brushes once he got closer to the actual bones, but for the moment, he had to remove the portion of the floor that still covered the grave and the layer of earth on top of the skelly.

"Are you sure I can't help?" Quinn asked as she peered into the dank hole.

"Positive," Gabe replied as he reached for a crowbar, sporting the look of a man determined to leave no tile intact. "You can make me a cuppa," he added with a smile. "Demolition is thirsty work. And after you make the tea, you should go take a walk. It's a beautiful day out, and you can use a bit of fresh air and exercise after sitting in the car all day yesterday."

"Yes, Dr. Russell," Quinn replied with a chuckle. Gabe really was becoming a dictator since the incident in New Orleans, but she secretly liked it. He did it because he loved her and their baby, and worried about them incessantly, although, at times, his high-and-mighty attitude grated on her nerves. "All right, I will take a walk before lunch, but for now, I will sit here and ooze moral support."

"Don't ooze too hard. I have hours to go before I get to anything even remotely interesting."

Quinn took a walk, as promised, and then had a lovely nap before returning downstairs in time for dinner. She couldn't cook anything, since the kitchen was out of bounds, but Cecily had invited them to dinner at her cottage as a thank you for taking her out the night before, and they both missed Emma. Gabe was shoulder-deep in the kitchen floor, his tools laid out on the remaining tiles at the edge of the opening. Quinn could see the gleam of bone as he used a brush to clear dirt from the skull. Most of the skeleton was already exposed, including the folded hands clasped around the hilt of a sword.

"A warrior," Quinn said as she bent to get a closer look. "An ancestor of yours?"

Gabe shrugged. "I don't know. Might be. He must have been very young, a teenager perhaps."

Quinn nodded in agreement. The skull didn't appear to be that of a grown man and the wrist bones indicated that he had been quite delicate. "I can't imagine someone with such fragile hands wielding that sword."

Gabe carefully extracted the sword. "It's not as heavy as you might think. It's a common misconception that medieval swords were weighty and cumbersome, but in truth, they were rather elegant and weighed no more than four pounds, on average."

"Let me see." Quinn pulled on cotton gloves and held out her hands. Whatever story the sword had to tell, she wasn't ready to hear it now.

Gabe passed her the sword. He was right, it wasn't as heavy as it had first appeared to be, and looked to be a fine piece of craftsmanship. This was a sword made for a warrior, a prized possession and a family heirloom. The hilt appeared too thick to fit into the hand that lay exposed in the dirt, but perhaps this boy had inherited his father's sword and had taken it into battle to honor the fallen.

"Do you think the skelly might be a squire?" Quinn asked, but Gabe shook his head.

"Why would a squire be buried with his master's sword beneath the kitchen floor? Doesn't make sense."

"No, it doesn't. A son, perhaps?"

"That's more likely, but why bury him here instead of in consecrated ground?"

"How long do you think he's been there?" Quinn asked. If the sword was anything to go on—centuries.

"If he was buried before the new house was built, then definitely several centuries. If he was buried after the new house went up, then considerably less. Just because he's holding a sword doesn't mean the sword belonged to him. Perhaps it was an antique that he was particularly fond of and wished to be buried with," Gabe speculated.

"Is there anything else?" Quinn carefully set the sword on the kitchen table and peered into the hole.

"Yes, actually. Because the grave was concealed beneath the floor, less moisture permeated the ground, since it wasn't exposed to the elements. There are bits of fabric, shriveled-up leather, strands of hair, and this!"

Gabe held up a rosary. The amber beads glowed in the late afternoon light, the amber still translucent and not a bit damaged by centuries underground. The links were tarnished but intact, holding the beads together as they had done since the rosary had been crafted.

"The cross must be solid gold to have lasted all this time without oxidizing." Gabe used the bottom of his T-shirt to carefully rub away the dirt. The crucifix shone in the sunlight as if it were newly minted, the figure of Christ delicate and intricately rendered.

Quinn accepted the rosary from Gabe and held it up to the light. "It doesn't look like a man's rosary," she said, admiring the craftsmanship and the honey-gold glimmer of the amber.

"Men used prayer beads," Gabe argued. "It's an expensive one, to be sure, not the rosary of a peasant."

Quinn shook her head. "I see a woman using this rosary—a wealthy woman."

"Perhaps. The fabric looks like it might be velvet. Either a man or a woman could have worn velvet and leather."

"Any jewelry? That would tell us for sure before we even send the bones to Colin."

"I don't see any." Gabe set down his brush and climbed out of the hole. "I'll have to finish up tomorrow. It's getting late." He picked up the sword and held out his hand for the rosary. "I'm going to lock these in Dad's study."

"Are you afraid that I will sneak downstairs in the middle of the night to get a head start?" Quinn asked, annoyed that Gabe wanted to lock up the artefacts.

"The doctor said you must avoid stress. This"—Gabe held up the sword—"is not an object devoid of stress."

"Leave out the rosary then," Quinn insisted. "How distressing can a rosary be?"

Gabe's eyebrows shot up, making Quinn laugh. "Are you joking?"

"Gabe, come on, you know I won't rest until I know what happened to this boy. Please. I'll set the rosary aside if I start becoming upset."

"No, you won't."

"I promise," Quinn pleaded. She had to know more. Already she was involved, and she wouldn't rest until she found out what had happened to this poor boy and how he had come to be buried beneath the kitchen floor with an object of war and a symbol of faith.

"I will let you have the rosary on one condition," Gabe said, eyeing her suspiciously.

"Which is?"

"You will only handle it in front of me, and if I see you getting worked up, I will take it from you. Agreed?"

"Dictator!"

"I prefer 'loving husband'," Gabe replied with a charming smile.

"All right. Agreed."

Chapter 5

Quinn woke up with a start. Moonlight streaming through the net curtains silvered everything in its path, including Gabe, who appeared almost otherworldly in its glow. The house was quiet, or as quiet as a centuries-old house could be when it creaked and groaned like an old man complaining about his aching joints.

She lay still and tried to calm her racing heart. She'd had the dream again. She was locked in the Talbot vault, and Brett Besson was taunting her through the locked door, condemning her and her baby to death. She knew her fear was irrational, but the darkness of the night contributed to the feeling of being buried alive. The beam of moonlight reminded her of the flashlight she'd used to illuminate the tomb and shine a light on Madeline's remains.

Quinn slid out of bed and padded to the door, careful not to wake Gabe. A small smile tugged at his lips, and his dark lashes rested against his lean cheeks as he slumbered on, worn out by hours of digging.

She belted her dressing gown and made her way downstairs. The ground floor was much darker than the bedroom, since the corridor had no windows, and the doors to the various rooms were firmly shut. Quinn felt her way along the passage until she found the door she was looking for—Graham's study. In centuries past, the study had been the heart of the estate, the room where all important decisions were taken and every farthing of estate funds flowed through. During Graham's time, it had been a room in which to smoke a cigar while sorting through outstanding invoices or read a fishing magazine. Graham Russell hadn't been much of a fisherman, but he'd subscribed to several fishing magazines, particularly ones dealing with fly fishing in Scotland, and pored over them endlessly, probably more to get away from his bossy wife than because he was planning a fishing expedition.

Quinn crossed the room and sat down in the old studded leather chair. It was a man's chair: hard-backed, solid, and uncomfortably firm. The two items from the grave rested on the desk. She'd promised Gabe she wouldn't touch them until they could do it together, but she was sleepless and frightened by her dream. And the artefacts beckoned to her. She had realized something when she'd discovered Madeline's remains in New Orleans. As much as she hated her psychic gift, she wouldn't give it up if she got the chance. Her ability took her on an emotional journey, and often left her heartbroken and trembling with rage at the injustice of the victim's fate, but it also gave her an opportunity to speak for the forgotten and the forsaken, and to give them a voice and a name once again.

Quinn studied the sword and the rosary, and opted to start with the sword. The rosary was small and delicate, and easily transported and stored, but she wouldn't dare leave the sword lying around, not with a curious little monkey like Emma in the house. It would be too dangerous, unless they purchased a lockable container long enough to accommodate the sword. The weapon weighed about four pounds, as Gabe had surmised earlier and later confirmed by weighing it on Phoebe's bathroom scale, and was approximately three feet long. It was a longsword with a cruciform hilt made for double-handed use. The steel blade, surprisingly uncorroded by time, glinted in the moonlight, reminding Quinn that it had probably claimed its share of lives and limbs. There had probably been an intricately patterned and possibly bejeweled scabbard that came with the sword, but there was no sign of it in the grave. The sword had been unsheathed, as it would have been when ready for battle. Whoever the young man had been, he'd been a warrior, and had been buried like one, even if his grave had been kept secret by those who interred him.

Quinn gingerly ran her fingers along the crossbar of the sword. The pattern was worn, but she felt the etching and the shape of the cool multi-faceted gem that adorned the center. The stone, the size of a pound coin, was a deep smoky blue, most likely a sapphire. This was not the sword of a foot soldier. It must have belonged to someone of consequence, someone who held a place in history, even if his name had been long forgotten. Quinn felt a tremor as the steel began to divulge its memories, taking her to a bloody battlefield.

Chapter 6

March 1461

Towton, Yorkshire

Guy's sense of smell was the first to reassert itself, which was unfortunate since the stink of blood, shit, sweat, and death was overwhelming despite the cold. The storm had raged all through the battle, from morning until well into the night. The snow and sleet had come down in sheets, blinding the soldiers and at times immobilizing them for what had seemed like hours, when in fact it had only been minutes.

The carnage was unprecedented. Guy had seen his share of battles, but he'd never seen anything that came close to what he'd witnessed this day. The dead and dying were piled so high the knights couldn't get around them, or lift their armor-clad legs enough to step over the fallen. The men were exhausted, not only from fighting but from battling the elements. Countless men had drowned as they tried to flee the battlefield, driven into the river by the pursuing enemy. The water had run red for hours, the scene reminiscent of a Biblical plague. It should have been an easy victory. How had it all gone so wrong?

With the army of the House of York vastly outnumbered by the Lancastrians, the outcome of the battle had been almost certain, until God had made His will known this Palm Sunday. Harnessing the power of the wind, the Yorkists had shot their arrows further and faster than the Lancastrians, whose own arrows were blown off course and fell at the feet of the Yorkist archers. The whoresons had actually used Lancastrian arrows against them, picking them up as they fell and turning them on the men who'd loosed them. And then the Yorkist reinforcements had arrived, with the Duke of Norfolk leading the charge. The Lancastrian army had been routed, leaving absolutely no doubt as to who won the day.

For a moment, Guy thought he must have died, since he could no longer hear the clash of steel or the screams of dying men and horses, but there was an almighty roar. The battle was over, so the roar had to be in his head. It throbbed and ached so badly he couldn't even open his eyes, which were nearly frozen shut from the sleet that had penetrated his visor. No, if he were dead, he wouldn't be this cold, or feel such searing pain. He was still among the living, if only just.

Guy tried to move his legs. They appeared to be pinned down by something heavy, likely a corpse, but were both still functional. His left arm felt numb, but his right arm was as heavy as a fallen log and the pain that gripped his upper arm when he tried to move it was so severe he nearly passed out again. He must have blacked out when he was wounded, but if he allowed himself to lose consciousness now, he'd be mistaken for one of the dead and left untended. It would take him hours, possibly even days, to finally die of his injuries or the brutal cold that turned his armor into an icy metal shell. Guy's mind ordered him to throw the dead weight of the corpse off his legs and rise, but his body wouldn't comply. He couldn't seem to find the strength to do anything but lie there like carrion, waiting to be pecked at by crows until he really was blind.

Opening his eyes took some doing since he couldn't use his hands to thaw the ice that had formed on his lids. Guy's vision was blurred and a wave of nausea threatened to turn his guts inside out. He turned his head just in time to retch into the blood-stained snow. There wasn't much in his stomach; he hadn't eaten anything since yesterday morning. He'd had some broth and bread to break his fast, but his body had burned through the meager meal by the time he was clad in his armor and in the saddle, ready for battle. And it had to be morning now, since the sky was just beginning to lighten, and the fury of the storm had abated, leaving behind an eerie calm broken only by the moans of the dying and the cawing of crows gleefully enjoying their gruesome breakfast.

Guy accidentally moved his arm and agonizing pain shot through his entire right side, making him cry out.

"Guy, thank Jesu," a voice from somewhere above him exclaimed. It pronounced Guy as *Ghee*, the way his French mother had. Few people called him that, so even though Guy couldn't quite make out Hugh's face, he knew it was his older brother bending over him. "Are you badly hurt?"

Guy had every intention of denying his injury, but when he tried to speak, agony laced his voice and he exhaled painfully. "Yes."

"Stay here. I'm going for help."

That nearly made Guy laugh. As if he could just get up and walk away. He was fairly certain his armor was frozen to the ground and even if it weren't for his injury, to so much as roll onto his side he'd struggle like a turtle that'd been flipped on its back.

"Is it over?" he mumbled.

"It is," Hugh replied.

His brother's grim expression told Guy everything he needed to know. He hadn't missed a last-minute miracle while he was unconscious. The Lancastrians had been trounced, and many of their comrades were either severely wounded, lying dead on this Godforsaken field, or rested on the riverbed, weighed down by their armor as the rushing water flowed over them as if they were nothing more than boulders. The grim thought made Guy sick again. He unwittingly leaned on his wounded arm to retch and the pain rendered him senseless, which at that moment was a blessing.

When he opened his eyes again it was very bright. A hazy winter sun glowed through the bare branches of a tree, its limbs black against the colorless sky. Beside him, Walter sat with his back against the massive trunk. The boy was fast asleep, his dirty cheek pressed against the leather of his doublet. Guy carefully reached out and pulled on Walter's sleeve. The boy came awake with a start and scrambled to his feet, as though ashamed at having nodded off.

"I'm thirsty, Walter," Guy whispered.

34

"Of course, sir. Right away, sir," Walter mumbled as he fetched a skin of wine and held it to Guy's lips.

Guy took a few sips and pushed it aside with his good hand. "Where's Hugh?" he croaked.

"He went to look for your brother, sir," Walter replied, a mournful expression on his face. He was only fifteen and hadn't yet learned the art of hiding his feelings.

"Did William fall in battle?" Guy asked.

Walter nodded miserably. "He never came back. I'm sorry, sir. Is there anything I can do to make you more comfortable?"

"You can take off my armor," Guy replied. His voice was barely audible and he felt sick and dizzy again. His armor weighed a ton and he could barely move.

"I have," Walter replied, clearly confused. "It's just there." Walter pointed to a pile of metal stacked to his left. Guy's sword rested alongside his breastplate, which glinted in the sun and appeared to have been cleaned of blood and gore.

Guy carefully raised his left hand and touched his head. Sure enough, his helmet wasn't there, but his head felt as if it were locked in a vise and was too heavy to lift. He moved his hand lower. Walter had removed what he could, but Guy was still wearing chainmail.

"I'm sorry, sir, but I will need help with the chainmail," Walter explained. "You're too heavy to lift and your arm is badly injured."

"What happened to my head?" Guy whispered.

"You took a mace to the head. I saw it myself. I had a devil of a time getting your helmet off. It's badly dented," Walter added. "I thought you were done for."

"I think I still might be," Guy rasped. He was going for humor, but sounded pathetic and filled with self-pity.

"You will recover, sir. I know you will," Walter sputtered. "I will look after you." The boy's wide blue eyes looked earnest in his freckled face. Walter was pale, the dark circles beneath his eyes a testament to exhaustion and hunger, and suffering. He'd seen too much for a lad his age, and would need time to come to terms with the slaughter he'd witnessed. Likely, he never would.

Guy felt a wave of affection for the boy. He was too young and sensitive to be a squire, but it was Walter's most sacred dream to become a knight, and he had been in the service of the de Rosels since he was eight years of age, as was the custom. He came from a good family, but his father, Lord Elliott, had died shortly after Walter was born, leaving his mother with seven children to raise, six of them girls. Lady Elliott had hated to part with her son, but understood the importance of having the boy properly placed in order to assure his training and future. Walter took his duties seriously and had nearly burst with pride when he was finally elevated from page to squire.

Guy's eyes slid to the left when he heard someone approaching. Hugh's face appeared above him again. Even in the bright light of day his skin looked ashen.

"William is dead, Guy. I'll need to find a wagon to bring you both home."

"What happened to Somerset?" Guy asked. Henry Beaufort, the Duke of Somerset, was not only the acting commander of the Lancastrian army in King Henry's absence, but also something of a friend and mentor to the de Rosels, despite his exulted rank. No soldier could match Somerset for bravery on the battlefield, and only the Earl of Warwick, Somerset's Yorkist counterpart, could be credited with the sort of military prowess and cunning that made Somerset a force to be reckoned with.

"Somerset escaped. Trollope and Northumberland fell," Hugh replied curtly. "Walter, see to your master. I will be back presently. I must have a word with Stanwyck."

"Yes, sir," Walter replied timidly.

Guy closed his eyes as silent tears slid down his temples and into his hair. William was dead. His oldest brother, who had been more like a father to him since the deaths of their parents, was gone, and now Eleanor was widowed. She'd suffered a stillbirth only two months since, and now she'd lost the husband she adored, and their son Adam had lost his father. The boy was only four, and likely wouldn't remember William once he reached adulthood. Guy barely remembered his own mother, who had died in childbirth when he was nearly six. The child never drew breath and had been buried with their mother on a beautiful spring day, a day so lovely and bursting with the promise of summer that Guy had only wanted to run and play and not stand with his head bowed as his mother was laid to rest. Their father had died a few years later of a fever that had burned hot and bright and took him in less than a week, leaving the de Rosel children orphaned, but not alone.

As had been previously agreed upon, John Ambrose, the Earl of Stanwyck, a great nobleman who'd had an affection for their father from the days of their youth, had become their patron. William, the new Baron de Rosel, and Hugh had already been in his service, William as a squire and Hugh as a page. Guy was taken on as a page and then elevated to squire after the required seven years of training. The brothers had squired for the earl until their knighting at the age of twenty-two.

Having been raised and fostered by the supporters of the House of Lancaster, the de Rosels had always pledged their allegiance to King Henry VI and his lady, Margaret of Anjou, and their French heritage had contributed to their loyalty to the French queen. There had never been any question about which side they'd fight on when the conflict between the houses of Lancaster and York escalated into open warfare with the ultimate prize being the throne of England. And now the Duke of Northumberland was dead, as were Sir Andrew Trollope and Lord Clifford, who had died before the battle of Towton during the retreat from Ferrybridge. The Lancastrian army was in disarray, as was their cause.

Guy tried to remain alert, but physical pain and emotional turmoil left him disoriented and confused. He fell into a restless sleep, plagued by nightmares of a never-ending battle in which he fell again and again, only to rise, bloodied and battered, to fight on, driven toward the river by his Yorkist foes. At the riverbank, the ground became slippery and uneven. He cried out in frustration as he lost his balance and tumbled backward into the icy river, the rushing water stealing his breath and pulling him down. He sank like a stone, his lungs burning, until his armor-clad body settled on the slimy bottom.

By the time Guy woke from his nightmare, Hugh had returned and sat on the ground next to Walter, exhaling loudly as he leaned against the tree trunk.

"Were you able to find a wagon, sir?" Walter asked.

Hugh nodded. "It's more of a rickety cart than a wagon, but it'll have to do. Walter, find us something to eat. I'm famished," Hugh said as he rubbed his eyes.

"Yes, sir," Walter replied. He looked like he was about to cry, but after a stern look from Hugh he set off, weaving between fallen knights and dead horses. Several fires burned on the outskirts of the field where Lancastrian survivors warmed themselves as they tried to regroup and account for their dead. The Duke of York's army had moved on after the battle. Walter heard it said that Edward had taken his victory to the city of York, where the staunchly Lancastrian population waited in terror for a reprisal from the enemy.

In the coming days, graves would be dug for the Yorkists who had fallen at the Battle of Towton, but today was the day Edward Plantagenet would celebrate his victory and solidify his claim to the throne. His cousin, Richard Neville, the Earl of Warrick, had proclaimed Edward king less than a month ago, but yesterday's battle had served to solidify his position. The balance of power had shifted, and every man who had survived the battle, Yorkist and Lancastrian alike, surely knew it.

Guy drifted off again, but woke with a start, unable to bear the recurring nightmare any longer. He was terribly cold and hungry, but he didn't complain. He was sure every man on that field felt much the same. He turned to Hugh. His brother appeared unhurt, but his face was gray with fatigue and his breastplate was smeared with blood. His dark hair was matted, and three-day stubble shadowed his jaw. Hugh's eyes flew open as though he felt Guy's gaze on him.

"Stay with me," Hugh commanded. "Do you hear me, Guy?"

Guy nodded. "I'd find it easier to stick around if I had something to eat."

"Walter will have a devil of a time finding even scraps of bread. There are hundreds of men here, and they are all hungry. I doubt the villagers have much left to spare. The sooner we leave, the better."

"Are we going home?" Guy asked. He found it hard to form the words due to the roar in his head, but had no desire to go back to sleep and face the demons with bloodied swords and empty eye sockets that sprang back to life to fight on and on.

"Aye, we are," Hugh replied. "We must bury William, and you're in no condition to do any fighting in the foreseeable future."

"Walter said Edward has gone to York."

"And a pretty welcome he's going to receive," Hugh replied with grim humor. "Last I heard, Edward's father and brother's heads, as well as that of his uncle, the Earl of Salisbury, still adorn Micklegate Bar. A gruesome sight for any man, let alone one whose family's remains grace the gatehouse. There'll be hell to pay, I wager, especially if Warwick has any say in the matter."

Guy thought on Hugh's words. The death of Richard Plantagenet, the Duke of York, in battle and the subsequent murder of his son, Edmund, the Earl of Rutland, at the hands of Sir

Clifford had changed the course of the war once and for all. Even loyal Lancastrians referred to Sir Clifford as 'The Butcher' after he killed the unarmed seventeen-year-old on Wakefield Bridge in cold blood, despite pleas by his own soldiers to let the boy live and take him prisoner instead. Sir Clifford had wanted to avenge the death of his own father at the battle of St. Albans, but his vengeance wasn't honorable, not by any standards of combat. Had he killed Rutland in battle, it would have looked very different for him.

Richard Plantagenet's death had left his eldest, Edward, first in line for the throne. Despite rumblings that Edward was nothing more than Warwick's puppet, his popularity had proved to be all his own, and he had succeeded where his father had failed in attempting to take the throne. The Earl of Warwick might have been the one to proclaim Edward king, but it was Edward's skill in battle, his youth, his bravery, and his charm that had paved his path to the throne, reminding the people of all that was missing in their current monarch, Henry VI, a man suited to ruling England about as much as a nun was suited to running whores.

Guy had seen King Henry from a distance several times, riding a docile mare as he wasn't a competent rider, an empty scabbard at his side. The man dressed in simple peasant clothes with his hair shorn close to the scalp. But it wasn't the manner of his dress that distressed his followers; it was the vacant look in his eyes, and the silly half-smile that played about his lips, as if he weren't quite sure where he was or what he was doing there. His wife, Margaret of Anjou, was the power behind the throne, but without the active support of her husband, she was fighting a losing battle, and a costly one.

"It isn't over. Not by a long shot," Hugh said, shaking his head. "Somerset will regroup, and Margaret of Anjou will launch a new offensive. She'll never give up, not as long as there's still breath in her body. She'll see her boy Prince Edward of Westminster on the throne if that's the last thing she does, despite the Act of Accord."

"It likely will be the last thing she does," Guy replied quietly. Prince Edward was quiet, pious, and utterly oblivious to the conflict he'd created through his lack of strong leadership. Some said he suffered from bouts of madness, but Guy had never come close enough to His Royal Highness to see for himself.

There were some who believed that Henry VI's son with Margaret of Anjou had been fathered by the Duke of Somerset's father, since the notion of their pious, simple-minded king bedding his fiery queen and begetting a son was incongruous and highly improbable. Few dared to say the words out loud, or lived long enough after making the insinuation to tell the tale. Margaret adored her son, and had fought like a lioness to safeguard the throne for him—a quest that had been declared virtually impossible with the Act of Accord of 1460, which allowed Henry to remain on the throne for the duration of his lifetime but disinherited his son, stating that the Duke of York would be next in line for the throne after Henry's death. Not a man in the kingdom believed that Margaret of Anjou would accept such a ruling. It had been a thinly veiled declaration of war. And now Edward of York was king, and Margaret of Anjou was on the losing side of history, as were the de Rosel brothers.

Chapter 7

July 2014

Berwick-upon-Tweed, Northumberland

Quinn pulled her hand away from the sword and leaned back in the chair. The Wars of the Roses had never been one of her favorite historical periods. The series of bloody conflicts that had claimed thousands of lives wasn't an uprising against tyranny or a defensive stance to protect England's sovereign borders; it was an endless struggle between vain, power-hungry individuals who were too fixated on the ultimate prize to do what was best for the country and the people they claimed to love. The conflict between the House of York and the House of Lancaster had spawned the sort of treachery one would only expect to find in a novel, with some of the main players changing sides more than once and sacrificing their loved ones for the promise of the throne. The Wars of the Roses were the original game of thrones, and few of the players walked away unscathed, or walked away at all.

Gabe could trace his family all the way back to the Norman Conquest of 1066, so it stood to reason that his ancestors would have been involved in the conflict that had divided the nation, just as it was to be expected that they would be loyal to the House of Lancaster. The north had remained staunchly Lancastrian, even after Edward IV won the throne and the Yorkists imprisoned Henry VI in the Tower of London. Had Henry's wife, Margaret of Anjou, accepted defeat, many lives would have been spared, but Margaret had fought on, spending most of her life in exile and mounting rebellion after rebellion until her son, Edward of Westminster, was killed at the Battle of Tewkesbury in 1471, putting an end to her longstanding campaign.

Many historians argued that the conflict was spurred by Henry VI's mental instability and inability to rule, but there were others who believed that the wars were caused by the very structure of the feudal system, sometimes referred to as Bastard Feudalism, which forced the gentry to support their liege lord rather than their king, and take up arms in support of whichever contender their liege backed at the time. The liege lords didn't have standing armies. They called on their retainers when they required military support. Some of the more powerful lords could raise a small army that consisted not only of knights, but of all vassals, who had no choice but to answer the summons of their overlord.

Quinn glanced at the beautiful sword. She knew that Gabe came from a distinguished family, but she hadn't realized the de Rosels had been titled once. Only sons of noble families, those not destined for the Church, had gone on to become squires and knights, and only wealthy families could afford the cost of armor, weapons, and destriers required for knighthood. Quinn was actually surprised that none of the three brothers had taken Holy Orders, but perhaps William de Rosel, who'd become Baron de Rosel upon his father's death, had decided to keep his brothers together after the loss of their parents.

Quinn reached for the bag containing the rosary. Perhaps it had once belonged to Lady de Rosel and had been buried with Guy de Rosel for protection, given that he hadn't received a Christian burial. Why would a warrior not be buried in consecrated ground? There were only a few reasons a person in the Middle Ages would be denied a Christian burial, the most common being suicide. Had Guy killed himself?

Quinn opened the bag and allowed the shiny beads to spill into her palm. Perhaps the rosary would tell her.

Chapter 8

April 1461

Holystone, Northumberland

Kate stepped out of the barn and stopped in her tracks, mesmerized by the glorious sunrise that painted the sky in breathtaking shades of crimson and gold. The sun shimmered as it made its ascent, its belly skimming the trees as it sailed slowly into the cloudless sky.

Kate watched the sunrise every morning, but she could never take its beauty for granted, especially on a glorious spring morning that heralded a gorgeous day to come. She balanced the milk pails in her hands and walked toward the refectory. Milking was her first chore of the day, followed by Prime. After breakfast, she worked in the stables or the laundry until Sext. Kate performed most of her chores alone, but she didn't mind. Even when she was in the company of the nuns, there was little idle talk. The Augustine order at Holystone Priory was not a silent one, but the sisters only spoke when something needed to be said or in prayer. They didn't require endless verbal intercourse to feel supported, understood, or cared for. Kate had never felt as accepted and cherished as she had since coming to the priory.

She delivered the milk pails to the kitchen, nodded to the sisters who were busy baking their daily bread, and was about to walk out when the other postulate, Mary, swept into the room. Mary was a girl who did everything with the maximum noise, even when her tasks were silent in nature. This morning, her sabots slapped loudly against the stone floor and she huffed as if she'd just run the entire length of the corridor. Mary's cheeks were stained with the rosy glow of excitement, and her wide brown eyes shone with curiosity.

"Catherine, the abbess wishes to see you right away," Mary blurted.

Kate longed to be addressed as Sister Catherine. She still thought of herself as Kate in her private thoughts, but she couldn't wait to be officially part of the order, a milestone that would take place in a fortnight when she would take her First Vow. Mary still had a year to go, but Kate had been at the priory for two years now, and her time as novice was finally at an end. Perhaps the abbess wished to discuss the vow-taking ceremony.

Kate's hand subconsciously went to her veil as she made sure no stray hair escaped the postulate's white headdress, and she followed Mary out of the refectory and toward the chapter house, where the abbess's office was situated. She'd only been there once, when her father, Lord Dancy, had delivered her to the convent two years before. Lord Dancy had not been happy to turn his only daughter over to the nuns, but it was his wife's greatest wish that Catherine be allowed to take the veil. Lord Dancy had three fine sons to carry on the family name; he had no need of a daughter to further his interests, Lady Dancy had insisted.

Kate had been fifteen at the time, an age when most girls began to contemplate marriage in earnest. She wasn't at all sure that she wished to devote her life to God, not when she could marry a fine lord and become the lady of the manor. The prospect of having her own home, lovely gowns and jewels, and servants to command was an appealing one, but her mother had won her over after a time. She hadn't explained her reasoning right away, but when Kate had proved stubborn and wouldn't entertain her mother's wish with due seriousness, she had finally revealed the truth and begged Kate to reconsider.

"Kate, you're very young and naïve and have romantic notions of marriage, but the reality is quite different. I was wed to your father when I was fourteen, only a year younger than you are now. Your father was twenty-one at the time, but he'd had little experience of women—or genteel women, I should say. He had no notion of how to woo a terrified young bride, nor did he bother to try. I don't wish to frighten you, but what happens to a woman in the marriage bed can be brutal, and I wish to spare you the indignities I've had to endure," Lady Dancy had said, her eyes shining with unshed tears.

"I've given your father seven children, and I consider myself blessed to have four who survived, but losing a child is not something a woman ever comes to terms with. I still grieve for your siblings every day, and pray for their immortal souls. A woman's life is not one of pleasure and comfort, it's a life of pain and suffering, no matter her station in life. I only wish to protect you, my dove. You will be happy with the nuns, and safe." Lady Dancy had taken Kate's hands in hers and smiled gently. "Do you trust me?"

"Of course I trust you, Mother," Kate had replied, her own eyes welling up.

She had only a vague notion of what her mother was talking about, but she'd heard Cook say that her brother Martin took liberties with the female servants, and being the heir to their father's title and estate, did what he wished, seeing the serfs in his father's employ as his for the taking. Kate didn't understand or ask too many questions. What Martin did was his business, and if their father didn't object, then it certainly wasn't up to her to pass judgment. It wasn't until she accidently walked in on Agnes in her travail that she finally understood what Cook meant by 'taking liberties,' and what those liberties led to.

Agnes had hidden in the barn when her time came, equipped with only a knife to cut the cord and a blanket to wrap the child in. She begged Kate to leave, but Kate couldn't abandon the poor girl, who was only sixteen, when she was frightened and in pain. Kate sat with Agnes for hours and brought her water to drink when the labor went on and on, leaving Agnes exhausted and weak. She'd never forget the agony Agnes endured to bring a baby girl into the world, a girl Martin refused to even look at or acknowledge as his own.

Lord Dancy sent Agnes away with nothing but the clothes on her back when she dared to speak the name of the man who'd taken her against her will and got her with child. He called her a liar and a harlot and threatened to have her whipped if she didn't clear off. Kate overheard Cook telling the scullion that Agnes had been found dead in a ramshackle barn three days later. The child had still been alive, but died the same day, having been exposed to the elements for too long. And a blessing it was too, Cook opined, nodding wisely, since no one'd want the poor mite, especially it being a girl, which was of little use to anyone. Agnes and the child were buried in a pauper's grave, with no one to mourn them or say a kind word in their memory since Agnes had been an orphan.

Kate observed Martin for days after Agnes's death to see if he was aggrieved by the news, but he didn't seem to care. Lord Dancy brought in a new serving wench from the village, and Martin laid his claim to her, telling his brothers to not even look at the new girl until he tired of her. Kate hoped that Geoffrey and Robert would chastise Martin for Agnes's death, but they didn't say a word, at least not within her hearing. Kate didn't expect much from Robert, who was sixteen and worshipped his older brother, but she had hoped Geoffrey would come to Agnes's defense.

At eighteen, Geoffrey was the kindest of her brothers, and the most affectionate toward her. He had entertained hopes of taking the Holy Orders from an early age, but their father repeatedly refused his request. Geoffrey had brought up the subject again after Agnes's death, appalled by his father's refusal to take responsibility for his son's disgraceful behavior and see to the welfare of Agnes and her child.

"We've enough priests in this country," Lord Dancy snapped. "'Tis not natural for a man to deny his needs. You'll do much better to make a fine marriage and advance the interests of your family. Once I find a suitable bride for Martin, it'll be your turn next. You'll not speak of this foolishness again, boy. Not ever."

Kate hadn't meant to eavesdrop, but now that she was of marriageable age she longed to know what was happening behind closed doors. Decisions were being made and alliances forged, and sooner or later it would be her turn, and she wished to be prepared.

Kate followed Geoffrey to the stables after his conversation with their father. She'd expected Geoffrey to look upset, but he seemed his usual self when she approached him.

"What are you doing here, Katie? This is hardly the weather for riding."

A heavy snow had been falling for hours, blanketing the muck in the yard with a pristine guilt of pure white as an unnatural hush had settled over the outbuildings. Everyone had hunkered down to wait out the storm, even the dogs, who were warm and snug in the kennel. Geoffrey wasn't going to ride either. He liked to go to the stables to be alone. They had grooms to take care of the horses, but Geoffrey enjoyed looking after his own horse, and spent hours brushing it down and exercising it when the weather was fine.

"I wished to speak to you," Kate said.

"You could have spoken to me indoors."

"I wanted to speak to you privately."

"And what private business do you have, little lady?" Geoffrey asked, smiling down at her.

"Geoffrey, is it not a sin what Martin did to poor Agnes?" Kate asked as Geoffrey took a handful of straw and began to brush down his horse. He didn't ask how Kate knew about Agnes, nor did he insult her by telling her that she was too young to fully comprehend the situation. Geoffrey's hazel gaze looked pained at the question, but he answered her truthfully nonetheless.

"It is, Kate, but Martin is our father's heir and can't be encumbered with a serf's bastard. Father will find him a bride soon, but until then Martin will sow his wild oats where he sees fit."

"Will the Lord not punish him for his sins?" Kate asked, perplexed. She lived in eternal fear of sinning and incurring God's vengeance, but her brothers didn't seem troubled by the stern words they heard from the pulpit week after week, words that threatened God's wrath for even a stray thought, much less a dishonorable deed.

"Katie, if the good Lord punished every man who lay with a woman out of wedlock, there'd be no one left to worship Him except the bastards they sired."

"Do women like Agnes have no recourse?" Kate inquired. She'd liked Agnes and grieved for her. She seemed to be the only one to take Agnes's senseless death to heart.

"Some lords find husbands for the women their sons disgrace, but Father was not kindly disposed toward the poor girl."

"Why? What had she done?"

Geoffrey shrugged. "I don't know."

Katie looked at his closed expression. He knew, but he didn't want to tell her. Suddenly, she had no wish to find out. The business of men was way beyond her understanding, but it was often cruel, unforgiving, and frightening.

"Do as Mother bids, Katie," Geoffrey said. "Before Father changes his mind."

"Why? What do you know?" A frisson of fear ran down Kate's spine.

"Katie, a daughter is only good for one thing, and that's to marry her off to form an alliance or settle a debt. You're fifteen, ripe for marrying. If you don't go to the priory, Father will have you wed as soon as he finds a suitable match. He's got his sights set on one of the Neville cousins, to strengthen our connection to the Earl of Warwick. The marriage would bring him one step closer to the Duke of York, who has his eye on the throne."

"What are you talking about?" Kate demanded. "How would marrying a Neville cousin bring father closer to the throne when King Henry is our sovereign?"

Geoffrey patted her cheek in a paternal matter. "Don't worry your pretty little head about it. It's way too complicated for you to understand. Just don't pass up your chance at freedom."

"Freedom? You think becoming a nun is a path to freedom?" Kate gaped at her brother. "Is that why you want to become a priest?"

Geoffrey looked momentarily shocked, but didn't bother to ask how she knew of his conversation with their father. "It is a freedom of sorts, Kate. Now, off with you. I'd like a few moments alone. I was supposed to practice swordplay with Robert, but I think we might have to wait until the weather improves."

Geoffrey and Robert never missed a day of practice. Sometimes Martin joined them as well, but Martin preferred to train with some of his own friends. They spent hours at swordplay, fighting until sweat ran into their eyes and their faces were flushed with exertion. There was a quintain set up in the yard, and they used that as well, taking turns jousting. For men in their position, war craft and politicking were some of the most important skills they could possess, and although her brothers hadn't had much opportunity to scheme and plot as of yet, they knew how to fight.

Kate returned to the house, kicked off her wet shoes, and climbed up to the solar where she curled up in the window seat. From her vantage point she could see the stable yard, the fields, and the woods beyond. This was her world, the only one she'd ever known. If she listened to her mother and Geoffrey, she would never see anything beyond the walls of a convent. But how could she ignore the advice of the two people she trusted most in the world? How could she dismiss the worry in their eyes when they spoke of her future? Gerard Dancy was not a cruel man—at least he'd never been cruel to her—but his dealings with Agnes had showed Kate that her father could be ruthless. She'd never felt the back of his hand or displeased him enough for him to use sharp words to her, being an obedient and respectful daughter, but Geoffrey had struck a chord when he spoke of her father's goals. Gerard Dancy was an ambitious man, and he'd use everything at his disposal to further his own ends. Already he was negotiating a marriage for Martin, looking for a bride among the highest-ranking Yorkist kin. Geoffrey would be next, and he was prepared to do his bit to further the family's influence despite his own wishes. Only Robert had a few more years of freedom before him. His future would not be decided until his older brothers were advantageously wed.

Kate hugged her legs and rested her head on her knees as silent tears slid down her cheeks. She was no longer a little girl; she had to start thinking like a woman. Perhaps going to the priory was the lesser of two evils. Kate wiped away her tears and stared blindly out the window. Her decision was made.

Chapter 9

Kate hurried along the empty cloister toward the abbess's office. Two more weeks and her future at the priory would be secure. Once she took her vows, she would belong to God, and not even her father would have a say over her life any longer.

She approached the arched doorway of the office, knocked softly, and was invited to enter. The abbess sat behind her desk, a folded sheet of paper with a broken seal lying before her. She was in her fifties, and had been at the priory since she was a girl of thirteen. The abbess was possessed of a patient, kind nature perfectly suited to her role as 'mother' to the women in her charge, and never behaved in a manner that was intimidating or unapproachable. She was sensitive to the needs of the postulates as well as the nuns, and always took the time to comfort and reassure when the situation called for it. This morning, the abbess looked tired and pale, and her mouth pursed into a thin line of displeasure.

"Good morning, Mother. You wished to see me?" Kate asked. The abbess normally greeted everyone with a serene smile and a kind word, but there was no smile today.

"Sit down, Catherine."

The seed of anxiety blossomed in Kate's belly as she perched on the edge of a chair. This wasn't a routine summons to discuss the vow-taking. This was something entirely different.

"Have I done something wrong?" Kate asked, her voice quivering with uncertainty. Why else would the abbess wish to see her, if not to punish her for some unknown transgression?

"No, you haven't done anything wrong, my child, which is not to say that a wrong hasn't been done to you," the abbess replied sadly.

"Whatever do you mean, Mother?"

"Catherine, a messenger arrived with a letter from your lord father last night. I didn't summon you right away because I needed time to think. I've pondered the situation all night, but I couldn't arrive at any solution that wouldn't hinge on deceit or disobedience. Your father wishes you to return home immediately."

"Why?" Kate cried. "I'm about to take my vows."

The abbess shook her head. Kate saw that she was genuinely distressed, and devastated by her own helplessness. Tears of sorrow welled in her eyes as she faced Kate across her massive desk.

"Catherine, I'm very sorry to tell you, but your brothers fell at the Battle of Towton on Palm Sunday. Martin and Robert died on the field. Geoffrey was grievously wounded and died of his injuries two days later. The forces of Lancaster were routed and the Duke of York is now confirmed as King Edward IV. I know you have Yorkist kin, and this would be very welcome news for you indeed, if not for the loss your family suffered on that battlefield. They say it was the bloodiest battle in Britain's history," the abbess added. "Thousands of men slaughtered on both sides. May God rest their souls." She crossed herself and Kate followed suit.

"God rest their souls," Kate muttered, reeling from the news. Her brothers were all gone, even Geoffrey. Kind, funny, ginger-haired Geoffrey who'd always teased her about her freckles and was the only one of her brothers to play a game with her or escort her when she rode her pony as a child. And Robert, who had hardly been more than a child himself. Oh, he'd fancied himself a grown man, but he had still been so naïve, and so foolish. She'd never felt kindly disposed toward Martin, even before Agnes's death, but his death was still a shock, and a loss. He'd been only twenty.

"Why does my father want me to come home?" Kate asked.

The abbess shook her head, but didn't elaborate. Lord Dancy wouldn't have explained his reasons to her. He'd sent a

53

summons, and she was meant to obey, but Kate understood her father's motives only too well. Now that a Yorkist king sat on the throne, new alliances would need to be forged and the fastest way to an advantageous alliance was through a mutually beneficial union. With her brothers gone, Kate was the only bargaining tool her father had left. Kate suspected that the abbess had considered telling her father that Kate had already taken her vows and was a full-fledged nun, but her conscience wouldn't permit her to lie, not even to shield Kate from what was to come.

"Catherine, your lady mother has been taken ill upon learning the news. She's been asking for you."

A terrible sob tore from Kate's chest. She was feeling sorry for herself and mourning her own future when her mother had just lost three of her beloved boys and needed the comfort of her only daughter. How selfish she was, how self-centered. No wonder God had seen fit to send her home before she had a chance to take her vows. She didn't deserve his love or his mercy.

"Catherine, I know you are devastated, and you have every reason to be, but there are many ways to serve God. You can serve him by helping your family during this difficult time. You must nurse your mother back to health and honor your father's wishes."

"Mother, please," Kate begged. "Ask my father to promise that I may return to the priory once my mother is recovered."

"I have no right to ask that of him, my child. Had you already taken your vows, I would have recourse, but you are still a novice, free to leave or be expelled. You are not yet bound to God, and I couldn't possibly tell your sire otherwise."

Kate steeled herself as sharp claws of disappointment tore at her soul. It wasn't until that moment that she understood how deeply committed she had been to taking the veil—not because she felt she had a vocation, but because at the priory she felt safe and in control of her own destiny. She was never coming back; she knew that. She would become her father's pawn the moment she stepped outside the walls of the priory. She'd be a means to an end, especially now that her brothers could no longer be instruments of Lord Dancy's ambition.

The abbess confirmed Kate's suspicions with her next words. "Catherine, the situation will be easier to bear if you don't fight it. Don't give your father reason to be cruel to you. Obey him in all things, and you will please the Lord."

"Thank you, Mother. I will do my duty by my family," Kate replied. "When must I go?"

"I sent the messenger to the village to find a bed for the night. He will come for you shortly. God keep you, child."

Kate closed the door behind her as she left the office. She'd intended to join the sisters for a final prayer, but instead retreated to her cell. She had nothing to pack since she'd renounced all her worldly goods when she arrived at the priory. The gown she'd worn had been given away, so she would have to travel in her habit, veil, and gray woolen cloak. Her only possession was the rosary her mother had given her the day she left home. Kate had always admired her mother's jet prayer beads, but Anne had given Kate a rosary made of amber. The polished stones were luminous and smooth, each bead unique in color and appearance.

"I got this for you in Newcastle," her mother had said. "I was going to get you a rosary like mine, but when I saw this one, it reminded me of you. The beads are sunny and beautiful, just like you are, and I want this rosary to bring you hope and light, even on the darkest of days. Say you like it," Anne had cajoled.

"It's beautiful, Mother. I will cherish it always."

"Think of me from time to time, Katie, and know that sending you away is one of the hardest things I've ever had to do."

Kate had been devastated by their parting. The priory allowed no visitors, so mother and daughter would never see each other again unless something went dreadfully wrong.

"I will think of you every day, and pray for your well-being," Kate had promised. "I will pray for father and the boys as well."

She had prayed for them every night. And now her brothers were dead, her mother was heartbroken and ill, and her father had lost the heirs to his title and lands. The time of reckoning was upon the Dancy family.

Chapter 10

Kate walked toward the gate. She hadn't told any of the sisters she was leaving; she didn't think she could maintain her composure when faced with their compassion and understanding. She'd deal with her disappointment and grief later, but for now, she had to get through the journey home.

She hadn't ventured beyond the priory gates in two years and the world outside suddenly frightened her. Men frightened her. She wondered who'd come to collect her. She hoped it wasn't Glen, one of her father's favorite men-at-arms. Glen was young, handsome, and skilled with a sword, but his insolent tongue and aggressive personality had always intimidated her. She wouldn't want to be alone with him for hours on end. Glen would do nothing to hurt her, not if he hoped to see the sun rise on another day, but it would be an awkward ride to say the least.

The path toward the gate was clear, but mounds of melting snow still dotted the landscape, and the ground was sodden. The weather had turned warmer since Palm Sunday, and the unmistakable smell of spring permeated the air. The sky was a pale blue, its vastness unmarred by even a wisp of a cloud.

Kate peered toward the gate. Her escort wasn't there yet, so she turned off the path and headed toward the Lady's Well. Kate made sure to keep to the well-trodden track so as not to get her feet wet. It would be an uncomfortable ride home if she were wet and cold. The track weaved through a grove of trees and emerged by a clear pool that was as smooth as a looking glass on this spring morning. The Lady's Well was a lovely, peaceful spot, said to have been originally used by the Anglo-Saxon Saint Ninian to baptize early Christians in its holy water. When the Augustine canonesses had first settled at Holystone in the twelfth century, they had dedicated the well to the Virgin Mary, and had looked after it ever since.

Kate folded her hands, bowed her head, and offered up a fervent prayer to the Blessed Mother. She prayed to God all the time, but at times, only a woman could understand what was in a girl's heart, and this was the place where Kate felt closest to the Virgin. She begged Mary to safeguard her on the journey home, to ease her mother's suffering, and to guide her father toward choosing a man who would be kind and gentle, should a marriage be contracted for Kate.

She crossed herself and rose to her feet. Feeling a little more optimistic, she squared her shoulders and walked away from the well without a backward glance, ready to face whatever the future held.

Kate breathed a sigh of relief when she recognized Osbert waiting patiently by the gate with two horses. He was in his late forties, and had been recently widowed the last time Kate saw him two years ago. Osbert's family had been in service to the Dancys for generations. They were kind, simple folk who were loyal to their lord and his family. She would be safe with Osbert on the journey home.

He kneaded his felt hat in his hands as he bowed to Kate in greeting. "I'm sorry for yer loss, me lady. Yer brothers were fine men, and brave soldiers."

"Thank you, Osbert. It's kind of you to say so. How are my parents?"

"Devastated, me lady. Yer lady mother has taken to her bed and hasn't risen since."

"I hope I can be of some comfort to her," Kate said as Osbert gave her a leg-up. She'd forgotten how awkward a sidesaddle was, but it was the only acceptable way for a young woman of good family to ride, so she had to make the best of it.

"Yer very presence will sustain her, me lady," Osbert replied kindly. He fitted Kate's foot into the stirrup and mounted his own horse, ready to leave.

"I do hope we get home before dark," Kate said as she took up the reins and followed Osbert toward the road. She didn't like the idea of being on the road after dark, not even with an armed escort.

"If we don't make too many stops, we aught be at the Grange before sundown, me lady. The sun's setting later, now it's springtime."

That was true, but despite the lingering light, most people returned to their homes in time for supper and remained indoors after they'd eaten. Having finished their work, they looked forward to well-deserved rest in the evening and spent the hours before bedtime sitting by the hearth or catching up on minor chores they hadn't got to during the day. In the summer, people sat outside, enjoying the lengthy twilight and the fragrant evening air, but it was still too cold out to enjoy such pursuits, and once the sun set, it grew pitch dark as well.

Kate and Osbert rode in silence for a time. Being a serf, Osbert knew his place and didn't speak to the mistress unless spoken to, and Kate had little to say, given her emotional state. The brief moment of optimism she'd felt after praying at the well had dissipated, now that she was on her way home. She grieved for her brothers, but she also grieved for herself and the future she'd been forced to abandon. She was frightened of what her father had in store for her, and wondered just how soon he intended to put his plans into action. If she knew her father, he wouldn't wait too long to solidify whatever alliance he was hoping to make, especially now that the Duke of York was on the throne of England.

Lord Dancy was the Earl of Warwick's cousin on Warwick's mother's side, and he mentioned his connection to the Nevilles at every opportunity. Kate now understood his boasting, given that her father was distant kin to the king himself, since Warwick was first cousin to King Edward on his sire's side. Lord Dancy didn't hold a position at court, at least not yet, but he was a very wealthy man whose fortune would sway many a potential in-law into considering his offspring's suit. With her brothers gone, Kate was now an heiress, and if she understood anything at all about the world, she had just become vastly more desirable on the marriage market. If her father managed to marry her off to a

Neville relation, his connection to the throne would grow even stronger, as would his influence.

It was close to noon when Kate noticed Osbert swaying in the saddle. At first, she assumed he was tired, but on closer inspection, he looked positively green at the gills.

"Osbert, are you quite well?" Kate asked.

"Aye, me lady," Osbert replied, but she could tell he was lying. His face was pale and glistened with sweat, and his eyes looked glassy and unfocused.

"I think we'd better take a rest."

"Thank ye, me lady."

"Was there sickness in the village?" Kate asked as they made for a copse of trees on the side of the road. Normally, she would have expected Osbert to help her dismount, but given his state, it seemed best to avoid contact.

"Not that I know of, me lady."

Osbert dismounted awkwardly and slid to the ground, leaning the back of his head against a tree trunk and closing his eyes.

"I'll get some water," Kate said, and walked to a shallow stream a few feet away. She knelt, cupped her hands, and drank, then splashed some of the fresh, cool water on her face. It felt pleasant and refreshing after several hours in the saddle. Her bottom hurt and her legs vibrated with tension. It'd been years since she'd spent so many hours on horseback.

She returned to the horses and searched Osbert's saddlebag for something to carry water to him. He had brought a bundle of food and a skin of ale. Kate decided to pour out the remaining ale and fill the skin with water. Osbert still sat leaning against the tree, his eyes closed and his hands folded in his lap, as though sleeping.

Kate walked back to the stream, rinsed out the skin, and filled it with the cool water. Osbert hadn't woken by the time she returned. She longed to get going, but the man looked so poorly she decided to give him time to rest. She walked about for a bit to stretch the soreness out of her back and legs. After a few minutes, her anxiety began to mount. She felt exposed and vulnerable. She looked at the position of the sun, judging the time to be well past noon. They had to get going if they hoped to get back to the Grange at a reasonable hour.

"Osbert," Kate said softly as she took the man by the shoulder. When he didn't respond, cold fingers of dread clenched her heart. She knew with certainty he was dead. "Osbert!" she cried, but there was no one to hear her save a few birds perched in the tree.

Kate yanked her hand away from the dead man. What was she to do now? It would be the decent thing to bring Osbert home so he could be buried next to his wife, but she couldn't possibly get him on a horse. It seemed wrong to leave him there by the side of the road, like a dead badger, but she didn't have a choice. Perhaps her father would send someone for Osbert's body tomorrow. She rummaged inside the saddlebag, searching for a blanket to cover him, but didn't find one. She'd have to leave him as he was, and hope the animals didn't get to him during the night and make a meal of his innards. The thought made her queasy and she turned away.

Kate considered taking the bundle of food and the skin of water, but changed her mind. If Osbert had sickened from something in the village, the food and drink might be tainted. But she had to take Osbert's horse. Her father would be angry if she left a perfectly good animal. Kate used a fallen log to mount, grabbed Osbert's horse by the reins, and returned to the road. She could still make it home before dark if she didn't make any unnecessary stops. With only her rosary for protection, she wished she'd taken Osbert's dagger. She'd never use it on anyone, but having it might have made her feel a little less vulnerable.

The road was deserted. Kate saw several farmhouses in the distance as she continued toward home, but didn't come across any travelers. The sky was a cloudless blue, and the sun still rode high in the sky, but the deceptive warmth of the April afternoon began to ebb as evening approached.

She came to a fork in the road and stopped, having no idea which way to go. She'd been this way only once before, when her father escorted her to the convent, and she hadn't paid much attention—not that there was anything to use as a landmark. It was all woods and fields. She'd passed a small hamlet about an hour since, but just rode right through, not wishing to attract attention to herself. Perhaps she should have stopped. She was hungry and tired, and the horses could have used a rest and bucketful of oats, as well as water. They were ambling along, having been on the road since early morning.

Kate remained at the crossroads for several minutes, trying to decide which way to turn, when she saw a lone rider approaching her. She experienced a moment of panic, but the young man didn't look threatening despite the sword at his side. He looked disheveled and weary, his doublet covered with rust-colored stains that could only be blood. Kate gripped the reins, but knew she wouldn't try to flee. She'd never outride the young man. Her horse snorted and pressed its ears back, as though sensing Kate's anxiety.

"Are you all right, Sister?" he called out. He smiled and his face went from somber to friendly, reassuring her.

"Ah, yes. I'm afraid I'm lost."

"Where are you headed?"

"I'm headed to the village of Belford," Kate replied. She didn't tell the young man that her father owned the village and everything beyond; there was no need for him to know that.

"My master is headed in that direction as well. Perhaps you can travel with us."

"And where is your master?" Kate asked. The boy looked too bedraggled to serve anyone of consequence.

"He's just over yonder," he said, pointing toward a wooded area down the road on the right. "I'm Walter Coombs, squire to Hugh de Rosel."

"De Rosel?" Kate asked. She was sure she'd heard the name before, but it might have been William de Rosel, not Hugh. And then understanding dawned. "Were you at Towton, Master Coombs?"

The boy nodded miserably. He clearly didn't wish to speak of what he'd seen and heard. Some squires were permitted on the battlefield, so perhaps he'd even fought alongside his knights.

"Was it horrible?" Kate asked, and Walter nodded again. He looked as if he were about to cry, but managed to get hold of himself.

"I've never seen such slaughter, Sister, or such suffering. It was beyond imagining."

"Was this your first battle?"

"Yes," Walter whispered. He seemed to rouse himself from his misery and looked purposefully at Kate. "Come with me, Sister. My master needs your help."

"In what way?" Kate balked, afraid to be alone with a knight and his squire, who'd do nothing to protect her should his master think to harm her.

"My master's brother is grievously wounded, Sister. He's dying," Walter replied. Tears filled his eyes. "Perhaps you can pray for him."

Kate turned her horse toward the boy and came alongside him. The wounded man needed her, and although she had been mercilessly ripped from her religious life, she could still offer comfort and assistance. Walter seemed relieved that she'd agreed to accompany him and trotted alongside her.

Kate didn't ask what side the de Rosels had fought for. It made little difference to her. She'd find out once she got home. *If she got home.* It didn't look as if she would arrive at the Grange this evening. Her father would be worried, and her mother would be frantic, but there was little Kate could do to put their minds at rest. She hoped that Hugh de Rosel would escort her home once his brother passed, or at least send Walter Coombs to show her the way.

Walter led Kate toward a ruin bathed in the golden light of the late afternoon. It must have been a church once, or more likely a chapel of ease, used by those who couldn't get to the parish church in the nearest village. All that remained of the one-room structure was dilapidated stone walls, each boasting an arched opening that must have been a window once. Several charred beams were all that was left of the roof, which looked to have burned away. The path that led to the chapel was uneven, roots and grass growing unchecked between the stones.

Three massive horses grazed lazily beneath the still-bare trees, and a wagon was just visible behind the eastern wall. A body wrapped in a cloak lay in the wagon, the feet hanging off the too-short wagon bed. Kate was about to follow Walter toward the arched doorway when a man emerged, hand on sword, eyes blazing.

"Who…?" He instantly dropped his hand and bowed. "I'm sorry, Sister. I didn't meant to frighten you. I saw a shadow and didn't know if our visitor was friend or foe. Hugh de Rosel, at your service."

The man wasn't very tall, but he was powerfully built and exuded strength and vitality. His light blue eyes crinkled at the corners when he greeted her, but his cordial manner was forced. He must have been around thirty years of age, but at the moment, exhaustion and distress made him look much older.

"I'm sorry I'm too late to be of any help," Kate said. She assumed Hugh de Rosel's brother had passed while Walter was away, and Hugh had waited for his squire to return before turning for home.

"You're not, Sister," Hugh replied, following her gaze. "My older brother, Baron de Rosel, died at the Battle of Towton. My younger brother was badly wounded. I would be most grateful if you would administer the sacraments to him before he passes. It would ease my mind to know that he died shriven."

Kate nodded. She wasn't qualified to administer last rites, but in situations where no priest could be found, any pious and God-fearing Catholic could step in. And this ruin had been a church once, so the dying man rested on sacred ground.

Kate made her way into the chapel. The man lay on a coarse blanket spread over the stone floor of the nave. His eyes were closed, and his skin had a greenish-gray tint, even in the golden light streaming through the empty windows. His black hair was matted and damp, and his dark stubble contrasted with his sickly pallor. The dirty rag that had been used to bandage his arm was soaked with blood and pus, and a terrible odor wafted from the wound.

"The wound's festered," Hugh de Rosel explained unnecessarily.

"Have you done anything to treat it?"

Hugh shook his head. "We bandaged it the best we could. We should have remained at the battle site. Someone might have been able to help Guy, but I wanted to get William home," he explained. "A body won't keep long, and my brother must be buried at home. He deserves that much. I thought Guy would pull through. He was coherent after the battle, but his condition has worsened in the days since."

Kate bent over the dying man and touched his forehead. He was hot to the touch and his skin felt papery and dry. He opened his eyes for just a moment and looked at her, but his eyes, a deeper blue than his brother's, were unfocused, and Kate was sure he didn't really see her. She unbound the filthy bandage and looked at the wound. The skin was sliced cleanly, most likely with a blade, but the wound was oozing blood and gore, and the arm was grotesquely swollen and burning hot.

"Do you have any honey?" Kate instantly felt foolish for asking. Of course they didn't, but maybe Walter could procure some before nightfall.

"No. I sent Walter to the village to get us some food. We've barely eaten since the battle. Guy hasn't had anything other than some wine."

"I got some mead," Walter piped in. "It's made with honey."

"Do you have a clean cloth?" Another foolish question. The men were filthy and didn't have anything with them save their armor, which she'd seen next to the corpse in the cart outside.

Kate exhaled audibly. She had clean cloth, but taking off her veil meant exposure. As long as she was decently covered, Hugh de Rosel saw her as a nun, but as soon as she took off her veil, she would become a woman—a woman alone with two strange men. But she couldn't allow Guy de Rosel to suffer, so she unwound her veil and tore it into several strips.

Both Hugh and Walter stared at her, their faces instantly transforming from expressions of reverence to obvious male interest. Kate kept her hair shoulder length, since it was uncomfortable to wear pinned-up plaits beneath the veil, but it was freshly washed and fell about her face in all its auburn glory.

She ignored the men and dipped a piece of fabric in the upturned helmet filled with water. She began to wash Guy's face. The cool water would hopefully revive him long enough to administer last rites. Guy moaned, but didn't open his eyes again.

"Give me some mead," Kate said to Walter, who was hovering just behind her. She cleaned the affected area with water

66

and then dabbed a generous amount of mead onto the wound. Honey was often used to combat corruption, so she hoped that the alcohol content mixed with the honey's healing properties might help, although she was fairly sure the man was too far gone. He had the same sickly look Osbert had had just before he died.

"He took a mace to the head," Hugh said. "The helmet saved him from certain death, but he isn't right in the head," he added sadly. "He spoke normally enough just after the battle, but then he seemed to go barmy and started talking pure guff. He said something about falling backward into a river of blood and turning to stone."

Kate nodded. The poor man was better off dead, but she fervently believed in the sanctity of life and would do everything in her power to help him. She pulled open one heavy eyelid. The blue eye stared back, unseeing. Guy de Rosel was beyond reach, but he'd opened his eyes before, and he might again.

"Sister, please, you must administer the sacraments while there's still time," Hugh pleaded as he leaned over her shoulder. He smelled of sweat, blood, and damp wool, but his bearing was that of a nobleman, even under the circumstances. Kate briefly wondered about the de Rosels' background. Hugh had referred to his brother as *Ghee*, but he was clearly English, his pronunciation clear and crisp, without any trace of a French accent.

Kate was about to explain that the sacraments could not be administered to a man who was not conscious to confess his sins or receive communion. She could, however, administer Last Unction and anoint the dying man with whatever was to hand. It would ease Hugh, but Guy de Rosel would not be fully shriven if he died. Perhaps this wasn't the time to mention this.

"Would you have any oil?" she asked.

Hugh shook his head. "Use the mead. It's the only thing we have."

Kate nodded and began. Both Hugh and Walter stood by Guy's side, their heads bowed as Kate anointed Guy's head with mead and prayed. He did not wake up.

"You both look exhausted. Perhaps you should rest," Kate suggested. "I will keep watch over him."

"We'll eat first. Please, share our meal, Sister." Hugh gestured toward the food Walter had brought back with him.

Kate gratefully accepted some bread and cheese. She hadn't eaten since she broke her fast at the priory that morning and she was famished. They drank water instead of the mead, which Kate was saving for Guy's wound, should he live through the night. The meal was a silent one since no one felt much like talking with Guy fighting for his life only a foot away.

As soon as they finished eating, Hugh folded up his cloak to use as a pillow and went to sleep, but Walter went outside. He planned to sleep by the cart, his sword at the ready should anyone try to help themselves to the armor or anything of value on Baron de Rosel's body. Kate felt sorry for the boy, but understood the necessity. And it was Walter's duty as a squire to look after the armor of his lords.

Kate positioned herself close to Guy, pulled up her knees, wrapped her arms around her legs, and rested her back against the wall, sitting in that position until the sun went down and the little chapel grew completely dark. She was tired, and shivered in the cold despite her woolen cloak. She looked up, staring past the charred beams at the sky above. It was vast, the stars and half-moon obscured by thick clouds. Kate hoped it wouldn't rain since there was nothing to shelter them inside the ruined chapel. She pulled the cloak tighter about her body and snuggled deeper into its folds, all set to keep her vigil.

She glanced at Hugh's silent form, thankful that he hadn't asked her any questions about herself or her family. He must be too tired and worried about his brother to wonder what a young nun was doing alone on the road to Belford, and she hadn't volunteered any information. A lie would sit heavily on her conscience, but she had no wish to tell him who she was, as he'd instantly realize that her relations fought for the opposing side.

Chapter 11

During the night, the sky cleared and the wind that moved stealthily through the trees died down. The clouds parted like heavy drapes, allowing Kate a breathtaking view of the starlit sky. Moonlight streamed into the roofless chapel, painting the walls in a silvery hue.

Guy de Rosel had settled into an uneasy sleep, his eyes moving rapidly beneath his eyelids. He moved his head from side to side, as if trying to escape the grip of nightmares, but the fever had a hold on him and wouldn't set him free, one way or the other.

Kate dabbed his brow with her damp veil and tried to get him to take a drink, but the water just ran down his chin instead of entering his mouth. She pulled out her rosary and resumed her seat. Her lips moved in silent prayer as her fingers moved from one smooth amber bead to the next. She prayed for Guy, who was in such agony, and for Osbert, for whom it was already too late. And she prayed for Hugh, who'd lost one brother and would most likely lose the other before long.

Kate fell asleep eventually, and woke as the gray light of dawn crept into the ruin. A dewy coolness had settled over the stones and what was left of the wood. She shivered and wrapped her arms around herself to ward off the chill.

A few more weeks and summer would be upon them, that brief, glorious season of sunshine and warmth. She'd spent the last two summers at the priory, working from dawn till dusk, with breaks only for meals and prayer. She'd enjoyed working in the vegetable garden and picking fruit in early autumn since the chores gave her a chance to spend some time outdoors. What would she do with all the empty hours of the day once she was back at home? Well-bred ladies didn't work in the garden or spend days pickling and stewing fruit and vegetables for the coming winter. Ladies sat in their solars, applying themselves to endless needlework and idle chatter, reluctant to step out into the sunshine for fear of ruining their milky complexions.

Kate ran a hand through her hair and rubbed sleep from her eyes before creeping outside to relieve herself. She returned to the church and used some of the water to wash her face and hands. That was the best she could do. She had no hairbrush, or anything to bind her hair, so she just left it loose to frame her face in thick waves.

"Who are you?" The whisper startled her. Guy de Rosel was watching her from the floor. His eyes were wide and clear, and he seemed fully conscious.

"Kate," she replied without thinking. "Eh, Sister Catherine," she amended quickly.

Guy reached out and took her hand. His hand was cooler than it had been during the night, and his grip was strong. "You prayed for me," he said, gazing up at her in wonder.

"Yes, I prayed all night. Well, most of it," she added, not wishing to exaggerate. "How do you feel?"

"Like a draft horse walked over me, then turned around and did it again," he replied. A hint of a smile tugged at his lips.

"How's your head?"

"It hurts, and my vision is blurred, but I feel less muddled," he said. "My arm feels like molten lead. I will never be able to wield a sword again, will I?"

Seeing fear and uncertainty in his eyes, Kate had no wish to tell him he might not live to see another battle, or even another sunrise. He believed he'd live, and that was as good as any poultice or potion.

"You will," Kate replied with all the conviction she could muster. "You'll need time to heal, and lots of practice, but you will wield your sword again."

Guy nodded. "I'm thirsty, Sister."

"Of course. I'm sorry. I should have realized…" Kate mumbled. She carefully lifted Guy's head and held a cup to his lips. He drank and drank, as if trying to douse the fire that raged within him. "Are you hungry?"

"Not really."

"You need your strength if you hope to fight off this fever. I'll give you tiny pieces. You don't even need to chew. Just swallow. Your body will do the rest."

"You're very comely for a nun," Guy said as he forced himself to swallow bits of bread soaked in mead.

"I'm not really a nun yet," Kate replied. "I was to take my vows in two weeks' time, but my father summoned me home. My brothers died on the same battlefield where you were wounded. My father has no sons left, just me," she added sadly.

Guy grasped her hand again. "I'm sorry, Kate, for both your losses. Do you mind terribly not becoming a nun?" he asked, just before she forced more food down his throat.

"Yes, I do. I wasn't sure at first, but I loved it at the priory. I would have been happy to spend the rest of my days serving God. But now, I will have to serve my father."

Guy nodded in understanding. "It's not easy to be a daughter, is it?"

"How would you know?" Kate asked, a smile tugging at her lips.

"I had a sister," he said. His expression turned grim and he looked away.

"Did she die?"

"She died because of me," he replied. Kate was about to ask more questions, but Guy's gaze grew clouded again, possibly from all the mead he'd just ingested. He closed his eyes, clearly exhausted.

"Rest," Kate said as she let go of his hand. "Just rest."

"How is he?" Hugh de Rosel asked from behind her. His hair was tousled from sleep and his beard had thickened during the night.

"He spoke to me. He seemed aware of his surroundings," Kate added.

"And his arm?"

"I don't think it's getting worse. I will change the dressing once it gets light."

Hugh shook his head. "There's only one other thing we can try now," he said, as he looked down on his brother. "I didn't want to do it if he was dying, but if there's even the slightest chance he will live…"

"What will you do to him?" Kate demanded. She felt protective of Guy, more so now that he'd spoken to her. She wasn't sure why she'd been honest with him, but something in his eyes had prevented her from lying to him. Geoffrey had advised her to always trust her instinct, and her instinct had been to trust Guy de Rosel.

"I will cauterize the wound."

She gasped. "No!"

"Sister, no amount of mead will stop the putrefaction from spreading. Guy will either live, or he will die, but we can't remain here any longer." Hugh added, "Will you help me?"

"Yes," Kate whispered. Her stomach clenched at the thought of hurting Guy so badly, but Hugh was right. She had nothing on hand to treat the infection. It hadn't grown worse, but it hadn't improved either. Guy was still feverish, and the wound was oozing pus, a sure sign that the putrefaction was spreading and would soon kill him.

"I will send Walter to gather some wood for a fire," Hugh said. He walked off, leaving Kate with Guy.

She reached for his hand and began to pray again, wishing she could give him some of her strength and vitality, and continued to pray as Walter and Hugh made a roaring fire in the nave. Its blaze seemed incongruous inside the chapel, especially since it was meant to be a healing flame and not a purifying, punishing pyre.

Kate removed Guy's bandage and exposed the ugly wound to the light. She held her breath as the stench of decay assaulted her, but didn't move away.

"I need you to hold his arm still," Hugh said. "Can you do it, or should I ask Walter?"

"I can do it."

"Probably best if you both hold him. He's strong as an ox when he wants to be. Walter, hold his shoulder in place and Sister Catherine can hold his lower arm."

Kate gripped Guy's arm with both hands and held it against the stone floor by the elbow and wrist. Guy's eyes fluttered open. He looked confused, but the sight of the glowing blade brought him to his senses and nearly undid him. His gaze filled with terror. "Please, Hugh, no," he pleaded.

"I'm sorry, brother, it's the only way," Hugh replied.

The searing blade came down on the open wound, filling the chapel with the stench of roasting flesh. Guy let out an inhuman roar and went rigid as a plank, then his legs began to quiver as Hugh held the blade over the wound. Guy jerked wildly and Kate brought all her weight down on his arm to keep him from yanking it away. Had Walter not been holding his upper body, Guy would have broken free. As it was, his eyes rolled into the back of his head and he mercifully lost consciousness, unable to bear the agony any longer.

Kate wiped away her tears with the sleeve of her habit once she was able to release Guy's arm. The puckered skin was red and raw and smelled of charred flesh.

"Let it cool completely, then bind it," Hugh commanded. "After that, we leave."

"I must return home," Kate told Hugh once she got hold of herself. "My parents will be frantic."

"You're coming with us, Sister. We can't manage without you. You have my word that I will deliver you to your father as soon as Guy is settled in his bed and William is in his grave."

"Seems I don't have a choice," Kate retorted.

"Walter can't look after him properly on the journey," Hugh replied, unfazed. "I need him to see to the horses and the armor. You're doing God's work," he added with a sour smile.

Kate didn't bother to argue. In truth, she couldn't leave Guy. He needed her a lot more than her father, and he would benefit from her ministrations, even if they were feeble. She watched as Hugh and Walter tied up the armor in bundles made of their cloaks and tossed them over her horse to make room in the cart.

William's corpse gave off a putrid odor, decomposition having set in. He'd been dead for four days, and even though the weather was cool, his corpse needed to be buried sooner rather than later. Kate tried not to look at what was left of William as she settled next to Guy, who was still insensible. Walter drove the cart, while Hugh led the horses ahead of them. The horses were spooked by the reek of death, so couldn't be downwind from the cart.

Kate brushed Guy's hair out of his face and laid a cool hand on his brow. His chest rose and fell evenly as he slumbered on. She couldn't bring herself to look at his arm, which was a horrid shade of crimson beneath the bandage. She prayed they would get to where they were going soon. She could smell her own sweat and fear beneath the putrid smells in the cart, and her head itched from lack of washing. She hadn't had a proper meal since leaving the priory, and she could feel that her courses were about to start. Her back ached, her belly cramped painfully, and her breasts were swollen and sensitive. She had nothing to use as rags if she began to bleed before they arrived at their destination, but couldn't raise the issue with the men.

They stopped only once to buy food and feed and water the horses, and then they were on their way again. Guy came to twice, but only for a few minutes at a time. Kate tried to get him to drink, since he couldn't manage any food, but he only took a few sips. When she spoke to him, he didn't reply, not even with a grunt or a squeeze of the hand. The day seemed to go on forever as the cart rattled along rutted tracks and muddy lanes. Kate's back groaned in protest and she tried to get more comfortable by leaning against the side, but had to fold her legs beneath her since William and Guy took up almost the entire cart.

It was nearly dusk by the time Hugh pointed out the shadowy bulk of Castle de Rosel in the distance. It stood squat and square on a hillside, overlooking the nearby town of Berwick, its crenellated tower dark against the lavender sky. The castle wasn't as grand as some Kate had seen. It was more of a keep, but it looked impregnable. Kate could see the dark outlines of arrow shafts, but several glazed windows that had probably been added later also graced the top floors. The light of a candle flickered behind one of the windows, but otherwise, everything was quiet and dark.

A chorus of barking erupted as they drew closer to the castle wall, and the gate swung open, revealing a nearly toothless old man holding a lantern. "Saw ye coming, I did. We was beginning to give up hope. The Earl of Stanwyck returned from the battle two days since. Suffered heavy losses. Thank the good Lord ye're home, Master Hugh."

The old man looked as though he were about to say something more when he spotted the bodies in the cart. "Lord Jesus, preserve us," he breathed and crossed himself before standing aside to let the cart pass. He shut the gate and followed behind the cart, shaking his head and muttering.

A boy of about ten ran from the stables, ready to help with the horses. His eyes sparkled with excitement, which turned to dismay as soon as he saw the contents of the cart. He looked ready to bolt, but held his ground, prepared to do his master's bidding.

Hugh dismounted with a grunt of relief, threw his reins to the boy without saying a word, then strode purposefully toward the keep. Walter helped Kate down from the cart before leading two of the horses toward the stables. Kate remained by the cart, uncertain what to do next.

A few moments later, a heavyset older woman rushed out the door. Her hair was covered with a veil and she wore a faded gown of brown homespun. She wiped her hands on the apron tied about her ample waist, as though suddenly remembering they were soiled from whatever she'd been doing when Hugh called for her. Lines of grief etched the woman's face as she slowly approached the cart and held out a work-reddened hand to gently touch William's body. She bowed her head in sorrow and crossed herself.

"Lord, have mercy on his soul," she said quietly as silent tears slid down her cheeks.

Hugh came up behind the woman and she turned and opened her arms to him. He walked into her embrace, burying his face in her shoulder. He appeared to be crying, and the woman, who was nearly as tall as Hugh but much wider, held him tightly and whispered words of comfort.

"Come now, me boy," she said as she held Hugh by the arms and gazed on him with love. "Ye must remain strong, Hugh. Ye're the master now."

Hugh nodded miserably. "Guy is barely holding on."

"I'll see to Guy, and to William," the woman said. She turned to Walter, who'd come out of the stable, having brought all the horses inside. "Walter, I know ye're tired, me lad, but if ye'd bring in some firewood I'd be most grateful."

She turned to Hugh and began issuing orders as if he were her subordinate, her earlier grief set aside while she took the situation in hand. "Hugh, get Guy to his room and lay him on the floor by the hearth. And get a good fire going in his bedchamber. Soon as ye can, lad. Alf, get water on the boil," she said to the old man, "and tell Aileen to bring clean towels. Walter, once ye bring in the firewood, see to his lordship's body. Alf will help ye."

"Shall I bring him to his bedchamber, Mistress Joan?" Walter asked.

"Don't be daft. That'll distress his wife and child. Bring him to the small chamber off the kitchen and lay him on the bench. And ye, come with me. What's yer name, then?" Joan asked Kate as she motioned for her to follow her into the keep.

Kate was about to reply when a young woman exploded from the doorway into the yard. Her fair hair was uncovered and hung down to her waist, and her dark eyes were wild with anguish. She was dressed in a gown of red velvet and her throat was adorned with a necklace of gold and rubies, the vibrant color pulsating with life in the face of death. The young woman wrung her hands and howled with grief when she beheld the body in the cart, then suddenly quieted and went deathly pale as if she were about to swoon. She swayed on her feet as she reached out to grab hold of the cart to steady herself.

Hugh rushed to her and took her in his arms just in time. The woman collapsed against him, sobbing. Hugh held her close, his hand stroking her golden hair as she cried. The gesture seemed to come naturally to him, speaking of a close relationship between the two.

"He fought bravely, Eleanor."

"He can't be gone," Eleanor moaned over and over. "Not my Will."

"Hugh, make sure the boy doesn't see his father like this," Joan said as she took charge of William's widow. "Come now, me lady. I'll see to his lordship's body. Come inside and get hold of yerself. Ye must remain strong for yer bairn, aye?"

Eleanor tried to get around Joan and back to the cart, but the older woman blocked her path and glared at her as if she were an errant child trying to grab a sweet. "Go back inside, me lady. Ye'll see yer lord when he's good and ready to be seen, and not a moment afore. Behave in a way that would have made him proud of ye." Joan whipped out a handkerchief and pressed it into the woman's hand.

Eleanor was still weeping, but softer now. She dabbed at her swollen eyes and wiped her streaming nose. "All right. I'll go inside," she whispered. She allowed herself to be led away by Hugh, who had his arm around her shoulders and spoke to her softly. Kate looked after them, her heart contracting with sorrow. No matter which side you were on, it was the women and children who bore the brunt of the fighting, left to mourn their losses and find their way in the world without their husbands and fathers.

Joan looked after the retreating figures and then returned her attention to Kate. She raised one eyebrow as she beheld Kate, still awaiting an answer.

"My name is Catherine Dancy. I was on my way home from Holystone Priory when I came upon Walter, who asked for my help."

"Well, God bless ye and keep ye, Mistress Dancy. Guy's wound looks well-tended to. Me name's Joan Wilbanks. Ye may call me Nurse or simply Joan, whichever ye prefer. We're an informal wee household. I was nurse to the de Rosel boys since the day they was born, and love them as if they was me own."

Like many people who'd been born and bred this far north, Mistress Wilbanks spoke a mixed dialect of English and Scots, and most likely boasted a few Scots in her line. Most people this close to the border did, since Berwick changed hands between England and Scotland with almost predictable frequency.

"And what were ye doing at the priory?" Joan asked conversationally as she stealthily took Kate's measure.

"I was a postulate, but my father summoned me home," Kate explained.

"Yer family lose someone at Towton?" Joan asked, instantly drawing her own conclusions.

"Three of my brothers."

"Oh, I'm sorry, lass. Ye must long to be with yer parents. Forgive Hugh for keeping ye from yer home. He wouldn't hold anyone against their will unless he were desperate."

"He didn't hold me," Kate replied. "I could have left, but Guy needed me."

"He still needs ye, by the look of him," Joan replied. "Help me get some food on the table, and then we'll see to Guy, unless ye're too weary."

"No, I wish to help."

Kate followed Joan inside. Despite the unwelcoming appearance of the keep, the interior wasn't as dark and dreary as Kate had imagined. Several sconces burned along the passage, lighting the way, and the room they passed was decorated with a tapestry and looked to be comfortably furnished, with fresh rushes on the floor and a fire burning in the grate. William de Rosel's widow was seated by the fire, her hands folded in her lap and her head bowed in sorrow. Hugh wasn't with her. He must have gone to do Joan's bidding and see to his brother.

Joan led Kate into a cavernous kitchen. A huge hearth took up the far wall, and a long, scarred table dominated the center. Two benches flanked the table, and several shelves held an assortment of bowls and jugs. A girl of about fourteen sat at the table, slicing turnips. She looked up and nodded, but didn't say anything. Joan made some elaborate gestures with her hands and the girl nodded again, more vigorously this time.

"Aileen's Jed's sister. That's the stable boy," Joan explained as she began to set the table. "The poor bairn's as deaf as a post. His lordship took the two of them into the household after their parents died a few years back. Kind he was, my William. And generous. He promised Jed his own parcel of land to work when he came of age, on account of letting other tenants work his father's farm since Jed and Aileen couldn't possibly manage on their own."

Joan set a plate of sliced pork, a wedge of cheese, and some brown bread on the table, and added a jug of ale. "That will do them for now. Had I known they'd be back today, I'd have prepared a hot meal, but Eleanor hasn't been eating much and we are all right with bread, cheese, and ale for our supper."

Joan grew silent and Aileen watched in horror as Walter and Alf carried William's body through the kitchen and into an adjacent chamber.

"Close the door," Joan barked at Alf, who was the last one out. "And Walter, wash yer hands before ye sit down to sup."

"Yes, Mistress."

A few minutes later, Hugh and Walter came into the kitchen. They'd washed their faces and hands, but must have been too hungry and tired to bother changing their clothes. Aileen vacated her seat at the table and took the turnips with her, retreating to the corner. Walter nodded to her, but Hugh paid her no mind, as if she weren't even there. He reached for the food and served himself first before passing the plate of pork to Walter. Both men looked up at Kate, as though expecting her to join them at the table.

"I'll eat something later, if I may," Kate said. "I'd like to see to Guy first."

"All right then. Come with me," Joan said.

Kate was famished, but she couldn't sit down and eat while Guy lay alone on the stone floor of his bedchamber. She couldn't understand why Joan wanted him laid on the floor, but didn't question her methods. Joan seemed like a woman who knew what she was about, and even if she didn't, she didn't seem likely to welcome advice from Kate.

She followed Joan down a narrow corridor toward a stone staircase. The stairs were dark and spiraled upward, but Joan knew her way by heart and didn't seem to require a candle. She led Kate to the uppermost floor and then walked to a door at the end of the passage. A single sconce burned in the corridor, casting shadows onto the stone walls and a low arched doorway that probably led to the roof. There was one more room, situated across from Guy's chamber, but its door was firmly shut.

Guy lay by the fire, his face flushed from the heat. His eyes were closed, but Kate suspected he was awake. A basin of water and some towels had been placed on a small table by the great bed, likely provided by Aileen. *Poor girl*, Kate thought as she waited to see what Joan planned to do. How awful it must be to live in a world of silence, a world in which she couldn't hear anything but her own thoughts. Kate wondered if Aileen had been born unable to hear, or been rendered deaf by an illness or an accident. It had been kind of William de Rosel to take in the children and guarantee Jed a future rather than keep him on as a groom for the rest of his days. Kate hoped William's heir, would honor that promise.

"Come now, me boy, let's get ye cleaned up," Joan said as she extracted a small knife from her pocket and sliced through Guy's blood-crusted tunic. She did the same to his breeches, leaving him completely naked. Kate looked away, embarrassed, but not before she saw his muscular chest, flat belly, and long, graceful legs.

"Give me a hand, Catherine," Joan said, handing Kate one of the towels. "Wet the towel and start at the bottom, with his feet."

Kate's cheeks flamed with embarrassment as her gaze traveled along Guy's torso toward a thicket of dark hair between his legs. She'd never seen an unclothed man before, and it was a revelation. She wasn't sure what she'd expected, but it wasn't the innocent-looking bit of flesh nestled there. How on earth did men beget children with that thing? Kate wondered as she soaped Guy's calves.

Joan gave her a pointed look and went to work on Guy's face and neck. She spoke gently to him, telling him of local happenings and promising to get him back on his feet as she washed the rest of him. Guy's eyes fluttered open when she touched his wounded arm.

"It burns, Nurse," he muttered.

"I know, me lamb, I know," Joan replied as she deftly lifted his upper body and pulled a clean shirt over his head. "But Hugh did the right thing. Ye'll be on the mend now. I just know it."

"Where's Kate?"

"I'm here," Kate answered and moved closer so that Guy could see her. Joan's disapproving look spoke volumes when Guy referred to her as Kate instead of Catherine, but the nurse said nothing and carried on.

"Don't leave me, Kate," Guy mumbled. "Stay with me until I sleep."

"Of course I'll stay," Kate replied. "Can you eat something?"

"I'll try."

"I have some broth," Joan interjected. "Broth is the best thing for him right now. Catherine, help me get him into bed."

"I think I'd best summon Hugh. He's too heavy for us."

"Nonsense. You just grab his legs." Joan lifted Guy off the floor as if he were no heavier than a child. Kate grabbed his legs

83

and helped Joan lay him on the clean sheets. Joan pulled the counterpane over him and smoothed back his hair. "How do you feel, pet?"

"Better," Guy replied. He grimaced with pain, but seemed afraid of offending his nurse, so put on a brave face. Perhaps her determination was exactly what he needed to recover from his injury.

"I'll get ye that broth. Ye stay with him, Catherine," Joan snapped, clearly annoyed that Guy preferred Kate to her.

It was well after midnight by the time Kate finally got into bed. She'd eaten, washed thoroughly, and was now wearing a clean shift Joan had brought her.

"Ye may wish to keep wearing that filthy habit, but if ye change yer mind, I've brought ye some clothes," Joan said as she laid out a sky-blue gown made of fine damask, complete with an embroidered stomacher. There was also a chemise, silk stockings, and a gauzy veil.

"These are very fine," Kate said as she looked at the items. "Whom did they belong to?"

Joan sighed. "They belonged to Marie de Rosel, the boys' mother, God rest her soul, but she no longer has need of them and ye do. She'd want ye to have them."

"Won't they object to me wearing their mother's things?"

"Marie's been gone for a long while now. I doubt the boys even remember what she wore. I kept her trunk. Shame to throw away such beautiful gowns, and ye never know when a comely young postulate will show up at the door," Joan said with a sour smile.

"Thank you, Mistress Joan," Kate replied, paying no heed to the sarcastic comment. She caressed the lovely bodice of the gown. The style was outdated, but the gown was still beautiful and well made, if a bit low-cut. Kate hadn't worn anything this fine since she left home, but the thought of wearing something that didn't cover her from head to toe was daunting after two years of living in a nun's habit.

"Ye'd best get used to it," Joan said, as if reading her thoughts. "Ye'll never be a nun now."

"No, I don't suppose I will."

"Once King Edward establishes his court, the ladies will display all their finery, hoping to catch his eye. He's still unwed, our new king, and handsome from what I hear. I doubt he'll marry one of his courtiers, not if Warwick has any say in the matter. Edward will be needing a foreign alliance to secure his throne, but to be the king's mistress is a great honor, and can be very lucrative for the family," Joan added. "Will your sire be taking ye to court then?"

"I doubt it, and I'm not looking to catch anyone's eye. Besides, I'm hardly worthy of the notice of the king."

"Ye never know. Ye never know," Joan repeated thoughtfully.

She left the clothes and walked out, leaving Kate to rest. Kate set aside the gown and climbed into bed. *What an odd household this is*, she thought as she lay sleepless. *The lady of the house is treated like a child, while the old nurse rules the roost and holds some rather astute opinions regarding the future of the Crown.*

Kate had yet to meet young Adam, who was four years old, but as she finally succumbed to sleep, she couldn't help wondering what the future held for the de Rosels now that a child was the head of the family.

Chapter 12

July 2014

Berwick-upon-Tweed, England

Quinn laid the rosary aside and stared at it thoughtfully. So, the rosary and the sword had belonged to two different people. It stood to reason that the remains they'd found were of Guy de Rosel, who'd been buried with his sword and Kate's rosary, but why was he buried in the kitchen? Hugh de Rosel had made it clear that it was very important to him to bury William properly at the parish church. Why would Guy not receive the same treatment, especially if his death was the result of a battle wound? And what had become of Kate? Was it possible that she'd given her most prized possession to a man she barely knew?

Quinn sighed. She couldn't wait to share what she'd seen with Gabe, but she'd have to brave his ire first. She smiled, feeling a bit smug. Gabe's curiosity about his ancestors would overcome his irritation. Gabe was a historian, first and foremost, and he'd want to hear every detail of what she'd seen. Quinn was sure that Gabe knew every name on his family tree and could recall the backstory, no matter how brief, on every person, but she wasn't ready to find out what had happened to Guy and Hugh de Rosel. She wanted to see for herself and watch their destinies unfold without already knowing how the story ended.

Quinn left the study and returned to the bedroom. Her earlier nightmare was forgotten and she could still get a few hours of sleep before it was time to get up. She curled up next to Gabe and was asleep the moment her head hit the pillow.

Quinn gazed up at Gabe, bleary-eyed. "What time is it?"

"Just gone eight." Gabe had just come out of the shower. Normally, Quinn would have appreciated the sight of him with his hair damp and a towel wrapped about his trim waist, but at the moment she was too tired to admire anything other than a cup of strong tea.

"Did you not sleep again last night?" Gabe asked as he bent to give her a kiss. "You should have woken me."

"I snuck down to your father's study," Quinn confessed.

Gabe's mouth stretched into a tight line as he crossed his arms and glared down at her. "You promised." He spoke quietly, but his voice was laced with anger.

"I had the nightmare again, and I just needed a distraction."

"You could have watched television or read a book. You didn't have to go sneaking behind my back. You're not taking any of this seriously. You are endangering yourself and the baby." He strode toward the bureau and grabbed the portable blood pressure kit. "Give me your arm."

Quinn sat bolt upright as irritation flared within her. "I'm not a child, Gabe, and I don't need to be lectured. Seeing into someone else's life is a lot less traumatic than reliving the nightmare of being locked in that tomb, thinking I'm going to die and you'll never find out what happened to me or our child. I would never, *EVER* endanger our baby." She didn't mean to get emotional, but tears of hurt slid down her cheeks and she wrapped her arms about herself in an effort to keep it together and prevent Gabe from getting the blood pressure cuff around her arm.

Gabe set aside the kit, sat on the edge of the bed, and drew her into his arms. "I'm sorry. I'm just worried about you. You seem so fragile these days."

"I'm not fragile." Quinn sniffed into his shoulder. "I'm as tough as a pair of old boots."

That made Gabe laugh. "Interesting comparison."

"My Grandma Ruth used to say that when my dad tried to bully her into taking things easier."

"All right then," Gabe said as he stroked her hair. "You're as tough as old boots."

"They're still fashionable boots though," Quinn mumbled, a hint of a smile tugging at the corner of her mouth.

"Blood-red Dr. Martens with a steel-reinforced toe," Gabe replied, smiling widely.

"You remember?"

"Of course I remember. You wore those bloody boots every day, and when you tripped and fell over me, you kicked me in the shin. It was like being kicked by a donkey. I limped for a week."

"How would you know? Have you ever been kicked by a donkey?"

"No, but I've been blessed with a very vivid imagination," Gabe relied, his impish grin fading as his gaze clouded with desire.

Quinn lay back and pulled him down on top of her. "Come here, then," she whispered. "I won't kick. I promise."

Gabe didn't need to be asked twice. He tossed his towel to the floor and covered her body with his own.

"You know, you're very fit for an academic," Quinn murmured as she ran her hands across Gabe's hard chest.

"And you're wonderfully round." Gabe lowered his head and kissed Quinn's belly before sliding his hand up her leg.

Quinn moaned with pleasure and arched her hips as flames of desire leaped in her belly. Gabe made love to her slowly and gently, as if she were made of glass. Afterward, she lay in his embrace, feeling languid and sated. Gabe's unwavering devotion banished her nightmares to the deepest recesses of her mind, exactly where she wanted them.

Chapter 13

"Gabe, do you know anything about Holystone Priory? It's not too far from here, is it?" Quinn asked as she pulled on a pair of track pants and a T-shirt.

Gabe rested his hip against the bureau, lost in thought. "No, it isn't too far. The Holystone Priory was the home of a cloistered order of Augustine nuns before it was looted and destroyed during the Dissolution of the Monasteries. It was built next to a Lady's Well, which was believed to be a place of great mysticism and power. My mum actually took me there when I was a boy," Gabe said. "I kept staring at the Celtic cross rising out of the water, expecting something to happen. I thought it was frightening."

"I didn't see a cross."

"The cross was erected during Victorian times, so it wouldn't have been there in the Middle Ages."

"Why did your mum take you there? Did she want to visit the ruins?" Quinn asked.

"No, we went directly to the Lady's Well," Gabe replied. "Come to think of it, it is really odd that she took me there. I'll have to ask her if she remembers. Why do you ask about Holystone?"

"The owner of the rosary was a postulate there."

"I wonder how she wound up here," Gabe remarked as he began to dress for the day.

"She was brought here by your ancestors, Hugh and Guy de Rosel. I didn't think she'd stay."

"Did she?"

"I don't know yet. I'm working on the assumption that the remains we found are Guy de Rosel. Kate nursed him after he was gravely wounded at the Battle of Towton."

Gabe's jaw tensed at the mention of Towton. The Wars of the Roses was his area of expertise, and the Battle of Towton, fought more than five centuries ago, still pained him since his ancestors had been on that battlefield and fought for the losing side. "What were they like, Hugh and Guy?" Gabe asked as he searched under the bed for his trainers.

"Guy was unconscious most of the time, so it's hard to say anything about his personality. He was handsome, though. Kind of looked like you when I first met you at that dig," Quinn added, smiling wistfully.

"And Hugh?"

Quinn shrugged as she tried to marshal her thoughts. "Hugh wasn't as attractive, but he had an air of competence about him. He was the type of man who got things done. He was a bit gruff too, but I suppose, given the fact that he'd just lost one brother and was about to lose the other, a little gruffness wasn't unexpected."

"And Kate? What was her surname?"

Quinn was about to reply when Phoebe's voice drifted up from the foyer. "Are you both up? I've come to collect some things."

"You go on, Gabe. I'll be right down. I'm curious about this visit to Holystone," Quinn added as she reached for her hairbrush.

By the time Quinn came down, Phoebe and Gabe were already installed in the front parlor, mugs of tea in hand. Phoebe still refused to go into the kitchen, so Gabe made tea and toast and set their breakfast on a low table before the sofa. Phoebe was buttering a piece of toast for herself, but held it out to Quinn while Gabe poured her a cup of tea.

"You look peaky," Phoebe said as she studied Quinn. "Nightmares still plaguing you?"

Quinn nodded.

"Can't your doctor prescribe something to help you sleep? You need your rest."

"I don't want to take any more medication than I have to," Quinn replied. "I'm taking enough as is. I'll manage. I try to kip during the day, while Emma's at school."

"Mum, do you remember taking me to Holystone Priory when I was a boy?" Gabe asked as he spread marmalade on his toast. "I must have been around six or seven."

"You were five," Phoebe replied. She looked away, clearly uncomfortable with the topic.

"Why did we go there?" Gabe persisted.

"I wanted to visit the Lady's Well and had no one to leave you with. Your father had gone fishing with some of his mates and didn't want you under his feet."

"Why did you want to visit the well?" Gabe asked. "It doesn't seem like your sort of place."

"I wanted to pray."

A hush fell over the room as Gabe gaped at his mother in astonishment. "But you're not Catholic," he finally said. "Why would you want to pray to the Virgin Mary?"

Phoebe sighed and laid down her uneaten toast. "I wanted to pray for a baby."

Gabe and Quinn sat in shocked silence, waiting for Phoebe to elaborate. She was the type of woman who went to church to socialize, not to pray. She had once quoted Karl Marx at a dinner party, saying that religion was the opium of the people. Graham had laughed at her and called her a 'closet socialist' in front of their friends. Phoebe hadn't liked that one bit, but she'd stuck to her guns. When Graham died, Phoebe had chosen to have him cremated instead of having a religious funeral service, a decision that hadn't sat well with Gabe.

"I suffered several miscarriages before Gabe was born," Phoebe explained, speaking mostly to Quinn. "I was devastated, and after nearly a decade of marriage I longed for a baby with a desperation only a childless woman could understand. In this day and age, they would have run tests and tried to figure out why I kept miscarrying, but fifty years ago the doctors blamed me. It was always, 'Did you lift anything heavy? Did you allow yourself to become agitated? Did you take too much pleasure in marital relations?' That sort of thing."

"Why would it matter if you enjoyed marital relations?" Gabe asked, baffled.

"Because, my dear boy, some doctors believed that an orgasm could bring on a miscarriage," Phoebe explained, making Gabe blush. "After my last miscarriage, they put me on the maternity ward. You know, just to drive the stake deeper into my heart. I lay there, watching besotted new mothers nursing their babies. I just wanted to die," she said with a sigh.

"I'm so sorry," Quinn said and reached for Phoebe's hand. "I can't even begin to imagine how painful that must have been for you."

Phoebe nodded. "There was a young woman in the next bed. Sheila, she was called. She said that she and her husband had been trying for seven years. She couldn't get pregnant. Then her mother told her to go pray at the Lady's Well at Holystone. She refused time and time again until she finally went. Had nothing left to lose, she said. Nine months later she gave birth to her first child. She went again, and had another baby shortly afterward. She swore it was a miracle."

"So you went?" Gabe asked.

"I went. I got on my knees and I prayed to the Blessed Virgin, and to whatever pagan gods inhabited that mystic place long before Christianity, to give me a living baby. I swore I'd never ask for anything again if I had one child that survived."

"And you had Gabe?" Quinn asked, stunned.

"Gabe was born less than a year later, healthy and strong. It was a miracle, in my book."

"Why did you go back?" Gabe asked. He glanced away when Quinn gave him a loaded look, implying that he was being obtuse.

"I wanted another child. I was happy and busy with Gabe, but he was getting older, about to start school, and I began longing for another child. I wanted a daughter, you see."

"I'm sorry it didn't work, Mum," Gabe said.

"No, it didn't. I prayed, but I wasn't granted another miracle. Perhaps it was because I'd promised I wouldn't ask again. Or perhaps because I was just too old by that point to get pregnant naturally. Nowadays, I would still be considered fertile, but in those days, a woman over thirty was considered to be 'past her prime.' We tried for several years, but I never got pregnant again. Still, I think my Gabe is a miracle, and I'll say so to anyone who asks," Phoebe concluded defiantly.

This was completely at odds with what Quinn knew of Phoebe's religious beliefs, but she didn't question Phoebe's story. Perhaps Phoebe had grown disillusioned when she failed to conceive again. Quinn's hand subconsciously went to her belly. A child was a miracle, and she was blessed to have conceived so easily.

"I'm sorry, Phoebe," Quinn said. It wasn't until she'd fallen pregnant herself that she'd really given any thought to what her mother and Phoebe must have gone through. Susan Allenby had been unable to conceive due to endometriosis, while Phoebe had conceived again and again only to lose her babies halfway through the pregnancy. Both Susan and Phoebe had managed to raise one child, but their paths to motherhood hadn't been easy—unlike Sylvia, who got up the duff after one encounter and thrown her baby away.

Chapter 14

April 1461

Northumberland, England

Guy opened his eyes and promptly cursed his brother, using language that would make most men cringe. The wound in his arm had begun to blister and ooze, and the pain of the injury combined with the burn Hugh had inflicted hurt him in ways he couldn't put into words. The slightest movement caused Guy to break out in a cold sweat and retch into the basin Nurse had thoughtfully left on the bed. He was, however, alive and at home, and for that he was extremely grateful.

He hoped Kate was still there. Her gentle touch and fervent prayers might not have saved him, but they had certainly helped, especially to lift his spirits, which had hit rock-bottom as he lay in the chapel ruin, staring up at the jagged bits of roof and dark heavens and believing it was the last thing he would ever see. And then he'd seen her, leaning over him, her hair brushing his face as she laid a hand on his head and blessed him.

Guy turned his head toward the door as he heard approaching footsteps. He hoped it was Kate, coming to check on him, but it was Hugh. He'd bathed and shaved, and his hair was neatly brushed. He was wearing a doublet of claret velvet, and William's ruby ring, which he seemed to have forgotten to return to Eleanor to keep safe for Adam.

Hugh pulled up a chair and sat down next to the bed. "You look better," he said.

"May you roast in the fires of Hell until you hurt as much as I do," Guy replied without heat.

"You're welcome. Our sweet Angel of Mercy tells me your fever has broken and you've managed to eat something other than broth and bread. That's excellent news indeed."

"I can't move my arm," Guy complained.

"You have to give it time. The sword cut deep, almost to the bone. How's your head?"

"It still hurts like the devil, and my vision blurs when I get tired, but I think it's improving."

"Praise the Lord," Hugh said, crossing himself. "I really thought I'd lost you, Guy."

The brothers grew silent as they remembered William, now safely buried in the cemetery of their parish church, St. Mary's. There were half a dozen de Rosels buried inside the church, but the more recently deceased were in the cemetery, the church being too small to accommodate any more tombs in its crypt.

"How's Eleanor? She hasn't been to see me," Guy said.

"She's in a bad way, Guy. Adam is frightened. Thank Jesu for Nurse. She's keeping him away from Eleanor by creating 'important' tasks for him to carry out. He's been helping Walter clean our armor and accompanied him to the blacksmith's to have your helmet beaten back into shape. It's as good as new."

"I keep expecting William to walk in and tell me that I'm a lay-about and we need to get in some sword practice," Guy said wistfully. "I never got to say goodbye."

"Guy, you're a seasoned soldier, not a blushing maiden. You know what happens when men go into battle, and you know the odds of coming back unscathed. Lord Dancy lost three sons at Towton," he added, looking gratified by Guy's stunned reaction.

"Did he indeed? How do you know?" The Dancys had fought for Edward, so Hugh's intimate knowledge of the family's losses took Guy by surprise, but he assumed that Hugh had heard that bit of gossip from someone left on the battlefield to tend the wounded. Many had lost their fathers, brothers, and sons that day, and many families had lost more than one loved one.

"I know, because their sister is in the bedchamber down the passage, looking very fetching in one of Mother's gowns."

Guy stared at his brother as the words finally penetrated. "Sister Catherine is Lady Catherine Dancy?" he asked stupidly.

"She is indeed."

"But she's a nun," Guy protested. "Why is she wearing Mother's gown?"

"The good Lord has smiled upon us, Guy. We lost William, but we gained something in the bargain. Lady Catherine was a postulate at Holystone Priory, not a full-fledged nun. She told Nurse. She was due to take her vows next week, as it happens, but her bereaved sire summoned her home as soon as he learned of the loss of his sons, and there's only one reason why a man needs his daughter," Hugh said, grinning.

"To marry her off to his advantage."

"Exactly."

Guy shook his head in confusion. It ached unbearably and he needed to close his eyes since everything in sight began to dissolve into swirls of mist, including his brother, whose head now resembled a large gourd. "I don't see what this has to do with us."

"You will, little brother. You will."

"Hugh, I…" Guy began, but didn't get a chance to finish the sentence as the lady in question poked her head around the door.

"May I come in?" Kate asked. "I wanted to say goodbye."

Sunlight from the window fell on her as she stood in the middle of the room. A golden haze surrounded her, probably caused by Guy's distorted vision, but to him she looked like an angel. Her glorious hair fell to her shoulders and framed her face, and her wide blue eyes held Guy's gaze as he looked upon her.

"Your brother is taking me home," Kate said as she approached the bed. "I'm so glad you're feeling better. I know you must be in terrible pain, but the danger's passed and Nurse will look after you until you're well enough to rise from your bed."

"Thank you, for everything," Guy mumbled, suddenly afraid that he might embarrass himself by getting teary-eyed. He felt ashamed of his weakness, but he didn't want her to go. Once Kate left, she'd be out of his reach, and the thought made him sick with longing. He'd never been in love, never even looked at a woman with any thought for the future, but he could imagine Kate by his side. She wished to be a nun; he knew that, and he would be prepared to never lay a finger on her if only she agreed to share her life with him. He would remain celibate, for he would never want another woman again if he couldn't have her.

"Guy? Guy?" Kate called to him. "He's exhausted. Perhaps we'd better leave him to rest." She leaned over him and kissed him gently on the forehead. "May God bless you, Guy de Rosel," she whispered. "And may he keep you safe."

"And you," was all Guy could manage. His head was splitting in two, and he could barely focus on Kate's face, which was a shame because he wanted to store it in his memory forever.

"I'll be back in a few days," Hugh said as he rose to leave. "Nurse will look after you, brother. Get well."

"Right," Guy muttered as he closed his eyes to hide the tears that stung his pride.

Chapter 15

July 2014

Berwick-upon-Tweed, Northumberland

"That's the last of it," Gabe announced as he finished bagging and labeling the bits of cloth, hair, and leather he'd found in the grave. A long box, looking for all the world like a Christmas present, rested on the kitchen table, and contained the bones of the medieval warrior who was about to embark on his final journey.

"Think he's even been to London?" Quinn asked as she eyed the box. It always amazed her that a living, breathing human being could be reduced to nothing but a box of bones.

"It's possible," Gabe replied. "It all depends on where his loyalties lay."

"I never knew your family was titled."

"Armand de Rosel, grandfather to William, Hugh, and Guy, was created the first Baron de Rosel. He would have received a Writ of Summons to attend Parliament, quite an honor in those days. The title passed to his son, Gilles de Rosel, and then to William. On William's death, four-year-old Adam became the next Baron de Rosel. And he was also the last. The family was stripped of the title when Henry Tudor took the throne."

"Fought for the wrong side, did they?" Quinn asked.

"They did. I know the history, but I can't begin to imagine what it must have been like to live in a time when the balance of power continually shifted, and choosing the wrong side could mean not only the loss of your title and holdings, but possible execution. Imagine the uncertainty. Putting aside the ongoing struggle for the throne, Berwick changed hands more than a dozen times during the Middle Ages, going from being English to Scottish and back again."

"Were there any Scots in your line?" Quinn asked.

"Not that I know of." Gabe looked at the box of bones, his head tilted to the side in thought. "Other than the fact that our man was buried with Guy de Rosel's sword, there's nothing to indicate that he was actually an ancestor of mine. He could have been buried here for any number of reasons. It would seem that someone was trying to hide his body, so chances are he didn't die in battle, or of natural causes."

Quinn rested her palm on the box containing the mortal remains of the knight. "Whoever buried him clearly held him in great esteem and gave him the honors due to a warrior. I'd wager he wasn't buried by his enemies."

"No, probably not, but why bury him beneath the floorboards? A Christian burial was very important, and still is for people of the faith. Burying someone in unconsecrated ground was seen as either an insult or a punishment."

"What did you do to deserve such a fate?" Quinn asked the silent bones.

"Hopefully, we'll get some answers from Colin. Once we know what ultimately killed him, we'll be able to start filling in the blanks."

"Gabe, would you mind if I shared this discovery with Rhys? It could make for an interesting episode of *Echoes*. I know Rhys has several good leads for the second series, but he'd love this."

"Quinn, you're on maternity leave," Gabe replied with an eloquent frown.

"I know, but I feel so restless," she complained. "I'm not used to doing nothing."

"You're not doing nothing, you're taking care of our baby and preparing for its birth."

Quinn sighed. "My nesting instinct hasn't kicked in yet. Right now, I just feel grumpy and listless. Besides, whether Rhys is interested in the story or not, we're still digging into the past. It's what we do, Gabe."

"All right," Gabe conceded. "You can discuss this with Rhys. As long as production is on summer hiatus, I guess he can't do too much damage. Have you spoken to Sylvia?" Gabe asked carefully. Relations with Sylvia had been strained since Gabe called the police on Jude when he'd disappeared with Emma.

"I have, but the conversations were brief and confined to inquiries about my health and the well-being of the baby. She's still upset about not being invited to our wedding. And about Jude, of course."

"Has the prodigal son returned?"

"Yes, Jude has come back to Sylvia's, but only temporarily. Seems he's moving in with his girlfriend, Bridget."

"Isn't that the girl who colored Emma's hair pink?" Gabe asked, his jaw tightening in that telltale fashion. He was still upset with Jude for taking Emma out without permission and not telling anyone where he was going. Thankfully, no harm had been done, but Gabe had been frantic, especially since Jude wouldn't answer his mobile for hours.

"Yes, that's her. Sylvia is rather in the dumps about it," Quinn replied. "Jude is her baby."

Gabe didn't reply as he surveyed the hole in the floor. The kitchen had been practically demolished. A large chunk of the black-and-white tiled floor had been taken up to extract the remains and the plumbing was exposed. There was still no running water, and the leaky pipe would need to be replaced, if the plumber could be persuaded to return.

"Is your mum ready to come back home?" Quinn asked as she organized the labeled plastic bags on the table.

"Not yet. I don't want her back in the house until the water is running and the floor has been retiled. I worry about her falling into the hole."

"Gabe, this place is a money pit," Quinn said carefully. She knew Gabe shared her sentiment, but it was still his ancestral home, and he might take offense at her description.

"I know." Gabe sighed. "I know. And so does Mum."

"Shall we get going?" Quinn asked, eager to return to London.

"There's one more thing I need to do before we leave," Gabe replied.

"What are you thinking?" she asked, fairly sure he'd had an idea regarding the remains. "I know that look."

"I'm thinking I need to find the floor plan for the original house."

"Do you think such a thing exists?"

"My family has been on this parcel of land since the Conquest," Gabe replied. "The original structure must have been a fortress, but they expanded it over the centuries and eventually opted for comfort over safety. This house was built in the eighteenth century. Perhaps there are plans for the modern structure somewhere in Dad's study."

"Gabe, how is it possible that this house was constructed without the remains being unearthed?"

"That's what I was wondering," Gabe replied as he headed for the study, determined to find the answer.

Chapter 16

April 1461

Belford, Northumberland

Kate breathed a sigh of relief when the twin roof peaks of the Grange finally came into view. She ached from being in the saddle all day, but Hugh didn't seem similarly affected and talked easily as they made their way toward the house. His demeanor had changed, possibly because he was no longer worried about Guy. He seemed lighter somehow, and more gallant. Kate was grateful to him for bringing her home, but she worried about her father's reaction to her Lancastrian escort. She didn't think her father would turn Hugh away, but she wasn't at all sure of the type of welcome he would receive, given recent events. Her stomach twisted with anxiety when Hugh dismounted and helped her down from her horse.

Isaiah came running out of the stables to take their horses and bowed to Kate from the waist. "Welcome back, Lady Catherine," he said solemnly. "Your father will be much relieved to see ye home safe."

"Thank you," Kate said and turned to Hugh. "We'd best go inside."

She gazed at the imposing façade of the Grange. It was built of gray stone and shaped like the letter E. The house had been commissioned by her grandfather, a man who had valued not only appearances but comfort and wasn't satisfied with the wattle and daub structure his own father had built. The rooms were spacious and light, and were adorned with tapestries, handsome furniture, and silver candleholders. When Kate had reminisced about her home during her time at the priory, she had always imagined it bustling with activity, but at the moment the place looked almost deserted. Most of the shutters were closed against the light and the yard was unusually quiet.

The entrance hall was cool and dark. No one had bothered to light the sconces or lay the fires despite the nip in the air. Kate looked around in dismay. Where was everyone? She opened the door to the front parlor, but it was empty, as were the dining hall and all the other rooms on the ground floor. Even the servants didn't seem to be about.

"Mother! Father!" Kate called out.

"Lady Catherine!" Mildred came rushing from the kitchen at the back of the house. She looked flushed and nervous as she curtsied to Kate and Hugh.

"Mildred, where are my parents?" Kate asked. She looked around anxiously. "Where's everyone?"

"Yer lady mother hasn't left her bed since news of the battle reached us," Mildred explained. "Lord Dancy is with her, and the servants are in the kitchen, having their supper. Yer father sent out all the men to search for ye, after ye failed to turn up, me lady, except Isaiah, on account of him being too old."

"Osbert died," Kate explained.

"Aye, we know. Matthew found him by the side of the road and brought him back to be buried. Yer father thought ye might have been taken hostage." Mildred gazed warily at Hugh, unsure of his role in Kate's disappearance.

"Mildred, this is Hugh de Rosel. He was kind enough to escort me home and will, of course, be spending the night. Please have a bedchamber prepared, and we'd like some supper. I need to see my parents, Hugh," Kate said apologetically.

"Of course, my lady. I'll wait in the parlor, if I may."

"I'll light the candles and get the fire going," Mildred fussed, flustered at being caught unprepared. "If ye come this way, sir."

Mildred led Hugh into the parlor and threw open the shutters. The purpling shadows of twilight filled the empty room, but did little to chase away the melancholy mood that seemed to permeate the house. Hugh lowered himself onto a wooden settle by the empty hearth and crossed his legs, the very picture of patience and calm.

Kate hitched up her skirts and sprinted up the stairs. Her heart squeezed with anxiety, but she was grateful to be home at last. She stopped in front of the closed door to her mother's solar and took a deep breath before knocking.

"Come," Gerard Dancy called out.

"Father, it's me," Kate said as she stepped into the room.

"Oh, Kate, praise the Lord," Gerard breathed as he came forward to wrap her in a fierce embrace. "We thought we'd lost you. Didn't we, Anne?"

He addressed his wife, but Anne didn't respond. She lay quiet and still among the blankets, her face pale and twisted in the meager candlelight.

"Where have you been, Kate? I sent Matthew, Glen, and Cecil to look for you. They found Osbert's body, but no trace of you," her father added gruffly. "He looked to have died of natural causes."

"After Osbert took ill and died, I set off for home on my own. I came across several knights returning from Towton," Kate explained.

"You met knights on the road?" her father demanded, his eyes narrowing with suspicion.

"Yes. One of them was gravely wounded, so I stayed to tend to him. His brother, Hugh de Rosel, escorted me home. He's downstairs in the parlor."

"Is he King Edward's man?" her father asked.

"No. They fought for King Henry."

Gerard glowered. "You dare to bring a Lancastrian knight into my household?"

"Father, Hugh de Rosel has been nothing but gallant and kind. I could hardly ask him to leave without inviting him in."

Gerard Dancy shook his head in dismay. "I suppose we'll have to put him up for the night. But in the morning, he leaves."

"I understand," Kate replied. She had no wish to talk about Hugh. There was so much in her heart. Her father didn't hold with sentiment or tears, but Kate needed to express her sorrow and offer him whatever comfort she could. "Father, I heard about…" Her voice trailed off. She couldn't bear to say the words aloud.

Gerard Dancy bowed his head in grief. "I never imagined… Your poor mother… I don't know how we'll get through this, Kate. It's too much to bear."

"What's wrong with Mother?"

"Your mother suffered some sort of apoplexy when she found out about the boys," her father replied, not bothering to lower his voice. "Her entire right side is immobile, and she can barely speak or eat. She sleeps most of the time, and even when she wakes, she's confused and lost in her own waking nightmare."

"Oh, Father," Kate said, taking his hands in hers. "I will tend to her. She will get better in time. I know she will."

"We must look to the future," Gerard said, pulling his hands out of Kate's grasp. "We must survive."

"Father, will you not come down and meet Hugh?" Kate asked. It seemed rude to leave Hugh all alone in the parlor, but her father shook his head.

"Maybe later."

Kate nodded. It was pointless to argue with her father when he was in such depressed spirits. She walked over to the bed and kissed her mother's cold cheek. "I'm home, Mama. Can you hear me?" But her mother didn't respond. Her face was as still and white as a stone effigy, and her hands, which had always been white and elegant, looked like gnarled claws atop the counterpane. Kate smoothed back her mother's hair. It had been a rich auburn, like her own, but now thick streaks of silver framed her face. Kate hardly recognized the woman in the bed.

"See to your guest," Gerard ordered. "And tell Mildred to send up some food. I'm famished."

"Won't you join us for supper, Father?" Kate tried again, but her father glared at her and turned away, not bothering to respond.

Kate returned downstairs to find Hugh gazing out the window, his hands clasped behind his back. He turned and smiled at her, clearly surprised to find her alone.

"I'm sorry, Hugh, but my mother is ill, and my father doesn't want to leave her side. Looks like it will be just you and me for supper," she said, hoping that didn't sound improper.

"I actually prefer it that way," Hugh replied. "I was a bit nervous about meeting your father," he confessed. "I thought he might be angry with me for detaining you instead of sending you home straight away."

"He was worried for my safety." Given her father's mood, he'd likely never meet Hugh de Rosel, so there was little point in mentioning Lord Dancy's displeasure. Hugh would be gone soon enough, his part in Kate's disappearance forgotten. "I'll tell

Mildred to serve supper now, since my father won't be joining us. You must be hungry."

"I am," Hugh admitted.

Kate led Hugh into the dining room and took a seat opposite him as Mildred brought out a platter of sliced pork, fresh bread, and buttered parsnips.

"I'm sorry, me lady, but Cook didn't have time to prepare anything more fitting. We wasn't expecting guests."

"I'm perfectly happy with pork and parsnips," Hugh assured her, smiling pleasantly. "And the company more than makes up for the lack of delicacies."

Kate blushed, unaccustomed to this side of Hugh. Perhaps now that he was done with soldiering for a while, he was behaving more like his normal self.

They shared a pleasant meal, and then Kate excused herself and went upstairs, leaving Hugh to enjoy a cup of wine in the parlor. She was tired from the long journey, and worried for her mother. Once Hugh left, she would dedicate all her time to nursing her mother back to health.

Kate decided to stop by her mother's chamber before going to sleep. Her father wasn't there. Perhaps he had retired. Kate sat on the side of the bed and took her mother's hand. It felt brittle and cold.

"Mama," Kate called. "Mama, it's me."

"Katie," her mother breathed. "My Katie."

"I'm home, Mama. I'll look after you."

Anne Dancy shook her head as silent tears slid down her cheeks. "Don't want to…"

"Don't want to what?"

"Don't want to go on," Anne muttered. Her speech was slurred, but Kate could still make out her words.

"Mama, don't say such things. I'll be here with you."

Anne shook her head again. "No, you won't, Katie."

"I'm not going anywhere."

"Kate, obey your father. Don't antagonize him. He's heartbroken."

"I know. I'll be a dutiful daughter to him. I always have been."

"I'll go to my boys," Anne mumbled as her eyelids fluttered. "They need me."

Anne was asleep within moments, leaving Kate more depressed than before. She adjusted the counterpane and bent down to kiss her mother's forehead. "Don't leave me, Mama," Kate whispered. "Please, don't leave me."

Kate turned when Mildred entered the room, carrying a candle. "I'll sit with her now, me lady. Ye must be worn out from yer journey."

"Where's Master de Rosel?"

"He's still in the parlor, me lady. His chamber is all made up for him. I told him so. Ye go on now."

There was nothing for Kate to do but go to bed. She snuggled beneath the blankets, but despite the feathery embrace of the mattress and the softness of the pillows, she couldn't get comfortable, not after sleeping on a narrow wooden cot for more than two years with only a threadbare blanket for warmth. The bed was too soft, the room too warm, and the atmosphere in the house heartbreakingly melancholy. Kate hadn't expected a happy homecoming, but the reality was even bleaker than she'd prepared for. She felt weepy and hollow, and strangely out of place in her own home.

She closed her eyes and waited for sleep to come. She tried to recall happy times with her brothers, to honor their memory, but Guy de Rosel was the last person she thought of before falling asleep. His face appeared to her, clear as day, and the anguish she felt at the thought of never seeing him again took her by surprise, possibly because he was as lost to her as if he were dead.

Chapter 17

Kate woke with a start. She had no idea how long she'd been asleep. For a brief moment, she thought it was time for the Midnight Office prayer, or Matins, but quickly remembered she was no longer at the priory. What had woken her was the opening of the door, followed by footsteps.

As her father approached the bed, the light of a single candle illuminated the lower half of his face, giving it a demonic appearance.

"Is it Mother?" she gasped, sitting up.

Gerard set down the candle on a bedside table and leaned over Kate. The anger burning in his eyes frightened her. "Did he force you?" he demanded.

"What? Who?"

"Did Hugh de Rosel force himself on you?" her father repeated, his face so close, Kate could smell wine on his breath. .

"No, he didn't." Her mind had been muddled with sleep, but now she was fully awake. She drew back from her father and pulled the counterpane to her chest, clutching at it with all her might in a desperate but vain effort to protect herself.

He slapped her hard across the face and she cried out in shock as her head spun to the side, blood filling her mouth when she bit her tongue.

"Father, what have I done?" Kate cried as he towered over her.

Her father didn't answer. He dragged her out of bed and pushed her down on the cold floor. She thought he might kick her and she curled into a ball to protect her middle, but he stood aside, panting with fury.

"Whore!" he spat out. "Get out of my house and never return. You're useless to me now. You're soiled."

"Father, I…"

"Get out!" he roared. "If I ever see you again, I'll kill you." He grabbed the candle and stormed from Kate's bedchamber, leaving her bewildered and shaking with shock.

What had she done? Why did he think she was soiled? Kate hastily pulled on her clothes, stuck her feet in her shoes, grabbed her cloak, and ran downstairs.

Hugh was in the yard, their horses saddled and ready. "Come, Catherine. We'll bide at the inn tonight, and tomorrow, I will return and try to reason with your father."

"What on earth did you say to him?" Kate cried as he gave her a leg-up and handed her the reins.

"I asked him for your hand in marriage," Hugh replied as he swung into the saddle. "I told him that I'd had the honor of getting to know you over the past few days and wished to spend my life with you."

Kate stared at him. "Is that *all* you said?" She couldn't begin to understand why Hugh would ask her father for her hand. Lord Dancy was a staunch Yorkist, cousin to the Earl of Warwick, and distant kin to the new king. He would never consider a suit from someone whose rank was beneath his own, particularly an avowed supporter of the House of Lancaster.

"Of course," Hugh replied, sounding deeply offended. "What else could I have said?"

"My father seems to have misinterpreted your meaning," Kate replied, her voice shaking with anger, hurt, and confusion. Only a few days ago she had been at the priory, her life measured, ordered, and calm, and now her father, who professed to love her, had accused her of being a whore and cast her out when she'd done absolutely nothing wrong, other than help a wounded man.

"Please don't worry, Catherine. I will speak to your father in the morning, but in the meantime, I will look after you, just as I did for the past few days. You are safe with me."

Kate had no choice but to follow Hugh out of the yard and toward the road to Belford. She didn't cry, but her insides twisted with misery and she wanted nothing more than to turn around, run up to her mother's bedchamber and beg her father to listen to her. He'd misunderstood, that was all. He would forgive her and apologize for the awful things he'd said to her.

But her bruised cheek told a different story. Surely her father should have known her better, or if he didn't, could have at the very least given her a chance to explain—not that there was anything to explain. She was innocent of any wrongdoing, as was Hugh. The most he'd done was help her mount her horse and dismount when they arrived. He had taken no liberties. He hadn't so much as touched her hand or looked at her with anything other than respect. He was Henry VI's man, that was true, but that didn't make him a blackguard.

When they arrived at the inn, all was quiet and dark. The shutters were closed against the night and the stable door was bolted. Thick clouds obscured the moon and fat drops of rain were just beginning to fall, a downpour imminent. Kate slid into Hugh's waiting hands and he set her on the ground and drew her cloak closer around her body as her teeth chattered with cold and anxiety. He threw the horses' reins to a bleary-eyed boy who'd materialized out of the darkness, then banged on the door of the inn until the proprietor came to answer, wearing nothing but his nightshirt.

"We need two rooms," Hugh commanded as he pushed past the man and drew Kate inside, out of the rain. The man followed them into the small parlor, his candle casting a pool of light on his tired face.

"I'm sorry, sir, but there's just the one room. The bed is big enough for you and your lady wife," the man added, as though reluctant to let them leave now that they'd woken him up.

"One room?" Kate balked.

"We'll take it," Hugh replied and dropped a coin into the man's outstretched hand. He turned to Kate. "I'll sleep on the floor. You've nothing to fear from me, Catherine."

Kate and Hugh followed the innkeeper to the upper story and into the room. "'Tis the best room in the house, sir," the innkeeper said proudly, pointing to the four-poster bed with an embroidered tester and a thick quilt. The mullioned window offered a view of the village green during the day, but at the moment, it was a black rectangle streaming with rainwater. Not a chink of light could be seen, with every house in the village tightly shuttered for the night. It was like gazing into an abyss—or perhaps the abyss was in Kate's soul. She'd never felt as adrift as she did at that moment, not even when she'd been lost on the road to Belford. Then, she'd had a home to return to. Now, she didn't belong to anyone.

"You and your lady will be comfortable here. Shall I have some hot water sent up?" the innkeeper asked. "Or some food?"

"There's no need," Hugh replied as he unbuckled his sword belt and threw his cloak over a chair. "Leave us."

"Good night, sir. Madam." The man bowed low and left them alone.

"Take the bed, Lady Catherine. I'll bed down on the floor."

"I'll take the floor," Kate said miserably. "I won't be able to sleep anyway."

"Of course you will. You need your rest. Now come, let me help you with your cloak." Hugh opened the clasp of Kate's cloak and tossed the garment next to his own. He then bent down and removed her shoes and set them beside the bed. "Lay your head," he said gently. "It will all come out all right in the end."

Kate hadn't meant to give in to her grief, but tears of hurt and anger slid down her cheeks. "He'll never forgive me," she cried, "especially not once he finds out that I shared a room with you tonight. I must go," she exclaimed, but Hugh's strong hands on her forearms stopped her.

"Catherine, darling, there's nothing wrong with us sharing a room. 'Tis the only one left, and we are betrothed, you and I."

"Are we?" Kate asked, staring at Hugh in confusion.

"Of course. Your father gave his consent, before he evicted me from the house," Hugh added with a sad smile. "He won't have you dishonored in the eyes of the world. He'd rather have you married to the likes of me."

"I haven't done anything to bring dishonor on my family," Kate argued.

"Of course you haven't. You're beautiful, and pure, and kind," Hugh said, brushing a stray curl out of her eyes. He leaned in and gave her a feather-light kiss on her lips. "You saved Guy's life, and now you can save mine."

Kate stared up at him, confused.

"Oh, Kate, I have been lonely for a long time. You brought something out in me, a depth of feeling I didn't realize I was possessed of. I want to love and protect you. I want you to be mine," he whispered as he pushed her back onto the counterpane.

"Hugh, no," Kate protested, but Hugh covered her body with his own as his kisses grew more ardent.

"Kate, I love you," he whispered, his eyes aglow with passion. "I'll make you happy."

"No, please," she begged as she struggled against him, but it was too late. Hugh had pushed up her skirts and was already fumbling with the laces of his breeches.

Kate felt his hand between her legs as he attempted to guide himself inside her. She tried to squirm away, but he was too heavy, and there wasn't anywhere to go. She cried out as he forced his shaft inside her, breaching her maidenhead and destroying any possible future she might have had in the Church or with any other man. Hugh began to move inside her, pushing deeper and deeper into her unwilling body. Honeyed words dripped from his lips as he made love to her, but Kate had to bite her lip to keep herself from howling in anguish. She didn't want this; she hadn't asked for this, and now there was no going back.

"Kate, try to relax. All I want is to make you happy. Please, darling, it's all right."

All the fight went out of her and Hugh thrust harder, making her cry out in pain, but he seemed to misinterpret her reaction as one of pleasure.

"That's my girl," he whispered. "I knew you liked me."

Hugh eventually finished what he was doing and rolled off her. He cupped her cheek and looked into her eyes, as though seeking affirmation that all was well between them. "I'll give you a good life. I promise," he said. "You will never have cause to regret marrying me."

Kate nodded mutely, too afraid to look at Hugh for fear that he'd see the panic and revulsion in her eyes. She didn't wish to marry him, nor did she think he could make her happy, but what choice did she have? Her fate was sealed.

Hugh fell asleep, but Kate lay awake for hours, staring up at the tester. Had she still been at the priory, she would have prayed, but God seemed to have forsaken her this night, and she was on her own.

She must have eventually dozed off because when she opened her eyes, it was morning, and weak sunshine was streaming through the dingy window. Kate sat up and looked around in panic. Hugh was nowhere to be seen. His sword belt was gone, as was his cloak. She was alone.

Chapter 18

July 2014

Berwick-upon-Tweed, Northumberland

Gabe brushed the dust off his jeans and reached for an old towel to clean his grimy hands. He'd turned his father's study upside down, but found nothing pertaining to the plans of the house. He had found many other 'interesting' tidbits, which had reaffirmed his belief that his parents' finances were in dire straits and that the repairs his father had planned never took place. There were estimates from various contractors, unpaid bills for services rendered, and an extensive list—written in his father's hand—detailing all the work that needed to get done to get the house up to scratch.

Gabe put the list out of his mind and returned his attention to the attic, which hadn't seen the light of day, or an electric lightbulb, for decades. There were countless pieces of broken furniture, Christmas ornaments from the Victorian period that were probably collectibles by now and might actually pay for some of the restoration, and boxes and boxes of ledgers and various other documents pertaining to the running of the estate. Gabe had been at it for about eight hours and he was ready to chuck it in. There were no plans.

"Damn it all to hell," Gabe grumbled as he descended the rickety staircase and headed straight for the bath down the corridor. Even his hair was covered in dust and cobwebs.

"You're a sight," Quinn said with a chuckle as she came out of the bath, her hair wrapped in a fluffy towel. "Anything?"

Gabe shook his head and stopped as particles of dust flew in all directions and making Quinn sneeze. "Nothing. I'm filthy and hungry."

"Would you like me to make some pasta?" she asked.

"Oh, no. We're going out to the pub. I've earned a pint or two, and you've earned a dinner out."

"And what have I done to earn such an honor?"

"You made love to me and did that amazing thing you do with your tongue," Gabe replied without missing a beat.

"Did I?"

"Didn't you?" Gabe asked with a wicked smile.

Quinn smiled back. "You know where to find me once you've bathed. I'm not touching you looking like that."

"I would never ask for such a sacrifice, but I bet medieval ladies welcomed their knights home from battle with open arms, despite the stench from days locked in their armor and the muck of the battlefield."

"And when you come to me clad in your armor after having taken the throne, I'll be all over you." Quinn giggled as Gabe smacked her bottom.

"Wait for me."

"Oh, I will," she promised.

Once they were settled in the pub with a pint in front of Gabe and a glass of mineral water in front of Quinn, she considered the problem with the house plans. "Have you looked online?"

"Of course I have. There's some information about Berwick Castle, but nothing much about the other houses in the area."

"Tomorrow, I'll visit the library. They might have something. Will you be returning to the trenches?"

"I don't know if it's worth it. There's so much rubbish up there, I can barely get around without having to create a path between the junk. If there's any useful information up there, it might take me months to find it." Gabe took a long pull of his ale. "Ultimately, it's not that important. Our man was buried within the walls of the house, indicating that he wasn't deserving of a Christian burial. But whoever buried him treated him with love and respect, so most likely he was buried by his family."

"The poor lad must have committed some unforgiveable sin," Quinn agreed.

"Can you tell me more about Guy?" Gabe asked.

"I've told you all I know so far."

"I'm dying to find out what happened to him. I just can't seem to reconcile what I know of Guy de Rosel to what we discovered, but I don't want you to get upset or emotionally involved. I know what a toll it takes on you."

"Gabe, I promise to keep a professional distance."

He gave Quinn a look of such stunned disbelief that she burst out laughing.

"All right, I won't," she conceded. "But I need to know what happened to him. And don't tell me what you know. Not yet."

"Can you tell me about Kate then?"

Quinn shook her head. "I need more time with the rosary. Kate's life turned upside down the moment her brothers stepped onto that battlefield. Their deaths changed everything, but so did her encounter with the de Rosels. I believe that her fate was intertwined with theirs, but I don't yet know how the story played out."

"It's a mystery."

"Not for long," Quinn promised. "Ah, good. I'm starving," she said as the waitress brought their food. "Want some chips?"

"I'm happy with my steak pie and mash," Gabe replied, eyeing his plate like a man who'd just come face to face with his long-lost love.

"Do I have time to visit the library before we leave tomorrow?" Quinn asked as she popped a piece of flaky fried fish into her mouth.

"Of course. I still have a few things to tidy up before we leave. Can you collect Emma on your way back from the library?"

"Sure. I might even take her with me. She can look at children's books while I troll the research section."

"She'd like that. I think she's getting a bit restless with Mum and Cecily."

"She misses us," Quinn said and smiled happily. It still gladdened her heart to think that Emma saw them as her parents and not just a couple who looked after her in lieu of her mother. They were a real family.

Gabe smiled at her across the table as though he understood what she meant. "It's wonderful, isn't it?"

Quinn nodded, suddenly overcome. She was always close to tears these days.

Chapter 19

Quinn glanced toward the children's section to make sure Emma was happy and occupied before returning to the folio she'd found on the history of Berwick. The library was small enough for Quinn to see Emma, who was sitting in a comfortable chair, her legs folded beneath her, a picture book in her lap.

Quinn leafed through the folio, searching for any references to Gabe's family or ancestral home. She didn't find anything, given that the family wasn't titled, so not worthy of mention in the history books, but she did find sketches of other wealthy homes.

"Well, this is interesting," she mumbled as she studied a drawing of a tower house from the fifteenth century. She went through all the source material she found, which wasn't plentiful, and called out to Emma. "Time to go, darling."

"All right," Emma said and returned the picture book to the shelf. "I wish I could read this."

"Would you like me to read it to you?" Quinn asked. "We have a few minutes to spare."

"No, I want to read it myself."

"You will be able to read for yourself very soon. By next year, in fact. Now that you're starting school, you'll be learning to read."

"I want you to teach me," Emma replied.

"I'd be happy to," Quinn said. She'd taught Emma her letters over the past few months, but they hadn't progressed to actually reading words. Quinn thought that Emma might be bored in class if she already knew how to read and had to wait for the other students to catch up. But if she wanted to start reading, Quinn could hardly refuse.

"All right then," Emma replied happily. "Let's go."

By the time they returned to the house, Gabe had already loaded their cases into the boot of the car and had cleaned the kitchen. He'd procured some yellow tape from somewhere and made a large rectangle around the hole in the floor, also winding the tape around the backs of chairs that he'd placed next to the opening to alert Phoebe not to cross the line. She knew the hole was there, of course, but might forget and walk toward the sink out of habit and fall.

"We are ready to go," Emma announced as she bounced into the kitchen.

"We'll just stop by Cecily's and say goodbye to Grandma. Shall we?" Gabe asked.

Emma nodded. She checked her backpack to make sure that her picture book, Mr. Rabbit, and several coloring books and pencils were all packed.

The stop at Cecily's cottage took longer than expected since Emma had to say a very thorough goodbye to Buster, who seemed sad to see her go. Once Emma left, he'd go back to his routine of daily 'walkies' with Phoebe, instead of running around happily as Emma tossed him a ball or chased him round the garden.

"Find anything at the library?" Gabe asked Quinn as they finally drove away.

"Not specifically pertaining to this house, but I did discover something else," Quinn said. "There were a few drawings of houses from the period. Several showed a cross on the East-facing section of the house."

"A chapel?"

"Yes, and our man was buried facing east."

"That's brilliant, Quinn. I should have realized there'd be a chapel at the keep. I found several prie-dieux in the attic and assumed they used the prayer desks in their chambers."

"Some people used prie-dieux in chapels, particularly if the chapel was too small to hold actual pews. I think that our man was buried beneath the chapel floor," Quinn theorized. "What I don't understand is how come no one had come across him before, especially when they built a whole new house in the eighteenth century."

"That I can explain," Gabe said as he swung the car onto the southbound carriageway. "My ancestors were tight-fisted sods who decided to build on the old foundation to save on costs. They built upward, but no one had any reason to dig below the foundation, and when they laid the pipes, they avoided the grave by sheer coincidence."

"Which would suggest that there was only one grave," Quinn said softly, so as not to frighten Emma.

"Perhaps there was more than one, but we'd have to demolish that entire section of the house to find the others."

"So, it is possible that our man got a Christian burial after all. The de Rosels might have had a priest who celebrated Mass at their private chapel and would have performed a funeral service."

"Yes, it's possible," Gabe agreed. "And that changes all our previous assumptions."

"For now," Quinn replied. "We've yet to see what happened to him."

With that, they dropped the topic because Emma was getting restless in the back seat. That usually meant she needed the toilet, or more likely, wanted to stop under the pretense of using the toilet to wheedle a snack and a drink from the rest area.

Chapter 20

April 1461

Belford, Northumberland

Kate drew up her legs and rested her forehead on her knees as hot tears spilled down her cheeks. She had no notion of what to do. Her father had evicted her and Hugh had abandoned her at the first opportunity, having taken her innocence and her honor. He'd spoken to her of marriage to silence her protests, thinking that in her gratitude she wouldn't object to him bedding her. He hadn't been rough or abusive, as her mother had predicted, but he had taken what he wanted all the same, sugarcoating his actions with words of love and devotion. His ardor had lasted only as long as it took him to destroy any future prospects she might have. He was probably halfway to Berwick by now, the promises of last night forgotten.

Now she'd have to fend for herself, but she had nothing of value, save her rosary, and she'd never part with it, not for all the world. Kate momentarily considered returning to the priory, but that was no longer an option, not when her thighs were smeared with Hugh's seed. More than anything in the world, she wanted her mother, but the woman who'd loved and cherished her was locked in a prison of suffering, unable to leave her sickbed. Anne would have reasoned with her husband last night and convinced him that Kate was innocent of any wrongdoing, but now there was no one left to champion her, not even the abbess. She was completely on her own and utterly bereft.

Kate angrily wiped the tears with her sleeve and looked around. She had to keep a cool head. The first thing she had to do was remove all traces of Hugh from her body. She felt disgusted and ashamed, and soiled. The water in the pitcher was cold, but Kate didn't mind. At the priory, they always washed with cold water, even on the most frigid days of the year. She found a linen towel and went to work, starting with her hands and face and moving downward. She grimaced with distaste when she washed between her legs and hastened to complete the task. Once clean, she dressed and plaited her hair. She didn't even have a hairbrush, or a spare chemise. The only thing she had in the world was Marie de Rosel's gown and the gray cloak she'd been issued at the priory. She also had her horse, if Hugh hadn't taken it.

Kate stilled when a soft knock sounded on the door. "Come," she called. A dark-haired girl of about eleven poked her head in the door.

"I hope I haven't disturbed ye, me lady, but Master de Rosel bid me bring ye something to break yer fast when the church bell struck the hour."

"Thank you," Kate said and beckoned the girl into the room.

The girl set a plate of bread and cheese on a small table and placed a cup of small ale beside it, then curtsied awkwardly.

"When did Master de Rosel go out?" Kate asked.

"'Bout an hour since. He left this for ye," the girl added, taking a note from her pocket. She'd clearly forgotten all about the note, and would have walked off with it had Kate not enquired about Hugh.

Kate unfolded the small square of paper. Hugh's handwriting was elegant, but his message brief.

Dearest Catherine,

Gone to the Grange to speak to your father. Will return before noon. Be ready to leave.

Your devoted Hugh

The girl looked on with interest as Kate read the note and stowed it in the pocket of her gown after refolding it.

"Bad news, me lady?" she asked, her eyes dancing with curiosity. She probably would have liked nothing more than to stay for a little chat to avoid whatever duties awaited her downstairs, but Kate wasn't about to discuss her situation with a child, no matter how much she longed to talk to someone.

"No. All's well."

"I'll leave ye to it then," the girl said, and backed out of the room.

Kate sat down and took a sip of the bitter ale. No, it wasn't bad news that Hugh hadn't deserted her, but she wasn't convinced it was good news either. At this stage, she wasn't sure what would constitute good news. Her life was irrevocably altered, and now that she was no longer at the priory she needed the protection of a man, be it her father or a husband. A woman on her own was helpless and vulnerable, and ultimately doomed to a life of poverty and deprivation. The only thing Kate was certain of was that she'd never resort to whoring to survive. So she either had to go begging to her father—who wasn't a forgiving man by nature, so appealing to him would be pointless given his harsh treatment of her—or agree to marry Hugh, if he still wanted her.

Kate finished her meal, grabbed her cloak, and headed for the door. She had some time before Hugh returned, so she would go to church. She needed guidance, and since she couldn't talk to her own mother or the abbess, she would speak to Father Phillip, who'd known her since she was born. Father Phillip had baptized her and watched her grow. He would be kind, understanding, and truthful.

Kate walked the short distance to All Saints' and pushed open the heavy door. The interior of the church was dim and cool, and for a second Kate thought it was empty, but then she saw Father Phillip emerge from the apse and head toward her down the nave. Father Phillip was in his sixties, gaunt, stooped, and gray. He walked slowly, as if in pain, but when he recognized her, his eyes lit with the warmth Kate had longed to see in the eyes of her own father, and a smile of welcome lit up his weathered face.

"Lady Catherine, I'm very sorry for your loss," he said as he approached her. "It's a tragedy to lose one child, but three is beyond words. Your parents must be beside themselves with grief. I've yet to see either of them."

"My mother's taken ill, and my father has been tending to her."

"Poor lady. She must be devastated. And your lord father, of course. What a blow," Father Phillip said, shaking his head in disbelief. "I will call on them later today to offer whatever comfort I can."

"I'm sure they'd be most grateful, Father."

"You seem in need of comfort yourself," Father Phillip said as he beckoned Kate toward the front pew. "Come, sit, my lady." Father Phillip paused while a hacking cough wracked his thin frame for several minutes and left him exhausted and trembling. His hand shook slightly when he mopped his brow with a much-used linen handkerchief.

"Are you ill, Father? Is there anything I can do to help?" Kate asked. "Should I fetch some water?"

"Thank you, child. I'm afraid it will take more than water to restore my health. I've written to the bishop. 'Tis only fair to give him time to find a replacement."

"Are you going somewhere?" Kate asked. Father Phillip had been at All Saints' since he was a young man, fresh out of the seminary.

The old priest chuckled, which turned into another coughing fit. "I'm going to stay right here at All Saints'. I will be buried next to Father Paul, who was the priest here before me. He was a good man, and taught me much. I still miss him."

Kate turned away for a moment to hide her tears. Father Phillip was dying, but he seemed accepting of his fate, and not at all bitter or frightened.

"Lady Catherine, don't grieve for me. I've had a long and happy life. I don't fear death. 'Tis but a stepping stone to the afterlife, and it will be glorious; I know it."

"Do you think my brothers are in Heaven, Father?" Kate asked, wondering if Martin had ever confessed his sins to Father Phillip. He had much to answer for, but he had died fighting for his king. Surely that earned him some measure of forgiveness.

"I'm sure they are, my dear," Father Phillip assured her. "Now, tell me about yourself. Are you back from the priory for good? Have you sacrificed your own desires to support your parents at this difficult time?"

Kate opened her mouth to speak, but a desperate sob tore from her chest. She hadn't meant to give in to self-pity, but for some reason, Father Phillip's kindness undid her.

"Father, I grieve for my brothers, and I'm sick with worry for my dear mother," Kate admitted reluctantly, "but today my grief is also for myself." She hung her head in shame, but Father Phillip patted her hand in a gesture of support.

"You've nothing to be ashamed of, Lady Catherine. Your brothers are beyond caring about the physical world, and your dear mother is in the hands of God. Now, tell me what's troubling you."

"Father, a week ago I was at the priory, preparing to take my vows. I was happy and at peace with the choice I'd made. I knew exactly what my life would be like, and I was eager to devote myself to the service of our Lord. Since then, I have lost not only my brothers, but my parents as well, and I'm about to marry a man whose motives I have reason to question. I feel as if God has forsaken me."

Father Phillip shook his head, his eyes full of sympathy. "My dear Lady Catherine, the Lord has not forsaken you. He loves you, and values you, which is why He's sending you where you're needed most, as He did with His own beloved son. Perhaps you would have served Him faithfully at the priory, but He clearly has a different plan for you. He has chosen this new path for you, and you must follow it, for you don't know where it'll lead. This man you are to marry, what has he done to make you mistrust him?"

"I think he manipulated the situation to his own advantage to ensure an outcome he'd hoped for, and has greatly angered my father." Kate decided not to elaborate on exactly what her father now believed, too ashamed to speak the words in the house of God.

Father Phillip smiled kindly. "He wouldn't be the first man to do that, certainly. Did he deceive you?"

Kate thought about that for a moment and realized she couldn't answer the question with certainty. Hugh had promised to escort her back home, which he had. He had told her father that she'd spent several days in his company, tending to Guy's wound, which was true. He'd also told her father that he wished to marry her, a proposal that seemingly came from the heart. Kate couldn't be sure what had led to her father's assumption that she'd lain with Hugh, but she was fairly certain that Hugh hadn't said such a thing straight out. Gerard Dancy had made an assumption based on something that Hugh had implied, intentionally or unwittingly, and had cast out the daughter who up to that day had always been virtuous and pure. Was Hugh to blame? Perhaps, but at the end of the day, he was the one who intended to stand by her, unlike her father who had cut her out of his heart based on nothing more than conjecture.

"No, Father, he didn't deceive me," Kate finally replied, somewhat relieved to have come to that conclusion.

Father Phillip smiled, as though glad to have planted seeds of doubt and made her reconsider the situation. "Is he so odious then, this man?" he asked, his eyes twinkling with mischief.

"No, he's not odious," Kate replied truthfully. Hugh was handsome, in his own way. He was neither stout nor balding. He had a pleasant face, with slanted light blue eyes and a strong nose that bespoke his Gallic ancestry. He was of above average height, and was strong and fit, a man used to days in the saddle and hours of swordplay. But there was one thing he wasn't—he wasn't Guy.

Kate was shocked by the rogue thought. Guy de Rosel wasn't hers for the taking, and until yesterday the very idea of marriage had been something vague and threatening. She supposed it still was, but Hugh had professed to love her, and seemed to think that what had passed between them last night was a symbol of commitment. She had no inkling of what went on between men and women, other than some second-hand knowledge gleaned from eavesdropping on her brothers and now her own unexpected experience. She couldn't expect what took place in the marriage bed to be pleasant or comfortable; her mother had made that clear enough. It was a woman's duty to lie with her husband and give him children.

As long as Hugh didn't hurt her intentionally or treat her unkindly, she had no grounds for complaint. Besides, any man her father would have chosen for her would take getting used to, even if he happened to be handsome and charming. Hugh had just lost his older brother, and Guy had been near death. She could hardly blame him for his lack of courtly manners, or his overly emotional response to the woman he thought had somehow saved his brother. Perhaps Hugh's feelings were genuine. What did she know of love? Geoffrey had once told her that love enters through the eyes. Perhaps that had been the case with Hugh. He had looked at her differently the moment she removed her veil, seeing her as a woman rather than a bride of Christ. And now he wanted to make her his bride.

"Do you think you could grow to love him?" Father Phillip asked, pushing his point further.

"I don't know, Father. It was my wish to become a nun. I hadn't considered loving a husband," Kate replied truthfully.

"My dear, very few people, men as well as women, get to live the life they envisioned. We must take what God gives us and make the best of it, if we hope to gain any measure of happiness. I know you had your heart set on a religious life, but if that's not to be, then you must apply yourself to being a good wife and mother, and being loyal to your husband. Do you think you could do that?"

130

"I suppose I'll have to, won't I?" Kate replied, resigned. She had no recourse, and if Father Phillip believed that the Lord had set her on this path, then she had no choice but to accept His will.

"You're a practical young woman, Lady Catherine, and I know you will do what's best. Your father will come to accept your marriage in time. He's very fond of you."

Kate nodded. "Thank you, Father Phillip. I knew you'd help me see that which had been hidden from me."

"It's not hidden, it's just not as clear as you expect it to be. Go with God, Lady Catherine, and do your duty without reservation or bitterness."

"Thank you, Father," Kate said. "You've made me feel infinitely better."

"That's what I'm here for."

Kate wished she could hug the old priest, but that would have been highly inappropriate. She knew she'd never see him again, and hoped his illness wouldn't cause him prolonged suffering.

"God bless you, Father Phillip," was all she said as she turned to leave the church.

"He already has," Father Phillip replied, and bent double as another coughing fit nearly brought him to his knees.

Chapter 21

By the time Kate returned to the inn, Hugh was back, pacing impatiently in the dooryard. He stilled when he saw her, and gave her an elaborate bow. "My lady, I have concluded my business with your father earlier than I expected," he said by way of explanation. "I'm ready to leave, if you are."

Kate nodded. She had no belongings save her rosary, so all she had to do was mount her horse and follow Hugh. He, however, had something in his possession that he hadn't had before. He stowed a silver coffer in his saddlebag, tied it securely, then turned to help Kate mount.

"What is that?" Kate asked, jutting her chin toward the small casket.

Hugh's eyes blazed and an angry blush stained his cheeks. He didn't immediately reply, but then looked at Kate, his stance defiant, and said, "That's your dowry."

"Really? Has my father sanctioned the marriage?" Kate asked. The notion of being forgiven by her father and accepted back into the family was overwhelming, but Hugh quickly dashed her hopes.

"No. He relinquished the dowry on the condition that neither one of us ever sets foot at the Grange again."

Kate felt the prickle of tears, but said nothing. Why was her father so angry? Hugh might not be his choice for his only daughter, but surely, if her father loved her, he could come to accept this union, even if Hugh was a Lancastrian. King Edward was victorious and well-liked. Hugh would have to accept the new king whether he wished to or not, so his politics were no longer relevant. Hugh de Rosel wasn't wealthy in his own right, or titled, but he was still young and his fortunes could change. Did it really not pain her father at all to lose her, or had he steeled himself to losing her when she entered the convent and no longer held her in his heart as he had when she was a little girl?

Kate sighed and followed Hugh out of the dooryard and toward the northbound road. She was setting off on a new life, but she felt no frisson of excitement or flurry of hope. She felt frightened and depressed, and the thunderous countenance of her new lord did nothing to lift her spirits.

Thankfully, Hugh's sour mood didn't last long. The sun had come out and a gentle April breeze caressed their faces as they traveled north. The trees were already in leaf, the juicy green of new foliage bright against the brilliant blue sky. Birdsong filled the air, and the sun on their shoulders was warm enough to make the ride more pleasant. Hugh held the reins in one hand and patted his horse's neck with the other, softly promising the mare a treat once they got home.

"I think my lady might be ready for a treat as well," he said, smiling at Kate. "Shall we stop in the next village? It's just over that hill."

"Yes, please."

Kate was glad when they reached the village and found a tavern. She was hungry and needed to answer the call of nature. By the time she returned from the privy, Hugh had ordered a hearty meal and a jug of ale to wash it down with. He seemed in good spirits and eager to talk, so Kate seized on his jubilant mood in an effort to draw him out.

"Hugh, may I ask you a question?"

"You may ask me anything you like, my dear." Hugh drained his cup of ale and refilled it. The stew he'd ordered was hot and fresh, and accompanied by a loaf of crusty bread straight from the oven. Hugh took a spoonful and sighed with contentment. He was a happy man.

"How old are you?"

"I'll be seven and twenty in July."

Kate lowered her gaze to her stew. There were things she wished to ask, but she wasn't sure how to broach the subject in a way that wouldn't anger Hugh. At his age, most men were either married or widowed, but she didn't get the impression that Hugh had been married before. He seemed devoted to his brothers, but there was something remote and private about his demeanor. 'A lone wolf,' her mother would have called him.

"You're wondering why I'm not wed," Hugh said. He tore off a chunk of bread and used it to soak up the gravy from his bowl.

"Yes, I am," Kate admitted.

Hugh finished his meal and leaned back in his chair, looking for all the world like a man at peace with himself. "After I was knighted—that was nearly five years ago now—William, being the head of the family, arranged a marriage for me with Eleanor's sister. Our fathers were distant kin, so we'd known Eleanor and Faye all our lives. We were to marry once Faye turned sixteen. Her father was very fond of her, and didn't wish to part with her too soon, especially since Eleanor was already wed and with child, and his wife had died the year before."

"Did you marry?" Kate asked.

Hugh shook his head. "Faye loved to ride and went out nearly every morning. A few weeks before the wedding was to take place, she tripped while in the stables. One of the stable boys had left a pitchfork on the ground and she didn't notice it beneath the straw. She grabbed onto a post to steady herself and cut her hand on a nail. It wasn't a deep cut and should have healed in a few days, but it festered. I fetched a physician from Newcastle, but the infection had spread quickly. She died within a week. Toward the end she was so delirious, she didn't recognize anyone, not even Eleanor. The day after Faye died, Eleanor's pains started. It was too soon and William feared she'd lose the babe, but Adam arrived safe and sound."

134

"Poor girl," Kate breathed. "Did you love her?" Hugh had spoken of Faye with affection, which led Kate to believe that he'd wished to marry her and hadn't simply been complying with his brother's wishes.

"I cared deeply about her. I'd known her all my life," Hugh replied. "Marriage to Faye would have been no hardship. She was a sweet and obedient girl."

"And did she love you?" Kate asked. She knew she was prying, but couldn't help herself. She supposed she was wondering if Hugh was worthy of a woman's love.

Hugh smiled wryly and reached for his cup of ale. "She loved Guy."

"Did you not mind?"

"Faye and Guy were close in age, whereas I must have always seemed older and more intimidating. It was only natural that she felt more at ease with him, but Guy was too young to marry, and it was William's wish that I marry Faye. We would have got on fine in the end." Hugh glanced toward the window. "It's well past noon. We'd best be on our way if we want to get home before dark. Are you finished?"

"Yes. Thank you. It was delicious."

"Nothing like a good meal to lift the spirits, eh?"

Hugh paid for their meal and they headed outside into the sunshine. Kate was about to mount her horse when Hugh turned her to face him. He leaned down and kissed her tenderly, smiling into her eyes. "We'll get on fine, you and I. You'll see. I'll give you no cause to regret marrying me."

I hope I can say the same, Kate thought as she forced herself to smile back.

Chapter 22

July 2014

London, England

Quinn eagerly set aside the stack of party invitations when she saw Dr. Scott's name pop up on the screen of her mobile. She and Gabe had dropped off the boxed remains and all the samples a few days ago when they'd returned to London, and Colin had promised to work on the skelly as soon as possible. He was up to his eyeballs in postmortems, he'd said, but his true love was forensic archeology, and he relished the opportunity to unearth someone's past through science. Colin's assistant, Dr. Dhawan, performed many of the tests, but Colin studied each skeleton in person, paying attention to every detail, no matter how minute.

"You two just keep tripping over bones, don't you?" Colin had joked as he accepted the box and the half dozen plastic bags. "And you found a medieval sword. Now that's something I'd like to see."

"I plan to show the sword to a medieval weapons expert we have on staff, but once he's finished his examination, you are welcome to take a look," Gabe offered.

"I'll gladly take you up on that," Colin replied. "I have something of a thing for medieval weaponry. I bet Logan would enjoy seeing it as well."

"Does Logan like history?" Quinn asked. Her brother had never mentioned an interest in anything that took place before the turn of the century, so Quinn wasn't sure. Their acquaintance was still new, and she was learning things about him day by day.

"If watching *Spamalot* constitutes being interested in history, then yes," Colin joked. "Logan is more of a science fiction buff. He likes all those apocalyptic disaster and clones-take-over-the-world programs." Colin shuddered dramatically and rolled his eyes.

"I can just imagine the epic battle for the remote at your house," Quinn quipped. "Do I suspect Logan usually wins?"

"We compromise." Colin chuckled.

"What does that entail?" Gabe asked.

"It means that we watch *Call the Midwife* followed by *Torchwood*. Everybody wins."

"Sounds like you two have it all figured out," Quinn said. "I'm more partial to *Call the Midwife* myself."

"Excellent program," Colin agreed as he glanced at his watch. "Well, I have an autopsy in a few minutes. Good to see you both. I'll ring you as soon as I have anything."

"Thanks, Colin," Gabe and Quinn said in unison.

Quinn answered the phone, her voice breathless with anticipation. "Colin, hi. Do you have something for us?"

"I do, indeed. Would you like to come by the mortuary?"

Quinn glanced at her watch. She was due to meet Gabe for lunch in an hour. Perhaps they could skip the meal and visit Colin instead. She knew that Gabe was as anxious for the results as she was. "Would noon be convenient?"

"Absolutely. See you then."

Quinn fired off a text to Gabe and returned to the party invites. Emma had asked for a *Frozen*-themed party, which wasn't the easiest of feats to pull off in August, but Quinn was determined to make Emma's first birthday with them as special as possible. She'd booked a private instructor at Queens skating rink. The instructor would teach the children to skate for half an hour, then give them another thirty minutes of free skating time. After, the kids would adjourn to the arcade, where they'd be allowed to play only age-appropriate games, and then on to the in-house restaurant for pizza and birthday cake.

"Quinn, I don't think that venue is geared toward children," Gabe had protested when Quinn brought up the idea. "They have a bar, and some very violent games. The other parents won't approve," he'd added lamely.

"Leave it to me," Quinn had replied with more confidence than she'd felt. "I have a plan for keeping the children in line. Besides, I seriously doubt there will be many hard-drinking, snooker-playing types at Queens at ten in the morning."

Quinn wasn't at all sure if her idea would work, but it was worth a try. She'd had no contact with Jude since the dinner Sylvia had invited them to, and thought this might be a way to make inroads with him. She'd asked Logan for Jude's mobile number and left him a voicemail, asking him to call her.

Jude had taken his time, but did return the call eventually. "What's up?" he'd asked.

"Hi, Jude. How did your tour go?" Quinn asked.

"All right." Jude wasn't a man of many words, but he'd called her back, and that was a start.

"Your mum said that you're between jobs at the moment, so I was wondering if you might be interested in a paying gig," Quinn said, praying that Jude wouldn't be mortally offended by her idea.

"What gig might that be?"

"We're having a birthday party for Emma on August ninth, at Queens," Quinn began. "She's turning five."

"So, you'd like my band to play some heavy metal for the kiddies?" Jude asked. He oozed sarcasm, but he hadn't hung up yet.

"No, actually, I'm in need of a prince."

"What?"

"Emma has asked for a *Frozen*-themed party and I thought that some of your friends might like to make some extra money by dressing as the characters and mingling with the children. I'll rent the costumes, of course."

"You must be joking," Jude sputtered.

"Well, if you have no need of money…"

"How much you payin'?"

"Fifty quid for two hours, for you and any willing victim," Quinn replied. Fifty quid was nothing to sneeze at, especially when all they'd have to do was some glorified child-minding and amateur skating. No triple-axel jumps required.

"Any nibbles and plonk included?"

"I'll spring for pizza, but there won't be any alcohol at a children's party."

"Is your wanker of a husband going to be there?"

"Yes, he's going to be there, and don't call him that. He was well within his rights when he called the cops on you, and you know it." Quinn wasn't about to apologize for Gabe's behavior. He had her undying support, now and always.

"All right. Fine. I'll think on it. How many people you need?" Jude asked.

"Four."

"Right. Let me ask around and see if anyone is desperate enough to make a complete ass of themselves."

Jude hung up without saying goodbye, but called Quinn two days later. "Okay, I have a couple of mates lined up. Bridget thinks it's sweet what you're doing for the kid. She liked Emma. So, here's the deal. Bridget will bring a friend, and they'll be Elsa and Anna. I'll do Prince Kristoff, and I have a mate who's willing to make a fool of himself as Olaf. That's two hundred quid, cash up front, lunch included, and if you post any photos of us on social media, I'll put a hit out on you."

"You drive a hard bargain, Your Highness," Quinn replied, smiling. The hardest part of the deal would be not posting photos on social media, since some of the children might like to be photographed with the characters, and their parents might post them despite promising not to.

Quinn couldn't help smiling to herself. Beneath Jude's prickly exterior, she could sense a thawing in his attitude toward her. Perhaps this could be the first step in establishing some sort of a relationship.

Quinn winced when she remembered the bond she'd thought she was establishing with Brett. He'd certainly led her up the garden path, but she'd be more careful with Jude.

"I reserve the right to strip search him before he enters the premises," Gabe had threatened.

"Don't be ridiculous," Quinn retorted. "Sylvia said Jude is clean."

"About as clean as a fireship," Gabe replied, still annoyed.

"Gabe, that's uncalled for. Comparing Jude to a pox-ridden prostitute is beneath you," Quinn said, putting her hands on her hips for emphasis.

"You're right. I'm sorry. I just worry about Emma."

"I know you do, but give Jude a chance. You did misjudge the situation last time."

"I made a judgement call based on the facts I had available to me. And I would call the coppers on him again," Gabe said. "Now, can we drop this? I'll be nice to Jude and his friends, but I will keep an eye on them. You can be sure of that."

"This ought to be fun," Quinn muttered, but allowed the subject to drop.

Chapter 23

"I'll never get used to this smell," Quinn said as she followed Gabe down the corridor to the mortuary. The usual stench of carbolic, decay, and desperation hung over the premises, making her wince. She felt sorry for the poor people who had to come to the mortuary to identify the remains of their loved ones. It didn't happen often, but when it did, it was usually the result of either suicide or violence, and the sight wasn't for the faint of heart, even when only the face of the victim was visible.

"You're not meant to be used to it," Gabe replied. "It's revolting."

Quinn knocked on the door and poked her head in. Sarita Dhawan was seated in front of the computer, typing rapidly. Her ebony hair was wound into a bun atop her head and her stylish glasses appeared to be sliding down her nose.

"Hello there," Sarita called out. "Dr. Scott said you'd be stopping by. He'll be back shortly. He just popped out to get a sandwich. Give me a moment to finish entering these autopsy results and I'll walk you through to the lab."

"Find anything interesting?" Gabe asked as they followed Sarita into an adjoining room where their skelly was laid out on a metal slab, completely reassembled and thoroughly cleaned.

"I'll let Dr. Scott fill you in," Sarita replied. "He'd have his nose out of joint if I stole his thunder."

"Ooh, there's thunder," Quinn said, rubbing her hands in anticipation. "I can't wait."

"Did you work with Colin on this?" Gabe asked, standing over the bones gleaming beneath fluorescent lights.

"I ran tests on the fabric, leather, and hair," Sarita replied. "Fascinating stuff."

"Sorry I'm late," Colin called out as he walked into the lab. He shook hands with Gabe and kissed Quinn's cheek before pulling on a pair of latex gloves and approaching the remains.

"So, what can you tell us about him?" Gabe asked.

Colin smiled happily, his eyes crinkling with good humor. "The first thing I can tell you about him is that he is a she," he announced, looking gratified by Gabe's shocked reactions.

"Are you sure?" Gabe asked. "I've never come across a Christian woman buried with a sword. Of course, there were Saxon women, and Celts, who were warriors, but women of the Middle Ages didn't often go into battle."

"It's not her sword," Colin replied, grinning as though he were thoroughly enjoying himself.

"How can you tell?" Gabe inched closer to the skeleton and stared down at the bones, as if they would suddenly reveal all to him. Of course, he already knew that the sword didn't belong to the woman on the slab, but scientific proof was what counted in archeological circles.

"Let's start at the beginning, shall we?"

Quinn and Gabe nodded eagerly.

"What we have here is a female, aged between twenty and twenty-five." Colin pointed to the bone at the base of the spine. "The shape of the pelvic cavity, the angle of the greater sciatic notch, and the mandible shape and its ramus all prove that she was indeed female. I have determined her age by scoring the epiphyseal closure of the sacrum to determine the age at the time of death. Her humerus bone is a maximum of thirty centimeters and the femur is a maximum of forty-three centimeters, which tells me that she was between four-foot-seven and five-foot-two."

"Fascinating," Gabe said as he studied the remains. "Go on."

"Based on Carbon-14 dating, I'd say she lived in the mid-to-late fifteenth century. And she was no warrior; she was a lady. If you look at her wrists, you'll see that they are very delicate. A person who routinely performs hard physical tasks, such as wielding a sword, develops ridges at the site where the muscle was attached to the bone and pulled over the years. I see no such ridges here. I think this woman came from a wealthy family. Her teeth are in excellent shape, which means she enjoyed a varied and plentiful diet. The bits of fabric and leather support my theory. The fabric is a fine velvet, which was dark blue in color originally. There are tiny bits of gold thread, and the stiches, or what's left of them, are very fine. A woman who wasn't well to do would be wearing homespun, dyed with basic dyes obtained locally. The homespun would have disintegrated after all these centuries, being more loosely woven and much thinner in texture. I would also venture to suggest that she had well-made shoes, not the coarse leather shoon worn by the poor, where both shoes were exactly the same and could go on either foot. The leather is from a calf, not a fully grown cow. Also a luxury."

"And her DNA?" Quinn asked. She'd seen strands of hair still clinging to parts of the scalp, which was now washed clean.

"Unfortunately, we couldn't get a whole follicle, but we ran whatever tests we could on the hair strands themselves. Our lass had auburn hair and light eyes—either blue or green. She was fair-skinned, as people with her coloring tend to be. Her DNA shows traces of Saxon, Norman, and Scottish ancestry, which, given the area where she was found, is very common."

"Did she have children?" Quinn asked as her hand automatically went to her stomach, where baby Russell was in the middle of a particularly exuberant somersault.

"I don't believe so."

"How did she die?" Gabe asked, fast forwarding to the most important question.

"I haven't a bloody clue," Colin replied, spreading his hands in a gesture of puzzlement. "She was as healthy as a horse, from what I can see. Her skull is intact," he added, caressing the gleaming skull tenderly. "There are no nicks on her bones, which would indicate a knife or sword wound. There are no fractures, recent or well healed."

"So, what would a very healthy young woman die of, if she didn't die in childbirth?" Gabe persisted.

"A fever, perhaps. The plague wasn't rampant in that area during the second half of the fifteenth century, so I don't think that would have been the cause. She might have drowned," Colin added thoughtfully. "A drowning would leave no visible traces after all this time. I can't help wondering why she was buried with a sword though," he continued, cradling his chin in speculation. "My theory would be that someone wished to honor her. Perhaps it was her husband's sword. If he died in battle, it might have been the only thing she had left of him, so it was buried with her. What I can't figure out is why she was buried in the kitchen."

"I think we can answer that," Gabe jumped in. "We believe the kitchen was, in fact, the chapel back in the fifteenth century."

"Really? That would make sense then," Colin said. "Was there just the one body?"

"As far as we know. We'd have to dig up that entire section of the ground floor to find out for sure."

"I don't think your mum would be too pleased with that plan," Colin said with a chuckle. "My mum goes ballistic if you so much as move one knick-knack out of place."

"She refused to stay in the house until we removed the remains," Gabe said.

"Understandable. It's not pleasant knowing you've been walking over someone's grave all these years. Well, do let me know when you have the sword back in your possession. I'm dying to see it."

"Will do," Gabe replied.

"Perhaps you and Logan can come to our place for dinner," Quinn suggested.

"That would be lovely. See you soon."

Quinn and Gabe thanked Colin and left the mortuary, grateful to be out in the fresh air and sunshine after the windowless confines of the morgue. They had time for a quick bite before Gabe was due to return to work, so they found a Costa and placed their order.

"You didn't seem surprised when Colin said the remains were those of a woman," Gabe said as he unwrapped his sandwich and added sugar to his coffee. He lowered his voice so the other patrons wouldn't hear him discussing such a grim topic, but a woman at the next table threw him a look of pure venom nonetheless and moved her chair further away, scraping the floor loudly in the process.

"I didn't know the skeleton was of a woman. I assumed it was Guy, just as you did."

"Do you think it's Kate?"

"I couldn't say. I've seen very little of her story so far."

Quinn felt reluctant to talk about Kate. She supposed that after getting emotionally involved with Elise, Petra, and then Madeline, she'd tried to keep Kate at bay and look at her through a lens of professional detachment. She had to avoid stress, for the sake of the baby, and she handled the rosary for brief periods and mostly during the early hours of the day, so as not to dream of what she'd seen when she went to bed. She had enough bad dreams as it was.

"Gabe, what do you know of Guy?"

Gabe shrugged. "I know that he existed, and I know that he was the brother of William and Hugh, and the son of Armand and Marie de Rosel. Not much else is known about him."

"Do you know when he died?" Quinn asked cautiously.

"Yes. Shall I tell you?"

"Not yet. And what do you know of William and Hugh?"

"Not a whole lot. William de Rosel died at the Battle of Towton, which you already know. He was thirty-two at the time, and left behind a son, Adam, from whom I'm descended. It was Adam de Rosel who changed the name to Russell in the sixteenth century."

"Why?"

"Probably because he wished to anglicize it. De Rosel sounded very French, and given the ongoing animosity between France and England it made sense to fit in, if he meant to remain in England. Previous generations of de Rosels had maintained their ties to France, but Adam put a stop to all that."

"Did Guy or Hugh ever marry?" Quinn asked.

"I tried to research my family history when I was a teen, but only found information on Adam's descendants. There's a family tree that goes back to the Conquest, but it makes no mention of either Guy or Hugh's nuptials. Perhaps they died before they had a chance to marry."

"Interesting."

"Do you think the woman might be Adam's mother, Eleanor?" Gabe speculated. "I know Colin said that she likely didn't have children, but it's possible that he's mistaken, especially after all this time. Perhaps she had a very easy labor that left no mark on her pelvis. The child could have come early, and been very small."

147

"Surely, even a small child would leave its mark if it was nearly full term," Quinn argued.

"What if she had a cesarean? The procedure would surely kill her, but since the child didn't pass through the birth canal, there'd be no way to tell that she'd given birth."

"I don't think cesarean sections were very common in the fifteenth century, but I know for a fact that it isn't Eleanor. She survived Adam's birth and suffered a stillbirth just before William died. She bore two children, and Colin would spot that immediately."

"I have to go," Gabe said as he finished his lunch. "Will you be all right?"

"Of course. When do you think you'll get the sword back from Dr. Edwards?"

"Today or tomorrow. I have to find a good hiding place for it, what with Emma nosing around for her birthday presents. Perhaps we can wrap it in a towel and hide it on top of the wardrobe. She can't reach up there."

"Neither can I," Quinn replied with a chuckle. "It won't be that easy to keep it away from me."

"You can't blame a bloke for trying," Gabe replied with a sigh. "You won't rest until you know what happened, will you?"

"Shall I stop now?" Quinn asked innocently, and was rewarded with the reaction she'd hoped for. Gabe was desperate to know what happened. "You're just as hooked as I am, Dr. Russell."

"They're my ancestors."

"Exactly. You owe it to yourself to discover their story. Bring back that sword."

"All right," Gabe capitulated. "I'll see you both tonight." He placed his hand on Quinn's belly as he kissed her, then left for work.

Chapter 24

Quinn stared into her empty cup and pondered what to do. It was a lovely day outside, and she didn't feel like returning to the empty flat. She knew she was meant to be taking it easy, but sitting around for hours on end with nothing specific to do raised her stress levels more than actually being productive. She wasn't someone who could spend hours watching television or gobble up one book after another in a futile attempt to keep her mind occupied. She did keep a stack of pregnancy manuals by the bed and consulted them every night, learning in minute detail what the baby might look like at any given stage and what developmental milestones were to be expected within the next week or two.

They'd started talking about baby names, but for some reason no name felt quite right yet. Since Phoebe kept insisting that the baby was a boy, they'd come up with several male names, but the only one Quinn was partial to was Alexander. Gabe hadn't mentioned it, but she was sure he wouldn't be averse to naming the child Graham, after his father. Quinn understood the sentiment, and would have loved to honor Gabe's dad in that way, but she just couldn't warm up to the name. To her, Graham was an old-fashioned name, not a name for a little boy, or even an adolescent. She wanted her child to have a name that was trendy and modern. She wouldn't object to giving Graham as a middle name, if it came to that. Perhaps she'd stop by Waterstone's and pick up a book of baby names.

Quinn was just about to leave the café when her phone buzzed. It was a text from Rhys, asking her to stop into the BBC offices to sign the renewed contract. He went on to say that he could overnight it to her if she didn't feel up to coming in person. Quinn glanced at her watch. She had hours until Emma needed to be collected from nursery school, and a walk was just what she needed. Waterstone's could wait.

On my way, Quinn texted back and slung the strap of her bag over her shoulder. She put on her sunglasses and headed out into the glorious afternoon, her mind on the fifteenth-century remains she'd so recently seen.

The BBC head office in Portland Place sparkled with reflected sunshine as Quinn approached. A number of people milled about outside, talking on their mobiles, sneaking a quick cigarette, or just enjoying a few minutes of sunshine before returning to their desks. Quinn signed in and took the elevator to Rhys's floor. His PA invited her to sit down.

"He's in a meeting, but should be wrapping things up," Deborah said, glancing at the clock. "Can I get you a cup of tea or some water?"

"Thank you. I'm all right. I'll just wait."

Quinn took a seat on the ultra-modern white leather sofa and checked her phone. There was a missed call from her mum and several new texts. Jill had sent a photo of a charming empire-waist frock in apple green. The caption read: *You like?*

Quinn responded: *I like. Keep it aside for me, and any peasant blouses you might have in my size. I can still get away with wearing those.* She glanced down at her stomach. She'd have to start buying maternity clothes soon. Her elastic-waist leggings were becoming too tight around the waist and she was uncomfortable. It was about time, she supposed. She'd just entered her third trimester.

Quinn scrolled through the unread texts and found a message from Sylvia. She wanted to know if Quinn might like to meet for lunch at the weekend. Sylvia omitted any mention of Gabe, which meant that she was still angry about the incident with Jude. Quinn sighed with frustration. Why did people have to make things so difficult? Gabe refused to apologize—not that he should have to—and Sylvia refused to see that Gabe was justified. They hadn't come face to face since the incident with Emma, and Quinn hoped that Emma's birthday party might give them the opportunity to bury the hatchet. She smiled wryly. She'd learned that expression from Seth. She hadn't spoken to him in weeks, and knew that she should reach out, but every time she thought of Brett, her stomach contracted with fear. She didn't want to revisit the events that had landed Brett in prison, and talking to Seth inevitably brought it all back.

Quinn's thoughts were interrupted by the opening of the door. Rhys stepped into the anteroom, followed by an elderly gentleman wearing a clerical collar. They were still talking, but Rhys gave Quinn a warm smile and beckoned to her.

"Reverend, this is Dr. Quinn Allenby. Or is it Dr. Russell now?" Rhys asked.

"I'm keeping my maiden name professionally," Quinn replied.

"Dr. Allenby, this the Reverend Alan Seaton. He's just written a best-selling book about the life of Richard III and given all the recent interest in Richard, the BBC has invited him to do an interview and an overview of his work. The reverend was there when they unearthed Richard's remains. Isn't that so, Reverend?" Rhys asked, inviting the man to enter the conversation. "And he's campaigning to have Richard interred at Leicester Cathedral."

Quinn suddenly felt as if all the air had been sucked out of the room. She knew the name sounded familiar, but hadn't made the connection until Rhys mentioned Leicester Cathedral.

"Reverend Alan Seaton?" she gasped, looking at the man closely. "Are you the same Reverend Alan Seaton who found an infant in September of 1983?"

"Yes, I am," the reverend replied shyly. "I'm amazed that you'd remember that story. You must have been an infant yourself at that time. I always did wonder what happened to those girls," he said, shaking his head.

"Sorry, how do you mean?" Quinn asked. Her knees suddenly felt like jelly and her stomach felt hollow and jittery.

"Quinn, you're white as a sheet. You'd better sit down," Rhys said. "Reverend, Dr. Allenby is the baby you found that day."

"You said 'those girls', Reverend," Quinn breathed as she stumbled to the sofa and sat down hard. Her mouth had gone dry and she suddenly wished she'd accepted the offer of a glass of water.

"Oh, I'm so sorry, my dear. I didn't mean to distress you. Yes, there were two babies. I assumed you knew."

Quinn shook her head. "But that's impossible. I saw the news article. My parents showed it to me. It said 'infant', not 'infants'."

"Deborah, get Dr. Allenby some water," Rhys barked. His PA sprang to her feet and ran to the water fountain in the corridor.

I must look as awful as I feel, Quinn thought hysterically.

"Perhaps we'd better continue this in my office," Rhys said as he accepted a cup of water from Deborah. "Come, Quinn." Rhys gave Quinn a hand up and steered her into his office, where he installed her in a comfortable chair and handed her the water before shutting the door on Deborah's curious stare. The Reverend took the other guest chair, while Rhys sat behind his desk.

"I'm so sorry," Reverend Seaton said again. "Are you all right, Dr. Allenby?"

Quinn nodded, too stunned to speak. She took several sips of water, but her mouth was still dry and her heartrate had accelerated, leaving her breathless. "Please, tell me what happened. From the beginning."

The reverend nodded and began. "It was a weekday in late September. It was still fairly early in the morning, so the cathedral was empty. We'd just opened, you see," he explained. "I was in the vestry, having a cup of tea and preparing for the morning service, when I thought I heard something odd. A mewling, you might call

153

it. I stepped out and saw a bundle in the front pew. At first, I thought someone had forgotten their jumper, but then I heard the whimpering and knew it wasn't a jumper at all. The baby got tired of fussing and let out a howl, the likes of which I'll never forget." He smiled at the memory. "You had some lungs on you, young lady."

"But I was there alone," Quinn clarified. "You said bundle, not bundles."

"You were alone. I picked you up and looked around, assuming the mother was nearby or maybe went to the ladies' room and thought it safe to leave you lying around. There was no one there. You quieted down and were studying me with as much interest as I was studying you. I'd baptized quite a few babies, so I could tell you were a newborn, and then I saw the note inside your blanket and realized that you'd been abandoned. I took you into the vestry and called the police. They arrived quickly, and brought a case worker with them. She took possession of you right away."

"What did she do?" Quinn asked, fascinated. She had never heard this part of the story.

"She was well prepared. She had clean nappies, a blanket, in case one was needed, and several bottles of baby formula. She changed you and fed you in the vestry while the officers searched for the mother. It was then that she told me she'd just come from the Leicester Royal Infirmary. A baby had been left in the waiting area of the Children's Emergency Department. The baby was wrapped in a blanket and had a note tucked inside."

"What did it say?" Quinn whispered.

"Quentin, born September twenty-seventh, 1983."

Quinn's hand flew to her mouth. "But why? Why was she left at the hospital?"

"The baby had difficulty breathing and had a bluish color about her when she was discovered by hospital staff. She was born with a heart murmur. The case worker assured me the child would

154

recover fully after surgery. Once it was well enough to leave the hospital, it would be put up for adoption, if the mother didn't come to claim it. She did study the note carefully, and was certain that the handwriting was the same."

"What happened to her?" Quinn cried. "Why did no one ever tell me I had a sister?"

"I can only assume your adoptive parents never knew. Clearly, you two were treated as separate cases. I don't know if any tests were ever performed to determine if you were indeed twins, but I'd say that the answer is obvious."

"Not to me," Quinn replied, shaken. "I found my birth mother less than a year ago. Quite by chance. We talked at length of the events that led to my birth and abandonment, but she never once mentioned a second baby. She wouldn't withhold something like that from me, would she?" Quinn asked, turning to Rhys, who looked as shocked as she felt. "Rhys, would Sylvia really not tell me?"

Rhys shook his head. "I don't know, Quinn. I'd like to say that Sylvia would never do such a thing, but I'm finding that I don't know her nearly as well as I thought I did. I've caught her in several lies as well, as of late."

"Really?" Quinn breathed.

Rhys nodded. "I'd rather not go into details."

"I understand." She turned to Reverend Seaton. "Reverend, did you ever follow up on what happened to us?"

"Once you entered the system, no one would tell me anything. I wasn't a relative and had no legal right to any information. I checked the papers for years, hoping for a mention of your case, but there was never anything. I must admit that I assumed you two would have been kept together, given the circumstances."

"You never saw an obituary for a baby named Quentin?" Quinn asked, holding her breath until the reverend shook his head.

"No. Never. The case worker assured me the baby would be all right. I had no reason to doubt her word."

"Quinn, would you like a moment alone?" Rhys asked gently.

"Please," Quinn muttered.

"Come, Reverend, I'll walk you out. We'll talk again soon. Would it be all right if Quinn contacted you should she need any further information?" Rhys asked.

"Of course. Anytime. And Quinn, if you wish to talk, I'll be in London for another week. I'd be happy to meet you anywhere you like."

"Thank you, Reverend. That's very kind."

Quinn buried her head in her hands as soon as Rhys and the reverend left the office. She was shaking all over, and could feel an angry flush spreading from her chest up to her neck and face. Her cheeks were flaming. Her heart was galloping like a terrified horse and she was short of breath.

"Do you have your heart pressure medication?" Rhys asked as soon as he came back into the office.

Quinn nodded, but didn't have the strength to find it. Rhys unceremoniously dumped the contents of her bag onto his desk and found the bottle. He checked the dosage, then took out a tablet and held it out to Quinn. She obediently took the medicine and drank the rest of the water, but it would take at least a quarter of an hour for the drug to take effect.

"You need to lie down," Rhys said, taking control. He led Quinn over to his sofa and made sure she was comfortable. "All right?"

"Yes," she murmured.

"I'm calling Gabe."

Chapter 25

Gabe rubbed his eyes with his thumb and forefinger. His head was pounding and he could use a stiff drink to calm his nerves, but it was past midnight and he'd be better off going to bed, if he could manage to relax enough to fall asleep. Quinn had finally dozed off, but her eyelids fluttered as if she were having a bad dream and she was whimpering in her sleep. Gabe could make out the tear tracks on her cheeks in the silvery moonlight. Her belly shivered like shifting sands, the baby now wide awake when its mother needed rest.

The news about Quinn's twin couldn't have come at a worse time, and Gabe felt a renewed burst of anger toward Sylvia. Would this never end? The woman had misled Quinn time and again, and still there were more secrets and lies. Gabe fervently wished Sylvia had never found Quinn. Quinn would have always wondered about her birth parents, as many adopted children did, but she wouldn't have had to deal with all the heartache and disillusionment meeting Sylvia had brought into her life.

Quinn refused to condemn Sylvia without first confronting her, but Gabe's mind was made up. Sylvia was poison, and he would do anything to keep Quinn from meeting with her. Of course, Quinn had a right to know the truth, but her blood pressure had been dangerously elevated when he'd fetched her from Rhys's office, and she'd been pale and shaky. Gabe had asked Brenda McGann to collect Emma from school and take her out for pizza to give him time to calm Quinn down and talk the situation through.

He'd meant to argue his case against Sylvia, but Quinn had been so distressed that he'd simply held her and let her cry until she'd eventually exhausted herself enough to allow him to make her some chamomile tea and draw her a warm bath. The bath had helped somewhat, but as soon as Quinn had toweled herself dry and climbed into bed, the tears had begun anew. The revelation that Sylvia had repeatedly lied to her and that she had a twin sister out there was simply too much for Quinn to absorb, and she'd returned to the same questions again and again, unable to make sense of the situation.

The conversation would resume as soon as Quinn opened her eyes in the morning, and Gabe needed to figure out a plan for Quinn to get her answers, but suffer no ill effects. Easier said than done. Gabe almost wished he could confront Sylvia himself, but it wasn't his place, nor would he have enough self-control not to wring the woman's neck. Perhaps he could ask Logan to mediate. Logan's presence might keep the conversation between Sylvia and Quinn from escalating into nuclear warfare, but it didn't seem fair to bring him into it. Sylvia was Logan's mother, and he didn't need to be confronted with these terrible secrets from her past.

Gabe sighed and went to check on Emma, who was sleeping fitfully, Mr. Rabbit clutched in her hand. She always sensed when something was wrong, and began to fret, terrified that the new development would somehow destroy her happy home. Poor child. She'd been through so much already. She didn't need this additional stress when she was about to start at a new school and share her parents with a new sibling. That was enough for any small child to deal with. Gabe tucked the duvet tighter around Emma's shoulders and left the room on silent feet. She was a light sleeper, and once woken, would take hours to go back to sleep.

Gabe got into bed, folded his hands behind his head, and stared up at the murky white ceiling. Preventing Quinn from confronting Sylvia would take an act of God. He couldn't keep that conversation from taking place, but perhaps he could offer Quinn a distraction before the epic confrontation. He'd fetch the sword back from the institute in the morning and let Quinn have a go. The distraction would help—he hoped.

Chapter 26

April 1461

Berwick-upon-Tweed, Northumberland

Guy came awake slowly, his lids fluttering like the wings of a butterfly before finally opening all the way. He'd been sleeping a lot, since there wasn't much else he could do in his weakened state. His arm still felt like a fallen log, and he experienced excruciating pain every time he tried to move it. This made everyday tasks difficult. Even eating had become a challenge, since he couldn't cut his meat with his left hand. Walter had to cut up the meat for him, like he would for a small child. Nurse had helped him bathe the day before. She was the only person in his life in front of whom he could never be embarrassed. She loved him for who he was, and had done so since he was an infant. Nurse was the closest thing he had to a mother, and although he'd never admit it to Hugh, he cherished her as he would a beloved parent.

Guy glanced toward the window to gauge the time. He was hungry, so it had to be getting close to suppertime. He also needed to piss, so he carefully slid off the bed and used his foot to slide the chamber pot from beneath the bed. After relieving himself, he congratulated himself on completing this important task on his own, and lay back down. He felt lightheaded and weak after standing for less than a minute.

When Walter quietly opened the door and peeked inside, Guy beckoned him to come in.

"Just checking if you're awake, sir," Walter said as he advanced into the room with a laden wooden tray. "With Cook's compliments," he added impishly.

"Pour me some wine, Walter. I'm thirsty."

Walter poured Guy a cup of wine and set the tray on the counterpane next to him. It contained a bread trencher filled with mutton, thick with gravy and onions. The gravy had soaked into the bread, making it too messy to eat with his hand.

"Shall I cut it up?" Walter asked.

"Please. Walter, I thought I heard hoof beats a few minutes ago." Guy took a mouthful of bread and mutton and began to chew. It was good, and hot, and he instantly felt better.

"Aye, you did, sir."

"Well, who was it?"

Walter's eyes danced with mischief, and he clearly couldn't wait to divulge whatever news he was withholding. "The master is back. And Sister Catherine is with him," he said, watching Guy for a reaction.

Guy stopped eating and stared at Walter, his eyes wide with concern. "Are they hurt?" he demanded.

"No, they appear to be quite well," Walter replied, smiling with glee.

"Walter, I'm going to box your ears if you don't tell me what you know," Guy said and resumed eating his supper.

"The master just informed Mistress Joan that Sister Catherine has come to stay. They are to be married as soon as arrangements can be made."

Guy nearly choked on the piece of bread he was chewing and took a long swallow of wine before turning on Walter. "You're really asking for it, you ungrateful whelp. I know you like a bit of a lark now and then, but I won't have you enjoying a laugh at my expense."

"'Tis no joke, sir," Walter replied, frowning. "Heard it with me own ears, I did."

"Ask my brother to come and see me." Guy pushed the empty plate toward the boy. "And get more wine. This flagon is nearly empty."

"Aye, sir."

Walter took the dirty crockery and departed, leaving Guy seething with irritation. He hated being cooped up in this room. The world went on without him, and if Walter was to be believed, it was moving a lot faster than it had only a day ago.

Guy was seriously contemplating getting out of bed and going in search of Hugh when his brother finally decided to grace him with his presence. He was clad in dark blue breeches and a matching doublet, his jaw was shadowed with stubble, and his thick hair was playfully tousled. It suddenly struck Guy that Hugh wasn't completely without appeal. Had he charmed Kate into agreeing to marry him?

"How're you getting on?" Hugh asked as he pulled up a chair and sat down next to the bed, looking very pleased with himself.

"Clearly not as well as you are," Guy retorted. "Is it true?"

"Oh, aye," Hugh replied, smiling. "Kate and I are to be married."

It's Kate now, is it? Guy thought sourly. "When?"

"As soon as arrangements are made."

"What sort of arrangements? All you need is a priest and a bride."

"Not quite. I intend to use this marriage to facilitate an introduction to the Earl of Warwick, or at the very least make myself known to him."

Guy gaped at his brother in astonishment, but decided to pursue the Warwick connection later. First, he needed to understand how this betrothal had come about.

"Has Lord Dancy given you his blessing, then?" Guy asked. He couldn't see someone of Lord Dancy's stature condoning a union between his only daughter and a Lancastrian knight of middling wealth. Surely, Lord Dancy would aim much higher when making a match for his daughter, and choose a husband from among his Yorkist cronies.

"Not exactly, but he'll come around to the idea in time," Hugh replied, that sly smile still playing about his lips.

"Meaning?"

"Meaning he didn't have much say in the matter. I had a quiet word with the doting papa last night and led him to believe that his daughter had allowed me to sample her favors. Of course, I would gladly marry the lady, I said, if Lord Dancy would bestow his favor and Catherine's sizable dowry on me. If he refused, I would let it be known that Lady Catherine was no longer a maid, and might already be with child. Lord Dancy was livid. He banished Kate then and there, leaving her no choice but to marry me, since she is now dispossessed. I did manage to convince him that it would be in his best interests to keep the matter quiet and allow me to marry the fair maiden, but I would only do my duty by her if a dowry was forthcoming. He refused to part with all of it, but the amount he gave me will keep us afloat for years."

"And when the money runs out?" Guy asked, his voice tight with anger.

"By that time, the old goat will have died, and Kate, being the only surviving child, will inherit the entire estate, which will, of course, pass to her loving husband. I'll have no claim to the title, but I will have the lands, the serfs, the house, and all within it. And I will have the Warwick connection, which I intend to work tirelessly to my advantage."

"In what way? Are you no longer loyal to Henry and Margaret?" Guy demanded.

"Guy, let's face it, the Lancastrian cause is lost. Margaret is a brave and cunning woman, and if she were a man, she'd make a formidable king, but Harry is weak and ineffectual. Some say that his madness has progressed and he's barely aware of what's being done in his name. King Edward is the future, and I would be a fool to pass up the opportunity to switch sides at a time when it won't be viewed as treason, but rather as good sense."

"William would not have approved."

"William is dead and I'm now head of the family," Hugh reminded Guy, not without anger. "If we are to survive, we must take advantage of this God-given opportunity."

"And what of the Earl of Stanwyck? He's our liege lord. We can't simply change sides," Guy argued.

"Stanwyck is no fool. He can see for himself which way the wind is blowing. He's ready to declare for Edward, and that makes our desertion of the Lancastrian cause a *fait accompli*."

"And what if Kate decides not to marry you and returns to the priory?" Guy asked, hoping Kate would do just that.

"I've taken care of that," Hugh replied with a smirk. "The thought no doubt crossed her mind, so I tumbled her and put an end to that plan. She can never return to the priory now. Her conscience wouldn't allow it. Besides, she might already be carrying my son," Hugh added as he got to his feet.

"You forced her?" Guy growled, outraged that the brother he trusted and respected would be capable of such a vile act against a lovely girl who'd been nothing but kind to them.

"Of course not. I'm not some thoughtless brute, Guy," Hugh retorted, his color rising. "And I am marrying her, so I only took what was rightfully mine."

"Hugh, you *will* make her happy, or you'll have to answer to me." Guy's tone brooked no argument and he glared at his brother with contempt.

"Happy?" Hugh echoed, looking genuinely puzzled. "What does a woman need to be happy? She'll have a roof over her head, my affection and protection, children, and expensive gowns. We must appear prosperous if we hope to get ahead and improve our fortunes, so she'll want for nothing. Of course she'll be happy."

"Do you love her?" Guy asked.

Hugh shrugged. "I desire her; that's enough. I'd like to think that in time I'll grow to care for her. I'm not like you and William, Guy. I'm not sentimental," Hugh explained without any rancor.

"Hugh, please, be kind to her," Guy said, his voice thick with feeling.

"I will be very kind to her, as long as she never gives me a reason not to be, as would any husband. I think I'll go visit my bride and see how she's settling in. I have an itch that needs scratching." Hugh winked at Guy, smiling at his own wit. "Don't be jealous, little brother. We'll find you a wife soon. In the meantime, Nurse can give you a hand. I'm sure she'd enjoy it." Hugh made a lewd gesture, leaving Guy in no doubt of what he meant, laughed uproariously, and left the room. Guy heard his laughter echoing through the empty corridor as he made for the stairs.

It should have been you who died, and not Will, Guy thought bitterly, and instantly regretted the sentiment. That was disloyal, and it was God's will who lived and who died, not his. He would miss Will though, not only as a brother, but as a mentor. William had been an honorable man, loyal to those he cared about and merciful to those he fought against. He had lived by his own code of honor, a code Hugh knew nothing about. Hugh had always been the most cunning and self-serving of the three of them, but William had believed that once Hugh grew into manhood, he'd

165

outgrow the tendency to scheme and manipulate. He had been wrong. Deceit was simply a part of Hugh's nature, just as decency had been a part of William's. Guy supposed that some would congratulate Hugh on his quick thinking and finding a way to turn the situation to his own advantage, but when Guy thought of Kate's sweet face and trusting gaze, he wanted to weep. She was innocent and kind, and not equipped to deal with a man like Hugh, who'd use his connection with her family to further his own ambitions.

Guy pressed his palms to his eyes as a headache began to build, blurring his vision. He was sure Kate had not lain with Hugh willingly. Hugh wouldn't rape a woman; that wasn't his way, but he'd surely manipulated the situation to make it easier to take Kate and practically impossible for her to resist. Guy prayed that Hugh hadn't hurt her and that he would try to be a good husband to her. Hugh hated complications, so it would make his life considerably easier if he had a sweet and compliant wife. He would treat Kate well enough as long as she showed him due respect and fulfilled her wifely obligations, but the idea of Hugh and Kate as a wedded couple still burned Guy's insides until he felt like he was going to be sick.

He had a brief vision of Kate lying beneath Hugh as he thrust into her again and again, and Guy's right hand instinctively went for his sword. He cried out in pain, reminded of his injury and the absurdity of his feelings. Kate wasn't his to protect or defend from her betrothed. Surely, she could have convinced her father to refuse Hugh if she didn't wish to marry him. Perhaps this was what she wanted, Guy reasoned, as he cradled his aching arm. He hardly knew her, and his desire to protect her was misguided and self-serving. He wanted Kate to see him as her champion, her lord, when in fact, he'd be nothing more than her crippled brother-in-law.

166

Chapter 27

Kate was in the Lady Chamber with Eleanor when Hugh came to find her. She supposed the room's name would make more sense if there were more ladies, but Eleanor had been the only woman to use the room since Marie de Rosel died nearly twenty years ago. The two women sat companionably as Eleanor mended Adam's hose, which he was forever snagging, according to her. Adam sat in front of a low table, his father's chess set before him. He didn't know how to play, but he enjoyed moving the pieces around the board, acting out a great battle in his imagination.

"Can you teach me how to play, Uncle Hugh?" Adam asked, looking up from his battlefield.

"I don't see why not," Hugh replied. "My father taught me to play when I was about your age."

"Your father taught you?" Adam asked, staring up at Hugh.

"Yes, he did. He was still alive then, as was my mother," Hugh explained.

"How old was my lord father then?"

"He was ten, but he no longer lived at home because he was a page to a great lord."

"And Uncle Guy?" Adam asked.

"Uncle Guy was hardly more than a babe in arms. He still wore a gown," Hugh replied with a wistful smile. "He toddled after me all day long, whining for me to play with him."

"He played chess?" Adam asked, his eyebrows disappearing into his hair in astonishment.

Hugh laughed. "No, he was too young to play chess. Guy had some wooden pegs that he wanted me to stack for him. As soon as I built a tower, Guy would knock it down. He seemed to find that particular pastime very amusing."

"Will I be a page to a great lord?" Adam asked, dismissing Guy from his mind.

"When the time comes. Is that what you want?"

"I want to be a knight like my father. I want to fight and slay evil King Edward and regain the throne for our rightful king."

"That's a noble sentiment, Adam, but by the time you're a knight things might have changed somewhat. King Henry is an old man."

"Then I'll fight for his son," Adam exclaimed, fired up. "I will avenge my father."

"I'm sure Edward of Westminster will be glad of your support," Hugh replied.

Adam nodded, as if confirming something to himself, and returned to the board, no longer interested in the conversation.

Hugh ruffled Adam's dark hair affectionately and approached the ladies. He gave a courtly bow to Eleanor and smiled at Kate. "Will you oblige me by joining me at the writing desk for a moment, my sweet?" Hugh asked.

"Of course." Kate rose to her feet, gladly setting aside the mending.

"I'm glad to see you two are getting to know each other," Hugh commented, his gaze on Eleanor. "I hope Kate will be of some comfort to you in your grief."

Eleanor nodded miserably as her eyes filled with tears. "I'm grateful for the company," she mumbled.

Hugh rested his hand on the small of Kate's back as he guided her toward the ornate desk situated beneath the window to capture the light. He was all smiles but had a purposeful look in his eyes. She obediently took a seat behind the desk when Hugh asked her to.

He pulled out a sheet of paper from a drawer and handed her a quill. "I'd like you to write a letter to the Earl of Warwick. Invite him to our wedding."

Kate gaped at him. She'd thought he wanted her to write to her father, to perhaps ask for forgiveness or more money, but this request came as a shock. "Hugh, I've never met Cousin Richard. Why would he want to come to our wedding? Surely he has more pressing business to attend to."

Hugh smiled at her indulgently. "I don't expect him to come," he replied, all patience. "He will decline the invitation, or more accurately his lady will, but Her Grace might invite us to visit them in Westminster or even at Middleham Castle. You are kin, after all. And if you assure your kinsman that your future husband is his great admirer and wishes fervently to be of service, surely he can find some use for me."

"Hugh, I really don't think…" Kate began, but Hugh silenced her with a severe look.

"Write the letter, Kate. Thinking is not required."

Kate cringed with embarrassment as she penned the letter, acutely aware of how sycophantic it sounded and how transparent her invitation was, but she could hardly refuse. Hugh had asked her to do it, and as of last night, he was her lord and master. Kate signed the letter with a flourish and handed it to Hugh, who reached for her hand and planted a kiss in her palm.

"Thank you, dearest. I'll send a messenger to deliver this tomorrow, and I'll have him stop off at Newcastle and ask Master Reynolds to pay us a visit," Hugh said, his earlier pique forgotten.

"Who's Master Reynolds?"

"He's a cloth merchant. His wares are vastly superior to anything you can find in Berwick. We're rather provincial here, on the border, so it's either Newcastle or Edinburgh if we desire quality goods."

"Master Reynolds comes with an added benefit," Eleanor interjected from her place by the hearth. "He brings his sister along, who's skilled with a needle and has keen eyes. She's made all my gowns since I married William."

The gown Eleanor was wearing that evening was made of rich brown velvet and trimmed with fox pelt. The color combination brought out Eleanor's lovely brown eyes and accentuated her fair hair and complexion. Mistress Reynolds was indeed gifted, but Kate had no desire for such finery.

"Two serviceable gowns will do, Hugh," Kate objected. "I don't require anything so fine."

Hugh looked at Kate in surprise, as if seeing her for the first time. She supposed it was unusual for a woman not to wish for beautiful things, but she'd spent the last two years at a priory, preparing to take her vows. She'd renounced worldly goods, and found it difficult to go back on her promise, especially when fashionable gowns exposed more flesh than she was comfortable showing after being covered from head to toe even when alone in her cell.

"Kate, I admire your sense of economy, but you can't spend your days wearing a sack gown or my mother's castoffs. You are to be my wife, and your appearance is a reflection on me and my place in the world. I might not be a great lord, like your father, but I won't have my wife looking like a peasant. You'll need several gowns, one suitable to be wed in and worn to an important occasion should one arise, and several for every day. And you'll need new undergarments, stockings, several veils, and a new cloak. That thing you wear looks like a moth-eaten horse blanket. I'm probably forgetting something, but I've no doubt Eleanor will be more than happy to assist you. She knows what a woman of your station will require. Don't you, Eleanor?"

"I'd be happy to help," Eleanor replied demurely, and cast a melancholy look in Hugh's direction. She pouted prettily until Hugh finally caught on.

"And, of course, you must order a new gown for yourself, Eleanor. And whatever else you require," he added. "Master Reynolds doesn't come this way often, so we must take advantage of his visit."

"Thank you, Hugh. I could do with a few things," Eleanor replied, a small smile tugging at her full lips.

"Shall we sup? I'm famished," Hugh announced. His eyes raked over Kate's body as his hand brushed against her thigh, giving a whole new meaning to his innocent words.

Kate blushed with embarrassment, but Hugh winked at her and moved toward the door. The prospect of sharing a bed with Hugh again tonight soured Kate's mood, but she obediently followed him. She could hardly refuse. She was his for the taking now.

Chapter 28

May 1461

Berwick-upon-Tweed, Northumberland

After more than a month at the keep, Kate began to long for something to do other than sit in the Lady Chamber and sew. Sewing and mending had their place, of course, but the hours of physical inactivity left her feeling sluggish and frustrated. She couldn't imagine devoting years of her life to mending hose. There was a flutter of activity before the wedding, but once the day passed, life settled into a more tranquil routine.

The wedding was held at the parish church in Berwick at the end of April. It would have taken place sooner had Kate's gown been ready, but Mistress Reynolds had caught a chill and couldn't finish the gown in time. Hugh had planned a feast to celebrate the marriage, but the Earl of Warwick sent his regrets, via a curt note from his duchess, and Hugh's liege lord had taken ill with the ague and couldn't attend. He sent a gift of two silver wine goblets with his son, Robert Ambrose, which Hugh accepted with great pleasure and displayed in pride of place on the mantel in the great hall.

Kate had also written to her father, asking after her mother's health and inviting her parents to the wedding, but received no reply. She hadn't expected one, but it still hurt her to know that her father had cut her out of his heart so completely. It was common knowledge that the Earl of Stanwyck had changed sides and swore allegiance to the new king, allowing Hugh and Guy to do the same. They were all on the same side now, and Kate hoped that her father might relent, but Lord Dancy was a proud man and wouldn't be manipulated by the likes of Hugh de Rosel. Accepting the invitation, or even replying, would open the door to a reconciliation, and that was something her father had no desire for, not even if it meant a reunion with his only living child.

With most of the guests unable or unwilling to attend, the wedding feast was a small affair, held in the hall of the keep. Guy made it to the service, but the journey took a toll on him since he flat-out refused to arrive at the church in the back of a cart. It was the first time he'd been astride a horse since the battle, and although he put on a brave face, Kate saw him wince with pain when mounting and dismounting. Guy could hold the reins with his left hand, but couldn't manage the rest without putting weight on his injured arm. He cradled it all through the wedding ceremony, but smiled warmly at Kate whenever their eyes met on the ride back. Kate asked Guy several times if he was all right, annoying Hugh with her fussing, but Guy assured her that he was well, and very happy for the newly-wed couple.

Guy refused to return to his room to rest after church and insisted on remaining downstairs for the celebratory feast, but he barely did justice to the meal Joan had prepared for the special occasion. There were several courses, including roast capon, baked fish, and mutton prepared on the spit, followed by a variety of sweetmeats and stewed fruit sweetened with honey and sprinkled with cinnamon, a spice worth its weight in gold and used only on the most special of days. Toast after toast was drunk to the happy couple, and Kate suspected that only a large quantity of wine kept Guy from howling with pain and crawling off to bed.

Kate was relieved when it was finally time to retire. Hugh had consumed too much wine and mead to trouble her with his attentions, and she looked forward to taking off the gaudy gown he'd insisted she wear and enjoying at least eight hours of alcohol-infused oblivion. The gown was a rose pink silk—a color Kate detested, but had been talked into by Eleanor and Mistress Reynolds—with a bodice liberally adorned with gold thread and gemstones. Kate knew she was being ungrateful, since Hugh had been very generous and complimentary of her purchases, but wished only to wear the two day gowns she'd ordered, one of deep blue wool and the other of rust-colored velvet. She'd tried to insist on an unfashionably high neckline and no adornment, but Eleanor and Mistress Reynolds had bullied her into agreeing to fur trim and a lower neckline, to please her lord. Still, the gowns were the most demure garments she owned, and she planned to wear them until they fell apart at the seams.

Once the wedding was behind them, Kate had to face a new hurdle—her increasingly uncomfortable relationship with Eleanor. While William was alive, Eleanor had been the undisputed mistress of the house, but now that he was gone and his title had passed to Adam, she still believed herself to be in charge. Kate supposed that as the mother of the next baron, Eleanor was well within her rights, but Hugh saw himself as the master—being that Adam was only four and could hardly be the head of the family—and he expected Kate to act the part of the mistress. Sensing Eleanor's growing resentment, Kate decided to diffuse the tension by presenting herself in the kitchen early one morning wearing her old sack gown. A morning away from Eleanor was just what she needed, and she was sure that given time apart, Eleanor might come to value Kate's companionship more.

"Good morrow, Mistress Catherine," Joan greeted Kate with some surprise. "Is there aught I can help ye with?"

"No, it is I who've come to help you, Joan."

"I'm coping just fine." Joan looked defiant, as though taking Kate's offer of help as a suggestion that she was failing in her duties.

"I didn't mean to imply that you weren't," Kate rushed to reassure her. "The truth is that I was busy from dawn till dusk at the priory, and I enjoyed the work. I long for something to do, Joan. Please, allow me to assist you in some small way. Surely there's something you'd like help with."

Joan gave Kate a gimlet stare, but quickly relented. She was getting on in years, and there was too much to do for two people. Aileen assisted Joan with the simpler tasks, like fetching water, washing out the crockery, and wringing out the laundry, but Joan did all the cooking and baking. Joan also made sure that every bedsheet, spoon, and morsel of food was accounted for. "Do ye enjoy baking, Mistress Catherine?"

"Please, call me Kate. And yes, I do enjoy baking. Shall I get started on the bread?"

"If ye like."

Joan didn't comment, but Kate was aware of her watchful stare as she mixed the ingredients, kneaded the dough, and shaped it into loaves. Kate carefully placed the loaves in the opening beside the hearth used for baking and turned back to Joan, eager for the next task. She was surprised to catch Aileen's baleful stare.

"Fetch some water," Joan said to the girl. She spoke loudly and made a gesture as if she were lifting a bucket to clarify her instructions. Aileen turned on her heel, grabbed the bucket, and left.

"She's in a mood," Joan commented. "Should be grateful to have a roof over her head and plenty to eat."

"Is she upset about something?"

"How should I know? Not like she tells me. I tell ye, it's lonely having no one to talk to all the long day. Aileen is like a shadow. I'd much rather have a nice, friendly lass to help me with the chores."

"What will happen to her? Once she gets older, I mean," Kate asked. Aileen was on the cusp of womanhood, and might be wondering what life at the keep had in store for her.

"I don't rightly know. It's up to Hugh, I suppose. That girl isn't much use to anyone, is she?"

"Well, I don't know about that. She's deaf, but she's not slow-witted."

"No, she's sharp as a knife when it suits her." Joan peered at the browning loaves. "Did ye bake at the priory?" She appeared to be satisfied with Kate's bread-baking skills and seemed open to allowing her to undertake other tasks.

"I didn't do much baking, but I learned how to do it as part of my training. Every nun and postulate had their assigned tasks, and mine was milking the cows and tending the vegetable garden. I also helped with the pickling and the making of jams and jellies."

"Is that so?" Joan seemed impressed. "If ye're still eager for something to do, mayhap ye can help me with that come autumn. I spend half me time preparing supplies for the winter months, and Aileen ain't much use. More jelly ends up in her mouth than in the jar."

"I would be delighted," Kate replied truthfully. "I quite enjoy making jam. I must admit that I've been known to help myself to a spoonful or two. Or three," she confessed.

"And who could blame ye? I enjoy sampling it meself," Joan added with a smile. "It's when the sampling turns into outright gorging that we have a problem."

"What should I start on next?" Kate checked on the loaves and looked around the kitchen.

"Perhaps ye can churn some butter, if ye feel up to it."

"Of course. It'll be my pleasure." Kate filled the butter churn with milk and took a seat on the bench set against the wall. The churn was surprisingly modern, and had a foot pedal instead of a hand crank. Kate set her foot on the pedal and began to rock the churn back and forth.

"Guy used to like coming to the kitchen when he were a little lad." Joan's face softened at the memory. "He said he wanted to help, but what he really wanted was a bit of company. He was often lonely, the poor mite."

"How old was he?"

"About six. My lady died when Guy was five and Margaret was three. I kept Margaret here with me while I worked, but Guy was left to fend for himself. William and Hugh had gone by that time, and he missed them something fierce."

"What were they like, as children?" Kate asked. She knew next to nothing about her husband and his family.

Joan laughed and shook her head in amusement as if she recalled some particularly amusing incident. "They were a handful, I'll tell ye that. Their lady mother, God rest her soul, compared them to horses once."

"To horses?" Kate asked, so surprised she stopped pushing the pedal.

"She had a funny way with words. His lordship brought her from Normandy. She spoke English well, but often translated sentences in her head from French, and they came out sounding odd. She didn't have too many ladies of her station to talk to, so that didn't help neither."

"Why?"

"People are wary of foreigners," Joan explained, as if that should be obvious.

"But the people hereabouts support a French queen."

"Aye, that they do, but a queen is a queen, and a French woman is a harlot and a witch, best avoided."

"That seems awfully harsh," Kate exclaimed. She could understand how lonely Marie must have been, if her own experience of life at the keep were anything to go by.

"She was beautiful, and kind. She left us too soon."

"So why did she compare her children to horses?" Kate asked.

"Oh, that. Marie said that Gulliume—that's what she called William—was like a work horse: strong, steady, and hardworking. Hubert was like a destrier, bred for war. And Guy was like a pony: gentle and sweet, and perfect for children."

"And Margaret?"

177

"Margaret was like a newborn colt—shaky and frightened," Joan replied, the smile having faded from her face at the mention of the little girl.

Kate liked the whimsical descriptions. She hadn't known William, but both Guy and Hugh had mentioned that he'd been loyal, decent, and honest. Hugh, from what Kate knew of her husband so far, was aggressive, ambitious, and morally ambiguous when it suited him. And Guy seemed sensitive and chivalrous.

"Funny how bairns born of the same parents can be so different," Joan mused as she deftly skinned a rabbit. "Those boys had their own personalities from the day they were born, and no amount of schooling or scolding could change them."

"What about Margaret?"

Joan shook her head in dismay. She never mentioned Margaret unless Kate asked about the child outright. Perhaps the memory was too painful. But Joan's next words quickly dispelled that notion.

"Margaret was clumsy, and oblivious to all around her. Not clever and canny like her brothers. That bairn had no sense of self-preservation, so someone always had to keep an eye on her, even once she got too old to be minded round the clock," Joan added.

"Guy blames himself for her death."

It was difficult for Guy to speak of his sister, but he'd shared with Kate that Margaret had drowned in the river when she was only five. She'd gone there with Guy, who had been distracted by something he saw and wandered off. He didn't see his sister slip on the mud and fall into the river. Margaret's desperate screams got Guy's attention, but it was too late. The waterlogged skirts had dragged the struggling child under before he got a chance to call for help. He'd nearly died himself, trying to rescue her, but she'd drowned nevertheless and her body hadn't been recovered until it washed up downriver and was found by one of the de Rosel tenants.

"More fool he if he does," Joan snapped. "Margaret was old enough to know not to come too close to the river. She just wasn't paying attention, as usual. It weren't Guy's fault."

"That's rather a harsh view of a child's death." Joan hadn't liked Margaret, that was clear, and wasn't ashamed to admit it.

"There are those who are taken from us through no fault of their own, and there are those who run toward their own end." Joan finished with the rabbit and reached for another one, whacking off its head before she carefully peeled the skin away from its body. The fur would not go to waste, not in a place that was cold and windy even in the warmer months. "Ye'd best check on those loaves afore they burn to a crisp."

Kate jumped up and hurried toward the hearth. She'd clear forgotten about the bread as she listened to Joan. There was much to learn, and some of the most important lessons would be taught here in the kitchen. Kate took out the perfect loaves and left them to cool.

"Now where's that foolish lass?" Joan groaned. "Ye'd think I sent her to get water from the river."

"Shall I go and see?"

"Don't trouble yerself. She's probably making cow eyes at Walter. As if he'd have anything to do with the likes of her."

Kate didn't reply. There was little point. Joan was a woman who spoke her mind and expected little opposition to her opinions. She was reliable, efficient, and capable, but kindness and compassion didn't appear to be part of her nature, which was odd for a woman who had been employed as a nurse.

Joan turned toward the door when Aileen bustled in, carrying the water, a happy smile on her face. Joan waited until Aileen set down the bucket before giving her a resounding slap. "I won't have ye dawdling. Ye hear me? No, ye likely don't, but ye understand the sting of the back of me hand. Now, get to work, ye lazy slattern."

Aileen nodded in contrition and took her place in the corner, reaching for a bowl of peas to shell. She kept her head down, but Kate saw the sparkle of tears on her thick lashes.

Chapter 29

August 2014

London, England

Gentle fingers of morning light caressed Quinn's face as she slowly came awake. She'd slept fitfully and had strange dreams, but this morning she felt much calmer. She'd cried for hours last night, soaking Gabe's T-shirt with tears as she tried to wrap her mind around what she'd learned from Reverend Seaton. She wasn't sure what hurt more, discovering she had a twin sister out there somewhere, or realizing Sylvia had betrayed her so completely.

Sylvia had known from the start how desperately Quinn longed to find her family, and Quinn had mentioned more than once how excited she was to find out she had siblings. She'd given Sylvia every opportunity to tell her there'd been another baby, a twin no less. But Sylvia's bland expression had never altered when Quinn spoke of siblings, and not a twinge of guilt had marred her features when she spoke to Quinn about the day she'd abandoned her. Sylvia appeared to love her sons. Why couldn't she have loved her daughters?

A child was such a gift, even if it wasn't one's own, Quinn reflected, as Emma's piping voice drifted from the kitchen, and Gabe's baritone answered her patiently.

"What am I getting for my birthday?" Emma asked for the hundredth time.

"You'll just have to wait and see," Gabe replied.

"But I want a puppy," Emma persisted.

"I know, darling, but there's no room for a puppy in this flat. Maybe we can get a puppy once we move."

"But I want a puppy now."

"It wouldn't be fair to the puppy to have nowhere to play," Gabe reasoned with her. "Would you want the puppy to be sad?"

"No, I suppose not," Emma conceded. "Can I have one when we move?"

"We will talk about it then."

"But I don't want to move to Berwick. I like it here," Emma whined.

"I like it here too," Gabe replied wistfully.

"So, why can't we stay? Is it because of Grandma Phoebe?"

"Partially, yes. Now, what would you like for breakfast today? Toast okay?"

"I want a boiled egg and soldiers," Emma replied. That was her favorite breakfast and she'd eat it every day if she could.

"All right. Boiled egg and soldiers coming right up."

"I want Quinn to make it," Emma replied defiantly.

"Are you saying that I can't be trusted to boil an egg?" Gabe demanded, pretending to be outraged. Quinn could hear the smile in his voice.

"I'm saying that Quinn makes it better," Emma replied, honest as only a four-year-old could be.

"Quinn is still sleeping. She's tired, darling."

"Why was Quinn crying, Daddy? Was she sad?"

"Just a little bit. It's all right to feel sad from time to time."

"What did Grandma Sylvia do? I heard you say her name."

"Grandma Sylvia likes to play games, and sometimes they are not fun," Gabe answered.

"What sort of game is it?"

"The kind of game only adults can play. It's a grown-up version of show and tell."

"Did Grandma Sylvia show or tell?" Emma asked.

"Neither, which is why Quinn was upset. Grandma Sylvia didn't follow the rules."

"Rules are rules," Emma intoned. "Miss Aubrey always says that when we don't want to do something at school."

"Rules are there for a reason," Gabe said. "Here's your egg and soldiers, and a glass of orange juice. Enjoy."

"Can I have coffee?" Emma asked.

"What? Why would you want coffee?"

"Because I'll be five soon and that's what grown-ups drink."

"I don't think you'll like it. It's bitter."

"So why do you like it?"

"Because I can't have whisky in the morning," Gabe joked, but it fell flat, given that his audience was slightly underage.

Quinn smiled. She loved listening to the two of them. Gabe and Emma's relationship had come a long way in the past few months, and they had a dynamic all their own, one that she at times hated to disrupt. Quinn had her own relationship with Emma, and she hoped it wouldn't change once the baby came.

Quinn finally got out of bed, pulled on her dressing gown, and padded into the kitchen. "Good morning, you two. Beautiful day."

"Are you done crying?" Emma asked.

"Absolutely. No more tears. See?" Quinn gave Emma a brilliant smile. "I have a very important assignment for you today."

"What?"

Quinn took a stack of birthday invitations from the drawer and showed them to Emma. "I will put these in your backpack, and you will hand them out when you get to school. Can you do that?"

"But I can't read," Emma protested. "How will I know whose invitation is whose?"

"All the invitations are exactly the same, so it doesn't matter who gets which envelope. Are you up to the task, Miss Russell?"

"Yes!"

"Excellent. Now, finish your breakfast and go get dressed. Your clothes are on the chair. I just need to speak to Daddy for a moment."

"Promise you won't cry?" Emma asked as she slid off her chair.

"Promise."

"How are you? Really?" Gabe asked as he wrapped Quinn in his arms and gave her a lingering kiss.

"I'm all right. Really."

"Quinn, about Sylvia…"

Quinn held up her hand. "Nothing to worry about."

"Why don't I believe you?"

"Well, you should. I've had a moment of perfect clarity," she announced, still smiling.

"I'm almost afraid to ask."

Quinn took a seat at the table and reached for one of Emma's leftover strips of toast. "Any chance of a cup of tea?"

"Of course." Gabe poured her a cup of tea and added a splash of milk. She could see the tension in his shoulders and the worried look in his eyes, and her heart turned over. She was so blessed to have a husband who loved her so much and worried about her well-being. Gabe was the only person, besides her parents, whom she'd trust with her life, and the realization overwhelmed her with gratitude.

'I love you," Quinn said simply.

"And I love you, but I'm still waiting to hear about this earth-shattering revelation," Gabe replied with a warm smile.

"When I asked Sylvia why she didn't want me, she said she gave me away because she couldn't love me," Quinn explained. "I was devastated by her answer, but also grateful for her honesty. It'd have made it worse if she'd said she wanted me desperately but couldn't find a way to make it work. I'd have felt like I missed out on a lifetime with my mother."

"Yes, I can see that. But how is this relevant?"

"What I realized just now is that the sentiment is not one-sided. I don't want Sylvia because I can't love her. You were absolutely right about her, Gabe. I built up my birth mother in my mind, imagining her to be this perfect woman, but in truth, Sylvia is someone I'd never choose to know had she not given birth to me. I don't trust her, and, let's be brutally honest here, I don't even like her. Just because I now know her doesn't mean I have to maintain a relationship with her or allow her to be a part of my life."

"So, what are you saying? Are you severing ties with her?"

Quinn shook her head. "No, not yet. I will speak to her about what I've learned, and if what the Reverend Seaton said is true, I will look for my sister. But I will no longer allow Sylvia to hurt me, nor will I permit her the chance to be my mother, or a grandmother to my children. She's lied to me once too often. Sylvia Wyatt can just be someone I know. Period."

"That's quite a turnaround from yesterday," Gabe said, watching Quinn. "What brought this on?"

"Perhaps I'm starting to think more like a mother and a wife and less like a single woman. Sylvia is not a priority for me any longer—you and the children are." Quinn laid a hand on her belly, smiling as it shifted beneath her hand. "I will not do anything to endanger this baby, or myself. I will approach this new hurdle like a work project rather than a personal quest."

"Who are you, and what have you done with my wife?" Gabe joked. "I'm glad to hear you see sense. That is the best possible attitude I could have hoped for. Will it last?" he asked carefully.

"I think so."

"What are you not telling me?" Gabe asked as he took a seat across from Quinn and sipped his coffee.

"I want it to be a coincidence, Gabe. I don't want that baby to be my sister."

"Really?"

"Gabe, you know how badly I wanted to know my parents and my siblings, but so far, meeting them has been a great disappointment. Sylvia is as wily as a fox. Seth is a good man, but, on some level, he'll always be a stranger to me, and my brothers have been a revelation, to say the least. If I truly have a twin sister, God only knows what she's like. Just because we shared a womb doesn't mean we have anything in common or will even like each other."

"You're afraid to get your hopes up."

"I suppose you could say that. Finding my twin, if that's who she is, would really prove to be an interesting case study for nature versus nurture. Would we be similar because of our genetics, or would we be polar opposites because we grew up in completely different families and circumstances?"

"There's only one way to find the answer to that question, and I think that perhaps you should wait until after baby Russell is born to start looking for it."

Quinn nodded. "I think you're right, but in the meantime, I can start doing the legwork, and the first port of call is Sylvia."

"I'm coming with you," Gabe said.

"Gabe, I love that you want to protect me, but this is something I must do on my own. I promise you I will remain cool, calm, and detached. Like I said, I'm done allowing Sylvia to hurt me."

"All right. But ring me, should you need moral support."

"You know I will."

Chapter 30

Quinn wasn't as calm as she'd hoped to be when she finally rang Sylvia later that morning. Her resolution not to allow Sylvia to hurt her anymore made her feel stronger, but the very topic she was about to broach made her heart beat faster. Could Reverend Seaton have arrived at the conclusion that Quinn and Quentin were twins without sufficient evidence? Surely, babies were abandoned every day, and it wasn't outside the realm of possibility that they'd be wrapped in a blanket with some sort of message from the mother. The case worker might have been mistaken about the similarity in handwriting, couldn't she? Quinn and Sylvia had spoken repeatedly about past events, and not once had Sylvia alluded to a second baby. No, it had to be a mistake and she was condemning Sylvia based on nothing but circumstantial evidence. A part of Quinn wished the conversation with Reverend Seaton had never taken place, but now that she knew about Quentin she had to find out the truth. Once she had her answer, she'd make a decision about Sylvia.

Quinn tried to sound normal when Sylvia picked up.

"Well, hello there, stranger," Sylvia said. "How are you feeling?"

"I'm well, thank you. I was wondering if you might like to come for lunch today, Sylvia. It's been some time since we saw each other."

"That would be lovely. Can I bring anything?"

Just some truth serum, Quinn thought bitterly. "No, just yourself. Would sandwiches be all right? I'm not much in the mood for cooking."

"Of course. I'll bring something for pudding."

"Let me guess; Rhys has been plying you with baked goods," Quinn joked.

"Actually, I haven't seen him recently. But more about that later. I'll see you around noon?"

"Great."

Quinn rang off and stared at her phone, thinking. She would conduct her own research, regardless of what Sylvia said. There was no reason to expect Sylvia to be honest with her, and she needed to be sure that she knew the truth of the situation before making any decisions. Quinn found Reverend Seaton's contact information and called the number.

"Reverend, it's Quinn Allenby," she began. "I'm sorry to disturb you."

"Not at all. Not at all, dear. I'm so glad you called. Please allow me to apologize once again. I was unforgivably tactless yesterday. I do hope you weren't too upset."

"I was a bit, but I'm all right now. I'd just like to ask you a few questions, if you don't mind."

"It's the least I can do."

"Do you recall the name of the case worker who came to collect me?" Quinn listened to the silence on the other end as Reverend Seaton considered the question.

"It was thirty years ago," he finally said. "I can't recall her name, but I know someone who would be able to. My wife, God bless her, has the memory of an elephant. I'll call her right now and ask. Can I ring you back?"

"Of course. You can even text it to me, if you prefer."

"I'm afraid I'm not that technologically advanced. I'm still old school, and prefer to speak to people in person."

"I'll wait for your call then."

Quinn disconnected the call and went to take a shower. After hearing back from Reverend Seaton, she'd go to the shops and pick up the ingredients for the sandwiches and something to make for dinner. She owed Gabe and Emma a home-cooked meal, and she was in the mood for pasta primavera. It was delicious, and a sneaky way to get Emma to eat her vegetables.

Quinn was toweling her hair dry when her mobile rang. Reverend Seaton.

"That was quick," she said by way of greeting. "Any luck?"

"If anyone would be able to remember, it'd be my Abigail. The case worker's name was Hetty Marks. Lovely lady, as I recall. I hope you'll be able to track her down."

"Thank you, Reverend. I hope so too. I just have one more question," Quinn said, wondering if what she was about to ask would make any difference to the outcome.

"Of course."

"Was it you or Ms. Marks who made the assumption that we were twins?"

"It was Ms. Marks. Why does that matter?" the reverend asked.

"It matters because Ms. Marks saw us both and also saw the notes. If she surmised that we were twins, her assumption would be based on that."

"Whereas mine would have been nothing more than supposition," Reverend Seaton concluded.

"Well, yes."

"I don't think Hetty Marks was the type of woman to jump to unsupported conclusions. Very no-nonsense, she was—a real brick, as we used to call girls like her in my day. I'd be surprised if she got it wrong. Anyway, I wish you luck with your search, Quinn. Ring me if you need anything else, dear," the reverend said before hanging up.

Quinn sighed. The conversation with Reverend Season had given her a valuable lead, but it also undermined her resolve to give Sylvia a fair chance. Regardless of what Sylvia said, Quinn had to discover the truth for herself. She pushed aside the notepad with the case worker's name on it and went to get dressed.

Sylvia arrived on time, bearing a box of lintzer tarts. "I had a terrible craving for sweets when I was pregnant," Sylvia said as she followed Quinn into the kitchen. "Particularly with Jude. I thought the kid would come out begging for sticky toffee pudding."

"Does he like sweets?" Quinn asked.

"Yes, he does, but he likes lager much more," Sylvia replied. "I did not have that while pregnant."

"I made some egg and cress and ham and tomato sandwiches, and a salad. I hope that's all right," Quinn added as she invited Sylvia to sit.

"Perfect. I'll have one of each. Are you experiencing any cravings?" Sylvia asked as she helped herself to some salad.

"Yes, I've been craving eggs. Perhaps I'm not eating enough protein. I've had an aversion to meat these past few weeks." Quinn reached for an egg and cress sandwich. "I do crave sweet things as well. I'm looking forward to those tarts."

"They are to die for. Logan always brings me some when he pops by, which is not as often when things are going well with him and Colin. How's Gabe? Has he found a job up north yet?" Sylvia asked, her tone carefully neutral.

"Not yet, but he's looking."

"I love your idea for Emma's birthday party. Sounds like a blast. I never got to have such girlie themes, not having a daughter." Sylvia looked sheepish when she realized how that statement had come out. "I didn't mean to sound insensitive," she added, stopping short of apologizing. She'd only spoken the truth, as she knew it, but the careless remark stung Quinn nonetheless.

"Quite all right." Quinn looked across the kitchen table at Sylvia. She looked happy and relaxed as she helped herself to another sandwich. Even now that Sylvia knew Quinn, she obviously felt no regret about missing out on their time together, nor did she try particularly hard to forge ahead with their relationship. Sylvia had been the one to seek Quinn out, but Jude and Logan were her priority, and always would be.

Quinn experienced a sudden thunderbolt of blinding anger. She was tired of her British reserve. She was half-American after all, and Seth wouldn't have minced words in a similar situation. He'd have come right out and confronted Sylvia head on, as would Quinn's biological grandmother. She must have been quite a firecracker in her day. Quinn felt a pang of regret at not having had more time with Rae Besson, especially before the Alzheimer's set in.

Quinn took a sip of water to steady her nerves and plunged in. Taking Sylvia completely by surprise was the only way to glean anything resembling the truth, and Quinn was no longer concerned with her feelings.

"By the way, Sylvia, when were you going to tell me I have a twin sister?"

Sylvia dropped her sandwich and paled visibly, confirming Quinn's suspicion that Reverend Seaton and Hetty Marks had been correct. Sylvia reached for her glass of water and took a long sip before finally meeting Quinn's gaze. "Quinn, I…" She faltered. "How on earth…?"

"Funny thing, that. I met a Reverend Seaton at the BBC offices yesterday. Quite a coincidence, as he was the very man who found me in that cathedral pew nearly thirty-one years ago. We got to talking, and he mentioned the other baby, the one that was left at the hospital on the same day with the same note. Quentin, was it? I see you have a fondness for Q names."

"Quinn, I don't know what to say." Sylvia looked cornered and frightened, but Quinn wasn't about to stop.

She felt a cool sense of detachment as she watched Sylvia, like an interrogator who'd do anything to extract information from a suspect. "How about you tell me the truth for a change? That would be very refreshing."

"I have told you the truth," Sylvia retorted. Angry spots of color bloomed in her cheeks, and her eyes glittered with resentment at having been caught out.

"Have you? Seems to me that you manipulated the facts to suit your own agenda, and that the men you accused of raping you remember a very different version of events. I suppose I should take your word over theirs, but they are very convincing, and have all proved to be more honest than you have been."

"Quinn, you're angry. I see that." Sylvia's placating tone only served to fuel Quinn's fury.

"Damn right, I'm angry, Sylvia. Who you slept with when you were a teenager is your own personal business, but not to tell me about a twin sister is a lie of a magnitude that should get its very own category. I'd file it under V for vicious, or D for diabolical."

"How about M, for misguided?"

"Sylvia, you're many things, but misguided is not one of them. Are you going to tell me the truth, or are you stalling for time while you try to work out an acceptable version of events in your head?"

"Is this why you invited me here today?" Sylvia asked. Quinn felt the shift in her attitude; she was about to go on the offensive and act the victim.

"Yes, it is. I needed to hear it from you first, before I began my own investigation. Will you tell me, or do I need to find out for myself?"

Sylvia sat back and studied Quinn for a moment, almost as if she were deciding if it was worth the bother. She must have realized that their relationship, fragile as it had been, was now broken beyond repair. No matter what story she spun, Quinn had caught her in a lie that was too big to explain away. Nothing Sylvia said could undo the damage, and no apology could ever soothe the hurt.

"Yes, Quinn, it's true. I gave birth to twins that day. As I said before, I never received any antenatal care, as I never went to the clinic, so I didn't know I was carrying twins until the midwife examined me during labor. I was shocked, I can tell you that. If dealing with one baby was terrifying, the thought of two sent me over the edge. I was seventeen, alone and scared."

"You didn't have to be alone. You had a father who loved you. And you could have gone through the proper adoption channels. The social workers would have helped you, and you would have had some say in who got your babies."

"Hindsight is always twenty-twenty, isn't it?" Sylvia replied. "I'm not proud of what I did, but there's nothing I can do to change that now."

"So, what happened?" Quinn demanded.

"You were born first. You were healthy and strong, but your sister, who was born twenty minutes later, wasn't as lucky. The midwife thought the reason she was bluish and had trouble breathing was because the cord had been around her neck, but that wasn't it. Even after an hour, she was still gasping for breath, and it was clear that something was terribly wrong. The midwife urged me to call an ambulance, but if I did that, all my careful planning and hiding would have been for nothing. Everyone would know I'd had children. So, I asked her to stay with you and took Quentin to the hospital. I put her down on a chair in a high-traffic area and pretended to go to the loo. Then I slipped out of the emergency waiting area and watched through the window. I waited until the baby was picked up by a passing nurse, who instantly summoned a doctor, then left. She was in good hands and would receive the care

194

she needed. I returned to my room and took you to the cathedral in the morning. You know the rest."

"What happened to her?" Quinn asked. She was shocked to the core by Sylvia's matter-of-fact recital of the facts. Her first priority had been protecting herself rather than getting medical help for a struggling baby.

"I don't know." Sylvia shrugged in ignorance. "I never went back. I assume she got adopted, just like you did."

Quinn stared at the woman who'd given birth to her. Quinn had seen many dangerous and corrupt people in her visions, but those people were usually driven by love, hate, jealousy, or fear. Sylvia was driven by self-preservation. She hadn't cared enough to make sure her babies got a good home, or even to make sure an ailing child recovered. She had simply walked away and gone on with the business of being a teenager.

"I think I'd like you to leave now," Quinn said. Her voice sounded cool and detached, and oddly, her heart was as well. She'd learned what she needed to learn. The end.

"Will we speak again?" Sylvia asked, clearly shocked by Quinn's unexpected behavior.

"Perhaps one day, but it won't be any time soon," Quinn replied. "I need time to come to terms with this, and to find my sister."

"May I call you?" Sylvia's voice shook with distress, but Quinn no longer cared.

"I'd rather you didn't. Thank you for the tarts," Quinn added as she escorted Sylvia to the door.

"Quinn, I'm sorry. Truly, I am," Sylvia said. "I wish I could meet you all over again, and start fresh."

"So do I, Sylvia. So do I."

Chapter 31

June 1461

Berwick-upon-Tweed, Northumberland

Kate carefully edged out of bed and pulled on the blue woolen gown. The weather outside was improving, but it was always cold within the castle walls and she found herself gravitating to warmer spots, sitting by the hearth or by the window when the sun was out.

She pushed her feet into her shoes and pinned up her hair before creeping from the bedchamber. Hugh was a sound sleeper and liked to sleep well into the morning hours, but Kate could rarely sleep past sunrise. She began her day by going to the chapel, which had become her special place. The chapel wasn't in use, since the family preferred to go to the parish church on Sundays and Feast Days. It was the only time during the course of the week when they came in contact with people from the neighboring estates, an opportunity not to be missed. Kate was accustomed to the slow rhythm of the priory, but Eleanor and Hugh chafed at the solitude and looked forward to socializing and exchanging bits of news and gossip with the neighbors.

Being bedbound, Guy hadn't gone to church the first few weeks he was home, but he'd been coming to services since the wedding, more because he was going mad with boredom than because he felt the need to commune with the Lord. Joan herded Aileen, Jed, and Walter as well, mindful of their spiritual needs, but Alf always remained behind, fearful of leaving the keep completely unattended. He locked the gates and didn't open them again until the church party returned.

The castle chapel had been added about a hundred years ago, centuries after the original keep had been erected on this parcel of land. It was small and silent, and had never been intended for use by all the inhabitants, only those who wished to pray in solitude. There was a wooden altar with a silver cross and two prie-dieux upholstered in worn claret velvet. The prie-dieux had seen their share of knees, mostly female, Kate surmised. The only light in the chapel came from a round stained-glass window set high in the wall above the altar. It was the chapel's only luxury, aside from the cross, and Kate often gazed up at it after finishing her prayers. The bright colors gave her hope, and reminded her of Holystone Priory and her happy time there.

Kate never complained, but she longed for the comfort of daily prayer. Her marriage wasn't unhappy by any means, but it wasn't at all what she had expected. Hugh was courteous, but he never really confided in her. He wasn't a man who was comfortable around women; he treated them much as he treated the dogs, with restrained affection and a complete indifference to their thoughts. He spoke to Guy at length, and sometimes chatted with Walter while they practiced in the yard, and even with Adam, whom Hugh had begun to teach fighting with a wooden sword, but never to Kate. Hugh was kind and affectionate to the boy, which allowed Kate to hope that he would be a good father to their children. Despite his frequent attentions, she hadn't conceived. It was early days yet, but she knew Hugh was disappointed, having assumed it would happen right away.

Kate didn't enjoy lying with Hugh, but she didn't dread it either. She knew his pattern by now and simply allowed her mind to drift until he was finished. He didn't expect much of her in the bedchamber. All she had to do was welcome him into her body and lie still until he was done. Hugh always kissed her afterward and went straight to sleep, leaving Kate to her own thoughts, which were often gloomy.

The Earl of Warwick was still very much on Hugh's mind; she knew that since she'd overheard him mention the earl to Guy on more than one occasion. The invitation to the wedding had been Hugh's opening overture, and he intended to try again when the time was right. Kate dreaded being used as bait to facilitate an introduction to the earl, since she'd never actually met him in person, and didn't relish being treated like a poor relation to be fobbed off at the earliest opportunity, but Hugh wouldn't be deterred.

She hadn't heard anything from her father, despite sending several letters, which Walter had dutifully delivered to the Grange. Walter always returned empty-handed, having been refused an audience with Lord Dancy, so he couldn't say with any certainty if her father had actually read the letters or simply thrown them on the fire. Kate was desperate for news of her mother, so when she'd sent the last letter, she'd asked Walter to stop into the church in Belford and inquire after Lady Dancy from Father Phillip. She was sad to learn that Father Phillip had passed away in May and a new priest had taken his place, a Father John, who was reluctant to share anything about the family with a young man he didn't know.

Walter, being a clever lad, had decided to stop into the tavern for a tankard of ale and a chat with the proprietor, who remembered Hugh and Kate quite well, and was eager to talk once enticed by the glimmer of silver. Walter was able to discover that Lady Dancy had died at the end of April, just about the time Kate and Hugh were married, having never recovered from the shock of losing her sons. Kate assumed that her father was stricken with grief, but even in his darkest hour, he still refused any communication from her. She prayed that, in time, Lord Dancy's stance toward her might soften, especially if Hugh proved himself loyal to the Yorkist king, which he fully intended to do.

Kate's only solace was her relationship with Guy. He'd recovered sufficiently after a few weeks abed, but his arm still pained him and he suffered from frequent headaches and occasional loss of vision. Guy managed everything on his own, but he could no longer wield a sword or lift anything heavier than a puppy. One of the Scottish Deerhound bitches had given birth a few weeks since, and Adam brought the puppies into the keep for company. He named them Angus and Hamish. Angus slept in Adam's bedchamber, but he generously gave Hamish to Guy to cheer him up. The puppy followed Guy everywhere, its warm brown eyes eager for attention.

Kate often bumped into Guy just as she was leaving the chapel in the morning, and they broke their fast together since Hugh and Eleanor were still abed. After breakfast, they'd go for a walk. Guy needed to regain his strength after so many weeks of immobility, so they walked a little further each day, sometimes going almost as far as Berwick Castle, which rose above the River Tweed like a giant beast, peering from behind the curtain wall punctuated by nine watch towers. Kate liked walking toward the castle and would have liked to go as far as the town, but since most people's loyalty in this part of England still lay with the House of Lancaster, it was best avoided for fear of confrontation. Kate and Guy usually turned back as soon as they came across the castle's inhabitants or townsfolk.

Guy often spoke to Kate of his childhood and ambitions for the future. Being the youngest brother, he'd always been overshadowed by William and Hugh, but now that he was nearly five and twenty, he was ready to think for himself, a development that Hugh wouldn't welcome. Despite Adam inheriting the title, Hugh enjoyed playing the lord of the manor too much to countenance any opposition from anyone. He'd stepped into William's shoes and meant to remain in charge until Adam came of age. There were moments, during the darkest hours of the night, when Kate allowed herself to believe that Hugh wouldn't be too heartbroken if Adam never reached adulthood. He'd grieve for the boy, since he seemed genuinely fond of him, but Adam's death would mean Hugh's ascension to the baronetcy, something he coveted above all else. Guy never spoke of Hugh's ambitions in that regard, but Kate knew he kept a watchful eye on Adam, and often frustrated Hugh by putting a damper on his plans. Guy was the voice of reason, whereas Hugh was the force for change.

Kate didn't have much say in any significant changes, but one aspect of her life she wished to improve was her relationship with Joan. Joan had been the true lady of the house in everything but name since the death of Marie de Rosel. She'd run the household and raised the children, and continued to rule the roost even after William married Eleanor. Joan should have stepped aside and allowed Lady de Rosel to take her rightful place in the household, but Joan was too set in her ways and Eleanor too timid to assert her rights. In truth, Kate didn't think Eleanor minded. She was the kind of woman who preferred to have someone else make the decisions for her, and deal with the consequences as well. She was only too happy to surrender the running of the household and even the raising of her son to the formidable Joan, who treated her like a dimwitted child, to be scolded and rewarded as the situation demanded, but Kate would have none of it. Eleanor was still Lady de Rosel, in name, but Hugh was the head of the family, which made Kate the acting mistress, and she would not permit Joan to usurp her place. Lady Dancy had taught her daughter much, by lesson and by example, and one of the most important pieces of advice, before the decision had been made to send Kate off to the priory, was that the mistress of the house should always keep her servants in line.

Joan had initially welcomed Kate into her domain, but did not take kindly to her interference once she realized Kate wouldn't get bored and return to spending her days with Eleanor in the Lady Chamber. Kate tried to suggest minor changes, or propose certain economies, which Joan wouldn't countenance just on principle. She would not give up her place without a fight, and Kate was beginning to suspect that she'd not adhere to any rules of combat. Joan tolerated Kate in her kitchen, but was often resentful and abrupt in her eagerness to drive Kate away. Kate supposed she could understand Joan's feelings, given that she'd ruled the roost since the days of the last Lady de Rosel, but some part of her refused to let Joan have her way. Kate was respectful and polite to the older woman, but she did insist on certain minor changes in the running of the household, which angered Joan and fed her resentment.

Kate noticed that Joan kept a watchful eye on everything she did, and at times seethed with baseless jealousy, as if Kate had stolen the affection of her boys from her. Joan was particularly possessive of Guy, whom she still saw as her ward. Kate and

Guy's relationship was innocent, but if Joan's sly looks were to be taken seriously, they had something to feel ashamed of. Or perhaps it was Kate's guilty conscience that troubled her and made her see something that wasn't truly there.

Guy never made inappropriate comments or touched her without good reason. He held out his hand to help her over a slippery patch, or kissed her on both cheeks when congratulating her on her marriage, but he never behaved like anything other than a devoted brother. Kate herself was the problem. Several times she woke in the night, her cheeks flaming and her heart beating fast, and she realized she'd been dreaming of Guy. In her dreams, Guy wasn't the brother she loved, but the husband she adored, and the ache in her heart when wakefulness abruptly yanked her back to reality was a testament to how she truly felt about him. She never dreamed of Hugh, nor did her body rouse to him the way it roused to Guy in her dreams, but Hugh was her husband, and she would be loyal to him in deed and thought, and Guy would forever remain her brother by marriage.

Chapter 32

After leaving the chapel, Kate headed to the kitchen. To her disappointment, Guy hadn't been dawdling outside waiting for her. Perhaps he'd decided to remain in bed a little longer since rain was coming down in a torrent and the sky was a threatening shade of greenish gray. A walk was out of the question, and for Kate, it was too gloomy to sew. She often got headaches when sewing by insufficient light, so she took advantage of sunny mornings to work on her mending and embroidery.

Joan nodded to her as she walked in, pushing a plate of sliced bread and a dish of butter toward her. Kate poured herself a cup of ale and buttered the bread. She was always hungry in the mornings and wished for something more substantial than bread. At the priory, they often had boiled eggs, a breakfast that kept her satisfied until the midday meal.

"Where's Aileen this morning?" Kate asked Joan, who was cutting up strips of meat and tossing them into a bowl.

"How should I know?" Joan snapped. "Haven't seen her yet this morning. Perhaps *her ladyship* has decided to sleep in on account of the foul weather."

Kate ignored Joan's sarcasm. It wasn't her place to criticize Joan's treatment of the help, but she often felt that Joan was unnecessarily unkind to the girl. Perhaps Aileen was ill.

"Is that for the dogs?" Kate asked, jutting her chin in the direction of the bowl of bones and gristle.

"Aye, it is. Now I'll have to take it out meself," Joan grumbled.

"I'll take it."

"Ye'll get soaked."

"A little rain never hurt anyone," Kate replied. She finished her breakfast and reached for the bowl. She liked going to the kennel. It was a pleasant way to spend a few minutes, surrounded by the castle dogs. They always wagged their tails and nudged her hands with their damp noses, eager to be acknowledged.

"Suit yerself," Joan replied, clearly glad not to have to go outside in the rain.

Kate let herself out the back door and ran across the yard to the kennel. Her hair was dripping by the time she got to the cover of the outbuilding and the hem of her gown was muddied. The hungry dogs greeted her like an old friend, and gathered around her in anticipation. Kate divided the meat equally among their bowls and stood back as they began to gobble up the food. She made sure they had enough water to drink, and opened the door, ready to sprint back to the kitchen. The rain had let up a bit, and a patch of pale blue sky was just visible beneath the leaden clouds.

Kate was about to cross the yard when she noticed a stealthy movement by the stables. Aileen slipped out the door, the hood of her cloak pulled low over her face. Kate couldn't see her eyes, but she saw her mouth, which was stretched into a happy grin. Aileen ran across the yard and disappeared through the door leading to the kitchen. She must have known she'd get a tongue-lashing from Joan, but she didn't seem overly concerned. Kate remained sheltered in the kennel and watched, wondering what had made Aileen so happy. A few minutes later, Walter emerged from the stables, wearing an almost identical grin on his boyish face. Walter began to cross the yard, so Kate left her hiding place and intercepted him midway.

"Good morrow, mistress," Walter called out cheerfully. His clothes were grubby, but he seemed very pleased with himself.

"Good morrow. Have you had your breakfast, Walter?"

"Not just yet. Glynis foaled last night, and I was with her until the early hours."

"Were you alone?" Kate asked, wondering why Alf wasn't there to help Walter deliver the foal. Strictly speaking it wasn't part of Walter's duties to assist with a birth. He only looked after the war horses, while Alf took care of the rest.

"Aye, all alone," Walter lied cheerily.

"Where's Alf?"

"His old bones need their rest, mistress, and Jed's too young to be of any help. Not to worry, the little fellow is healthy and beautiful, and I'm famished."

"Walter, was Aileen with you all night?" Kate demanded. Walter looked like he was about to deny the charge, but Kate gave him a severe look, warning him not to lie to her.

Walter reddened and lowered his eyes. "She was. She only wanted to help."

"Do you two often spend time together?" Kate could understand Walter's need for companionship, and being close in age, it made sense that he and Aileen would develop a friendship, but given what had happened to Agnes, Kate worried about Aileen. The girl was vulnerable and shy. Any attention from Walter could easily turn her head and lead her down a dangerous path.

"From time to time," Walter replied carefully. "I'd never do anything to hurt her," he sputtered. "We're friends, that's all."

"So what do you do together as friends?" Kate asked. She had no desire to accuse Walter of inappropriate behavior, but she seemed to be Aileen's only champion at the castle and she wouldn't allow the girl to be mistreated.

"We just talk."

"Talk?"

Walter looked stricken, as if he'd suddenly realized he'd revealed an important secret. He stared at the tips of his boots and twisted the lowest button of his doublet.

"Walter, is Aileen really deaf?"

Walter nodded. "She is, but not completely, and she can read lips. It's easier for her to pretend to be stone deaf, this way no one can punish her if she doesn't hear something and doesn't respond right away. She's scared."

"Of what?"

"Her father used to beat her about the head when he were drunk. He was a cruel man, mistress. Over time, Aileen began to lose her hearing. Had he not died, she might have lost it completely, due to the beatings. He never beat Jed as severely, but he took pleasure in punishing Aileen. She reminded him of his wife, he said, and since the poor woman was beyond his reach, he went for Aileen instead."

Kate's eyes filled with tears. How cruel people could be. No wonder Aileen was frightened and reluctant to admit that she could hear something. It was easier to pretend to be completely deaf, especially when dealing with Joan, who'd berate her all day long if she suspected Aileen could actually hear her.

"Don't worry, I won't tell anyone, Walter. Aileen's secret is safe with me."

"You're a kind lady, mistress," Walter replied. "Unlike some. And you've nothing to worry about," he added, blushing furiously. "It isn't like that with Aileen and me. We just get lonely sometimes, not being part of the family. It's hard to be an outsider."

"Yes, I understand," Kate replied. She knew just how Walter felt. "You must miss your family."

Walter nodded. "I do. I wish I could visit them sometimes."

"Have you asked Hugh if you may?"

Walter shook his head. "I'm here to serve and learn, not enjoy myself. Once I finish my training and become a knight, I'll be my own master, at least in my own home. I'm grateful to have a place, since my father died and my mother can't afford to support me, having fallen on hard times. I have six sisters, all under the age of twelve. They'll need a dowry when the time comes. Maybe by that time, I'll be able to provide it, at least for the younger ones."

Kate clapped Walter on the shoulder in a gesture of support. She'd led a peaceful and sheltered existence, never realizing how difficult life was for some. Leaving the priory had been a rude awakening, in more ways than one.

Kate walked with Walter to the kitchen door. She heard Joan's harsh voice as they approached, cursing Aileen for being late. Something clattered to the floor. Kate yanked open the door and faced the older woman, who had a wooden spoon raised above Aileen's head. The girl was cowering, her hands above her head for protection against the impending blow. A wooden bowl lay upturned on the stone floor, spilled milk beginning to soak into the crevices between the stones

"Joan, Aileen was ill. Now, let her be and get about your chores." Kate hadn't meant to sound harsh, but Walter's explanation of Aileen's deafness left her trembling with fury. She'd keep an eye on Joan to make certain she didn't strike Aileen again.

Joan's eyes narrowed in anger, but she didn't argue. "Aye, mistress. Whatever ye say."

Chapter 33

"Do you still miss the priory?" Guy asked as he and Kate followed the path that ran along the riverbank. The sun shone brightly after the downpour of the day before and the river sparkled playfully as it flowed past Berwick castle and wound into the distance. The dew on the grass hadn't burnt off yet, and the leaves dripped moisture, still wet after the night's rain.

Hamish ran around in wild circles, ecstatic to be out and about. Guy didn't bother with a lead, since the puppy was too small and frightened to run far. It was more interested in trying to wedge himself between Guy's ankles as he walked, nearly tripping him more than once.

"You foolish pup," Guy scolded it affectionately. "Keep this up and I'll take you back to the castle."

The puppy yapped happily and ran after a squirrel. Kate smiled at his exuberance. She wished she could feel so free.

"I don't miss the priory as much as I miss my family," she finally replied. "My mother most of all. The loss of her left a hollow space inside me that will never be filled. And Geoffrey too." Kate sighed. "I miss Geoffrey."

"Which one was Geoffrey?"

"He was the middle one. It's not right to say it out loud, but I loved him the most, probably because he was the kindest."

Guy nodded in understanding. "You've no reason to feel guilty for loving Geoffrey best. I loved William. I miss him every day. There are times when I'm not completely awake yet, and I think of something I must tell Will, and then I remember that he's gone, and I begin to mourn him all over again."

"I wish I'd known him."

"So do I. But if Will hadn't died, you wouldn't be here. He'd not have allowed Hugh to force this marriage."

Kate didn't reply. She'd initially believed that her father had misinterpreted Hugh's comments, but she knew better now. Hugh had known what he was about when he escorted her home. He'd planned it all, and had admitted to it once when in his cups.

"No, I don't suppose I would be," she finally said.

"He is kind to you, isn't he, in private?" Guy asked, concern in his eyes. Kate could see that he genuinely cared.

"Yes, he is," she reassured him. "Sometimes I still can't believe how it all worked out. The Church teaches us not to question God's will, but at times it's difficult to understand why certain things happen."

"It's not God's will; it's the will of man," Guy replied, his tone bitter.

"How do you mean?"

"Do you think it's God's will that thousands of good men should die fighting over who's the rightful king? Each claimant believes God is on his side. But I don't think God cares, one way or another. If He did, He'd let His will be known and not allow the senseless slaughter. Instead, you have powerful men fighting for more power and more wealth under the pretense of doing God's will."

"You don't believe their cause is just?" Kate asked, surprised by the cynicism of Guy's argument.

"I believe that every man on a battlefield has his own cause, and it's not the divine right of their champion. The nobles fight for power. The knights fight for their lord, even if they don't agree with his chosen side. The common men fight because they have no choice. They've been called to arms by their lord and they have no right to refuse. Their only hope is that they'll live to see another day. When all is said and done, thousands of women are left widowed and children are left fatherless and defenseless. Some manage to survive, but many don't. Can that really be a part of God's plan?"

"I don't know, Guy. I never thought of it that way. I never questioned anything before. I did what I was told and worried about not being dutiful enough." *And this is where it got me*, Kate thought, but didn't speak the words out loud. "I wonder if my brothers ever felt this way."

"Probably not. They would have benefited greatly from Edward taking the throne, so they were fighting to further their own interests. That's always good motivation."

"Will you fight again?"

"I must. I've taken an oath of allegiance to the Earl of Stanwyck. He's my liege lord and I owe him my service. As soon as I regain full use of my arm, I'll take up the sword again."

"Even if you don't support the cause he's fighting for?"

"Even if I don't support the cause. I have a duty, as does Hugh. We're bound for life."

"My mother said that women are victims of circumstance and their fathers' scheming, but I now see that men are just as trapped by the expectations of their station. Is anyone truly free?"

"I don't think so. Everyone owes their allegiance to someone, whether it's their sovereign, their lord, or the Church. Even the king is at the mercy of his supporters. Edward can lose the throne just as easily as he gained it should Warwick turn against him. He's nothing but a puppet, his strings pulled by his illustrious cousin. Your cousin."

"That borders on treason, Guy," Kate remarked, surprised that Guy would even voice such thoughts.

"Will you tell on me?" Guy asked, suddenly towering above her. "Will you see me executed for sharing my thoughts with the only person I truly trust in this world?"

"You can say anything to me. I would never betray you. I'd risk my life for you," Kate exclaimed. She hadn't meant to say so much, but once the words were out, she realized they were true. She'd do anything to protect Guy.

Kate's cheeks grew uncomfortably warm as Guy's gaze softened and a smile tugged at his lips. She'd betrayed herself, just as he'd probably hoped she would when he'd challenged her. Her breath quickened. Guy was too close. She could smell the wool of his doublet and the musky scent of his skin. His eyes darkened with desire and he leaned toward her, his arm encircling her waist.

Kate pushed Guy away and took a panicked step back. If she didn't put some distance between them, he'd kiss her and then she'd be lost. If she ever allowed herself to give in to her feelings for Guy, there'd be no going back. She belonged to Hugh, regardless of how he'd come to possess her, and the only way out for her was death, either Hugh's or hers.

Kate cried out as something soft squelched beneath her foot and a miserable howl pierced the air.

"Oh, I'm so sorry, Hamish," she cried. She'd stepped on the puppy's paw and its eyes were huge with pain. Kate bent down and picked up the little dog and held it to her bosom. Her eyes filled with tears, partly for the dog and partly for herself. The puppy howled for a little while longer, but then burrowed its nose into Kate's bodice. "I think we should be getting back."

"As you wish," Guy replied, looking shamefaced.

"Guy, I…"

"Kate, forgive me," he interrupted. "I was out of line. It'll never happen again. Please say we can still be friends."

"Of course we can still be friends. You're my only real friend in this place," Kate added to lighten the mood between them. "You're the only person who actually talks to me."

"Because you're the only one who listens," Guy replied. "Hugh only tells me things to hear himself speak. And I can't reveal my thoughts to Walter. It wouldn't be fair to put him in that position."

"What about Joan? I thought you trusted her."

"Nurse loves me the way she'd love a little boy. She doesn't see me as a man grown, and never will. She thinks she needs to protect me."

"From what?"

"From you," Guy replied just as they reached the keep.

Chapter 34

August 2014

London, England

"What's your plan for the day?" Gabe asked Quinn as he buttoned his shirt.

She was still in bed, having slept badly again. Her conversation with Sylvia played over and over in her mind, making her wish she could just archive it somehow. She wasn't sorry about confronting Sylvia, but the whole episode had left her rattled.

"I have an antenatal yoga class this morning, and then I'll stop by the BBC. I never did sign that contract."

"When is our next antenatal appointment?" Gabe asked as he ran a hand through his damp hair. Their gazes met in the mirror and he turned to face Quinn. "Why do you look so worried? What are you not telling me?"

"Nothing. I just have a bit of a headache and my ankles are swollen."

Gabe didn't reply. Instead, he disappeared into the bathroom and returned with the blood pressure monitor. "Give me your arm, then."

Quinn reluctantly held out her arm. If it were up to Gabe, he'd take her blood pressure several times a day, but worrying about it all the time actually led to a spike. Quinn felt her best when not focusing on the preeclampsia and behaving as any other pregnant woman would.

"One twenty-eight over eighty," Gabe announced as he removed the cuff. "Your blood pressure is elevated."

"Only just. And what do you expect after the past few days? Anyone's blood pressure would be elevated," Quinn replied defensively. "I'll call the clinic and move up my appointment."

"To tomorrow," he said, watching her with a steely gaze.

"To tomorrow."

"I'm ready, Daddy," Emma called from the other room.

"So am I. Let's go, love."

Quinn lay back and closed her eyes, but knew she wouldn't be able to sleep. So she took a long shower and made herself a healthy breakfast before heading out to the yoga class.

She normally didn't like yoga, but the antenatal class was different and made her feel more centered and relaxed. She'd met several other pregnant women there who were always happy to go out for a cup of tea and a chat after class. It was nice to talk to other expectant mothers, since Quinn didn't have any friends who had small children. Quinn gladly accepted the invitation to tea after the class, especially since Alison would be coming along. Alison was suffering from preeclampsia, and had been diagnosed with it during her first pregnancy as well. She was happy to answer any questions Quinn had, and assured her that as soon as the baby was born, the symptoms would disappear. Alison was a week away from her due date, and seemed to be feeling well, but her obstetrician had scheduled her for a cesarean.

"I would, of course, prefer a natural birth, but I'm not one for heroics," Alison said as she sipped her Chamomile. "The only thing I care about is having a healthy baby. Everything else is secondary."

"I admire your attitude," Quinn said. "I think I would be really upset if I wasn't given a choice."

"Quinn, you of all people know how many women and children used to die in childbirth. I'm grateful there are ways to reduce the risk. I will take longer to heal after the birth and have a permanent scar, but I will walk out of that maternity ward alive, my baby in my arms. Nothing else matters."

Quinn nodded and placed her hand over Alison's. "Thank you, Alison. You are right. I didn't think of it that way. I felt as if I failed somehow by allowing this condition to get the better of me."

"Never think that. The only way you can fail is by not taking proper care of yourself. Promise you'll come and see me once I'm back home from the hospital. I'd like us to keep in touch, Quinn."

"I absolutely will, and I'm sure the little ones will enjoy their play dates as much as we will."

By the time she left the tearoom and headed to Rhys's office, she felt completely restored and was sure her blood pressure had levelled off.

Rhys was expecting her when she arrived. "Quinn, have a seat," he said solicitously. "Would you like a cup of tea or some mineral water?"

"I'm all right, thanks," Quinn replied as she looked over the contract.

"I need you to sign a release form as well," Rhys announced. "Since the series finale deals with your own family, we need to have it on record that we have your permission."

"Of course."

"Quinn, I really am sorry," Rhys said as he glanced over the forms and replaced them in a file folder. "I had no way of knowing…"

"I mean to find my sister, Rhys."

"So is it true, then? Have you confronted Sylvia?"

"Yes, yesterday. Her reaction was all the answer I needed," Quinn replied bitterly.

"Why? Why did she split you two up?"

"Sylvia said my sister had difficulty breathing, so she left her at the hospital, and took me to the cathedral."

"Not the most sound decision, but given that she was only seventeen and had just given birth to twins, I don't suppose she was feeling very pragmatic," Rhys remarked.

"Rhys, I don't blame her for that, but I do blame her for not telling me. We've known each other for almost a year now and she never thought to mention that I have a twin sister. Had I never run into Reverend Seaton, I would have gone through my entire life never knowing I have a twin."

"Yes, that was unfair of her. What will you do?"

"I've decided I need to take a step back. I've asked Sylvia not to call me."

"And the boys?"

"I don't see why I can't maintain a relationship with them. They are my brothers, after all, and they are grown men."

Rhys nodded. Quinn could see there was something on his mind, and he appeared to be debating whether to share his thoughts with her. "Have you eaten?" he asked.

"Not since breakfast. I had a cup of tea after my yoga class, but I'm getting peckish."

"Can I take you to lunch? I'm hungry, and I hate eating alone."

"Don't I know it." Quinn chuckled. "Sure. I'd love to have lunch with you."

"Any particular cravings?"

"Don't laugh."

"Never."

"Fish and chips," Quinn confessed. "Gabe would have a coronary. He's making sure I stay away from fried, salty foods."

"Dictator," Rhys said with a laugh.

"He's worried about me," she replied, suddenly feeling defensive on Gabe's behalf. He was driving her mad, truth be told, but she understood his reasons and tried not to row with him about his overprotectiveness. He was motivated by love.

"You're very lucky to have a man like Gabe. He's one in a million."

"That's quite a compliment coming from you."

"It's the truth."

Rhys waited until they were settled in The George with plates of food in front of them before broaching the subject he'd clearly been waiting to bring up since Quinn had walked into his office. She knew him well enough at this point to be able to tell when something was weighing on his mind. Rhys sprinkled some salt over his chips and bit one, chewing thoughtfully. "Quinn, there's something I'd like to discuss with you."

"I would never have guessed," Quinn joked as she bravely moved the salt pot to the other side of the table to avoid temptation.

"It's about Sylvia."

"I'm shocked."

"You're laughing at me," Rhys replied with a smile.

"Sorry. Please go on," Quinn replied, contrite. At times, Rhys took himself too seriously, and she couldn't help teasing him.

"As you know, Sylvia and I have been seeing each other for the past few months," Rhys began. "I…" His voice trailed off as he seemed to search for the right words to express his feelings. Rhys was never at a loss, so this could only mean one of two things: either he was in love and wanted to take things with Sylvia to the next level, or he wanted to break things off. "I'm going to be a dad," he suddenly finished, nearly making Quinn choke on her fish.

"Sylvia is pregnant?" Quinn gasped, stunned. She certainly hadn't expected that. Sylvia was almost forty-eight. A natural pregnancy at her age was unlikely, though not unheard of.

"No, she isn't," Rhys replied. Quinn tried to hide her smile behind a napkin when she noticed Rhys's girlish blush. "It's not Sylvia. We actually never took things that far."

"Ah. Being chaste, were you?"

"I wasn't in any rush to jump in the sack. Given our history, I wanted to be sure a relationship with Sylvia was what I really wanted before going to the next step. I didn't want to hurt her," Rhys explained.

"I'm not judging you. Only you know how you feel."

"When I first contacted Sylvia, I had unresolved feelings about what happened the night you were conceived. I wanted, in some small way, to atone for what she'd been through, and to get to know her as a human being. I like her; I genuinely do."

"But you don't love her," Quinn supplied.

"No. It could never work between us. We are just two very different people who find ourselves at different stages in our lives. I enjoy Sylvia's company. I like her boys, and I certainly like you, but I can't see a future for us, not a romantic one."

"So, who is the lucky lady?"

"Haley Madden."

"The Haley Madden who played Elise in the first episode of *Echoes*?" Quinn asked, smiling. She recalled Rhys's face when Haley had come into the room to audition. He'd sat up straighter, and his eyes had lit up as he watched her read. Quinn had known at that moment that Haley got the part.

"Haley and I didn't get together until after the shooting finished. It would have been unprofessional, and I had no wish to put her in an uncomfortable situation if she had no interest in going out with me. She was seeing someone at the time of the shoot, but they'd broken up by the time the episode was completed," Rhys explained.

"And now she's pregnant."

"I was shocked at first but, truthfully, I'm thrilled. I didn't think I'd ever have children, but the thought of being a father makes me deliriously happy," Rhys admitted.

"Is she as giddy as you are?" Quinn asked gently. She didn't know Haley and couldn't presume to know how she felt, but for a woman in her twenties at the start of her acting career, a baby might not fit into her plans.

"She's really happy. She said that was one of the reasons her previous relationship broke up. She wanted to start a family while she was still young, but her boyfriend didn't. I'm over the moon, Quinn. I really am."

"Well, in that case, I'm really happy for you. Congratulations to you both."

"I've asked Haley to move in with me, and she's agreed."

"Big step."

"I know, but it just feels so right. I've always been a bit commitment shy. I like my space, and my freedom, but at this moment, I want nothing more than to have a family of my own."

"Well, I have a very important piece of advice for you, Rhys Morgan."

"What's that?"

"Don't bake for her. Haley won't thank you if she gains several stone."

"I know. She already warned me about that. All baked goods are prohibited. I'll have to find a new hobby."

"I hear knitting is gaining popularity among the male population," Quinn quipped.

"I was thinking of joining a gym, actually. I'll need energy to run after a little one."

"You certainly will," Quinn agreed. "Have you told Sylvia?"

"Not yet. I haven't thought of a way to break it to her gently."

"Just be truthful with her. Nothing hurts more than someone trying to deceive you and playing you for a fool. Sylvia is a big girl; she'll understand."

"Do you really think so?" Rhys asked, looking hopeful.

"Like you said, you want different things. Sylvia's already had her children, more children than either of us knew, and you are just starting out."

"I hope it's a girl," Rhys said. His eyes were glowing with excitement and Quinn felt a wave of affection for him. "But a boy would be grand too. My mum will be thrilled." Rhys glanced at his watch. "We'd better finish up. I have a meeting at two. This has been lovely, Quinn." He paid the bill and got up to leave. "Keep me in the loop, will you?"

"About?"

"About your search for your sister. I'll help in any way I can. Do you have any leads?"

"I have the name of the social worker."

"That's a start."

"It is."

Quinn said goodbye to Rhys and turned for home. She'd had her doubts before the conversation with Rhys, but now she was sure. She had to call Seth. He had a right to know that he had another daughter out there somewhere, and he had to hear it from Quinn.

Chapter 35

Quinn propped up her cheeks with her fists and stared down at the mobile phone lying on the kitchen table. It looked harmless enough, but at the moment it was an object of acute anxiety. It'd been easy enough to decide that she must call Seth, but somehow the act didn't follow naturally. She'd spoken to Seth only twice since leaving New Orleans, and although they'd had a fairly easy relationship while she was there, now that there was an ocean between them it was hard to recapture that feeling, especially after what had happened.

Quinn genuinely wanted to hear his voice and share the news with him, but for some reason her hand just wouldn't move toward the phone, no matter how many times she willed her hand to lower and pick up the object. She supposed it was because she couldn't not ask about Brett. That would be like avoiding a two-thousand-pound elephant in the room. Thinking of Brett still hurt, and probably always would. She'd opened up to him and let him in, believing he'd felt the same about her. She'd misjudged her brother just as she'd misjudged Luke. They had both taken her completely by surprise when they'd betrayed her.

Quinn sighed and pushed the phone away. She simply couldn't do this today. When she thought back to her time in New Orleans, her breath caught in her throat and a great big lump welled up in her chest. Not only had she nearly died, but she'd had several confrontations with Luke, who'd come all the way from Massachusetts to see her and try to win her back. Luke could be like a dog with a bone when he genuinely wanted something, and what he wanted was to go back to the life he'd left behind. With his American girlfriend gone and his teaching commitments about to end, he'd longed to return to the life he'd taken for granted. And now he was really coming back, all set to teach the autumn term at the institute while he waited for his next grant to come through. Quinn and Gabe had had a blazing row about it just the other day, and although Quinn had fought tooth and nail to make her point, she knew Gabe was right.

"You can't possibly take him back," Quinn had fumed. "It's not fair."

"Quinn, be reasonable. I have no grounds to refuse his request. Luke, for all his personal shortcomings, was a good employee—a fine lecturer and an experienced archeologist. As head of the department, I can't allow my personal feelings to get in the way of good judgment."

"This is not my idea of good judgment. He can get a job elsewhere."

"Archeologists are not exactly in high demand. Or haven't you noticed? I've had two job offers in the past two months, both of them offering a pittance. I'd make a better living driving a bus or fixing leaky sinks."

"He can stay in the States," Quinn said with a pout.

"I can't prevent him from coming back, Quinny," Gabe replied softly.

"No, you can't," she conceded. "Monica must be doing cartwheels of joy, especially since her marriage appears to be on the rocks."

"I'm not intimately familiar with the state of Monica's marriage, but yes, she's happy that Luke is coming back."

Quinn rolled her eyes at Gabe. "You know all."

"Do I?" he asked sheepishly.

"You only pretend not to listen to gossip, but every good administrator knows that it's a valuable source of information and knowing what's going on under one's nose can only be beneficial if you don't want to get caught with your pants around your ankles."

Gabe cringed. "A charming image. Yes, I hear things, whether I want to or not."

"And?"

"And Monica is separated. She caught Mark in a lie about going out of town on a business trip and things unraveled from there. He'd been seeing someone else."

"She's always had a thing for Luke, and now that they are both single..."

"Then things should work out splendidly for all involved. Monica and Luke will pair off and, in their newly discovered bliss, forget their resentment toward us and live happily ever after."

"You're laughing at me," Quinn said with a frown.

"I wouldn't dare." Gabe chuckled, finally getting Quinn to smile.

She knew she was being ridiculous, but she was pregnant, hormonal, and allowed to throw a temper tantrum once in a while. Wasn't she?

She decided to check with Jill, who wasn't pregnant or hormonal, but she was temperamental and loved to put on a good show of bad temper. She said it was therapeutic.

When Gabe left for work after their argument, Quinn rang Jill. "Morning, coz. How are things in the world of high fashion?"

"Meh!"

The response was so unexpected that Quinn burst into a fit of giggles. "What does that mean?"

"It means that I've gone off this whole idea of owning my own shop. It seemed glamorous and exciting when I first conceived of the idea, but the reality is bleak and depressing. I've had a grand total of three walk-ins in the past two days. Only one of them actually bought something. I made a whopping two quid."

"Are you reconsidering your prospects?"

Jill sighed. "I am. The lease on the shop expires in January. I think I might just have a 'going out of business' sale and close my doors right after Christmas. There doesn't seem to be much point in hanging around. And how are things with you?"

"Well, I called to have a little moan, but I see that you're not in any position to cheer me up."

"Are you kidding? I love other people's misery. It's the best antidote to one's own," Jill joked. "Bring it on. Too bad you can't come over and have lots of wine. I could use a drink. Or six."

"I can match you glass for glass with mineral water, but then I'll be cursing you all night when I have to pee every five minutes."

"Ah, the joys of pregnancy. How's the little bean?"

"Fine. It likes to play rugby between midnight and three a.m., with my bladder as the ball."

"I'm so jealous," Jill moaned. "I want a baby, Quinny."

"Can Brian be persuaded?"

Quinn could almost hear Jill smile across the space between them. "He's mentioned us moving in together."

"Is that what you want?" Quinn asked carefully. In some respects, Jill was more traditional in her views than Quinn.

"I always imagined doing things the old-fashioned way. I thought I'd meet a nice bloke, get married, buy a rambling mansion and hire a staff of nannies for when the heir apparent arrived, but I don't think that's likely, Quinny." Jill giggled merrily. "Living together is not a bad idea. Brian is the type of bloke who puts down his roots. Once I have him in my clutches, he's not going anywhere. Then I'll just plan a wedding and tell him when to show up. A baby will be the natural next step."

"What about the rambling mansion and a host of nannies?"

"On a civil servant's salary?" They both laughed, knowing how likely that was. "Speaking of which, are you going to stay at Gabe's bachelor pad for the duration?"

"Only until the baby is born. Gabe is having second thoughts about moving up north. If Phoebe agreed to sell the manor, Gabe and I would be able to get a bigger place in London. That would be a dream come true. Gabe loves his job, and Emma and I would be only too happy to remain here. And speaking of Gabe's job, guess who's coming back? Luke."

"No! Really?"

"Yes. Gabe rehired him. He'll be teaching several classes next term."

"You never have to see him. It's not like you'll be working at the institute."

"No, I won't be returning to the institute for a while. The program has been renewed, so Rhys has three more episodes in the works. I'll be quite busy after the baby comes. I hope Rhys allows me to take my maternity leave. You know how dogged he is."

"I never thought I'd say this, but he cares about you, Quinn. He won't push you too hard, especially since he's now involved with your family. He might become your stepdad in time."

"Rhys's going to be a dad," Quinn blurted out. It wasn't really her news to share, but since Rhys had been seeing Sylvia and Jill knew all about the relationship, Quinn had some small right to discuss his affairs, in this instance.

Jill gasped. "You're joking. Sylvia is pregnant? At her age?"

"No. He's moving in with someone else. He's not in love with Sylvia, so he thought it was time to move on. His girlfriend is an actress he met while making the program."

"He certainly didn't waste any time, did he?"

"He's over the moon," Quinn said, smiling when she recalled Rhys's blissed-out expression.

"Well, I wish him luck. Having a newborn at fifty can't be easy. I hope he'll be a hands-on dad and not someone who just pops in, coos to the baby for five minutes, and then stares into his phone for the rest of the night. Does he love the mother?"

"I think so. He's really excited."

"How's Sylvia taking it?"

"I have no idea. I haven't spoken to her. We've had a bit of a situation."

"Do tell," Jill urged. "What has she done now?"

"She had twins and didn't tell me I have a sister." Quinn was no longer smiling. Tears of hurt filled her eyes and she grabbed a pillow from the sofa and wrapped her arms around it for comfort.

"She what? Please tell me you're joking."

"I'm not. I found out completely by accident. There's a woman out there called Quentin who is my twin sister."

"Do you know where she is?" Jill asked. All the humor gone from her voice, she sounded stunned and subdued.

"No. Sylvia never bothered to look for her. She left the baby at a hospital because she had trouble breathing, and never looked back. My sister might have died, for all I know."

"Oh, Quinn! How awful for you. Is there anything I can do?"

"Just be there for me when I need a good cry."

"I'm always here. You can cry as much as you like. But seriously, what are you going to do?"

"I'm going to look for her. How can I not?"

"I can't wait to meet her. Have you told your parents?" Jill asked. Jill's father and Quinn adoptive father were brothers, so Jill was acutely aware of how this news might affect her aunt and uncle.

"No, I haven't. Finding Sylvia and then Seth was difficult enough for them. They feel threatened, especially my mum, even though I told them time and again that no one could ever replace them in my affections. They think they weren't enough somehow. They were always enough, but I just had to fill in the blanks. And now I have," Quinn added bitterly.

"Seems like there's one more giant blank you need to fill."

"And I will, but I'm not going to say anything to Mum and Dad until I know more. So please don't mention anything to your parents. I don't want Mum and Dad to find out just yet."

"My lips are sealed. I haven't been speaking to my mum and dad as often as I used to," Jill confessed.

"Why not?"

"Because I'm getting older and they are worried about my future, a topic that creeps up in every conversation. I'm in my thirties, unmarried, childless, and the proprietor of a failing business. My mum never stops reminding me that by the time she was my age she had three children."

"Times were different."

"Yes, they were, but this is the only reality they understand. 'You'd better get a move on, old girl, or it'll be too late. Mark my words. Your brothers are younger than you, and they have six children between them.' That's what Dad said to me last time we spoke. You'd think there's a line of willing men outside my door and I'm just refusing them all on principle. If Brian asked me to marry him, I would. And I would gladly produce a baby nine months later, but times have changed, and now men want to take their future wives out for a test drive before they commit to a lifelong lease. I bet Brian will want to live together for several years before he finally decides it's time to make things legal. He's not in a rush. His biological clock is not ticking like an undetonated Wehrmacht bomb."

"Jill, it will happen for you. Just be patient."

"I know, but in the meantime, I have to close down my shop and salvage what's left of my pride. Then, I have to find a job in forensic accounting. Talk about coming full circle."

"Gabe and I were attracted to each other when we met on that dig nine years ago. Had I not been blinded by Luke, we might have wound up together, but we both had other relationships and other heartbreaks. In the end, we got together, as we were meant to do. And now we're older and wiser, and more determined to make things work. We came full circle, because we were meant to. You might be going back, but it's never really to the same place or with the same result."

"I hope you're right, Quinny. There are so many women out there who are middle-aged and alone. Did their time never come, or did they miss the signs?"

"Jill, I've known you all my life, and you're not the type of person who'd ever miss the signs. You're not going to be middle-aged and alone. You will make Brian so happy that the thought of leaving you will never cross his mind. This time next year, we'll be planning your wedding."

"From your mouth to God's ears." Jill sighed. "I have to go. I think an actual customer is walking in."

"Bye." Quinn rang off and set aside her phone. Talking to Jill always made her feel better, if only because they could complain to each other and not feel pathetic about it. Quinn had been supportive and encouraging of Jill, but she could understand her worry. The business failing was a tremendous blow, and Brian, although a nice bloke, just didn't have the same drive and passion for life as Jill did. Quinn couldn't imagine the two of them happily spending their lives together, but it wasn't her decision to make. Jill had disliked Luke, but it'd taken Quinn nearly eight years to see him for what he really was—a liar and a cheat. She hoped Jill wouldn't end up disappointed. She deserved to be happy, and if Brian was her choice, Quinn would support her.

Chapter 36

December 1462

Berwick-upon-Tweed, Northumberland

Kate left the chapel and headed for the Lady Chamber. She'd decided a while back that if she wanted to get along with Joan, it was best not to step on her toes. They each had their roles, and it was her, not Joan, who had been overstepping her boundaries. Once Kate stopped popping into the kitchen, her relationship with Joan improved somewhat. The older woman simply wanted reassurance that her position within the family was secure, and Kate was more than willing to give it as long as Joan gave her word that she wouldn't be unkind to Aileen. Joan had been taken aback by the request, thinking it a rich woman's whim, but she'd readily agreed, eager to get Kate out of her hair. She still heard Joan berating the girl and calling her names, but Joan hadn't hit her again, at least not in Kate's presence.

The corridor was completely silent as Kate walked toward the Lady Chamber. She knew it'd be empty at this time of morning. Eleanor was still abed, as was Adam, Joan was in the kitchen with Aileen, and Alf and Jed were likely already about their morning chores. Hugh and Guy had left nearly a month ago, having been called on by their liege lord to help quell the Lancastrian uprisings in the north.

Hugh had been happy to go. He'd been restless and irritable, and Kate had secretly welcomed the separation. Tonight she would write to him to tell him of the happenings at the keep, which were few. Adam had fallen ill with a fever, but recovered quickly. The weather had been inclement, but Hugh would know that being not that far from home. Kate and Eleanor had called on the Duchess of Stanwyck to find out news of her husband and son and spend a pleasant afternoon in the company of other women. In her letter, Kate would carefully ask after Guy, hoping her inquiry didn't sound too eager or too personal.

She shivered as she sat down by the unlit hearth. She'd have to wait for Jed to bring in some firewood and start a fire. The room was cold and gray, and lonely. Kate stared wistfully at the large snowflakes falling steadily outside the window. It'd been snowing for several days now, and the snow in the yard was knee-deep. When the castle was this silent and still it felt like a tomb, devoid of any life or hope. Kate closed her eyes and recalled the days when Guy used to meet her outside the chapel. He'd stopped doing that after their near-kiss, finding excuses to remain in his room, or going out to the yard to practice with Walter for hours on end. Determined to regain full use of his arm, he spent each morning sword-fighting with Walter or Hugh, or practicing with a quintain. Some days, he came back in clutching his arm and grinding his teeth from the pain, but he carried on, convinced that with enough effort, he'd be battle-ready soon.

"I won't be a cripple, Kate," he'd said when Kate begged him not to push himself so hard. "I won't be useless. I can't spend the rest of my life sitting around, doing nothing. I'd rather die honorably on the battlefield."

"Is it really an honorable death if you don't believe in the cause you're fighting for?" Kate had challenged him.

"It's more honorable than pining after your brother's wife," Guy had replied.

That was the most honest thing he'd said to her since that day by the river, and the most painful. If Guy pursued her, he wouldn't be the man she believed him to be, and if he didn't, there was not a glimmer of hope in her already bleak life that anything might change. Guy's resolve appeared to be driven by his desire to get away from her because he couldn't stand the strain. They'd been doing a careful dance of avoidance, the steps becoming familiar to them both as the weeks wore on, but they could no longer deny their feelings for each other, or successfully hide them

231

from the rest of the family, a suspicion that was confirmed by a conversation with Eleanor only yesterday.

"It's so dull here without Hugh and Guy," Eleanor had complained as she sat by the fire, her crewel work in her lap. "I swear, some days I think I will expire from boredom."

"Yes, it's very quiet," Kate agreed.

Eleanor gave Kate a piercing stare. "Yet you seem lighter somehow since they've gone. Why is that?"

"No reason that I can think of."

"I can. You're happy that Hugh's not here," Eleanor observed. "Come now, Kate, what is it about your husband that vexes you so? I'd give anything to trade places with you. Anything at all."

"That's because you loved William," Kate replied patiently.

"And you should love Hugh. He's a fine man, Kate. He's strong, handsome, and ambitious. He's more ambitious that my Will ever was, God rest his soul. Will was too decent for his own good at times. Had he been as clever as some, he might have doubled our holdings and filled our coffers."

"We are comfortably off," Kate argued.

"Comfortably off is not the same as rich, is it, and where would we be without your dowry? We still have to economize if we hope to make that money last. Why, I'm sick to death of boiled mutton and mashed turnips. I'd like to have a table as fine as that of the Duchess of Stanwyck. I'm still tasting that marzipan," Eleanor said, closing her eyes and sighing wistfully. "I've never tasted anything so divine." She sighed. "Maybe Hugh will distinguish himself somehow. They say that Edward is generous to those who are loyal to him. He's been giving out lands and titles like Christmas sweets."

"I only want Hugh and Guy to return to us unharmed," Kate replied, doing her best to keep her patience in check. Eleanor was beginning to grate on her.

"Do you? Both of them?" Eleanor scoffed. "I don't think you'd be too heartbroken if you found yourself a widow. Well, let me tell you, Kate, there's no glory in being widowed. You become nothing. Less than nothing. You have no husband, no position, no money of your own, and no prospects. If Hugh cared anything for me at all, he'd find me a husband. I'm done with my mourning, and I'm still in my prime. I can even still bear children. So why shouldn't I remarry?"

"No reason that I can think of."

"Oh, there is a reason. Hugh will never allow me to take another husband. He's too shrewd for that. If I marry, my husband will become father to my son and assume control of the de Rosel estate until Adam comes of age. And if anything were to happen to my boy, God preserve us, he would get it all. No, Hugh will keep me here until I shrivel up and die, unless the situation changes."

Kate was about to protest, but saw the truth in Eleanor's words. Eleanor wasn't as naïve or trusting as Kate had first assumed, and now that she was out of mourning, her mind had turned to her future and she didn't like what she saw. But Eleanor wasn't one to make demands, at least not outright. Bluntness wasn't the way to influence Hugh. Eleanor never argued or did anything to anger him. She was all feminine frailty when he was around, bringing out his chivalrous side. Hugh was in control of Eleanor's fate, and she'd do anything to keep him sweet—a skill Kate had yet to learn—but Kate was sure her sister-in-law would get her way in the end. If Lord Dancy died, Hugh would inherit the entire Dancy estate, making it easier for him to let Eleanor go since he would no longer be dependent on the de Rosel lands for survival.

"Hugh should really do something about Guy," Eleanor continued.

"How do you mean?"

"I mean that Guy is five and twenty, and still unwed. He's a fine-looking man, if not wealthy in his own right, but if Hugh found him an heiress, that would bolster all our fortunes. Of course, the only way an heiress's family would consider Guy would be if her reputation were slightly tarnished. Guy could follow Hugh's example, and bag himself a noble lady," Eleanor said with a sly smile, clearly referring to the circumstances of Kate's own marriage. She studied Kate's mutinous expression. "You don't look pleased with my suggestion. Don't you think it's time Guy took a wife? I wager that his giving his affections elsewhere would make you none too happy. I see the way he looks at you. It reminds me of how Hugh looked at me when I first married Will. That's the thing with brothers, they always want each other's toys."

"It's not my decision whether Guy marries or not, so it matters little if I'm pleased with the idea."

"No, you don't get to make any decisions," Eleanor agreed. She never stopped reminding Kate that she wasn't the mistress of Castle de Rosel. Of course, Eleanor was mistress in name only, but that seemed to be enough for her. It gave her that small bit of authority that she so desperately needed.

"I don't want to sew anymore today," Kate said. "My head is beginning to ache. I think I'll go rest for a bit."

"Suit yourself," Eleanor replied. "I prefer being here to sitting in my room. At least here I'm not completely alone. Lord, I even miss Walter, that impudent little whelp." She sighed. 'I think he finds me beautiful."

"I've no doubt he does." Kate left the Lady Chamber and went to her room. She didn't really have a headache, but she couldn't bear Eleanor a moment longer. Normally, she wasn't this bad, but being cooped up in the castle while the snow fell made her irritable and argumentative.

Kate meant to come down for supper, but changed her mind. If Eleanor chose to be waspish, she'd have to dine alone. Kate hoped that Eleanor got the hint and would try to restrain herself in the future.

Chapter 37

The following morning, Kate had already finished mending the torn hem of her chemise by the time Eleanor appeared in the Lady Chamber, having broken her fast with Adam. She smiled warmly and took her customary seat by the hearth. "I slept well last night, so I'm in better spirits," she announced.

Kate lowered her gaze to her work and smiled. She suspected that was about as close as Eleanor would ever come to an apology, but Kate was glad that she realized how spiteful she'd been the day before. With just the two of them together day in and day out, their emotional well-being depended on them getting along, even if they'd never truly be friends.

"I do hope the snow stops soon," Eleanor said as she glanced toward the window. "Adam's restless. A young boy needs exercise and fresh air."

"Why don't you ask him to give Alf a hand?" Kate suggested. "Alf's been clearing a path from the kitchen to the stables and kennel every day since it started snowing. He's got a bad cough and his chilblains are painful. Joan's been putting ointment on them, but I don't think it's working."

"Why's Jed not helping him?"

"Jed's taken to his bed. Aileen is looking after him."

"Oh, I do hope it's not catching," Eleanor gasped. "I must warn Adam to keep away from him."

"It's just a chill. He's on the mend," Kate explained.

"Well, that's good then. I've told Adam time and again that he's not to fraternize with that boy, but Adam still seeks him out."

"Adam doesn't have anyone to play with."

"I know." Eleanor sighed. "Adam should have had brothers and sisters, but God didn't see fit to bless me with another child. I lost a daughter not long before you arrived. And now with Will gone…"

"I'm sorry, Eleanor. It must be very difficult for you."

Eleanor's gaze misted with unshed tears. "I'm just lonely, Kate. I'd been with Will since I was a girl of fifteen, and now I'm all alone. Another few years and Adam will be taken from me. I'll see him a few times a year, but he'll no longer be mine. And then he'll become a squire, and a knight. He'll be a grown man and I'll be an old woman. I just can't accept that nothing of importance will ever happen to me again."

"You mustn't think like that. You're still a young woman. Things might change."

"I'm three and twenty, Kate. I only have a few good years left in me. And I do so long for more children."

Kate nodded. At least in this, she and Eleanor were of the same mind. Kate longed for a child. She might not love Hugh as Eleanor had loved Will, but she would love his baby because it'd be her own. The thought of holding an infant to her breast, loving it and rearing it had her nearly bursting with longing. And although every woman wanted to give her husband a son, Kate wished for a daughter because a girl would remain with her for much longer than a boy. She'd have her girl for at least fifteen years.

Kate squinted hard as she tried to thread her needle. She was finding it more and more difficult to see the eye of the needle and sometimes it took a dozen tries to get the job done. Eleanor helped her from time to time, but Kate didn't like to ask. She finally managed to slide the thread through the tiny hole and was about to return to her mending when she experienced a wave of nausea so strong it took her breath away. Her hand instinctively went to her stomach, which seemed to be in the process of turning itself inside out.

"Kate, you're as white as a sheet," Eleanor exclaimed.

"I feel a bit sick," Kate replied. Her forehead grew clammy and a sour taste assaulted her mouth, which was suddenly full of saliva.

"Nurse," Eleanor called to Joan, who happened to be passing by the Lady Chamber. "Kate's unwell."

Joan set down the basket of linens she'd been carrying and stepped into the room, her gaze fixed on Kate, who was now panting and grasping the armrests of the chair.

Joan's eyes narrowed as she studied Kate's face. "Come now. Let's get ye to bed. I'll make a brew of mint tea to settle yer stomach."

"I hope it helps," Kate moaned.

She thought she'd be sick before she reached the room, but she made it to her bedchamber and climbed into bed. Moments later, another wave of nausea assaulted her, and this time she couldn't fight it. Joan pushed the chamber pot in front of her just in time. Kate wretched violently and lay back on the bed, gasping for air.

"How long have ye been feeling unwell?" Joan asked as she removed Kate's shoes and pulled the counterpane over her. "Here, let me tuck ye in. Ye're shivering. I'll bring ye a hot brick in a tic."

"I've felt a bit queasy these past few days," Kate confessed.

Joan's round face lit up with a joyful smile. "Hugh will be pleased as punch when he learns of yer condition. I was sick every day for the first three months with me first one, but she were a bonny wee lass when she finally arrived—healthy and strong. A little discomfort is a small price to pay for having a healthy bairn."

Kate tried to focus on what Joan was saying. It had never occurred to her that Joan might have had her own children. She'd never mentioned any, and the three de Rosel boys seemed to be the loves of her life.

"You had children?" Kate muttered.

"Oh, aye. I had two girls," Joan replied as she added a log to the fire. "They died of a fever, aged two and four."

"I'm sorry. I had no idea."

"Why would ye?" Joan shrugged. "Not like ye ever asked."

Kate mentally acknowledged the truth of this. She'd never asked Joan about her life, partially because she had been raised not to get too personally involved with servants, and partially because there was something about Joan that put her on guard. Joan could be all softness and understanding one minute, and all sharp angles the next. She treated everyone that way, so at least Kate knew it wasn't something she'd done to offend the woman.

"You must miss them very much," Kate said in a conciliatory tone. She'd have to make an effort to be kinder to Joan, especially since she still had such a hold over Hugh and Guy.

"I did, but then William was born, followed by Hugh, and then Guy came along a few years later, and Margaret three years after him. They became me children, and still are." Joan turned away from Kate. "Ye rest now. I'll bring ye that mint tea, and then some broth later. Ye're just about due for yer courses, so we'll know for certain."

Kate didn't bother to ask how Joan knew it was nearly her time of the month. Joan knew everything, and kept tabs on everyone, which was at times comforting, and at times unnerving, but Kate did pray that Joan was right in her assumption that she was with child. She laid her hand on her flat stomach, wondering if Hugh's seed had finally taken root. He would be so pleased. Kate allowed her thoughts to stray to Guy. She knew he'd be happy for her, and the thought of his blessing made her value him all the more. That was how Guy was—selfless and devoted.

Kate remained abed for three days, fighting nausea, weakness, and chills, but by the fourth day she began to feel better. The chills abated, the nausea passed, and she regained her appetite.

She craved meat, which was unusual for her. Joan brought her some beef broth, but Kate wasn't satisfied with that, so Joan made a rich stew that she flavored with onions, wild garlic, and carrots. She'd added bits of stale bread to the gravy to make the stew thicker and more filling. Kate had two bowls, and might have eaten a third had there been any left to spare. The stew had to feed everyone else in the castle.

"Ye're looking better," Joan remarked. "There's color in yer cheeks, and yer ferocious appetite is a good sign."

"I've been praying for you," Eleanor said when Kate finally joined her in the Lady Chamber. "It'll be such a pleasure to have a child about again, even if it isn't mine," she added sadly.

"It's early days yet," Kate replied.

She was brimming with joy, but at night, when she retired to her room, doubt set in. What if Joan was wrong and there was no baby after all? *Joan knows what she's talking about*, Kate thought. *My courses are nearly a week late and I've been unwell for days. It's finally happened.* Kate grinned in the darkness. She was so happy, and for the first time since marrying Hugh, she felt more at peace. Perhaps the good Lord had finally seen fit to reward her for her faith.

Kate's courses came with a vengeance two days later, leaving her moaning with pain as severe gripes twisted her innards into knots and made her curl into a ball in an effort to alleviate the agony.

Joan gazed upon Kate with contempt when she brought more rags. "Good thing ye didn't write to Hugh," she said, ignoring Kate's suffering. "Imagine his disappointment, the poor lamb. Ye'd best get with child, and soon," she advised, glaring at Kate as if she'd somehow refused to allow herself to become pregnant.

"What can I do?" Kate moaned.

"I have some potions I can make up for ye. Helps make the womb more receptive to a man's seed," she replied knowledgeably. "Ye'd best let me help ye. I won't have my Hugh left without an heir."

Kate nodded miserably. She'd gladly take the potion. Now that she'd had a taste of maternal happiness, she felt an even greater emptiness than before. When Hugh returned, she'd try to be a better wife to him and not cringe inwardly when he reached for her in the night. She'd welcome his touch and pray that her resolve paid off.

Chapter 38

December 1462

Bamburgh Castle, Northumberland

The sky was an impenetrable gray, the heavens so low it seemed as if they would just keep sinking until they skimmed the snow-covered ground. Guy moved closer to the fire, desperate for its meager warmth. Numerous fires dotted the open ground surrounding Bamburgh Castle. The men stomped their feet and moved around to keep warm. It'd finally stopped snowing, but the air hadn't warmed up enough to allow the accumulation to melt. A thick blanket of white covered the earth, making the disgruntled soldiers even more miserable, especially those who didn't have tents of their own and had to sleep rough night after night.

The castle sat on a hill just above them: massive, forbidding, and impregnable. A few knights jokingly implied that they'd rather be besieged than cool their heels out in the open, exposed to rain, snow, and gusts of cold wind that left their faces numb. The rations were inadequate as well. King Edward saw to the welfare of his men, but in the dead of winter, sufficient supplies were hard to come by. They weren't starving by any means, but men needed meat to maintain their strength, not porridge or slices of bread spread with drippings, which only made them hungrier for something more substantial.

No one had imagined they'd be back at Bamburgh so soon. The Lancastrians had surrendered the castle to Warwick's forces back in July, but in the months since, they'd regrouped and mounted an armed rebellion. Bamburgh Castle was one of three Northumbrian castles serving as strongholds for Lancastrian supporters since the Battle of Towton, and Warwick meant to see the rebels crushed. If he didn't, the rebellion might spread south and threaten Edward's reign, which thus far had been successful. Warwick had managed to negotiate a short-lived truce with the

242

Scots, with whom England was at war, and used the two-month respite from fighting to put down the resistance building at Bamburgh, Alnwick and Dunstanburgh castles.

Bamburgh Castle had been under siege since the beginning of December. Cut off from the world, the Lancastrians were running low on supplies and surrender loomed with utter inevitability, but they still held out, infuriating the Earl of Warwick and making him more determined to bring the rebels to their knees. Guy hoped the siege would end by the end of the year. He dreamed of going home for Christmas and spending the holiday in warmth and comfort. He'd been as ready to fight as he'd ever be, but spending weeks out in the open with nothing to do but watch the castle was taking its toll. Guy's arm ached almost constantly, and his headaches had returned, brought on by gusting wind and changes in the weather. He didn't complain about his suffering to anyone, but there was no glory in starving the enemy out, only boredom.

He'd accompanied Hugh when he'd presented himself to Warwick and his brother, John Neville, Marquess of Montagu, upon arrival at Bamburgh Castle a fortnight ago. The Neville brothers were well aware of the connection between their families, and Hugh would be damned if he allowed this opportunity to pass without trying to at least find some favor. Warwick and Montagu had been gracious enough, now that they were all on the same side, but had treated Hugh and Guy with the respect due to knights, not the warmth accorded to family. Hugh had fumed at the rejection, but Guy simply put the Nevilles from his mind. He expected nothing. The two Neville men were too experienced in the ways of the court and too shrewd in the art of warfare not to see through Hugh's feeble efforts. They would not take any interest in their distant kin by marriage unless they had something to gain by the association, and Hugh and Guy de Rosel had nothing to offer men who had everything.

"There you are," Hugh said as he settled next to Guy. His cheeks were ruddy with cold, and he seemed to be in a worse mood than when he'd left Guy about an hour since. "Here, have something to eat." He had brought a loaf of bread, some roast pork, and a skin of ale. "The meat is not as fresh as it should be, but tastes better than horsemeat." Hugh chuckled without mirth. "I hear they've started in on their horses," he said, his chin jutting toward the castle. "They're starving."

"They must be freezing too," Guy said as he accepted the meat and bread. "They must have burned though the firewood by now, and most of their furniture."

"They're still warmer than we are," Hugh scoffed. "I've never been this cold for this long. Lord, I long for my bed, and the warm, pillowy breasts of my wife." He sighed as he tore off a chunk of pork with his teeth.

The pork tasted rancid, and Guy stopped eating his share after the first bite. He'd rather be hungry than sick. Several men in the camp had the runs and groaned loudly as they hurried toward the areas designated for the purpose.

Hugh grimaced and threw the pork on the fire. "I'm not eating this maggot-ridden carcass. The bread will have to suffice." He took a long pull of ale and passed the skin to Guy, who was chewing on his own stale heel of bread with little enthusiasm. "And what is the point of all this?" Hugh asked, making an expansive gesture that encompassed the castle and the surrounding area swarming with Yorkist soldiers. He'd clearly been drinking with some of the other knights and was feeling loose-tongued and riled up. "They'll surrender in the end anyhow; they might as well spare us all the suffering. The Duke of Somerset and Sir Percy know full well that reinforcements are not coming, not in time to help them anyway. Margaret of Anjou is in Scotland, trying to raise an army. Much good it will do her."

"Don't underestimate the woman," Guy replied. "She managed to recapture Bamburgh two months ago, with the assistance of the French. Not an easy feat."

"And promptly lost it again. She's an admirable woman, I'll grant you that, but she doesn't have enough support to pose any real threat to Edward, and Warwick is too experienced a tactician not to anticipate her every move."

"Margaret will never give up, not as long as she has her boy to think of," Guy replied. "She'll see him on the throne, or she'll die trying."

"Likely the latter," Hugh scoffed. "She's just ceded Berwick Castle back to the Scots on behalf of her husband and put Robert Lauder of Edrington in charge. I hope Kate understands the implications of this and keeps well away from the castle. You know how she likes to walk."

"Surely she'll come to no harm," Guy replied.

"I'd like to think not, especially if she's with child."

"Is she?" Guy asked. "Have you had news from home?"

Hugh shook his head. "No, I haven't had any news, not since the last letter, but I would be very pleased to find my wife with child on my return," Hugh replied hopefully. "I really thought she'd have given me a son by now. Or a daughter, at the very least."

"So, why are you so worried about your yet-to-be-born children?" Guy asked. Hugh was holding something back; that much was obvious.

"I've heard some talk."

"What sort of talk?"

"Warwick visited Kate's father after the Battle of Towton to express his condolences on the death of Dancy's sons. The two have maintained a steady correspondence since then, it would seem," Hugh explained. He stared into the flames, his elbows resting on his thighs and his body unusually tense.

"Why does that matter?"

"It doesn't, really. It only matters because Warwick's had news of Dancy, which he was only too happy to share with me when he saw me earlier while inspecting the camp. He actually stopped to talk to me for a minute, an honor I could have done without in this particular circumstance. No doubt he just wanted to watch me squirm."

"What news?"

"Dancy's remarried, and his new bride, who is twenty-five years his junior, has given him a healthy son. I know you're not very financially minded, brother, but even you can grasp the ramifications of this union."

"Kate will never inherit as long as the boy lives," Guy said, his tone wooden.

"Even if the whelp doesn't live, Dancy's wife is young enough to give him a dozen more sons. I won't see a farthing off my father-in-law. Not as things stand now. Had Lady Dancy lingered…"

"God rest her soul." Guy crossed himself in memory of Kate's mother. He knew Hugh didn't mean to be cruel; he was just being practical, as Hugh was wont to be.

"There is one thing I miss about my lady Margaret," Hugh said, lowering his voice so no one could overhear. "She allowed the men to plunder. I was making out very nicely for a while there," Hugh reminisced. "And would have profited even more had it not been for William's tender sensibilities."

"William was a man of honor," Guy flared.

"William was our father's heir. He inherited the title and the estate simply by the virtue of being born first. He could afford to be sanctimonious. And now Adam is Baron de Rosel," Hugh reminded Guy bitterly. "What am I to leave to my children, Guy? Unless I distinguish myself in battle, I have no hope of ever attaining a title or lands. And if we can't plunder, how are we to fill our coffers?"

Guy shook his head in dismay. With two older brothers, he hadn't given much thought to his own prospects, but it was time he did. He was going to be six and twenty, a middle-aged man.

"We must find you a worthy bride, Guy," Hugh said, clapping Guy on the shoulder.

"I've no desire to marry," Guy replied. "I've nothing to offer a wife."

"You're young—relatively—and not too ugly, and you come from a distinguished family that's related by marriage to the king himself. You might have a weak arm and difficulty seeing straight, but as long as your prick still works, you should acquit yourself well enough."

Guy raised an eyebrow in mockery of Hugh's words. "Hugh, I think we best end this conversation now, while we're still on speaking terms."

"I'm only looking out for you, Guy."

"And I'm looking out for you," Guy replied acidly and left the warmth of the fire. He was cold and his feet were wet, but he needed to walk to release some of his ire. As he moved further from the walls of the castle he saw several women making their way toward the fires. The women were of varying ages, but they all had one thing in common: they were widows, fallen on hard times. The women were huddled in their cloaks against the cold, but their eyes were full of intent, scanning the men and evaluating which of them might be more likely to respond to their advances. For as long as the siege lasted, they had a steady supply of customers, and the coin they earned would last them until the spring, if they were lucky.

Some of the women made their way toward men they'd serviced before, and some just walked between the fires, striking up flirtatious conversations with the soldiers. Most of the women didn't have to walk far before someone took them up on their offer. Since the camp was situated on completely open ground, there was nowhere to go for privacy. Only the higher ranks were allocated tents. The foot soldiers took the women right there, laying them down in the snow, or simply unlaced their breeches and let the women do their work.

Guy shook his head as a lass of about twenty approached him, smiling shyly. "Good evening, sweeting," she said quietly. "Are you interested in a bit of company?"

"Not tonight," Guy replied, not wishing to offend her. She was a comely lass with abundant dark hair and luminous eyes. She'd find the company she was seeking soon enough, possibly even with Hugh, who'd availed himself of the harlots at least once or twice a week. Guy didn't judge him, but for some reason, he felt angry on Kate's behalf.

Chapter 39

August 2014

London, England

"Perhaps you should wait until you know more before you tell Seth," Gabe suggested as he set the table for dinner. "He's been through enough. Don't you think?"

"Yes, he has, but I just feel awful about withholding this from him," Quinn replied.

"Have you been able to track down Hetty Marks?"

"I have, actually. She still lives in Leicester, and has a Facebook page. I sent her a message. I hope she responds."

"What about searching for Quentin on Facebook? There can't be that many women named Quentin residing in the UK," Gabe suggested.

Quinn transferred some cheesy pasta into a bowl and set it on the table. "I did a search for a Quentin. I got eleven results in Great Britain. Most of them were teenagers, and there were two women who appeared to be well over forty. None of them looked like they could be the right one."

"Perhaps she moved abroad, or isn't a fan of social media."

"That's possible, of course, but most people these days leave some sort of electronic footprint."

"That they do. I'll tell Emma dinner is ready," Gabe said, effectively putting an end to the conversation.

Quinn set the salad bowl on the table and poured Emma some milk. Her hand began to tremble and she nearly spilled the milk on the table as a terrible thought occurred to her. She might not have found anyone named Quentin who fit the profile because her sister might be dead. She'd assumed, and desperately wanted to believe, that her twin had been treated and released after Sylvia left her at the hospital, but what if her medical issue had been more severe? What if Quentin had never left that hospital alive? Child mortality in twentieth century Britain was very low, but it still happened. And given that Sylvia hadn't thought to seek help for Quentin immediately, she might have wasted precious moments that made the difference between life and death.

Quinn kept this awful thought to herself while they ate. There was no sense telling Gabe about her fear. Hetty Marks would know if Quentin had survived, and if Ms. Marks answered the message Quinn had sent, she'd put her mind at rest, one way or another.

Quinn forced herself to put Quentin out of her mind for the moment and smiled as Emma went on and on about her upcoming party. She was so excited. Emma had made a lot of friends over the past few months, and was finally beginning to feel like she truly belonged. Even her Scottish accent, which had been quite strong when they'd met her in Edinburgh, had softened as she unwittingly imitated the pronunciation of those around her. Emma was beginning to sound more like Gabe, who still had a trace of a northern accent, but after years of living in London almost sounded like a bonafide southerner.

"Is Grandma Sylvia coming to the party?" Emma asked.

"I think we'll just have the children," Quinn replied. "It won't be any fun for the adults."

"But she is my grandma," Emma protested. "And Jude will be there."

Gabe and Quinn exchanged looks.

"Grandma Phoebe is coming down for your birthday," Gabe announced.

"But what about Grandma Sylvia? And what about Grandma Susan and Grandpa Roger? I miss them."

"Sweetheart, you know they live in Spain," Quinn explained patiently.

"Why? Why do they live in Spain?" Emma demanded. "They are not Spanish."

"My dad has severe arthritis, Em. Living in a warmer climate helps him feel better."

"Will he die if he comes back? Like Grandpa Graham?" Emma asked, her eyes round with worry.

"No, he won't die, but if he remains here permanently he'll be in quite a lot of pain. He can come and visit from time to time though."

"Grandma and Grandpa Allenby came for the wedding, and they are going to come for the new baby," Emma reasoned. "Don't they think my birthday is important?"

"Of course they do. I'm sure they'll send you a lovely present."

Emma stared at Quinn balefully and stabbed at the lettuce on her plate. She was clearly hurt, but Quinn wasn't at all sure what to say. Her parents were comfortably off, but they couldn't afford to fly back to England for every occasion.

"I'm finished," Emma announced, pushing her plate away. "Can I go to my room?"

"Of course. Wash your hands first," Gabe reminded her. Emma stomped off and Gabe turned to Quinn. "It's all right," he assured her. "Emma has to get used to dealing with disappointment. It's a part of growing up."

"She's only going to be five, and she's had to deal with so much pain already."

"I know, but your parents are not coming, so Emma can either accept that as fact or feel bad and allow her disappointment to ruin her party," Gabe reasoned.

"Should I have invited Sylvia?" Quinn asked, and giggled when Gabe's eyebrows shot upward.

"After the conversation you two just had? I think not. Let it be, Quinn. Emma will have a wonderful party regardless."

"I know. I just want it to be perfect for her. It's her first birthday with us, and five is kind of a big deal. It's a rite of passage, since she'll be starting primary school next month."

"Don't remind me. The pressure is on to make a decision about the move," Gabe replied.

"Have you spoken to your mother about it?"

"She's moved back home, but she hasn't been herself, Quinn. I think she's depressed."

"She's still grieving for your dad."

"Of course she is, but it's more than that. It's almost like she can't stand being in that house. She's even taken up gardening, which she hates, just to get outside."

"She's lonely, that's all."

"It's a lonely place," Gabe replied with a sigh.

Chapter 40

January 1463

Berwick-upon-Tweed, Northumberland

The half-light of dawn was just beginning to chase away the darkness of night when Kate came slowly awake. She'd drunk more than usual last night, having been invited to Stanwyck Hall along with Hugh, Guy, and Eleanor to celebrate the end of the Bamburgh Castle siege. The Earl of Stanwyck had entertained all his knights and their spouses at a gathering that had begun at noon and turned raucous by nightfall. Hugh had been in fine spirits, but Kate sensed a suppressed anger in him, and feared it might be directed toward her, although she couldn't see what she'd done to give offense since he hadn't seen her since November and her letters to him had been brief and not overly detailed.

Hugh and Guy had returned the day before—tired, hungry, and desperate for a wash after camping out on the field outside Bamburgh Castle for over a month and not bothering to shave or partake in anything more than a compulsory wash. Even Walter had sported a sparse beard, of which he'd been exceedingly proud. Joan had spent hours heating water, while Alf and Walter carried up steaming buckets to Hugh and Guy's rooms, along with their newly sharpened daggers so they could shave. They'd emerged by suppertime, looking like they'd shaved a decade off their appearance. Aileen had put an arm over her nose when she collected their clothes and hose. No words had been needed to express how foul they smelled. Walter had had to wait his turn for a bath, but he'd been pleased as punch when he finally got his turn and washed away the sweat and grime of the past weeks. He'd considered keeping the beard, but Aileen had shaken her head when he asked if he should let it grow, and handed him his dagger and a small looking glass, making a shaving gesture with her hand. Walter had taken her advice. They'd all had a pleasant supper together, and Hugh and Guy had regaled everyone with stories of the siege. Even Adam had been allowed to join the adults so he could enjoy the evening until being sent off to bed.

Now, the morning after the Earl of Stanwyck's supper, Kate carefully inched away from Hugh so as not to wake him.

His arm shot out and grabbed her about the waist. "Don't go," he said sleepily. "I've missed you."

Kate froze. Hugh's words could mean only one thing and every fiber of her being screamed in protest. He'd had a go at her as soon as he was done with his bath after returning from the siege, then again after supper, and last night when they'd returned from the feast in the early hours. Kate's tender flesh was sore and her thighs were sticky with Hugh's seed.

"Hugh, please," she whispered in desperation.

He rolled on top of her, pinned her wrists to the bed, and gave her an unfocused stare. "Please what?" he growled.

Kate was surprised that after the amount of wine and mead he'd consumed last night he was even awake, much less coherent. "Please, not again," she said, her voice barely audible. This was the first time since they'd married that she'd shown a reluctance to perform her wifely duty.

Hugh's eyes opened wide, no longer clouded with drink and sleep, and his mouth twisted into a grimace of fury. The slap that followed left Kate reeling, more with shock than pain. Her teeth rattled with the force of Hugh's anger and tears sprang to her eyes. He had never struck her before.

"Not again?" Hugh hissed as he pushed up her nightdress and drove his knee between her legs. "Not again? You ungrateful bitch. You should be thankful that I still want to fuck you, seeing as you've given me no children in nearly three years of marriage." He rammed into her with the full force of his body and Kate cried out in pain. Thrusting hard, he muttered under his breath, "And now your sire's gone and got married, and begot himself another brat. You know what this means, sweetness, don't you? You're useless to me. You'll inherit nothing."

Kate whimpered as Hugh drove into her again and again, his desire fueled by anger.

"I'll ride you as often as I want when I'm at home, and if you ever try to deny me again, you'll suffer a lot worse than a slap. Is that clear?" he demanded when he finally finished and rolled off her.

"Yes," Kate whispered.

"I can't hear you."

"Yes," she said louder.

"Yes, what?" Hugh taunted her.

"Yes, my lord."

"That's better. Now get out of my sight."

Kate grabbed her clothes and ran from the room, tears streaming down her face. Hugh had never shown such cruelty toward her before, not even when he'd been disappointed or upset. His eyes narrowed and his jaw tightened in anger when she displeased him, but he'd always kept a rein on his feelings and managed to maintain a veneer of civility. The weeks away had done something to him. Kate wasn't sure if it was the frustration of the siege or the news of her father's marriage and new child, but Hugh was smoldering with resentment, and she was the easiest target for his fury.

She stepped into the still-dark Lady Chamber and pulled on her gown with shaking hands. It took her several minutes to do up the laces of the bodice since she couldn't seem to coordinate her movements, and her legs were wobbly. Her hair tumbled down her back, making it more difficult to tie the bows. Once the garment was finally fastened, Kate sat down heavily on the settle, still shaken, and squeezed her legs in an effort to stem the pain. Her womb throbbed from Hugh's onslaught and she thought she might be bleeding. She considered going into the kitchen get some water to wash, but Joan would already be up, stoking up the fire in the great hearth and putting on broth to warm for their breakfast.

Thinking of her father, Kate wished she could have a cup of mead to numb the pain in her heart. He hadn't replied to any of her letters, not even the one she'd written after her mother died. Gerard Dancy had cut her out of his heart, and now he'd cut her out of his family. His newborn son stood to inherit everything and Kate was dispossessed. Hugh wouldn't see another pfennig of Lord Dancy's great wealth unless her baby brother didn't survive, which was something she could never wish for, not even to avoid Hugh's wrath. Her father was forty-four. He could still have several children—siblings Kate would never meet. She longed to visit the Grange and meet her stepmother and hold her baby brother, but that was not to be. Ever. She was completely and utterly dependent on her husband, who at this moment loathed her and blamed her for his disappointed hopes.

Kate shivered. Her feet were numb and her arms broke out in gooseflesh. The keep was as cold as a tomb. It was cold even on the warmest days of summer, but in the beginning of January, when the wind howled outside and snow drifts came to the knee, it was practically uninhabitable. . She abandoned the Lady Chamber and walked down the corridor toward the chapel. It was no warmer there, but it was a place where she felt secure and more at peace. She was a few feet from the door when Guy's face loomed out of the dark, the whites of his eyes illuminated by the tiny flame from his candle.

"Kate, are you all right? I thought I heard you crying." Guy held the candle up to Kate's face. His hand went to her cheek, gently touching the reddened spot Hugh had slapped. "Why did he hit you?" he asked softly.

"It was my fault," Kate replied. "It's nothing. Go back to bed, Guy."

"I'll be right back," Guy said as he disappeared down the corridor.

She pushed open the door and stepped into the dark chapel, but didn't kneel on a prie-dieu. Instead, she wrapped her arms about her and stood still, listening to the moaning of the wind outside.

Guy slipped into the chapel a few moments later. He wrapped a fur from his bed around Kate's shoulders and touched the flame of his candle to the tall candles beside the altar. Then, he turned to study Kate's face as she huddled into the warmth of the fur.

"Why did he hit you?" he asked again.

"I tried to deny him," she confessed.

"I see." Guy looked murderous.

"It was my fault, Guy. Please, let it be," Kate pleaded, suddenly terrified that he would confront Hugh. His interference, although no doubt well meant, would only make things worse for her.

Guy gently brushed a stray curl from her face and tucked it behind her ear. "I never see you with your hair down," he said. "I've forgotten how glorious it is. You are glorious," he whispered.

"Guy, don't," Kate said, but her treacherous body leaned toward him, seeking his touch.

Guy caressed her cheek and then his lips found hers, brushing them very lightly before he drew back, his eyes still blazing. "I could kill him for hurting you. He had no right."

"He had every right. He's my husband and he can do what he wants. You know that. Besides, he's angry," Kate explained unnecessarily.

"I know. He had great financial expectations from this marriage, but it isn't your fault things didn't work out as he'd hoped."

"No, it isn't, but Hugh can hardly slap my father, or Warwick," Kate replied with a wry smile. "I'm the only one he can take his anger out on."

"That doesn't make it right," Guy protested stubbornly.

"Few things in this world are right, Guy, especially for those who depend on others for their livelihood."

He nodded. "Hugh wishes me to marry."

"It's only right that you should," Kate said, but her heart contracted at the thought.

"I don't want to. I could never fully give myself to a wife when my heart longs for you."

"Don't say such things. I belong to Hugh. I'm his in the eyes of God and man, and I will remain his until one of us is in our grave. I will not betray him, Guy."

"I'd never ask you to," Guy replied. "But perhaps it's time for me to seek my fortune elsewhere."

"Oh, Guy." Kate reached out and cupped his cheek. The thought of life without Guy was unbearable, but he was right. If they remained in the same place long enough, denying their feelings for each other would become harder and harder, and eventually, Hugh would see the truth and punish them both.

"I'll ask my lord Stanwyck to release me from my obligations for a year or two. He's a good man; he'll understand."

Kate nodded. "God bless you, Guy de Rosel." *How I wish I'd never laid eyes on you*, she added silently.

Guy kissed her hand and left the chapel, his footsteps unnaturally loud in the quiet of the passage.

Chapter 41

Kate spent the rest of the day trying to avoid Hugh. She simply couldn't bear to look at him after what had happened that morning without her feelings showing plainly on her face. The acute hurt would eventually become a dull ache, this episode becoming just another entry in her list of painful experiences. Hugh's name would be right beneath that of her father. They were two men who should have protected her, but instead they coddled their pride, and used their manhood to dominate the weak.

Kate sighed and retreated to the Lady Chamber. Hugh rarely came in there, preferring to spend his day in more active pursuits.

"It was wonderful last night, wasn't it?" Eleanor asked. She was standing by the window, watching Adam build a snow maiden with Jed's help. The boys' laughter drifted from below, making Kate feel even more isolated in her misery.

"Yes, it was," she replied as she sat down and rummaged in her work basket for the next garment to be mended. It seemed that for every item she worked on, another two showed up the next day.

"You know what I liked best?" Eleanor asked, her tone dreamy. "The minstrels. Oh, I do enjoy the music. Will used to play the lute when we were first married. He used to write songs dedicated to my beauty," she added with a wistful sigh. "And he hired minstrels to play for us once a year at the New Year. The earl always invited everyone for a Christmas celebration, but Will liked to have a celebration of our own. Those moments are the ones I miss the most. They were so pure and joyous."

"My father used to bring in minstrels as well," Kate replied, thankful to talk of something neutral. "My mother loved to hear them play, and she allowed all the servants to take part in the celebration. She said that everyone was entitled to enjoy the beauty of the music."

"Sounds like she was a gracious lady. I don't even remember my mother. She died when I was a child." Eleanor tore her gaze away from the window and took her seat by the hearth, rubbing her arms to warm herself. "I hope Adam doesn't catch a chill out there. Hugh says I should stop coddling him, but I worry so."

"The cold won't hurt him, Eleanor. It'll only make him stronger. Hugh and Guy just spent a month living outside and they're no worse for it."

"Except maybe in temper," Eleanor replied, smiling. "Hugh was a right old bear until he bathed and had a proper meal."

"Yes, that he was," Kate agreed.

Eleanor was just about to say something when Joan appeared at the door, her round face creased with worry and her hands clasped nervously in front of her bosom.

"What is it, Nurse?" Eleanor asked. "Is something amiss?"

"Yes, me lady. It's Aileen. She's gone missing."

"Whatever do you mean?"

"I haven't seen her since yesterday."

"Perhaps she's still abed," Eleanor suggested.

Joan shook her head. "No, I checked. Jed said she still hadn't come to bed by the time he fell asleep last night, and her bed hasn't been slept in since."

"Was she upset about something?" Kate asked. This wasn't like Aileen. She returned to her quarters as soon as Joan dismissed her for the day, eager for rest and time to herself.

"She's been acting a bit odd these past few weeks, but that's nothing unusual for Aileen. She's such a moody thing; one minute she's smiling to herself like she's got a precious secret, and the next she's down in the mouth, sulking in the corner. She did seem quieter than normal yesterday. I thought she was just tired from lugging all that water and doing the extra laundry."

"Have you told Hugh Aileen is missing?" Kate asked.

Joan shook her head. "I had no wish to get the girl in trouble, but now I'm worried. I've looked for her everywhere."

"We'd best tell Hugh and Guy," Eleanor said, rising from her seat. "They'll know what to do."

Hugh staggered down the stairs, looking the worse for wear after last night's festivities, but he instantly took charge, too petty to allow Guy to take the lead.

"Joan, search the storerooms thoroughly. Maybe Aileen's hiding down there for whatever reason. Kate and Eleanor, check every room in the castle. I'll have Alf and Walter search all the outbuildings. Guy, go up on the roof. If she left the castle and is still within sighting distance, you'll see her. Maybe she got hurt and couldn't make it back."

"Aileen never leaves the castle on her own," Joan protested.

"There's always a first time," Hugh snapped. "I'll go speak to Jed. Maybe he can shed some light."

"I've spoken to him already. Don't frighten him, Hugh. He's just a boy," Joan warned. "I don't want him thinking something's befallen his sister without any actual evidence to the fact."

Hugh glared at Joan. "Why would I frighten him? I just want to speak to him. Get on with it, old woman, and stop wasting time."

Joan bristled at Hugh's tone, but turned around and went on her way, heading down to the ground floor and the storerooms.

Eleanor turned to Kate. "I'll check the rooms on this floor."

"All right. I'll search all the bedchambers." Kate walked up the narrow spiral staircase, followed by Guy, who was heading to the roof. "Do you think she's all right?"

Guy shrugged. "I can't see why she wouldn't be. That girl is like a frightened rabbit. The furthest she ever goes is to church, and only when accompanied by Joan and Jed. I think we'll find her sleeping somewhere," he added with a smile. "Don't worry. We'll find her."

"Of course we will," Kate replied. "I just can't imagine where she might have got to."

"We'll find out soon enough."

Kate left Guy at the landing and turned toward Marie de Rosel's bedchamber. She couldn't imagine that Aileen would go in there, but she had to check.

Chapter 42

Guy jogged up the steps to the low doorway leading to the roof. In the past, the roof had served not only as an observation tower where sentries could look out for approaching enemy, but also as a vantage point for the archers. Thankfully, Castle de Rosel hadn't been under attack in several decades, and no one went to the roof unless they wanted to enjoy the glorious vista that spread as far as the eye could see. Will, Hugh, and Guy used to climb up there when they were boys, pretending to loose arrows in defense of their home. Guy liked to look at the distant hills and the sparkling ribbon that was the River Tweed. It was deep and wide, a watery highway for fishermen and soldiers alike, when the situation called for it.

Guy had stopped looking at the river after Margaret's death. To him, the river was no longer beautiful. It was a painful reminder of his negligence, and a harbinger of death. Margaret had been gone for nearly twenty years, but Guy could still see her sweet face, and her wide, cornflower blue eyes that had gazed upon him with such trust. He'd been her favorite brother, the one she trusted most, and he'd let her down, distracted by the sight of a group of knights, in full armor, heading to some battle somewhere along the Scottish border. They had been magnificent, tall and proud, their armor shining in the sunlight as their powerful horses carried them effortlessly to war. Their squires had trotted behind them, their breasts swelled with importance as they followed their masters. Guy had stared after them open-mouthed, desperate to grow up faster so he could enter into the service of the Earl of Stanwyck and take his rightful place among the military elite of Britain. And now he was a knight, just as he'd dreamed he would be, but it brought him no joy, only shame because he was no longer a boy of eight and now he understood that his only purpose in life was to kill.

Guy pushed open the door and stepped onto the snow-covered roof. It was square and flat, surrounded by thick, crenellated stonework. He saw the deep footprints immediately, left by small feet, and turned around to see where Aileen had gone.

He froze when he saw her in the northwest corner, sitting in the snow, her back leaning against the stonework and her head falling sideways. Her legs stuck out in front of her and her arms hugged her middle, as if she were in pain. Guy knew the girl was dead before he approached her. Her skin was bluish, and the crows had already gotten at her. Her face was a grotesque mockery of the girl she'd been only yesterday, her eyes nothing more than hollow sockets, and her cheeks pockmarked by eager beaks. Guy turned away, feeling ill, but not before he noticed that the snow on the parapet above Aileen's head had been cleared away. She had leaned against the stonework, far enough to brush the snow away along the furthest part of the stone. She'd either been looking for something, or she'd meant to throw herself from the roof.

Guy walked to the opposite side of the roof and glanced down, his gaze searching for Hugh. Hugh was just coming out of the stable, his stride purposeful as always.

"Hugh, come up here!" Guy shouted. "Alone!"

Hugh appeared a few moments later, out of breath from running up the steep spiral staircase. When he saw Aileen's body, he sighed and shook his head in disbelief. He approached the girl and looked at her carefully, not appearing in the least revolted by the sight of her mutilated face.

"How did she die?" he asked at last. "I don't see any signs of violence."

"I think she meant to throw herself off," Guy said, pointing to the lack of snow on the stone.

"Clearly she didn't. So how did she kill herself? I can't imagine she sat here till she froze to death."

Guy had known from the moment he saw Aileen's body that she'd taken her own life, but it wasn't until Hugh had spoken the words that the magnitude of what Aileen had done really sank in. She had committed suicide—a mortal sin in the eyes of God. Perhaps that was why she'd done it here, on the roof, where she'd hoped not to be found.

"We'll have to inform Father Joseph," Hugh said as he continued to stare at Aileen in heartless fascination.

"You know what he'll say."

"Yes. We'll have to bury her at a crossroads at midnight with a stake through her heart."

"I won't do it, Hugh."

"What do you suggest? There's no place for her in consecrated ground. We must obey the Church in this."

"Well, I won't. She was an innocent girl who found her life too heavy a burden to carry. I won't dishonor her in that way. Let's bury her in the woods. No one need ever know. She has no family, aside from Jed, and he won't tell anyone."

Hugh turned around to look at Guy, an expression of pure contempt on his face. "You've grown soft, brother. No, let me rephrase that. You've always been soft."

"Do as you wish," Guy spat out and left the roof before his anger had a chance to overflow. "I'll send Alf to help you with the body."

"Did you see anything?" Kate asked as she came out of one of the bedchambers. She froze when she saw Guy's face.

"Don't go up there," Guy replied.

"Why?" she whispered. "What's happened to Aileen?"

"She's killed herself, Kate."

"Why?" Kate cried as her hand flew to her mouth in shock. "Why would she do that?"

"I don't know. Perhaps she saw no good reason to go on."

"She was eighteen," Kate whispered, shaking her head as if she could chase away the truth. "She had her whole life ahead of her."

She pressed herself against the wall when Hugh came awkwardly down the steps holding Aileen in his arms. Thankfully, her face was turned inward, so Kate couldn't see the full ugliness of the girl's death.

"Come away, Kate. Come away," Guy said as he tried to pull her away from the staircase. But she wouldn't budge. She stared at Aileen's body in horror, her hand reaching toward the girl.

"Get her away from here," Hugh barked as he reached the landing. "Move, you stupid woman."

Kate reacted as if she'd been scalded by boiling water. She turned on her heel and fled, disappearing into the nearest bedchamber.

"You didn't have to be so harsh," Guy said. "Kate was overcome with shock."

"If I need advice on how to treat my wife, I'll be sure to ask for it. But for now, keep your own counsel, brother, since I have no need of it." Hugh leaned against the wall and took a deep breath. "Help me get her down. She's heavy and stiff."

Guy took Aileen by the ankles while Hugh grasped her beneath the arms. They carried her down in silence, each lost in his own thoughts.

Chapter 43

Dinner was a subdued affair. Joan served cold meat and cheese, accompanied by yesterday's bread and a jug of ale. She hadn't had any time to prepare a hot meal, since it had fallen to her to see to Aileen's body. Everyone was in shock, but Kate sensed Hugh seething beneath his quiet exterior, outraged that this shame had been brought on his household. Guy ate in silence, his gaze never meeting anyone's, but Kate felt his warm hand on hers when no one was looking, a gesture of comfort and support. She was relieved when Joan came in to clear away the remnants of the meal.

"Well, what have you got to say for yourself, Nurse?" Hugh asked. He was normally more respectful to Joan, but at the moment, he couldn't be bothered to control his temper.

"I think we should speak in private," Joan replied.

"Speak now. I've no patience for games, and they'll all find out the truth anyhow." Hugh jutted his chin toward Guy, Kate and Eleanor, indicating who he meant.

"All right." Joan sighed. "Aileen was with child. About six months gone, I'd say. I found yew berries in her pocket. They are poisonous, so she would have died quickly. I think she brought them along in case she couldn't find the strength to throw herself off the tower."

"Who's the father of her bastard?" Hugh roared, his face turning puce with anger.

His vehemence surprised Kate. Hugh had barely noticed Aileen, at least in Kate's presence, but she quickly realized the reason for Hugh's fierce reaction had nothing to do with the loss of a young girl. They were a small household, and there were only three people who could have got Aileen with child. As master, Hugh would have to find out who was responsible and mete out the punishment—something he wouldn't relish, given his relationship to the possible miscreants.

"Excuse me," Kate said and left the room. She grabbed her cloak and walked out to the stables.

Walter was sitting on a bale of hay, his head resting against the wooden planks of the wall and his eyes closed. His cheeks were wet with tears and his lower lip was bitten to the quick. His eyes flew open in surprise when he heard Kate enter the stables and he angrily wiped his cheeks with the back of his hand.

"Walter, are you all right?" Kate asked as she drew closer to the boy.

Walter shook his head. His face contorted with anguish and his hands balled into fists. "How could she do it? How could she commit a mortal sin? She'll never be at peace now. She'll burn in Hell for eternity. Didn't she know that?"

"Walter, did you lie with Aileen?" Kate asked, deciding to be blunt. If Walter was the father, Hugh would skin him alive, but he was the likeliest candidate.

Walter shook his head again. "We were friends; that was all. I never touched her."

"She was a comely girl, and I think she had feelings for you," Kate persisted in the hope that he would tell her the truth.

"Aye, she was comely, and she did have feelings for me, but I had no wish to hurt her. I could never offer her a future. I must marry where my family chooses when the time comes."

"Many men marry where they are told, but that doesn't stop them from satisfying their needs elsewhere before they do."

"I never touched her, I told you," Walter spat out. "I cared about her."

"Then help me figure out who did this to her. Aileen was with child."

Walter sniffled and wiped his nose on his sleeve, but he showed no surprise at Kate's revelation.

"You know who the father is, don't you?" she asked.

"There's only one person it could be," he replied bitterly.

"Who?" Kate's stomach contracted with fear. If Walter said that Hugh had forced himself on Aileen, she wouldn't be able to remain a wife to him. She didn't know what she'd do, since Hugh owned her, but she'd find a way. She wouldn't stay at Castle de Rosel a moment longer. Kate stared down Walter, waiting, but he seemed reluctant to name the father, despite his loyalty to Aileen.

"Walter, please, you must tell me who did this to her," Kate persisted.

"He didn't do anything to her, at least nothing she hadn't wanted done," Walter replied stubbornly. "She wanted it. She told me so herself."

"Was she not afraid of the consequences?"

"She thought he'd look after her."

"Who was it?" Kate held her breath. She couldn't bear for the father to be Hugh, but if Walter named Guy she'd feel even more broken. She had no right to blame Guy for desiring a bit of affection. He didn't belong to her, nor did he owe her anything at all, but if he had lain with Aileen, it would still feel like a terrible betrayal, especially since Aileen would have been at his mercy and in no position to deny him. Kate didn't believe Guy capable of taking advantage of a vulnerable disabled girl, at least not the Guy she knew, but people had a way of hurting each other in ways that weren't always planned.

"It was Emmett Walsh," Walter finally said.

Kate released her breath in a rush. *Thank you, Father*, she thought. *Thank you. Thank you*. It wasn't until that moment that she realized how little she trusted Hugh, and how desperately she loved Guy and needed him to be innocent of using Aileen, even if she had been a willing participant.

"Who is Emmett Walsh?" she asked, dragging her errant thoughts back to the issue at hand. She'd never heard of the man.

"Emmett is the lad who brings the hay," Walter explained. "For the horses," he added, seeing Kate's puzzled look. "We don't make our own hay. We get it from the farmers on the estate."

"Oh, of course." She'd never given much thought to the horses and their dietary needs.

"Emmett comes once every fortnight and brings a cartload of hay. Aileen always made sure to find her way to the barn when Emmett arrived. That's where she lay with him."

"Would this Emmett have married her, had he known about the child?"

Walter raised an eyebrow, reminding Kate that she was awfully naïve for a woman of her station. "No serf can marry without his lord's permission. I don't think the master would have refused had Emmett asked, but he's already married. He was wed a year ago and his wife just birthed twins in November."

"Did Aileen know that?"

Walter shook his head. "Aileen never goes to the village, and being nearly deaf she isn't one for gossip. She had no idea."

"I see. Did you not warn her?"

"I didn't know he was wed until it was too late. I don't go into the village much, and I sit with the family in church, so I never paid him any mind. Besides, it seems his wife was laid up for months during her pregnancy. She was very ill, so she never came to church. Aileen never saw them together. She was devastated when she found out. She was in love with him."

"Did she confide in you?"

Walter nodded. "Aye, she told me. She was frightened and didn't know what do to. I told her to speak to Mistress Joan. She'd have advised her. She knows about such things."

"How do you mean?"

"She has sway over the master," Walter explained. "She'd have asked him to go easy on Aileen. Master Hugh would not have turned her out."

"I'll have to tell Hugh," Kate said. "He might wish to speak to you about this matter."

"Do what you must. I don't care a jot what happens to Walsh," Walter replied brutally. "I hope he burns in Hell."

Kate sighed and left the stables, heading back inside to find Hugh. She had no wish to speak to him, but he needed to know.

Hugh was still in the hall, drinking ale. He looked murderous, and the drink wasn't helping matters. Guy was standing by the narrow window, his hands clasped behind his back. He looked pale and tired, and upset. He'd been the one to break the news to Jed while Hugh saw to the body. The boy was now in the kitchen, being comforted by Joan and Alf.

"Walter says that Aileen was spending time with Emmett Walsh," Kate said, getting straight to the point. She had no wish to draw this conversation out.

"Who the devil is Emmett Walsh?" Hugh drawled.

"He brings the hay," Guy replied. He was a lot more familiar with the tenants on the estate. Hugh only collected tithes and gave the occasional blessing to a marriage or a child, following the example of William, who'd been a benevolent lord.

"I want him brought to me," Hugh ordered as his fist thundered on the wooden table. "I'll show him the meaning of de Rosel justice."

271

"He's newly married and has two-month old twins," Kate said quietly. "Hugh, please be merciful. He didn't force her."

"Be quiet! I'm master here and I will punish him as I see fit."

"What will you do to him?" Guy asked, turning from the window.

"Aileen was our property. And her child would have been our property as well. This worthless maggot robbed us of two serfs. He will pay for taking what's not his."

"What will you do to him?" Guy repeated. He hadn't raised his voice, but Kate could sense his anger.

"I'll have him gelded. He's already produced two pups. He'll not enjoy his wife's favors again, or anyone else's."

"That's not justice; that's cruelty," Guy retorted. "I won't permit you to do that."

"I'm not asking for your permission. No man's died from having his balls snipped. He'll still be able to work and pay his tithes."

Guy rounded on him. "Hugh, I will not allow you to torture a man. He's not the first or the last to lie with a woman that's not his wife. Aileen chose to take her own life. He didn't murder her. She could have come to us. We'd have looked after her. She knew that."

"So, how would you have me punish him?" Hugh asked, his voice suddenly low and silky. "Or do you suggest I simply let him use what's mine whenever his feels like it?"

"Have him flogged, but don't take his manhood," Guy said quietly.

"Since you're in favor of leniency, you soft-hearted fool, you'll do the flogging."

"I won't."

"You will. I'm master of this house, and you answer to me. You will give him thirty lashes. And if you refuse, I'll double the number."

"You can't do that," Guy snarled, staring at Hugh as if he'd never seen him before.

"Sixty lashes. Go on, argue some more, and I'll make it one hundred."

"I no longer recognize you, Hugh," Guy said, his voice dripping with contempt.

"I no longer have to answer to father or to William. I'm finally my own master, and I will do as I see fit. Now, have Walsh brought here and administer the punishment. Sixty lashes."

"As you wish, brother." Guy turned on his heel and strode out the door.

"What are you staring at?" Hugh demanded when he turned toward Kate. "Get out!"

She didn't need to be told twice but fled the hall and locked herself in one of the vacant bedchambers on the top floor. She couldn't bear to look at Hugh, nor could she bring herself to witness the punishment when the man was flogged in the yard. As she listened to the whistle of the whip and the young man's screams, in her mind's eye she saw droplets of blood landing in the snow and blooming into red flowers of pain. She knew the man couldn't go unpunished for what he'd done, but Hugh's pleasure in causing him suffering and taunting Guy made her sick with disgust. He would have gelded the man had Guy allowed him to, and that was what scared her the most. He didn't care about Aileen or her baby; he wanted to exercise his power over another human being, the way he'd done with Kate that very morning. Hugh had grown harder and meaner since their marriage, and she feared what the future would bring now that he could no longer rely on inheriting her father's estate.

Only a few minutes after the screams abruptly came to an end, Kate heard the thunder of hooves on the frozen ground and knew with sickening certainty that Guy was gone. Tomorrow, Alf and Walter would bury Aileen in the woods, Hugh's one concession to Guy's wishes, and this terrible episode would be over, but the scars it left would last a lifetime.

Chapter 44

August 2014

London, England

Quinn wiped the gel off her stomach while Dr. Malik turned off the ultrasound machine and recorded the results of the scan in Quinn's chart. Gabe stood by quietly, waiting for the final word from the doctor, but Quinn had seen the relief in his eyes when he watched their baby cavort on screen. He'd been really worried.

Dr. Malik turned back to Quinn and Gabe and gave them a reassuring smile. "Everything looks good. Your blood pressure is slightly elevated, but not enough to be of concern, and your ankles are swollen, but it has been rather warm these past few days. Try to drink more water and keep an eye on the ankles. Ring me if the swelling gets worse. I see no reason for complete bed rest as of now, but I'd like you to rest at least two hours every day. Are you resting?" she asked, peering at Quinn over her rimless specs.

"Not as much as she should," Gabe piped in, earning himself a look of reproach from Quinn.

"I will rest more," she promised.

"I'd like to see you in a fortnight," Dr. Malik said as she said her goodbyes and rushed off to see the next patient.

"See, all is well," Quinn said as she got off the examining table and slipped her feet into her shoes.

"Thank God. Would you like me to come with you?" Gabe suggested. "I still have a bit of time."

Quinn had heard back from Hetty Marks two days ago. . Hetty was in London visiting her sister, and had suggested they meet in person, which had left Quinn fluttering with nervous excitement. They had arranged to meet by the Albert Memorial at noon.

"Gabe…"

"All right. I understand. Ring me when you're through."

"I will. And thanks."

Quinn took a taxi to Hyde Park. It was too far to walk, and as Dr. Malik had observed, it was a hot day. Even in her light summer frock, Quinn was perspiring. The green expanse of the park beckoned to her to enter its coolness, but she had to wait by the memorial. It was the easiest spot to meet someone since it was open and elevated, the perfect vantage point.

The air shimmered with heat, and was thick with the aroma of freshly mown grass and flowers. Birdsong carried on the light breeze, but was quickly drowned out by the sound of a giggling toddler. Quinn looked at the little boy and her heart filled with longing. She couldn't wait to meet her baby. She wanted to hear it giggle just like that, and feel its weight in her arms as she held it close, enjoying that intoxicating baby smell that all little ones seemed to have. *Eau de Bébé*, Jill called it.

Quinn walked up the steps in front of the memorial before taking a drink of water from the bottle she always carried. The water was tepid and Quinn made a face, which elicited a chuckle from the elderly woman who was just walking up the steps.

"I remember you making a face just like that when I gave you a bottle. The formula wasn't warmed through, and you were very displeased, as I recall."

"Ms. Marks," Quinn said, smiling at the woman. She looked exactly like her profile photo on Facebook. Round blue eyes, ruddy complexion, and thick salt-and-pepper hair cropped close to her head. Ms. Marks wore a long cotton skirt with a pattern of bright red poppies against a cream-colored background, and a beige top.

"I'm thrilled to see you, Quinn. Or should I say Dr. Allenby? What an honor. I looked you up after I received your message. I've only just recently learned how to use Messenger. My word, you've come a long way from that squalling infant," she said as she studied Quinn with undisguised interest.

"Should we walk or would you prefer to find a shady bench?" Quinn asked.

"If you feel up to walking, I'm game," Ms. Marks replied. "And please call me Hetty."

They walked away from the memorial and deeper into the park. "I've only just found out about my sister," Quinn began. "I had no idea my mother gave birth to twins. She never thought to mention the fact."

"So you've met her then."

"Yes, very recently. She's not what I expected," Quinn confessed.

"Few people ever are. I'm glad you contacted me, though. I always did wonder about you girls."

"Please tell me everything, as you remember it."

Hetty nodded, a faraway look in her eyes as she recalled the details of that day. Her account was very similar to that of Reverend Seaton, and Quinn was disappointed that Hetty couldn't add much to what she already knew.

"You see, I took a leave of absence shortly after the two of you were found. My mother fell and broke her hip, and needed looking after, so I spent nearly a year in Manchester. That's where I'm from, originally. By the time I returned to work, your cases were closed."

"Did you never look at the files?" Quinn asked.

"I was no longer the case manager, so I had no access to the information. Adoption files are confidential."

"Do you know anything at all about my sister?"

"I know that she had surgery and remained in hospital for several weeks, under observation. By the time I returned, she'd been discharged and adopted. That's all I can tell you, love."

"Did she look like me? Were we identical?"

Hetty smiled kindly. "You were newborn babies. Even if you were identical, it'd be pretty hard to tell at that stage, especially as I never saw you side by side. I suppose you looked alike, but I can't tell you anything more than that. I'm sorry."

"Is there any way to find out who adopted Quentin?"

"I'm sorry, pet, but finding your sister won't be easy. Had your mother gone through the proper channels, there'd be a record, and your sister would have had a surname at birth. As your mother decided to leave you girls just lying about…"

"I see. Thank you, Hetty."

"I do wish I could help you. I always thought it was wrong that they split you up, but I suppose they thought it best to get you adopted as soon as possible without waiting for your sister to recover. Not many people wish to take on babies that are ill, and I believe your sister might have had a congenital heart condition. They thought you'd have a better chance on your own, and looks like they were right."

"Yes, my parents are wonderful. I got very lucky. I can only hope my sister can say the same."

"Have you searched the internet for a Quentin of about the same age?"

"I have, but no joy," Quinn replied.

"What's your next step then? Is there anything I can do?"

"I suppose I'll visit the hospital where Quentin was treated. Perhaps someone might remember her, or maybe I can even get access to her file. As her sister, I could be considered next of kin," Quinn speculated.

"Well, I don't know about that, but you can certainly try. I think your mother might have a better chance, as the birth mother, you know."

"Do you think so?"

"It's worth a try, isn't it? Oh, I do hope you find her, Quinn. I can't imagine life without my sister. We've had our ups and downs, as sisters do, but there's no one in the world who understands me the way she does."

"Since Quentin and I didn't grow up together, I can't expect that we'd share that sort of bond," Quinn replied, envious of Hetty's relationship with her sister. She'd always longed for a sibling, but she was grateful for Jill, who was as close to a sister as Quinn could hope for.

"No, you didn't, but you shared a womb, and parents. You must have something in common."

"I'd like the chance to find out."

"I hope you'll get it. It's so much easier to find someone in this day and age, with computers and such. I'm sure you'll find her trail."

Quinn and Hetty talked for a while longer, and then Hetty said her goodbyes and rushed off to meet her sister for lunch at a nearby pub. Quinn found a shady bench and sat down, needing a few minutes to ponder what Hetty had said. The truth of the situation was that Quinn was as far from discovering what had happened to Quentin as she had been a few days ago. She would never seek help from Sylvia, who had never bothered to find out what had happened to her baby. She'd just walked away—from both of them. She didn't deserve to have her daughters back, and Quinn would keep whatever she discovered to herself. In truth, Sylvia would be of no use anyway, since her name wasn't listed anywhere as the birth mother, and she had no legal connection to the children she'd abandoned.

Quinn supposed her only option was to visit the hospital where Quentin had been left, but what were the chances that anyone would actually tell her anything? She left the park, purchased a fresh bottle of water, took a few minutes to hydrate, and set off for home. She'd clear forgotten that Logan and Scott would be coming by tonight to take a look at the sword. She'd stop by the shops on the way home and pick up a couple of salmon fillets. Served with jasmine rice and steamed asparagus, they would do very well for an impromptu dinner.

Quinn took her mobile out of her bag and rang her mother. She'd promised to call after the doctor's appointment. She momentarily considered telling her mum about Quentin, but quickly changed her mind. She'd keep that bit of information to herself until she knew more. Perhaps it was unfair of her not to share this monumental news with her parents, but since discovering her psychic gift at a young age, she'd learned to be secretive, more for her parents' sake than her own. She had no wish to upset them or cause them unnecessary pain, since they were already questioning their place in her life and thinking that somehow they'd never been enough.

Chapter 45

"That looks delicious," Colin said as he helped himself to a piece of salmon. "And what's in that sauce?"

"It's plain yogurt with a bit of dill and lemon juice," Quinn replied shyly, taken aback by the praise. No one except Gabe ever complimented her cooking.

"Outstanding," Logan agreed as he popped another forkful of fish into his mouth. He swallowed and gave Quinn a brilliant smile. "So, are we going to acknowledge the five hundred pound elephant in the room named Quentin or are we going to talk about fish some more?" he asked playfully.

"I wasn't sure if you knew," Quinn replied.

"Oh, I know. Mum has been ranting and raving about your confrontation for days."

"Logan, did you know about Quentin before?" she asked, watching his face for clues.

Logan shook his head. "I didn't know about either of you. I love my mum, Quinn, but I don't pretend to understand her. There are parts of her she keeps to herself and always has done, even while my dad was alive."

"May I ask you something?" Quinn said, hoping he wouldn't take offense at her prying.

"I think you're entitled to some answers," he said as he continued to eat, unperturbed.

"Did your parents have a happy marriage?" Sylvia rarely mentioned her husband, who'd died of cancer several years before Quinn and Sylvia met. She seemed to mourn him, but not deeply, not the way Susan would mourn Roger Allenby if he passed, or the way Grandma Ruth mourned her Joe. He'd always been there, in her heart, and in everything she did, and she hadn't feared death, knowing they would be reunited at last. That was the sort of love Quinn strove for and the kind of marriage she aspired to with Gabe. Perhaps Sylvia was someone who wasn't capable of very deep feelings, but she did seem to adore Jude and felt very protective of him.

Logan didn't answer immediately. He took a sip of wine and held it in his mouth for a moment before swallowing. "I thought they did, but knowing what I now know, I'm not so sure. Their marriage was very quiet."

"Meaning?" Colin asked, his eyebrow furrowing in confusion.

"Meaning they just got on with it. They never rowed or disagreed. They kind of just rubbed along, like two coworkers who must share an office space."

"That's a good thing, surely," Colin said, still looking puzzled.

Logan blessed Colin with a brilliant smile, a smile that spoke volumes, and laid his hand over his partner's. "Would you want us to have a quiet relationship?"

Colin blushed prettily. "No, I suppose not. That kind of relationship doesn't have much passion, does it?"

"No. When neither person is invested enough to get excited about anything, it's as good as being dead."

"Hmm, I never thought of it that way," Gabe interjected. "My parents went at it hammer and tongs when I was a kid."

"And I bet they had great make-up sex afterwards," Logan concluded.

"Well, I can't attest to that, thankfully, but I can honestly say they loved each other. My mum was devastated when Dad died. She misses him sorely, even the parts of his character she found irritating."

"Quinn, what about your folks?" Logan asked.

Quinn chuckled and smiled at him. "No, my parents did not have a quiet marriage, but they did get on, and still do. They are not shy about showing affection though, and they feel comfortable to disagree and defend their point of view. It doesn't undermine their relationship; it makes it stronger."

"I don't think my dad knew Mum at all, now that I think of it," Logan said, shaking his head. "She kept a lot to herself, as we now know. She likes secrets."

"Will there be more revelations, do you think?" Quinn asked, suddenly worried.

"Lord, I hope not. This is about as much as I can handle," Logan joked. "So, what's our plan?"

"Our plan?" Quinn gazed at Logan across the table. She hadn't expected him to want to help, but she'd accept his assistance gladly if it was on offer.

"Well, you are planning to look for her, are you not?" he asked as he helped himself to more rice.

"Yes, but it's proving rather difficult. I have no legal ties to Quentin, and neither does Sylvia. And all this happened nearly thirty-one years ago. Hetty Marks, the Social Services case worker I met with this afternoon, suggested I start at the hospital."

Logan shook his head. "That's a dead end, if you ask me. In 1983 the records would still have been hand-written, so accessing the NHS database would yield no results. Given that this case is three decades old, the files from that period would no longer be kept on-site."

"Where would they be?" Quinn asked, alarmed. She hadn't considered that.

"The files would have been archived. They're either still in the building or have been transferred to some other facility. In any case, no one on staff would let you anywhere near them."

Quinn felt a pang of disappointment. Her plans had been tentative, but now she didn't even have a starting point. She pushed away her plate, no longer hungry.

"Can I have some pudding?" Emma asked as she came into the dining room, dragging Mr. Rabbit by the ear. "I finished watching the film."

"I think pudding is an excellent idea," Gabe said. "How about we clear the table and bring out pudding for everyone? Emma, will you help me?"

"Mr. Rabbit is tired," Emma replied.

"I bet he's weak with hunger too," Logan joked. "I can look after him while you help your dad."

Emma gave Logan a loaded look, but handed over the toy and accepted the bread basket from Gabe. "Go put that in the kitchen."

"What's for pudding anyway?"

"Banofee pie," Gabe replied with a smile of anticipation.

"Did you make it yourself?" Colin looked impressed.

"Is my name Rhys Morgan?" They all laughed at the joke. "No, I bought it on the way home, so I know it's good."

"Bring it on," Logan said. "Emma, do you like banoffee pie?"

Emma shrugged. "It's all right, I suppose. I like ice cream better."

"We have ice cream too," Quinn said. "I wouldn't let you down."

Emma lit up. "I'll have that then and you can all have your banana toffee thingy."

"We'll show you the sword as soon as Emma goes to bed," Quinn promised quietly after Emma disappeared into the kitchen. "We don't want her to know where it's kept."

"Would she go looking for it?" Colin asked.

"She might, just out of curiosity. Let me give them a hand," Quinn said. She collected the dirty plates and headed toward the kitchen. "After ice cream, it's off to bed with you," she said, smiling at Emma, who was taking out an extra-large bowl for herself.

"But I want to stay up."

"You have school tomorrow."

"I'm not tired."

"But Mr. Rabbit is," Gabe replied. "Or is he to sleep alone tonight? He might get lonely."

Quinn pinned Gabe with a disapproving look, and he shrugged. One of the things they were learning as parents was to watch what they said because Emma didn't miss a trick.

"Is that why you two sleep together?" Emma asked. "Who will I sleep with once I'm too old to sleep with Mr. Rabbit?"

Quinn patted Gabe on the back as he nearly choked on a sip of water. "There, there, Daddy. We've got time yet. Here, Emma, why don't you bring these plates and forks to the table?" she suggested. "Can't eat the pie with our hands."

"That would be exceptionally rude," Emma announced, making Gabe and Quinn exchange looks and burst out laughing.

"I suppose it would be," Gabe agreed. "Come, let me help you."

"Are you going to have a smart mouth too?" Quinn asked her belly as she took the kettle off the hob and made a pot of tea. "I suppose I'd be surprised if you didn't, with Gabe and me for parents, Emma for a sister, and your odd assortment of grandparents." She sighed and patted her stomach affectionately.

Once Emma finished her ice cream and was sent to bed under protest, the adults were finally able to resume their conversation.

"I think I might be able to help with the search," Colin said. "Neither of you can access the files, but I might be able to. As a doctor, if I request a file that I think might be relevant to a case I'm working on, I have a good chance of getting it."

"Would no one require authorization?" Gabe asked.

"The case is thirty years old. I think at this stage, no one would particularly care."

"Would you be willing to do that?" Quinn asked.

Colin turned to Logan with a playful grin. "Feel like taking a drive to Leicester on Friday?"

"I hear Leicester is lovely this time of year," Logan replied. "We'll play at being day-trippers."

"Excellent. Friday it is then. Now, let's see that sword."

Chapter 46

January 1463
Stanwyck Hall, Northumberland

Guy didn't get very far when he left Castle de Rosel behind on that cold December evening. He'd left in a fit of temper, only to realize a mile down the road that he'd taken neither his armor nor any coin. Returning home with his tail between his legs was out of the question, so he continued on to Stanwyck Hall to beg his liege lord's hospitality.

The Earl of Stanwyck listened to Guy's account over supper and smiled indulgently at the young man, gesturing for the serving girl to pour them more wine.

"Guy, you're welcome to remain at Stanwyck Hall for as long as you wish. Lord knows we have plenty of room. I'll send one of my men to fetch your armor, weapons, and personal possessions come morning and assign you a squire to look after your needs, but as your lord, I must offer a piece of advice, one you're not going to like. Your brother William was a good and decent man. He inspired obedience and respect, but Hugh must govern by fear. He's not the type of man to breed loyalty. Gelding the man would have been cruel, I agree with you there, but Hugh did right to punish him. Whether the girl was willing or not, she wasn't his for the taking. His actions led to her death, whether that was his intention or not."

The earl held up his hand to silence Guy when he was about to protest.

"Now, I know what you're going to say. If every man who lay with a woman that's not his wife were flogged, there'd be no one left with an unstriped back, and you're right, but different rules apply to different ranks of society, and as a serf, this Walsh is your property, not your contemporary. Had Hugh not punished him, he'd appear weak and ineffectual, much like our deposed sovereign. And you see what befell him when he failed to strike to defend his position. Guy, I admire your sense of decency. You remind me of William, but if you hope to survive, you must steel your heart to the pain of others. The girl is gone, the culprit punished, and your conscience clear of any wrongdoing."

"Is my conscience clear?" Guy asked.

"Guy, what ails you is not the flogging you had to administer—deep down you know it was just—but your brother's treatment of you. It rankles, I understand. I too had an older brother once. Hugh's not known for his tact or his kindness, and his temporary position as lord of the manor burns his gut more with every passing day. Having you there, judging him, only makes that flame stronger. What you need is a bit of distance, and not just from your brother."

"What do you mean, my lord?"

The earl raised one shaggy eyebrow, staring at Guy until his cheeks warmed. "I'm not blind, Guy, and neither is Hugh. You're hopelessly in love with his wife, and you need to conquer those feelings. She's not yours for the taking any more than a serving wench was Walsh's to enjoy. Now, tonight, I will send a girl to your room. She's comely and sweet, and you will make use of her as a man should. That's an order, not a request, since you're still in my service. If you refuse, you will insult my hospitality."

"Yes, my lord," Guy muttered and gulped down the remainder of his wine.

"Now, off to bed with you. You might not be tired, but I'm an old man and I need to rest my bones. They seem to creak louder with every passing winter," the earl complained as he rose laboriously to his feet.

"You're still in fighting form, my lord."

"Aye, as long as my squire dresses me, lifts me onto my horse, and hands me my sword. I'm getting too old for this, Guy. I think I'll sit the next one out, and the one after that. My son can represent the Stanwycks in battle. It's only right that he should. None of us are immortal, are we?" The earl patted Guy on the back and smiled at him, as if Guy were his own son. "I envy you, my boy. Your whole life is still ahead of you. Don't waste it pining for things you can't have."

"Yes, my lord. Sleep well."

The ear winked at Guy as he turned to leave the hall. "And I hope you don't sleep at all," he replied with a lewd smile, leaving Guy in no doubt of what he meant.

Guy retreated to his chamber and sat down by the hearth. He'd consumed a lot of wine during supper, but not enough to dull his senses or calm the turmoil he'd felt since that morning when he found Kate crying, her cheek bruised. The earl had been right in everything he'd said. Guy resented Hugh, and despised him for his ill treatment of Kate. But no matter how bright his anger burned, Kate belonged to Hugh, and Guy had no right to chastise his brother for his treatment of his wife. If Hugh chose to take a whip to Kate or ride her until she bled every night, Guy had no right to intervene. The kindest thing he could do was leave. Perhaps his absence would mellow Hugh's temper.

Guy had every intention of sending the girl away after extracting a promise that she'd tell the earl that Guy had availed himself of her body, but when she knocked on his door and entered the room, quietly standing before him, he changed his mind. She was indeed comely, with large blue eyes and long, lustrous red hair. The earl had chosen well, selecting a lass that resembled Kate, in coloring if not in feature. Guy gazed upon the girl and suddenly all the frustration and loneliness of the past several years came crashing down on him, overwhelming him with desperation. It'd been years since he'd enjoyed the touch of a woman, but tonight he would give in to his need. He was a man, and he had a man's desires, and if they couldn't be satisfied with the woman he worshipped, they'd be satisfied by one who was willing.

Guy held out his hand and the girl came to him, smiling and eager. "How do you like it, my lord?" she asked, cupping his cheek tenderly.

"How do *you* like it?" Guy asked, smiling back. He might have no feelings for her, but he'd not treat her unkindly.

The girl slid her hand downward and into his breeches, wrapping her slender fingers about his shaft and moving her hand skillfully. "I like it long and hard, my lord," she purred.

"What's your name?" Guy asked as a bolt of desire shot through him, leaving him breathless with lust.

"Rose," the girl whispered and sank to her knees in front of him, her rosy mouth opening to receive him.

"Rose." Her name turned into a moan on his lips. It didn't take her long to accomplish what she'd set out to do, but she remained on her knees in front of him, looking up at him with the eagerness of one who was just getting started.

"Come here," Guy bid her and pulled on the laces of her bodice.

"Aye, my lord," the girl replied with a coy smile. "I think I will."

Guy spent nearly a month at Stanwyck Hall, enjoying the hospitality of his lord and the welcoming embrace of Rose, who came to his chamber nearly every night. He lost himself in her body, but his heart remained untouched. At times, he closed his eyes and imagined Kate lying beneath him, moaning with pleasure and begging him for more. Rose didn't mind. She understood that Guy's heart would never belong to her, and had no expectations of him. She was a serf, the earl's property, and his to give where he saw fit. Once Guy was gone, Rose would return to her normal duties, which might include anything from scrubbing pots to servicing the earl or his son. Guy never asked what she had done before he came, and they never spoke of what she'd do after he left. He simply accepted the earl's gift and tried to make Rose's time with him as pleasant for her as he could. He made only one request of her, that she protect herself against pregnancy. Many a man wouldn't care if he got a bastard on the girl. Her child would simply be one more serf for his lord, but Guy couldn't bear to leave a child of his behind. Rose inserted a vinegar-soaked rag into her quim before coming to him, to prevent his seed from taking hold. She wrinkled her nose prettily at the smell, but Guy didn't mind it. It was a small price to pay for his peace of mind.

At the beginning of February, just after Candlemas, the earl summoned Guy. He was sitting by the hearth, his feet propped on a tapestry-covered stool, a goblet of wine in his hand. The earl's son, Robert Ambrose, sat across from his father, enjoying a cup of wine.

"Guy, my boy," the earl greeted him. "Have a cup of wine."

Guy pulled up a chair and accepted the wine from the serving wench hovering nearby. It was too hot by the fire, but Guy didn't move, not wishing to offend his lord.

"I've written to Dick, and had a reply just this morning."

"Dick?"

"Richard Neville," the earl replied, chuckling. "He's the Earl of Warwick to you, but Dick to me. I've known him since he was old enough to ride his pony. I've asked him to take you into his service for a period of one year. Should you wish to remain longer, you only have to ask. You're to report to him at Middleham Castle. Robert will be travelling that way in two days' time. You may travel with him."

"Thank you, my lord," Guy replied, genuinely grateful for the earl's understanding. He didn't have to release Guy, but the older man had a soft spot for him, having been great friends with his father.

"You may take your squire with you. You'll need him, and it wouldn't do to arrive at Middleham looking like a poor relation. You're my knight, and you will make me proud. Hmm?"

"Yes, my lord."

"I'll miss having you about, my boy. And I know a redheaded lass who'll pine for you once you're gone." The earl chuckled, but his son's mouth tightened with displeasure.

Guy paid him no mind. "I thank you for your generosity, my lord."

"Think nothing of it. There are plenty more where she came from. A man needs comely females about the place, doesn't he, Robert?"

Robert didn't reply.

"Robert was sick in love with Rose when he was a lad of thirteen," the earl explained. "She was all of ten then, working in the kitchens. I promised him that he could have her as soon as she became a woman. He had to wait three years, but once she came to his bed, he held on to her for five years. Wouldn't let anyone near her. I think he still loves her," the earl teased.

"I have a wife now," Robert retorted. He avoided his father's playful gaze and stared into the flames.

"When did having a wife ever stop anyone from enjoying a satisfying tumble? I have a wife too." The earl laughed good-naturedly. "My wife is only too grateful to let some poor wench service my needs, especially now that she's too old to bear sons. I hope Rose was to your satisfaction," he said, watching Guy intently.

"She was most pleasing, my lord."

"Good. You do look a bit happier, not like a dog that's been kicked by its master, as you did when you first arrived."

Guy cringed inwardly at the comparison, but didn't say anything. He was excited to be leaving Stanwyck Hall at last, and putting some distance between himself and Hugh—or more accurately, between himself and Kate.

Chapter 47

July 1463

Norham Castle, Northumberland

A few months after presenting himself at Middleham Castle, Guy found himself back in Northumberland, just a few miles from home. Norham Castle, one of the border strongholds of the Yorkists since 1462, had been besieged by the Lancastrian army under the leadership of Ralph Percy. With support from the regent queen of Scotland, Mary of Gueldres, and troops newly arrived from France, Margaret of Anjou had been on the move, ready to lay claim to the north. The siege had been in its eighteenth day by the time the Earl of Warwick and his brother, Lord Montagu, arrived with reinforcements. The fighting had been fierce, and this time, no quarter was given, as it had been after the sieges of 1462 when the leaders were pardoned by His Majesty and allowed to keep their lands and titles. The Lancastrians had been defeated, and justice was swift.

Guy stood at the back of the crowd assembled in the bailey, waiting for the prisoners to be brought forth. A platform had been erected, elevated high enough so everyone could see clearly. They were meant to see, and to reflect on the fate of those who had chosen the wrong side. Today, they would pay for their deeds, and their loyalty to a sovereign they'd sworn their allegiance to long before Edward IV took the throne. Guy still bristled when he thought of his final encounter with Hugh, but he had to give his brother credit. Hugh had been right to trust his instincts and change sides after the Battle of Towton. Had they not, it could have easily been one of them up on that platform, or both, with Adam dispossessed and stripped of his title by association. The king was weary of fighting, and Warwick was growing tired of putting down uprisings in the north, a simmering cauldron of dissent always ready to boil over in rebellion.

A hush fell over the crowd as Warwick's men brought out the leaders of the rebellion. They were dressed in breeches and shirts, their feet bare, and their faces gray in the golden sunshine warming their shoulders for the last time. They were no longer wealthy, powerful men, but defeated soldiers, frightened but defiant to the last.

Guy hadn't witnessed many executions, but he was keenly aware of the difference between the executions of felons and soldiers. When a felon was executed, the crowd jeered and often threw rotting fruits and vegetables at the condemned. They viewed the execution as a spectacle, something to break the monotony of their lives and discuss for several days afterward, especially if the death proved to be a particularly gruesome one. When the executions of soldiers were witnessed by other soldiers, the atmosphere was solemn. The men stood around silently, wary and watchful. They understood all too well that these were men of honor who had fought for their king and risked their lives for their beliefs despite the danger to themselves and their loved ones. All too easily, the positions could be reversed, and any man in the crowd could be facing the axman, his death watched over by his sworn enemies and regarded as a casualty of war. Many of these men, particularly those of high rank, would not receive a Christian burial, at least not right away. Their heads would be mounted on spikes as a lesson to those who chose to take up arms and challenge the unstoppable force that was Warwick's army.

Guy stood shoulder to shoulder with several other knights, their eyes fixed on the platform. He winced as the *thwack* of an ax was followed by a thud as the first head hit the basket set beneath the condemned. The executioner held up the head for all to see, the lower half of his masked face the only part visible, set in grim lines.

No one enjoyed this, least of all the victorious Warwick, who'd been denied the opportunity to bury his own father and brother after their executions several years back. Warwick had traveled the length and breadth of the country, putting down rebellions, relieving sieges, forging alliances, and seeking truces.

He rarely saw his countess or his daughters, who were nearly of marriageable age, something Warwick must have been keenly aware of as he toiled tirelessly on behalf of the king.

Guy had heard the talk at Middleham Castle while he was there. Warwick meant to marry his daughters to the highest ranking nobles in the land, the Duke of Clarence and the Duke of Gloucester, brothers to the king. Should Edward die without leaving a son, one of Warwick's daughters would become the Queen of England, most likely Isabel since it was rumored that she was meant for George, Edward's middle brother. Warwick fought like a lion, because in the end, he'd be the power behind the throne regardless of whether Edward had a son.

Guy waited until the executions were over, then joined a few other men for a game of hazard in the great hall. The wine flowed freely, provided by Warwick himself to help the men forget what they'd just witnessed. Except for the squires, they were all seasoned soldiers and had seen death in all its forms, but one didn't easily forget half a dozen beheadings. Guy accepted more wine from a serving wench and tossed it back as if it were water. A part of him wished he could visit Castle de Rosel and see the family before heading north tomorrow. Warwick meant to pursue the fleeing Scottish army to teach them a lesson, and the Yorkist forces would set off first thing in the morning, marching for southern Scotland.

Guy set down his cup and stepped out into the corridor. The earl would give him permission to leave for a few hours if he asked it, but he wasn't at all sure he wished to go. He knew he had to make peace with Hugh. They were brothers, and the rift between them had not been caused by anything more serious than wounded pride. Hugh would welcome Guy back, as Kate had said in her letters.

It was Kate that Guy was afraid to see. Rose had been the first in a string of casual dalliances, but Kate's face was the last thing he saw before he fell asleep at night, and her name the first word that came to his lips when he woke. He missed her sweet smile and her serious eyes, and he envied his brother bitterly. Hugh didn't appreciate the rare woman he had. Had Guy been the one to marry Kate, he wouldn't care if she gave him sons—although imagining his babe at her breast made him sick with longing. He would value her and love her for all his days, and be happy to remain at home, just to be close to her.

Guy sighed and returned to the hall, having changed his mind about seeking out Warwick. He had no wish to go home, not until he was ready. Hugh, damn his eyes, was right. It was time he thought of marrying. He needed to assure his own future and stop mooning over his brother's wife, who'd be forever out of his reach. Guy staggered away from the gaming table and found a quiet place to bed down. He needed sleep, but when he closed his eyes, all his saw was Kate's beautiful face and a basketful of severed heads.

Chapter 48

September 1464

Berwick-upon-Tweed, Northumberland

Kate stepped outside and turned her face up to the sun. It wasn't becoming for a woman to have a sun-tinted face, but she allowed herself a few moments on sunny days, just to enjoy the warmth on her skin. She tried to take a walk every day after breakfast, even on stormy days, desperate to get away from the keep, and from Hugh. She no longer walked toward the castle, and hadn't done so in years since the castle warden held it in the name of Lancaster and she suffered harassment when encountering the inhabitants. The north was still largely Lancastrian, except for pockets of Yorkist support, so Kate had to be mindful of where she went. Normally, she headed toward the woods, which were safe enough if one didn't encounter any poachers. She only wished to be alone so she could drop the façade of contentment and allow her true emotions to surface.

She was glad Guy was gone. She missed him sorely, and longed to hear his voice and confide in him, but the situation with Hugh would cause friction between the brothers, and she never wanted to come between them. Hugh had grown more abusive since the day he'd slapped her in their bed. Gone were the tender words and courtly manners. Something had snapped inside him when he learned of Gerard Dancy's marriage, and his fury was directed at Kate.

Some men didn't deal well with disappointed hopes, and Hugh was one to dwell on his failings. He'd given his forty days per year service to Lord Chadwick, but chose not to fight a single day more. Instead, he spent his time on the estate, trying valiantly to increase output and raise rents to generate more income. The Earl of Stanwyck had granted Hugh a tract of land for his service, a gesture which Hugh deserved, and greatly valued. The land had been mostly forest, but Hugh had commandeered men from the estate to clear the trees once the harvest was in and they could be spared for several hours a day. Now the land was being farmed, and there were several new tenants, which had lifted Hugh's spirits—until his gaze fell on his wife, who had yet to conceive.

Kate's heart nearly broke when she saw Hugh with Adam, who was nearly eight. Adam was a fine boy, and resembled his uncles in coloring despite his mother's fairness. Hugh poured all his affection into the boy, spending hours teaching him how to handle his sword and playing chess in the evenings. Adam needed a father figure, and Hugh desperately wanted a son. Hugh was always solicitous and courteous to Eleanor, who had recovered from her grief and regained her beauty. Eleanor was only twenty-five and still marriageable, but Kate could see that Hugh dreaded the idea of Eleanor remarrying because he feared losing his home and the income from the estate. He'd held on to the monies he'd received for Kate's dowry, fearful of spending the lot should he find himself dispossessed.

Kate could understand his fear and his resentment, which made her respect him all the more for the affection and attention he showed the boy who would one day leave him with nothing, and to the boy's mother. It wasn't until a few months ago that Kate had begun to suspect that Hugh might harbor more than brotherly love for Eleanor, but she tried to suppress the gnawing unease in her gut and told herself he was just being kind to his brother's widow. But Eleanor was beautiful, and Hugh was displeased with his wife, more so every day, so it stood to reason that his attention would turn to the only other woman who was there, pouting and acting as coy as a young bride in his presence.

Kate sat down on a tree stump to rest and sighed with irritation. Eleanor had never become the friend and confidante Kate had hoped for, but would Eleanor really try to come between Kate and Hugh in her desperation? She was lonely, she'd admitted that, but would she take Hugh as a lover if the opportunity presented itself? Kate suddenly realized that the possibility didn't distress her as much as she'd thought it might. At least if Eleanor took Hugh to her bed, he might leave Kate alone, a prospect that wasn't at all displeasing given his treatment of her of late.

Kate got to her feet and began to walk back toward the keep. The bright sunshine of earlier had dissipated and storm clouds were rolling in, signaling another dark and cold day within the walls of the keep. Kate hurried her steps as the first drops of rain plopped on her nose and cheeks and began to spot the fabric of her gown.

She saw Hugh hurrying inside just as she came through the gate. His hand was on the small of Eleanor's back, and the two of them were laughing and carrying on like they didn't have a care in the world. For a brief moment, Kate thought they looked right together.

Chapter 49

August 2014

London, England

Gabe splashed whisky into his glass and sat down on the sofa. The television was on mute, the constant stream of colorful images going unnoticed as he stared into space. Quinn and Emma were already asleep, but although he was physically tired, his mind was going a mile a minute, too restless to settle on any one problem. He needed to talk to someone, and normally, he'd talk to Quinn, but she was already tense and upset and he didn't want to add to her mounting stress. He knew he was driving her mad with his overprotectiveness, but he couldn't help himself. He was scared. He had to physically restrain himself from dashing to the bathroom for the heart-pressure monitor every time she looked flushed or appeared to be agitated, and now her ankles were swelling and she was often short of breath.

Gabe had also noticed Quinn peering at things as if she couldn't see clearly, and extracted a promise that she would inform Dr. Malik of this new development at the next antenatal checkup. He wasn't someone who prayed routinely, but since finding Quinn unconscious in that vault in New Orleans, he'd prayed for her and their baby's well-being almost daily. Liver and renal failure weren't common, but they did happen in mothers with severe preeclampsia, and although most symptoms disappeared after the delivery, in some cases, they continued after the pregnancy and required continued treatment.

Gabe glanced at the clock. It'd just gone ten, so his mother would still be awake. He tossed back the whisky, grabbed his mobile and keys, and left the flat. He'd talk to his mother and take a walk—two birds with one stone.

"Hello, son," Phoebe said when she answered on the second ring. "No, you didn't wake me," she added before Gabe could ask.

"Hi, Mum. How are you? Plumbing all right?"

"Yes, the water is running clear and the hole in the kitchen has been filled in and retiled. I still can't bring myself to step on that part of the floor. I feel like I'm walking over someone's grave."

"Well, you sort of are, but it's empty now, so you'll have to get used to it, I suppose. Are you keeping busy?"

"I'm trying," Gabe could envision the downward curve of her mouth and the sagging of her shoulders as she replied. "The house feels so empty without your father."

"Are you eating?"

"Yes, but I've no desire to cook anything, not when there's no one to eat it with. I eat toast and eggs, mostly. That suits me fine."

"Mum! You can't subsist on eggs."

"They're a good source of protein," Phoebe objected. "And they are quick and easy to make. What's the sense of doing a Sunday roast or making chops for one person?"

"We're going to feed you up while you're here," Gabe promised. "I can't wait to see you, Mum."

"Gabe, are you all right? What's on your mind?"

"Why do you think there's anything on my mind?" Gabe asked, a smile tugging at his lips. She always knew.

"Because you sound particularly downtrodden tonight. I can hear it in your voice."

"I'm just tired," Gabe replied. "And frustrated."

"With what?"

Gabe quickly filled Phoebe in on what'd been going on with Quinn. Phoebe listened intently, not saying anything until Gabe finished.

"Gabe, it's only natural that Quinn should want to find her sister and feel angry with Sylvia for withholding such crucial information."

"I know that, Mum, but I'm worried about her. Her blood pressure is spiking, she has terrible headaches, sometimes her vision gets blurry, and her ankles are swollen. She should be taking it easy, not obsessing about the mess her mother made thirty years ago. And she gets really angry with me when I fuss," Gabe added grumpily.

"I know and you know the only reason you fuss is because you're worried about Quinn and the baby, but it probably makes her feel like an errant child. Quinn is a grown woman, and she would do anything to protect that baby. If she tells you she feels up to doing something, then you must take her at her word."

"So you think I'm being overbearing?"

"I wouldn't go as far as to call you overbearing, but I'd say maybe a little over the top. I know you're worried, son, but you must trust your wife's judgement."

"You always put me straight," Gabe replied with a chuckle.

"That's what mothers are for, dear. Now, what else is bothering you? That was just the tip of the iceberg," Phoebe said. Gabe heard her sigh as she usually did when snuggling deeper into her favorite chair.

"Mum, I've been offered a promotion at work, and a significant pay raise. I've been invited to sit on the Board of Directors."

Phoebe didn't immediately reply, as though processing what he'd said and drawing her own conclusions. "Darling, you don't need to move up here. I know you want to be here for me, and you feel it's your duty to look after your old mum, but I won't have you doing so at the expense of your life. You have a successful career in London, as does Quinn. Emma loves it there and is about to start school. You have friends, and Quinn has her brothers. I won't have you uprooting everyone just to make me happy."

"But I want you to be happy, Mum," Gabe said, sounding like a whiny child.

"Gabe, I'm happy knowing you're happy. As it happens, I've been thinking about the house. I don't like being here on my own. It just doesn't feel like home anymore. When your father died, it was lonely at first, but now, after the discovery in the kitchen, it feels sinister somehow."

"What are you saying, Mum?"

"I'm saying I wouldn't be averse to a place like Cecily's."

"You mean at the retirement village?" Gabe asked, perking up.

"Those cottages have everything a person my age needs. There are no endless flights of stairs, there's a little garden, and there are loads of people my age. And they have activities. I can take up watercolor painting or do Pilates."

"Do you even know what that is?"

"Don't patronize me, son. I might not be overly active now, but I was quite athletic in my day. Your father always said I had stunning legs."

"And he'd know," Gabe joked. Graham Russell had adored his wife, but he'd always noticed pretty women, especially those that were fit. "Mum, I think that would be ideal," he said, suddenly more hopeful about the future.

"It would, but I can't bring myself to sell the family home. Some big developer is going to come in and build luxury flats, or something equally ghastly. The land has been in the Russell family for centuries. It's your children's legacy."

"Mum, unless Quinn and I move to Berwick and spend a fortune restoring the family home, it will be a ruin by the time my children are old enough to understand what a legacy is. We have to either go all in, or let it go out of the family, and the choice is yours."

"Gabriel, you're a historian, for the love of God. How can you feel no connection to the land of your ancestors?" Phoebe exclaimed.

"I do feel a connection to the place, but uprooting my family and playing 'lord of the crumbling manor' is not my life's plan."

"That's it then," Phoebe conceded. "I'll call an estate agent after I return from London. We'll sell the house and land, pay the death duties, and use the remaining funds to buy me a cottage at the retirement village and you a bigger flat in London."

"Are you sure you're all right with that, Mum?"

"Your father is probably spinning in his grave, but yes, I'm all right with it. There's no use holding on to the past if the past has no hold over you."

"It'll be better for everyone. You'll see."

"I've no doubt of that. I just feel a little guilty, that's all."

"I know. I do too. Who's going to look after Buster when you come down for Emma's birthday?"

"I'll leave him with Cecily for a few days. I'm actually looking forward to visiting London. It's been too long. I'd like to go to the National Gallery, and maybe see a show."

"I'll get tickets. Is there anything specific you'd like to see?"

"I'd like to see *King Charles III*. I heard great things about it," Phoebe replied.

"Consider it done."

"Thank you, son. And plan something romantic for you and Quinn. You two can use a night out. I'll be happy to mind Emma."

"Quinn would like that. Goodnight, Mum."

Gabe disconnected the call and turned for home. He did feel better after talking to his mother, but a nagging sense of guilt gnawed at his insides. His mother was right; Graham Russell would be spinning in his grave if he knew. Gabe sighed. Moving up north would accomplish one thing that staying in London wouldn't: it would get Quinn away from Luke once and for all.

Chapter 50

November 1464

Westminster Palace, London

The rain fell in sheets, soaking everything in its path and leaching every bit of daylight from the rooms. Braces of candles were lit despite the early hour, and a fire burned in every grate, adding a bit of coziness, but not nearly enough heat to warm the chambers.

Guy and Sir Anthony Hayes, one of Warwick's most trusted knights, stood guard at the antechamber on Warwick's orders, doing their best to look bland and disinterested in what was happening inside as the earl's voice thundered from behind closed doors. Warwick didn't bother to hide his displeasure at being thwarted, and anyone who passed close enough to the door could hear exactly what was being said. All Guy and Anthony could do to protect the earl's privacy was advise the passersby to move on and not linger in an ill-disguised attempt to hear more.

Guy had arrived at Westminster Palace a few weeks ago as part of Warwick's retinue. The earl had recently returned from abroad, having been involved in negotiations with France regarding a bride for King Edward. The object of the discussions was Bona, the daughter of Louis, the Duke of Savoy, and the sister-in-law of King Louis XI. Pleased with the outcome of the proceedings, the earl had been eager to share the news with Edward.

The ride from Middleham had been a merry one, with the earl regaling his escorts with stories of the French court and enjoying the journey as they passed through peaceful villages and sleepy hamlets. Warwick had appeared not only happier, but healthier. He'd looked gaunt and tired after the siege of Norham Castle and the subsequent foray into Scotland, but after weeks of being wined and dined by the French, he'd seemed more his old self, bursting with vitality and brimming with self-importance. That had been before he found out on his arrival in Westminster that he'd been negotiating on behalf of a bridegroom who was already wed.

"Who does he think he is?" Warwick roared from the antechamber, addressing his brother, George Neville, the Bishop of Exeter. "A monarch does not marry on a whim, and in secret! Elizabeth Woodville is a beauty, no one is contesting that, but he could have simply bedded her, or even set her up as his mistress if he's so smitten. He could have fucked her until he tired of her—and he will tire of her—while still doing his duty to the Crown. He didn't have to marry the wench, by God! Think of it," Warwick continued, his ire not having diminished an iota since learning of the marriage several weeks ago. "A Lancastrian widow, with two children, who's of advanced years, and comes from a long line of no one of consequence. What was he thinking?" Warwick's voice growled like distant thunder, too far away to do any damage, but still threatening.

"She bewitched him," the bishop replied in a calmer tone. "There's talk about her, and her mother too. Powerful witches, both of them."

"I've heard the gossip, George, but nothing that can be proven," Warwick replied with disgust. "There's no evidence of witchcraft. I've searched."

"Edward married her. Isn't that proof enough of her sorcery?"

"Not the sort that can stand up before a court," Warwick snapped. "Even the emasculated relics who make up the ecclesiastical court know the difference between sorcery and lust. I've no doubt they felt the stirring of it once or twice."

"Come now, Dick. Sometimes an accusation is enough, you know that as well as I do," his brother replied. "Once an idea is planted, it takes root."

308

"Edward won't listen. He's besotted. He's always liked a pretty face, but this is the most irresponsible thing he's ever done. To marry for love!" Warwick raged. "Men like us don't marry where our hearts take us. We do our duty, we advance the interests of our family, we think with our heads and not our cocks. If every nobleman in England married for love, where would we be?"

Happy? Guy thought sourly. He had no business passing judgment on his sovereign, but he envied the man. Edward was clearly in love with his queen, and she returned his affections. The two of them glowed in each other's presence, like twin flames reflected in a dark pool. Where there was love like that, children followed. That was the consequence of desire, genuine desire, the kind that quickened the heart and stirred the blood. Elizabeth Woodville didn't just do her duty by her lord, she relished it; it was obvious. Guy had never seen a married woman who looked so sensual, so eager. It was all right there in her eyes, in the way her lips parted when she gazed upon her lord, and the way she arched her back, making her breasts appear bigger and rounder. She made no attempt to hide her desire, and Edward preened and strutted when she was around, glorying in her love and stoking her passion.

What would it feel like to be that happy, to be loved and to be able to return that love openly and honestly? Even Warwick, who raged against Edward's choice of bride, knew love. His countess adored him, and waited for his return like a blushing new bride. Her gaze followed her husband about the room, and if he happened to glance her way or bestow her with an absentminded smile, she glowed like the moon, her joy at his attention obvious. Warwick had not married for love, but he did care for his wife. He had a devoted woman to come home to, a woman who cloaked him in her love and saw to his every need, and he was shrewd enough to appreciate that.

Warwick's voice rose again, his anger not yet waning. "George, if I don't find a way to end this marriage soon, it'll be too late. Once she gets with child, he'll never let her go. And if she has a boy…"

"She might be with child already. She's proven herself to be fertile."

"That's what I'm afraid of."

The bishop sighed with impatience. "If she has a son, the succession is assured, and if she bears a daughter, Edward might still be persuaded to put her aside and marry elsewhere. Bide your time, brother. Edward needs you. He needs your support. You are the 'Kingmaker'. He might have strayed, but he'll always remember what you've done for him. Accept this situation and find a way to turn it to your advantage."

Warwick's reply was softer, more reasonable. "I plan to. I made him a king, and I can just as easily unmake him if he humiliates me like that again."

"Careful there, Dick. Careful," the bishop advised him in a soothing tone. "You were always quick to anger, but we can still benefit from this. You can benefit from this."

"Well, you know what the price of my allegiance is, George, and it had best get paid in full."

Guy and Anthony stood to attention as Warwick strode past them with a brief nod of acknowledgment. The bishop followed, his robes billowing behind him in the draft from the nearest window.

"Let's go find some wine," Sir Anthony suggested. "We're no longer needed here."

Guy followed Anthony, who had a nose for food and drink and always managed to get them fed and watered.

"I do hope we remain at Westminster for a while," Sir Anthony said as he settled himself before a fire in one of the salons and called for refreshments. "I like it here."

"Why?" Guy asked.

"Because it beats traipsing through mud and eating gruel in the barren fields of Godforsaken Scotland, or putting down rebellions and starving the enemy, and ourselves, in the equally inhospitable north. Here, there is ample food, lovely women, and endless intrigue. I'm in heaven." He sighed theatrically.

"I'm from the north," Guy retorted, offended.

"I know, Guy, but you're slightly less savage than some other Northumbrians I know. You're almost good company." Anthony chuckled and slapped Guy on the back. "I'd like to skulk here long enough to discover what our diabolical earl has in store for the comely Elizabeth Woodville."

Guy accepted a cup of wine from a serving wench and stared into the leaping flames. He stretched his feet out toward the hearth and took a long pull of wine while Anthony flirted with the girl, plying her with compliments and making her blush prettily. Anthony was bent on seduction, and Guy wasn't about to interrupt, given that the girl seemed to enjoy Anthony's attentions. Instead, Guy pondered what Anthony had said.

Diabolical. Surely Anthony was judging the earl too harshly. Guy liked and respected the man, and had seen for himself how much Warwick had sacrificed to keep Edward firmly on the throne. He'd worked tirelessly for the king, only to find himself deceived and humiliated by the very man he'd trusted. Edward had wed Elizabeth Woodville at the beginning of May, but kept the marriage a secret for nearly six months, allowing his cousin to negotiate on his behalf and make promises that could no longer be honored. Warwick felt a fool, and he wasn't a man who'd tolerate being made a laughingstock. The palace was rife with tension, the halls devoid of laughter and gossip, at least when Warwick was around.

Anthony might enjoy the politicking, but Guy wanted no part of the scheming that went on every day, behind nearly every door. He suddenly missed home with an ache that pierced his heart. He missed the cold, inhospitable north, and he missed his family, even Hugh. His year in Warwick's service was almost up. Perhaps it was time to return home.

Chapter 51

August 2014

London, England

Sun streamed through the window, falling on Emma's princess bed linens and caressing Mr. Rabbit's face. He looked forlorn sitting there on the bed, waiting for Emma to return from school.

Quinn reached for the bunny and stroked his long ears. How long would it be before Emma outgrew her favorite toy and began to take an interest in more 'big girl' things? Brenda, who had two teenage sons, said that turning five had been the turning point for her boys, a time when they'd begun to leave babyish things behind and long for more grown-up toys and activities. Would it be the same for Emma? The thought made Quinn melancholy. She wished she'd known Emma when she was a baby, and then a toddler. She'd missed out on all the sweet things that came with babyhood. Of course, she'd never have wished for Emma to lose her mother sooner, but had Jenna been honest with Gabe, he'd have become a dad a lot sooner, and Quinn would have known Emma, if not had the chance to raise her.

As she replaced the rabbit on the bed and finished putting away Emma's clean clothes, Quinn wondered if Emma would be jealous of the new baby. Would she act out, or would she love her sibling and feel lucky to have a brother or a sister? Quinn had longed for a sibling all her life. Funny that now that she had three, or four if you counted Quentin, she didn't feel any of the joy and camaraderie she'd thought she would—but then again, she hadn't grown up with any of them, so perhaps it was too late to establish that sort of bond.

Quinn closed the drawer and let herself out of the room. She headed to the kitchen for a glass of water. She had to remind herself to drink enough during the day since Gabe wasn't there to shove a glass in her hand every few hours. She smiled. Gabe fussed over her like a mother hen, and when she didn't want to throttle him, she liked it.

Quinn poured herself a glass of mineral water and added a slice of lemon. A bit of vitamin C couldn't hurt. Her mobile began to vibrate on the counter. It was Logan. She set the glass down, afraid to spill her drink. Her hand shook with trepidation as she reached for the phone. Logan had promised to call once he and Colin left Leicester, and as it was already late afternoon, this had to be the call she had been waiting for.

"Logan. At last. Any joy?" Quinn asked. She took her mineral water, walked over to the kitchen table, and sat down.

"Yes and no," Logan replied. He sounded pleased, so she let him talk. "Colin is driving, so I'll give you the rundown. The files are still stored on site, albeit in the cellar. Colin had no difficulty gaining access once he showed his identification and explained the situation. Finding the file proved to be the difficult part. I wasn't allowed in, obviously, so Colin had to go it alone, poor dear," he said, and Quinn could hear him smiling. "The records are filed alphabetically, and since Quentin didn't have a surname at the time of admittance, it took some doing. Colin had to go through all the files for 1983 before he found it. It was filed under 'X', as in 'Quentin X'."

"So, what did it say?" Quinn asked, breathless with anticipation.

"Baby Q had surgery on October first, 1983. Colin says the surgery went well and there were no complications. She was discharged from hospital on October sixteenth into the care of Mrs. McGee. As luck would have it, Mrs. McGee still resides at the same address, so Colin and I paid her a visit. Lovely old girl," Logan added. "She and the late Mr. McGee fostered dozens of children in the eighties and nineties, and she still keeps in touch with most of them."

Quinn sighed with relief. It was nice to know Quentin had been looked after by someone caring. Foster children wouldn't bother to stay in touch with someone who'd been unkind to them, or treated them as a nuisance. "How long did Quentin stay with Mrs. McGee?"

"Not long. About two months."

"Where did she go after that?" Quinn asked. Two months seemed like a very short time to stay with a foster family. Adoption was a lengthy process.

"You are going to love this," Logan said as he drew out the suspense. "Quentin was adopted by Dr. Ian Crawford, the very man who operated on her. The adoption went through very quickly, because, let's face it, what better home could this child have asked for?"

"That's very fortunate," Quinn exclaimed. "So, we are looking for Quentin Crawford?"

"Well, that's where things get a bit muddled, love," Logan replied, obviously getting to the not-so-successful part of the story. "We looked up Dr. Crawford and found that he's deceased. Died two years ago at the age of eighty-three. The obituary mentioned his children, Michael and Karen, who both happen to be doctors. We found them online, and even if Quentin became Michael—which could happen, you know—or if her parents changed her name to Karen, neither one is the right age. They are both in their late forties."

"And there are no listings for Quentin Crawford?" Quinn asked, her heart sinking.

"Sorry, no. They might have renamed her, of course," Logan suggested. "There are other Crawfords in Leicester, but we didn't have time to look them all up. I think your best bet would be to contact Michael and Karen Crawford and find out what happened to their sister."

"Thank you, Logan, and give my love to Colin. You guys are the best."

"It was our pleasure, sis. After all, she's my sister too. I'll gladly come with you to speak to the Crawfords when you're ready."

"I'd like that," Quinn replied. She ended the call and propped her cheek with her hand while she mulled over what Logan had said. She supposed the expedition to Leicester had gone as well as could be expected. Logan and Colin had found out more than she would have ever discovered on her own. *Rome wasn't built in a day*, Quinn thought to herself, smiling at the saying.

So far, they'd laid the foundation. Quentin had had a successful surgery, had spent time in foster care—evidence of her well-being—and had then been adopted by a prominent surgeon. It was highly possible that the Crawfords had decided to choose a different name, unlike Quinn's own parents who'd retained Quinn's birth name. Perhaps they'd worried that Quentin's mother would return for her and wanted to leave no trail to follow. They had no way of knowing that Sylvia never attempted to look for her daughters.

Quinn took a sip of her mineral water and leaned back in her chair, feeling more relaxed than she'd felt since finding out about her twin. Quentin was out there somewhere, and they would find her.

She vacated her chair when she heard the scrape of a key in the lock. Gabe and Emma were home. Emma's birthday party was next weekend, but this weekend they were free.

Quinn gave Emma a hug and kissed Gabe, wrapping her arms about his neck and smiling into his eyes. "Fancy a ride to Leicester tomorrow?" she purred.

"Not really, but I know you won't give me a moment's peace until we go, so yeah, sure." He kissed her soundly and held her close. "Fill me in over dinner. I'm starving. Didn't have time for lunch today," he explained as he loosened his tie.

"Why are we going to Leicester?" Emma asked, looking up at the two of them, her eyes round with curiosity. "Does it have anything to do with my birthday?"

"No, darling," Quinn replied, "but it does have something to do with mine."

Emma exhaled loudly in disappointment. "I still want a puppy, you know," she reminded them before going to wash her hands.

"We know," Gabe and Quinn replied in unison.

Chapter 52

August 2014

Leicester, Leicestershire

The sunshine of the previous day had given way to pissing rain, making the drive to Leicester less than picturesque. Emma was huddled in her child seat, disgruntled at having to go on this boring expedition the weekend before her party instead of shopping for a new frock and picking out party favors. Quinn had promised her they would do all that tomorrow, but Emma was determined to sulk. Gabe hardly spoke on the drive, no doubt worrying about the outcome of their enquiry. Regardless of what they discovered today, the search was just beginning, and wouldn't end until Quinn found her sister.

Only Logan was chipper as ever, prattling on about his job and making funny faces at Emma to cajole her out of her bad mood. He'd instantly agreed to come back to Leicester when Quinn texted him, but made excuses for Colin, saying his boyfriend had plans with his mum. Quinn was grateful to Logan for his support and his cheer, particularly because they were genuine.

"Are you not rattled by any of this?" Quinn had asked when they spoke last night.

"Nope. Why should I be?"

"Quentin is your sister too, as you pointed out earlier."

"If we find her, I'll be thrilled to meet her and get to know her. But if we don't, I'll go on with my life as before. I can't feel a sense of loss over someone I've never met."

"But what about your mother?" Quinn had persisted. "Will this not change your relationship with her?"

"Not in the least," Logan had replied. "She did what she did. Period. What's the point of judging her now, thirty-one years after the fact? She's my mother, and my mother she will remain. It's different for me, Quinn. She never abandoned me. She loved me and raised me, regardless of what she'd done in the past. I understand how you feel about her, and I won't like you any less if you never want to speak to her again."

"Really? You won't resent me?"

"Not in the least."

"What about Jude?"

"What about him?" Logan had asked.

"Does he know about Quentin? Does he care? Does he have any thoughts on my relationship with Sylvia?"

"Jude doesn't know. Mum didn't tell him, and I saw no reason to apprise him of the situation. Jude has his own demons to battle, as I'm sure you know. Once we find Quentin, I'll fill him in. As far as you and Mum go, I don't think he cares one way or another. Jude's too self-absorbed to give either of you much thought."

Put like that, Quinn had felt more at ease. She hadn't spoken to Sylvia and she owed Jude no phone call. If Logan didn't find it necessary to tell him about Quentin, then she had no business calling him either. She would call Seth though, after they returned from Leicester.

The rain tapered off as they approached Leicester and the sun eventually came out, drying out the sidewalks and sparkling on the still-wet grass and leaves. Everything looked more cheerful and welcoming in the sunlight, but the modern office building where Dr. Karen Crawford had her surgery was gray and unwelcoming, the type of structure that could house anything from a school to a detention facility.

Gabe rolled into a parking space out front. It was Saturday afternoon, but Dr. Crawford had office hours, and Quinn had made an appointment first thing that morning. The doctor might have no time to speak to her, but with a half-hour appointment booked, she'd have no excuse.

Quinn turned and gave Logan a weak smile.

"Are you ready?" he asked.

"I'd better be," she replied. "I am nervous though."

"Me too," Logan confessed. "I hope she'll be amenable to answering a few questions."

"There's a playground two streets over," Gabe said. "Emma and I will wait for you there. Good luck, you two."

"Thank you, darling," Quinn said, and kissed Gabe's cheek before she got out of the car.

"See you later, Quinn," Emma called out. "Bye, Logan."

"Bye, princess," Logan said and high-fived her.

Gabe helped Emma out of her child seat and they set off for the playground while Quinn and Logan entered the building and took the lift to the third floor. The reception area was pleasant, with several potted plants and leather sofas in dove-gray for the waiting patients. Modern prints hung on the walls, adding a splash of color to the otherwise colorless room. Two receptionists sat behind a glass partition, their gazes fixed on computer screens.

"Sure you want to do this?" Logan asked as he took a seat on the sofa after they checked in at reception.

"Of course. Aren't you?"

"I am, but to be honest, I wish I didn't know these things about my mother. As much as I want to believe that nothing's changed, it has. I realized that last night after speaking to you. I'm grateful to have you in my life, and I hope to get to know Quentin, but I can no longer trust my mother unquestioningly as I did before. I keep wondering about the sort of woman she is, what else she might be withholding, and how much my dad knew. For a while there, I rooted for her and Rhys to make a go of it, but now I see that it would never have worked. Deep down, he doesn't trust her either, and he's beginning to question the accusation of rape she'd leveled at him."

"I'm sorry, Logan. I really am. I'm still trying to come to terms with the woman she is. Sylvia is not at all the mother I envisioned."

"No, I don't suppose she is. Come on. Let's get this over with," Logan said as a nurse called Quinn's name and led them down a narrow corridor to an examining room.

"I'd actually just like to talk to Dr. Crawford," Quinn told the nurse. "Perhaps we can speak in her office."

The nurse looked surprised, but acquiesced to Quinn's request. Quinn and Logan exchanged nervous smiles as they headed toward the doctor's office.

Karen Crawford looked up from a file she was perusing and smiled in welcome. "Please, have a seat."

Dr. Crawford styled her hair in a chic blond bob and wore perfectly applied makeup. Beneath her white lab coat was a smart silk blouse in an unusual shade of blue-gray that exactly matched the doctor's eyes. She was a woman who took pride in her appearance.

"How can I help you today?" she asked pleasantly, assuming an air of someone who couldn't wait to hear what the other person had to say.

"Dr. Crawford, my name is Quinn Russell, and this is my brother, Logan Wyatt. Nearly thirty-one years ago I was abandoned at Leicester Cathedral by my birth mother. A few weeks ago, I discovered, quite by chance, that I'm actually a twin, and that my sister, Quentin, had been left at the Royal Infirmary on the same day. I believe you know who I'm referring to."

Dr. Crawford's eyes grew round and she studied Quinn more openly, no doubt searching for a resemblance to her twin. She was silent for a few moments, then nodded, her unblinking gaze still fixed on Quinn. Her face underwent a series of expressions, ranging from surprise to sadness, and eventually to something that might have been a grimace of contrition.

Quinn's heartrate accelerated as she waited for the doctor to speak. What she said, however, wasn't quite what Quinn had expected.

"Are you currently on blood pressure medication?" Dr. Crawford asked. She came around the desk and reached for a blood pressure cuff on a nearby shelf. "May I?"

"Why?" Quinn asked, annoyed.

"You're a pregnant woman whose blood pressure just spiked in front of my eyes. Before I answer your questions, which I will do gladly, I must make sure you are well enough to have this conversation and your child isn't in any danger."

"I'm fine," Quinn retorted. "I'm just nervous."

"That's understandable. Slightly elevated," Dr. Crawford said as she took off the cuff and sat back down. "Can I get you a cup of tea?"

"Yes, please," Quinn replied, defeated. Everyone felt the need to mother her and it annoyed her to no end.

Dr. Crawford rang reception and asked for some tea, then turned back to Quinn and Logan. "I'm sorry for the delay, but I am a doctor, first and foremost."

"Understood," Quinn replied. "Now, please tell us about Quentin."

"What would you like to know?"

"Everything," Quinn replied. "You must recall the adoption, having been a teenager at the time."

"Yes, I do. It was an odd time for my family."

"How so?" Logan asked.

The receptionist brought it a tray loaded with three cups of tea, a jug of milk, and a sugar bowl. Quinn added a splash of milk to hers and took a sip. It did calm her and allowed Dr. Crawford a moment to compose herself while she made her own tea. She took a sip, then set the cup down, ready to explain.

"When Quentin was discovered in the emergency area of the Royal Infirmary she was in a bad state. She had difficulty breathing caused by a severe heart murmur. She might not have survived had her mother not brought her to the hospital when she did. My father fell in love with that little girl the moment he saw her, or more accurately, he fell in love with the idea of being her savior," she added bitterly. "You see, my dad, God rest his soul, loved attention and publicity, and adopting an abandoned little girl whose life he'd saved was the jewel in the crown of his achievements. He was enamored of the idea."

"Are you saying it was all a publicity stunt?" Logan asked.

"Not a conscious one, but if you knew my dad, you'd understand."

"What about your mother? How did she feel about adopting Quentin?" Quinn asked.

"My mother was nearly fifty when Quentin came into her life. She'd raised her children, supported her husband's career for nearly thirty years, and had been looking forward to some time to herself, to enjoy life. She thought Dad would scale back his hours and they would travel, or take up a new hobby. They both enjoyed golf, and Mum had this idea of visiting some of the world's most famous golf resorts. She had no desire to start all over again at her age, but once my father made the announcement to the press, she could hardly refuse. It would have made Dad look bad."

"Had he not consulted her?" Quinn asked, shocked.

"Not really. My father never consulted anyone. He presented them with a situation that they had no choice but to deal with. So, Mum did what she did best. She dealt."

"How?"

"She hired a nanny. She just wasn't up to taking care of a newborn. Sleepless nights, teething, daily trips to the playground; she was past all that. She was very much involved, but more in a managerial capacity. The nannies did all the hands-on work."

"Nannies?" Logan asked.

"Yes, there were several."

"So your mother never made peace with your father's decision to adopt Quentin," Quinn interjected.

"No, she didn't. She cared for Quentin deeply, as did my father, but adopting her had been an impulsive decision that near tore our family apart. My brother and I were ready to go off to uni. We resented Dad for springing this new sibling on us and couldn't wait to leave, which we did as soon as we could. Michael went first, and then I left home a year later. We saw Quentin when we came home, but we never developed a close relationship with her. At the time, she seemed to us to be an interloper in our family. Of course, we were young and selfish, and focused only on our own needs."

"So, what happened?" Quinn asked. She noticed that Karen spoke of Quentin only in the past tense. She hadn't mentioned any current feelings or circumstances.

"Mum died just after Quentin turned seventeen. She'd been ill for some time, and spent the last few months of her life in hospice care. Quentin had been planning on going to university, but suddenly changed her mind. She asked Dad for a sum of money, which he gladly gave her, out of guilt I presume, and took off. We haven't seen her since. She didn't even come for Dad's funeral."

"Are you in touch with her?" Quinn asked.

"No."

"So how would she know about the funeral?" Logan asked.

"She would have found out through our solicitor. Dad arranged for a very healthy trust fund for Quentin. She would never need to work if she had no wish to."

"Does she?" Logan asked.

"No idea. Like I said, we haven't seen her since she was seventeen."

"And you're okay with that?" Quinn asked, her blood pressure rising again.

"No, I'm not, and neither is Michael. We were beastly to her, and we feel awful about that. We tried reaching out to her over the years, but she never replied."

"Do you know if she's well?" Quinn demanded.

"As far as we know, she's all right. I'm sorry I couldn't be of more help. Seeing you brought it all back," she said, blowing her nose delicately on a tissue.

"May I ask you one more question?" Quinn's heartrate increased and she held her breath without realizing it. "Are we identical?" Karen would know the answer to the question that had been plaguing her since she found out about her twin.

"No, but you look very much alike. Seeing you was a shock."

"Can you give us the details for the solicitor?" Logan asked.

"Of course. He's right here in Leicester. Would you like me to call him for you? He's not in the office on Saturdays, but I believe he'd see you as a favor to me."

"We would greatly appreciate that," Quinn replied coolly. She had nothing more to say to this woman who'd been so selfish and unfeeling toward an innocent child and a neglected teenager. It seemed that Quentin's life hadn't been nearly as charmed as they'd first assumed.

Dr. Crawford pulled out her mobile and made the call. She spoke to the solicitor and turned to Quinn and Logan. "He can see you in a half hour. Here's the address. His name is Louis Richards."

"Thank you for your time," Quinn said as she got up to leave. She heard the disdain in her voice, but didn't care. She'd never see this woman again.

"Cheers," Logan said as he followed Quinn out the door. "God, what a cow," he said as soon as they exited into the street. "I wouldn't want to keep in contact with her either. I bet she'll still charge the NHS for the appointment. After all, she took your blood pressure, didn't she? What is it, Quinny?" he asked, noticing her pained expression.

"For years, I agonized about finding my birth parents instead of appreciating the wonderful parents I had. I see now how foolish and selfish I've been, especially since Quentin wasn't as lucky."

"Quinn, don't beat yourself up. You're only human, although Saint Quinn does have a nice ring to it," he said with a wicked smile. "We all need to know where we came from, even if our origins are not very exciting."

"But I was wanted and loved. It seems that no one really wanted Quentin."

"Still, I'm sure she had a better life than most unwanted children. I wouldn't say no to a trust fund myself," Logan added.

Quinn ignored his flippancy and reached for her mobile to call Gabe. The solicitor's office was within walking distance, so there was no sense in Gabe interrupting Emma's play time.

"Gabe, we'll meet you at the playground as soon as we're done. I don't imagine it will take long. I'll fill you in later," Quinn assured him. "All right, Logan. Let's go."

She didn't protest when Logan wrapped his arm casually about her shoulders. He didn't say anything, but she appreciated the gesture of support. What they'd learned so far upset her, and she didn't hold out any great hope for their interview with the lawyer. Solicitors were notoriously tight-lipped, so Quinn didn't imagine he'd tell them much.

Logan pulled her close and lightly kissed her temple, nearly making her cry.

Chapter 53

It took Quinn and Logan less than a quarter of an hour to reach the address Dr. Crawford had given them. On the ground floor, a discreet brass plaque by the door announced the offices of Richards and Saunders, Esqs. Logan rang the bell, since the door was locked, and they were buzzed through. It being a Saturday, there was no receptionist at the front desk. The office was quiet and dim, the lamps not having been lit in the reception area.

A nondescript-looking man in his early fifties came out to greet them. He was dressed casually, like someone who'd been enjoying a Saturday afternoon at home when he was rudely interrupted and yanked into the office.

"We're sorry to have disturbed your weekend," Quinn said as she accepted a seat opposite the massive mahogany desk in Mr. Richards' office.

"It's no trouble, Mrs. Russell. It's not every day that I get this type of phone call," Mr. Richards said, smiling kindly at Quinn and Logan. "How shocking this must have been for you both. May I ask how you came to learn about Quentin?"

"Yes. Reverend Alan Seaton of Leicester Cathedral told me there'd been another baby, left at a different location on the morning he found me in his church. My birth mother confirmed that she'd given birth to twins the night before and had taken my sister to a hospital."

"That is quite correct. You do look like Quentin," he added with a wistful smile.

"So you know her well?"

"Well enough. Her father and my father were great friends—golfing buddies. I'd known Dr. Crawford all my life, so by extension, I knew Quentin since the day Ian decided to adopt her."

"Did you handle the adoption?" Quinn asked.

"My father did. I was still a student in those days. It went through very quickly, if I recall correctly."

"Mr. Richards, where is Quentin?" Quinn asked, hearing the blood rushing in her ears. She was excited, nervous, and apprehensive all at once.

"Mrs. Russell, I am not at liberty to disclose personal information about my client. Surely you know that."

"But under the circumstances!" Logan exclaimed.

"Mr. Wyatt, I give you that the circumstances are extraordinary, but I can't break the attorney-client relationship. I can tell you that your sister is well, and I can offer to pass on anything you wish to send to her, like a letter or an email. Whether she chooses to respond is entirely up to her."

"Can you tell us if she's in the country?" Quinn asked.

"I'm really not sure. I haven't been in contact with her for some time."

"Is she married? Does she have any children?" For some reason, it was important to Quinn to know that. In some far-fetched fantasy, she could already see herself and Quentin sitting side by side in the garden as their children played on the lawn, laughing and chasing each other. Cousins. Friends.

"I can't answer that."

"Can't you give me her contact information?" Quinn demanded. Surely it couldn't hurt to send Quentin a direct email. It wasn't as if Quinn would show up at her door or accost her on the street.

"I'm sorry, but I can't. That information is confidential."

"We've tried to find her online, but there wasn't a single hit for anyone named Quentin who might have been her," Quinn persisted.

"Perhaps she's not on social media," Mr. Richards replied, his face expressionless.

"Even individuals who are not on social media leave an electronic footprint," Logan argued.

The lawyer didn't respond.

"Can you at least reach out to her and let her know we are searching for her?" Quinn pleaded.

"Certainly, I will do that. It would help if I had something to forward to her, as well as your own contact details, if you wish to leave them."

Quinn sprang to her feet. "I will write her a letter and post it to you *forthwith*," she said crisply, using the legal term with great sarcasm. "Thank you for your time."

"I'm sorry I couldn't be of more help." Mr. Richards uttered the words, but clearly didn't mean them. He'd likely put Quinn out of his mind as soon as they left his office until he received the letter from her.

"I bet you are," Logan grumbled under his breath as they left the solicitor's office. "Home?" he asked as they walked toward the playground.

"Home. There's nothing more to learn here."

"Is it me, or was he particularly guarded?" Logan asked.

"It wasn't you. He gave us nothing."

"Quinn, have you considered the possibility that Quentin might already know?"

Quinn stopped walking and turned to face him. "Know what?"

"Know that she is a twin. Surely, Dr. Ian Crawford saw the news and read the papers and put two and two together. Two babies, found on the same morning, wrapped in similar blankets, with identical notes attached to the folds. It doesn't take Sherlock Holmes to deduce that they might be related."

Quinn lowered her eyes to the ground. Logan was right. The news had come as a thunderbolt to her, but Quentin might have known about her twin all along. Perhaps she had no interest in finding Quinn, and wouldn't wish to meet her now. She shook her head. "No, we have to operate on the assumption that Quentin doesn't know. Karen seemed genuinely surprised. If her parents knew Quentin had a twin, surely Karen would know as well. She was old enough to hear the talk, even if they didn't tell her directly."

"I suppose it's possible that the good doctor only wanted the one baby, and had no wish to defend his decision to separate the twins. His wife would have put a kybosh on that adoption right quick if he wanted to adopt both of you."

"I suppose." Quinn sighed. "As a student of history, I know that people are always motivated by self-interest, but it still amazes me sometimes how selfish human beings can be. Did no one care about us? About what we might mean to each other? They separated us and gave us away, like a litter of puppies. Even our own mother couldn't care less about keeping us together."

"I'm sorry, Quinn. I can only imagine how that knowledge must hurt," Logan said kindly. "Do you believe in destiny?"

"To some degree. Why?"

"My mother found you by accident. She saw that article about your house being broken into for grave goods. Right?"

"Right."

"Then you ran into Reverend Seaton at Rhys's office, having gone there that day on a whim. What were the chances of that happening?"

"Very slim."

"Perhaps the universe, or destiny, is pushing you toward finding Quentin. You've found your birth mother and your natural father in less than a year, after decades of wondering about them. And now you know you have a sister. We might not have a lot to go on, but we got further in the past two days than we thought possible. We know something about Quentin and her life after she was abandoned. We have a way to contact her. Perhaps you should just write that letter and take a step back. Let her come to you. I know she will."

Quinn gave Logan a watery smile. "Even if we never find Quentin, I'm really glad to know you, Logan."

"Me too, sis."

Chapter 54

On the ride back, there was no discussion of what had transpired. Emma would have been full of questions, being permanently attuned to every conversation between the adults, and Quinn needed a little time to process what they'd discovered in Leicester. When Emma was finally in bed, she filled Gabe in on everything she and Logan had learned, and everything they hadn't.

"Logan is right, Quinn. You've made significant strides in the past few days. Be patient. I know it's hard, but you must allow this situation to play out naturally. The lawyer will pass on your letter, once you've written it, and then Quentin will contact you."

"Sure of that, are you?"

"Very sure. I do think you owe Seth a call."

"I know. I keep putting it off."

"Quinn, I know you dread calling him, but he's your father, and he deserves to know what you've discovered. Besides, I'm sure he's desperate to hear from you. He was so excited to have met you, and so looking forward to becoming a grandfather."

Quinn nodded, but didn't reply.

"Quinn, Brett is in prison. He can't hurt you anymore," Gabe reasoned as he smiled in understanding. He took Quinn's hand in his and began to massage it gently to help her relax.

"Yes, he can. Knowing that I put him there will haunt me for the rest of my days."

"Brett's actions put him there. Surely you know that."

"Of course I do, but had I not delved into family history and planned to make it public, things would have never gone that far. We all have secrets, and this was his, and I was about to trumpet it from the rooftops. People have killed for less."

"You can't blame yourself. You couldn't have known that Brett shares your psychic ability."

"No, I couldn't have," Quinn replied sulkily. "But I think Seth blames me for losing his son. If it weren't for me, Brett would be getting ready to start his freshman year of college, shopping for school supplies, and looking forward to making new friends. Instead, he's in prison, only about two months into his sentence, with a decade of nothing but fear, resentment, and misery stretching out before him."

"Seth doesn't blame you."

"How would you know?"

"I know because I spoke to him at length while you were in the hospital. He was ashamed, immensely relieved that you were going to be all right, and shocked to have learned that Brett was capable of such cruelty, but not for one second did he blame you or wish you hadn't come into his life. He loves you, Quinn, and what he fears most is losing both his children."

"Why must you always be so sensible?" Quinn asked, elbowing Gabe in the ribs. He'd put things into perspective for her, the way he always did, making her feel selfish and irrational for not calling Seth sooner.

"It's a curse I must live with."

"Don't look so sheepish, Dr. Russell."

"I've never actually seen a sheep looking shamefaced. Have you?" Gabe asked, making Quinn laugh when he tried to imitate a mortified-looking sheep.

"No, can't say that I have. It is a silly expression, isn't it? You know what else is a silly expression?"

"Tell me."

"As nervous as a turkey on Thanksgiving. Seth said that once and it made me laugh."

334

"Why did you think of it now?"

"Because that's how I feel about calling him."

"No matter how the conversation goes, your fate will never parallel that of a Thanksgiving turkey, despite the fact that you're becoming as plump as one," he quipped, rubbing her rounded belly affectionately. "Now, pick up that phone and call the poor man."

Quinn reached for her mobile while Gabe heaved himself off the sofa.

"I'll give you some privacy, shall I?"

"Thanks."

Quinn selected Seth's number from the contacts and pressed the call icon before she had a chance to change her mind. He picked up on the second ring.

"Quinn! How are you, sweetheart? I'm so glad you called."

"Hi. Sorry it took me so long. How have you been?"

"I've been better," Seth replied, with his usual American forthrightness.

"Is it Brett?" The last thing Quinn wanted to talk about was Brett, but she could hardly pretend that her brother didn't exist. She was glad that Seth understood and didn't go into detail.

"Brett's doing as well as can be expected. It's my mother. She passed away on the fourth of July."

"Oh, I'm so sorry. Why didn't you call me?"

"I didn't want to upset you. And it's not as if you would have come for the funeral," Seth replied. There was no reproach in his voice, just sadness and acceptance of the situation.

"No, but I would have liked to express my condolences. I know you two were close. How did it happen?"

Seth sighed. "Mom always loved the fourth of July. It was one of her favorite holidays. She said she liked it because it was all about food, fun, and family. There was no religious connotation or a marketing campaign to make it more than it was. It was a day to celebrate freedom, and that's something everyone could get behind. I always had a big barbecue at my place on the fourth, with a DJ and a caterer, but this year I wasn't in the right frame of mind for a party. I brought Mom over from the nursing home, and Kathy came over. We had some hot dogs and burgers and then went to watch the fireworks on the river. They usually have two barges that put on a dueling display. Mom loved that. It was her favorite part. The fireworks were spectacular this year. Truly amazing." Seth exhaled loudly. "Sorry, I'm a bit emotional."

"Take your time."

"After the fireworks display, I drove Mom back to the home. She was lucid, Quinn. More lucid than she'd been in months. We talked for almost an hour, just like we had before the Alzheimer's set in. She asked about you. She was sorry she never got a chance to get to know you better, or meet your baby. She asked to see your picture, and I showed her pictures of you and Gabe and Emma. She cried. She knew she'd never see you again."

Quinn brushed away tears as she listened to Seth. She had known when she left New Orleans that she'd never see her grandmother again, but the knowledge that Rae was gone forever still hurt. She wished she could have spent more time with her.

"I saw her to her room and waited until the nurse helped her to bed. Then I left. They called me a few hours later. Mom died peacefully in her sleep."

"I'm sorry, Seth. I wish I'd been there for you."

"Me too. It would have been nice to have at least one of my children at the funeral. I was glad she never knew about Brett though. That would have killed her. She adored him, and always asked about him during her moments of lucidity. She asked about him that night, but I couldn't bear to tell her the truth. I told her he was out with his friends, too grown up to hang out with his dad."

"You did what you had to do," Quinn interjected. She couldn't fault Seth for lying to spare his mother's feelings.

"I know, but it still felt wrong. She asked me which college he was going to and I lied through my teeth. The only true thing I told her that day was about how glad I was to have met you and how I hoped to be a part of your life, and the life of my grandchild."

Quinn heard the longing in Seth's voice. He missed her, and she suddenly realized she missed him too.

"Mom left something for you in her will."

"Really? That was kind of her."

"Yes, she added an addendum back in May. She penned it on one of her good days and asked the nurse to give it to me to pass on to her attorney. She left you her pearl set. You might not recall, but she wore it the night of the party. It's a three-strand pearl-and-diamond necklace, a pearl-and-diamond brooch, and matching earrings. You might think it outdated, but she wanted you to have it."

"I will wear it with pride," Quinn replied, and meant it. Touching Rae's jewelry would bring visions of her grandmother, but Quinn would welcome them. She never got to know Rae Besson in life, but she'd still get a chance to be close to her in death.

"I didn't want to send the items by mail, in case the package got lost. I will bring them to you in person, as soon as you're ready to see me. Are you?" Seth's voice trembled with anxiety. He probably knew the odds of being rejected, but put himself out anyway, desperate to keep the connection between them from being severed forever.

"Yes," Quinn replied. The word just slipped out, but she wasn't sorry. She did want to see him. They'd got on well in New Orleans and had been on the way to establishing a lasting bond when Brett decided to do away with her. Now that she was actually speaking to her father, she felt the depth of his love for her and his boundless longing to see her. "Seth, there's something I need to tell you."

"Yes?" Uncertainty laced his voice, as though he expected her to backtrack on what she'd just said.

"You'd better sit down."

"I'm sitting already. Lay it on me, kid."

"Sylvia gave birth to twins in 1983. You have another daughter."

Seth sucked in his breath and held it for a moment before letting it out slowly. It came out shaky and loaded with emotion. "How long have you known?"

"I found out quite by accident, about two weeks ago. I know I should have rung you sooner, but I wanted to be sure."

"And are you?" Seth's voice was watery, as if he were crying.

"Yes, Sylvia admitted to it when I confronted her."

"What do you know of your sister?"

"Not a whole lot, but I'll tell you everything I've learned so far." Quinn quickly related the details she knew about Quentin, without elaborating on her strained relationship with her adoptive family.

"Oh, Quinn, I'm overwhelmed. Another daughter. What a gift. After what happened…you know…with Brett, I felt forsaken, broken. I thought I'd lost you for good. But this news… It's as if I've been restored to God's grace. It's as if he's telling me that not all is lost."

Quinn felt a stab of guilt. She'd been so selfish, thinking only of her own needs and feelings. Seth had lost so much when he found out what Brett had done, and she'd nearly finished him off by effectively cutting him out of her life. "Seth, I'm sorry. Truly, I am. I was scared and hurt, and desperate to get away. I never meant to hurt you. You've been nothing but good to me. Do you think we can start over?"

"You've got nothing to apologize for, sweetheart. You've been through something awful, and it was partly my fault. I should have paid more attention, spent more time talking to Brett about his feelings. Maybe I could have prevented what happened, but I was oblivious, too excited to have found you to pay attention to my son and the hatred that was brewing inside him. Quinn, I want nothing more than to be your dad, in whatever capacity you're comfortable with. And I can't wait to meet Quentin. Will you keep me informed of what you discover?"

"Of course I will. And Seth, if you want to come visit, after the baby is born, I'd be very glad to see you."

"Can I bring Kathy?"

"Of course. I'd love to see her again. She was so kind to me, to all of us."

"Quinn, thank you for calling. You have no idea how happy you've made me. I love you, sweetheart."

"I..."

"You don't need to say it, not if you don't feel it. The fact that you want to give me another chance is enough. I'll speak to you soon, yeah?"

"Yes, I promise. I'll ring you next week."

"Deal. Goodnight, my girl. And give my regards to Gabe and Emma. I look forward to seeing them as well."

"Goodnight."

Quinn disconnected the call and set her mobile aside. Why had she been so reluctant to call Seth? It seemed silly now. She felt good after speaking to him, and loved, something she never felt from Sylvia. Seth was right; perhaps not all was lost. Sylvia wasn't the mother Quinn had dreamed of, but she had an amazing brother in Logan and a father who genuinely cared for her. Perhaps, in time, her family would grow. She still held out hope for Jude, and her heart filled with longing at the thought of meeting Quentin. No, not all was lost.

Chapter 55

December 1464

Berwick-upon-Tweed, Northumberland

The bleak light of a winter dawn was just creeping in through the arrow-shaft window when Kate woke with a start. The fire had burned down during the night and the temperature in the room had plummeted. Her breath escaped from her mouth in gossamer clouds and she burrowed deeper beneath the covers and furs that were piled on the bed to keep her and Hugh warm during the night. Something had woken her, but for a moment, she wasn't sure what it was since all was quiet and still.

Kate turned onto her side and was about to go back to sleep when she felt sticky wetness between her legs. She lifted the covers to discover she'd started her courses during the night and her nightdress as well as her side of the bed were soaked with blood.

"Oh, no," she gasped, before she had a chance to stop herself.

"What is it? What's wrong?" Hugh demanded drowsily. Being a soldier, he was attuned to any sign of danger, and even a gasp from his wife was enough to bring him to wakefulness.

"It's nothing. Go back to sleep."

Hugh reached out to her beneath the blankets. When his hand came away covered with blood, he looked concerned for a second until the truth dawned on him and he cringed with disgust.

"I'll clean it up," Kate hastened to assure him.

"Useless bitch," Hugh hissed as he glared at her, his gaze burning with hatred. "It doesn't matter how many times I fuck you, you still won't breed."

"I'm s-sorry, Hugh," Kate stammered. Her courses were about a week and a half late and she'd harbored some hope that she might be with child. She hadn't said anything to Hugh, but he kept his own mental calendar, always acutely aware of when she was due to bleed. She'd been late several times over the past few years, but despite fervent praying and hoping, her courses always came in the end.

"You're sorry?" Hugh spat out, his features contorted with rage and disappointment. "And what's that worth?"

Kate knew he was upset, but she hadn't anticipated the depth of his anger. Hugh's eyes flashed with malice as he shoved her viciously, sending her flying out of bed and onto the stone floor. She tried to break her fall with her hand, but landed painfully on her left hip, crying out as the jolt of the impact reverberated through her wrist and up into her arm. The icy stone beneath her burned her skin, and she wept softly as she curled into a ball on the hard floor.

"Oh, for the love of Christ," Hugh growled and swung his legs out of bed.

He stood over her for a moment, glaring down at her with undisguised hatred. Kate tried to edge away from him, fearful that he might kick her, but instead, he bent down and grabbed her by the hair, dragging her face closer to his own. "I've just about had it with you, you know that? From now on, I'll fuck you from the back, like a dog, because that's what you are—a useless, barren bitch. God put you on this earth for one reason and one reason only, to bear children, and you couldn't even do that, could you? Oh, go ahead and cry, and then run to the chapel to pray. Much good it will do you."

Hugh let go of her hair, grabbed his clothes and stormed from the bedchamber, still cursing her under his breath.

Kate began to tremble violently, her teeth chattering both from shock and the cold. She finally managed to scramble to her feet and hobble over to the ewer and basin on a low stand in the corner. The water was ice cold, but Kate cleaned herself as best she could and affixed the rags she used during her courses between her legs before getting dressed. She then stripped the sheet off the bed and assessed the damage. The blood had soaked into the mattress and would need to dry out before the mattress could be turned over to hide the ugly stain. That was the only way to salvage it and get a few more years of use from it.

Kate submerged the sheet in the basin and watched in despair as the water turned bright red. It'd need to soak for at least an hour before it could be washed out. She wiped her streaming eyes with the back of her hand and sat down by the hearth, clutching her shawl about her shoulders. The acrid smell of ashes stung her nose and she was numb with cold, but she didn't budge. She couldn't go to the chapel and pray, not today. Hugh had hit a nerve when he ridiculed her piety. She was tired of praying. She'd prayed for her brothers, and they'd died. She'd prayed for her mother, and she'd never recovered. She'd prayed to be reconciled with her father, but he'd cut her from his life and replaced her with new children. And she'd prayed to get pregnant so her husband would at least see some worth in her, but she'd never conceived. Her womb remained empty and hollow as her years of fertility slipped away. What was the sense of praying?

Christmas was a week away, a time of celebration and hope, but she only felt an all-encompassing dread. She'd never felt as alone as she had this past year, and the prospect of living out her life in this keep with her resentful husband and her distant sister-in-law left her desolate and depressed. She thought about Guy every day, and wondered where he was. They hadn't had word from him in months, and Kate worried for his safety. Guy had sworn that he'd fully recovered the use of his right arm, but she knew the truth. His arm tired quickly and began to tremble with the strain of wielding a heavy sword. In a prolonged battle, he'd be at a disadvantage, especially if confronted with a skilled and tireless opponent.

In his last letter, Guy had mentioned that he was quartered at Westminster Palace as part of Warwick's personal guard. Kate supposed it was kind of the Earl of Stanwyck to provide Guy with an opportunity to serve Warwick, but she wished he'd ordered him back home instead. Hugh missed Guy dreadfully, and took out his frustration and guilt at driving his brother away on Kate. He barely spoke to her these days and chose to spend the long evenings in conversation with Eleanor or playing chess with Adam, who took gleeful pride in beating Hugh nearly half the time. Hugh smiled indulgently and told Adam that he'd allowed him to win, but they both knew the truth and enjoyed the battle of wits.

Sadly, Adam would be leaving them in a few months, going to Stanwyck Hall to begin his term as page to the earl, and their family would shrink once more, leaving just the three of them in residence, a prospect Kate didn't relish.

Eleanor had become openly coy and affectionate with Hugh. She touched him lightly on the arm, or sat closer than necessary, claiming she was cold and needed to be closer to the fire. Her obvious loneliness was her excuse for blatant flirting. Hugh, in turn, was chivalrous and solicitous, treating Eleanor with the kind of respect he no longer bestowed on his wife. The two of them made Kate feel humiliated and ostracized, and whether their conduct was intentional or simply the result of their forced closeness, Kate often wished she could just disappear and leave them to it. There had been a time when death seemed like a terrifying and cruel punishment, if it came too early, but lately, in Kate's mind, it had taken on the qualities of a kind stranger who might take her away to a place where she'd no longer be unhappy or unwanted. She'd slip out of her skin and escape the hollow shell she had become—an abused wife, an unloved daughter, and an unfulfilled woman who had never become a mother, and be reborn in a place that promised eternal salvation and the everlasting love of God. Perhaps God would take her soon, if she were lucky.

Kate finally forced herself to stir. It was fully light outside and high time she started on the day's chores. With Aileen gone and Joan getting on in years, there was more for her to do, and

Eleanor never bothered to lend a hand with cooking, baking, or laundry. Kate's wrist hurt and had begun to swell and her hip throbbed where she'd landed on it, but she ignored the pain. She washed out the sheet, then limped down the stairs and toward the kitchen where she could hang it by the fire to dry.

Joan stopped kneading the dough when Kate walked in, her eyebrows lifting in surprise and her lips pursing. Kate realized she must have red-rimmed eyes and a pink nose from crying. She pretended not to notice Joan's questioning stare and smiled politely in greeting. She didn't need Joan's pity. She just wanted to get on with her day as if nothing had happened.

"Sit yerself down and have some breakfast," Joan said as she brushed flour off her hands. "Hugh's already eaten. He's outside chopping wood, the poor lad. 'Tis cold out there, and it snowed during the night. It takes some doing to get Hugh out of bed this early in the morning. Might he be angry about something?" she mused as she studied Kate's impassive face, her eyes straying to the wet sheet steaming by the hearth.

Kate accepted a cup of hot broth and a slice of bread and applied herself to her breakfast. She wasn't about to take the bait.

"Adam's excited about Christmas," Joan went on. "Hugh promised him a dagger this year, and a sword by the time he turns fourteen."

"What does an eight-year-old need with a dagger?" Kate asked.

"'Tis not about need, but about rite of passage. Adam will be going to Stanwyck Hall come spring, and it'll look good in front of the other lads if he has something of value, especially if it's a weapon."

"I'll miss him," Kate said truthfully.

"Aye, so will I, but 'tis the right time. Jed will be leaving us as well."

"What? Why?"

"William promised him a parcel of land when he came of age and Hugh means to honor that promise. Jed needs to learn to farm it, so he'll go live with one of the families on the estate. They can use the help, and Jed will get an education. And then he'll be ready to wed."

"How will Alf manage without Jed?" Kate asked. Walter did much to help the old man, but if Stanwyck called Hugh to arms, Walter would go with him, and Alf would be left to manage on his own.

"Oh, I expect Hugh will bring in a new lad."

"He should find someone to help you as well. It's been nearly a year since Aileen died."

"He's offered. I'm just not ready to train another lass, I suppose. Too much bother, if ye ask me. If they're too young, they can't handle much in the way of housework, and if they're a bit older, they only have eyes for the lads and want a home and hearth of their own. I thought Aileen might stay a while, being damaged and all, but even those who're deaf and dumb can't keep their legs crossed."

Kate bristled at Joan's spiteful comment, but said nothing. There was little point. She finished her meal and rose laboriously to her feet. She had mending to do, and wanted to take advantage of the bright morning light. Though she still saw well at a distance, she could no longer sew or embroider by candlelight. She dared not say anything to Hugh about her failing eyesight for fear of appearing even more useless than he already believed her to be.

Kate had been at her mending for nearly two hours when she heard the frenzied barking of the dogs. She glanced out the window to see what all the fuss was about. A lone rider came trotting through the gate, his face endearingly familiar, even from a distance.

Guy. Kate dropped the shirt she'd been working on and sprang to her feet. Her hip hurt even more after sitting for a prolonged period of time, but she had to welcome Guy home.

She heard Hugh's booming voice. "Nurse, you'd best prepare something grand for supper tonight. Our lad's come home!" Whatever animosity he'd felt toward Guy had been replaced by relief at seeing his brother home and unharmed.

Eleanor, who'd been working on the same piece of embroidery for the past two weeks, made no move to rise, but her eyes never left Kate's face, watching with interest as Kate tried to hide her joy and rearrange her features into a semblance of bland indifference. "You must be glad Guy's home. He will keep Hugh sufficiently distracted to give you some respite."

Kate wasn't sure what Eleanor was implying, but decided not to ask for clarification. Eleanor was probably just trying to get a rise out of her.

Kate limped from the room and stepped out into the snow-covered yard. Hugh was already there, clapping Guy on the shoulder and calling to Alf to see to Guy's horse. Adam stood just behind Hugh, suddenly shy of his uncle, his eyes alight with excitement and curiosity.

"Adam, Jesu, you've grown. I hardly recognized you. I'm glad I came home before you left us for good. When's that to be, then?"

"Just after Easter, Uncle Guy. I'm to enter the Earl of Stanwyck's service."

"I envy you. Some of the happiest years of my life were when I was a page. The earl has several boys in his service at a time, so you'll make friends and learn sword fighting and jousting."

"Uncle Hugh's been teaching me."

347

"He's a quick study," Hugh said, placing his hand on Adam's shoulder and smiling down at the boy. "He really makes me work. My reflexes are not what they used to be."

Adam's already pink cheeks reddened with pleasure. "I still have much to learn," he mumbled.

"That you do, but I've no doubt the earl will be very pleased with your progress," Hugh replied kindly.

Kate remained in the shadowed doorway and rested her head against the cool stone of the archway, not wishing to interrupt. From where she was standing, Guy and Hugh looked like the most devoted of brothers, and Hugh bore no resemblance to the angry, violent man he'd become.

She took a deep breath and stepped out of the shadows before Guy could see her skulking. Smiling in welcome, she walked toward him. He'd changed. She noticed that right away. His face was leaner, the stubble shadowing his cheeks making him appear older and harder, and his stance more assured, more aggressive. When their eyes met, Kate noticed the greatest change of all. Gone were the innocence and vulnerability, replaced by awareness and skepticism.

Guy smiled and held out his hand to her, but his smile slipped as his gaze roamed over her. "Kate, I'm glad to see you looking so well," he said.

She knew she didn't look well, and he must have noticed her fear of greeting him too eagerly, her swollen wrist, and her pained gait. She must have looked haggard, pale and downtrodden, but she thanked Guy all the same and withdrew her hand from his before Hugh could make more of the gesture than it was. "It's wonderful to have you home, especially in time for Christmas."

"I timed my arrival." Guy's boyish smile lit up his eyes and reminded Kate of the young man she'd met several years ago. "The Earl of Warwick was kind enough to release me from his service a month early. He had no immediate need of me and thought I might enjoy spending Christmas with my family."

"That's very considerate of him," Kate replied, surprised. She'd never met Warwick, but the tales she'd heard, even from her own father, always painted the man as calculating and driven, not sentimental.

"He's a surprising man. He can be ruthless, single-minded, and unforgiving. But he's also loyal to those he loves, keenly aware of his men's needs, and devoted to his family."

"And what of this business of the king's marriage?" Hugh asked as he led the way into the house. "I hear Warwick is incensed."

Kate trailed after the men, eager to hear what Guy had to say. Her life had been so monotonous this past year that news of the court was not to be missed.

"I'll tell you all about that later. I could use a wash, and I'm famished," Guy declared. "I spent the night at a tiny inn about three hours south of here, and the only thing the landlord could offer me by way of breakfast was some congealed gruel and watered-down ale."

"I'll have Nurse bring you some hot water and then you can join us for dinner. I hope you're not too good for the likes of us now, having supped at Westminster Palace and rubbed shoulders with the king," Hugh joked as he patted Guy on the shoulder once again. He looked genuinely happy, an emotion so rare in Hugh that Kate barely recognized it.

"I only saw the king from a distance," Guy replied as he began to ascend the stairs.

"And his queen?" Hugh called after him. "I heard she's a rare beauty."

"Aye, she is that." Guy looked like he wanted to say more, but changed his mind and made his way up to his chamber.

Chapter 56

Kate used her uninjured hand to carry the pitcher of hot water to Guy's bedchamber. Joan had much to do in the kitchen, so Kate had offered to bring up the water as an excuse to get Guy to herself for a few minutes. She found him sitting by the cold hearth, his boots tossed carelessly aside and his cloak and doublet on the coffer seat beneath the window. He looked tired and drawn, and held his right arm against his side as if it pained him.

"It gets stiff from the cold," he explained.

"How are your headaches?" Kate asked quietly as she set the pitcher down on the stand.

"Still there. They're quite severe at times, especially when it's stormy outside," Guy replied. "I wasn't much use to Warwick. He was glad to see the back of me. There's only so much guard duty one can perform."

"I'm sure he valued your service."

"Warwick was duty-bound to retain me for a period of one year. He needs all the support he can muster in the north, and the Earl of Stanwyck is a valuable ally who can raise a good-sized army when called upon. Warwick took me on as a favor to him, nothing more."

"Surely, a loyal man, even if not as proficient with a sword as some, is still better than two skilled fighters with divided loyalties."

"I suppose, but it's a bitter truth to swallow that you're no longer as useful as you once believed yourself to be. I can still fight for my liege, but I'm not strong enough to survive a prolonged battle."

"Oh, Guy," Kate breathed. She thought Guy had learned to see his own worth in Warwick's service, but the swagger she'd seen earlier was nothing more than defiance and a refusal to allow

Hugh to guess at his insecurities. Guy was still a valuable asset to his lord, but it seemed his confidence had been undermined by his injury and his faith in himself would not be restored unless he distinguished himself in battle or died trying.

"Enough about me. I've missed you, Kate." Guy crossed the room and stood close to her. Too close. She took an involuntary step back, earning a rueful smile from Guy. "How have things been at home?"

"The same." Kate shrugged. "Nothing much changes around here." She didn't mean to sound ungrateful or displeased with her life, but there was an edge of bitterness to her voice. Guy's gaze slid down to her waist, and then back up again, making her cringe with shame. She shook her head. "I'm not with child. Hugh is angry, Guy. He blames me."

"I'm sorry, Kate. I know how much Hugh wanted children. It might still happen," he added, but his optimism rang false.

"I don't hold out much hope. Not anymore. Hugh believes me to be barren, and now that he doesn't stand a chance of inheriting my father's fortune, he sees me as nothing more than a hindrance to his plans for the future. If I were to die, he'd be free to marry again, and believe me, he wouldn't tarry."

She was grateful that Guy didn't insult her by arguing that she was wrong and Hugh loved her and would mourn her. She'd always been able to talk frankly to him, and he did the same in return. Being able to speak openly, even if only for a few minutes, reminded her once again how emotionally isolated she'd become and how desperately she longed for a sympathetic ear.

"I must be going. Hugh will wonder what I'm doing up here," Kate said. She poured the hot water into a basin and motioned toward it. "You'd better wash up before the water grows cold. I'll see you downstairs. The food is simple, but it's plentiful, and you look half-starved," she joked. The only part of Guy that looked hungry were his eyes, which were fixed on her as if he were trying to memorize her every expression.

"Not a day went by when I didn't think of you," he said. He didn't come closer or demand a response. He was simply stating a fact.

Kate bowed her head. She wanted to tell him how much she missed him and how happy she was that he was back, but taking such a liberty would lead to more truths and more revelations, so she nodded in acknowledgement and fled Guy's chamber before he could see the tears quivering on her lashes.

By the time he came down a half hour later, Kate was calm and composed. She sat at the table with her hands folded demurely in her lap as Hugh said grace. He was in such high spirits that he'd invited Joan, Alf, Jed, and Walter to share their meal, and treated them as honored guests rather than individuals he'd bullied for years and rarely thanked for their service.

"A toast to my brother's homecoming," Hugh exclaimed as he raised his goblet in Guy's direction. "I'm so happy to see you, brother."

"And I you," Guy said, his gaze on Kate.

Chapter 57

Kate left Guy in the company of Eleanor, Hugh, and Walter after dinner and retired to her bedchamber. Her head throbbed as if someone had used it as a war drum and her belly twisted with menstrual cramps. She could barely move her wrist and her hip was bruised and stiff. She undressed down to her chemise, climbed into bed, and pulled the furs up to her chin, grateful for their warmth and the deep silence of the chamber.

She closed her eyes. Seeing Guy had brought her immeasurable joy, but also deep pain. She'd never fallen in love with Hugh, but she'd tried to be an obedient wife. This morning, Kate had realized with startling clarity that she hated the man. She'd been naïve when she allowed Father Phillip to convince her that Hugh was an honorable man and she should be a devoted wife to him despite her reservations.

Looking back after nearly four years of marriage, Kate now saw clearly how Hugh had manipulated events in order to gain her family's connections and fortune. She wondered how different things might have been had Hugh been the one wounded at Towton rather than Guy. But then, Guy would never have taken advantage of the situation as Hugh had. Guy would have escorted Kate home, thanked her for her help, and ridden out of her life.

She huddled deeper into the covers, pulling her legs up against her belly to staunch the ache. Her heart had soared at the sight of Guy, and her spirits had lifted just knowing he was well and safe, but the chasm between them was as unbreachable as ever. If he chose to remain at the castle, hiding her feelings for him would prove difficult, especially under the watchful gazes of Eleanor and Joan. She had to be twice as careful and maintain a constant guard where Guy was concerned.

After a restorative nap, Kate came down for supper. She was physically better, but the pall of misery hadn't lifted and she tried to keep her eyes from sliding to Guy as she took a seat at the table. Hugh was jubilant. He'd received a message from Stanwyck

Hall inviting them to come an hour earlier for the annual Christmas celebration. Kate suspected the invitation had been issued as soon as Guy's squire, lent to him by the earl, returned to Stanwyck Hall and reported Guy de Rosel's return. The earl would wish to hear all the latest news and enjoy court gossip before the rest of his guests arrived. Current information wasn't easy to come by, isolated as they were so far up north, and Guy's account of what was happening in the capital wasn't to be missed.

"Will there be minstrels and mummers?" Adam asked for the tenth time. This would be his first time attending a Christmas celebration with the adults.

"Yes, Adam, there will be minstrels and mummers," Hugh replied happily. "And the earl plies his guests with rare delicacies and fine wine."

"What about bear baiting? I'd like to see that."

"Adam, I don't think bear baiting is an appropriate activity on the day we celebrate the birth of our Lord," Eleanor admonished him.

"And minstrels are?" he demanded.

"Christ's birth is a joyous occasion, to be celebrated with music and feasting. Bear baiting is a sport, bloody and common, not at all the kind of pastime our Lord would have approved of."

"Did they have bear baiting in his day?" Adam asked, earning himself a reproachful look from his mother. Hugh looked amused.

"I daresay, Our Savior, who was kind and gentle, would not have approved of the torture of any creature," Eleanor replied to Adam sternly.

"Well put, Eleanor," Hugh said with nod of agreement. "No bear baiting, Adam, but I think the dice might come out later in the evening."

"Gambling on the day of the Lord's birth is a vice," Eleanor cried.

"So it is, my dear. So it is. Adam, you can't play."

"And you?" Eleanor demanded, turning to Hugh.

"I think the Lord will forgive me," he replied, putting an end to Eleanor's righteous indignation with a severe look. She could lecture Adam, but she had to keep her own counsel where Hugh was concerned. He was the head of the family, and she was there on his sufferance, even if her son was the rightful heir to the estate.

"Will there be many people?" Adam inquired, seemingly oblivious to the tension he'd created between Hugh and his mother.

"Nigh on fifty, I'd say," Hugh replied. "What do you think, Guy? He's had that many in the past."

"Sounds right," Guy replied. He seemed distracted.

"Eleanor, have you a gown to wear?" Hugh asked, his question surprisingly intimate. Men didn't ask such things of ladies they weren't married to, especially in front of others.

Eleanor blushed and nodded. "I have the green damask trimmed with sable. It's most appropriate for Christmas."

Guy turned to Kate as though expecting her to tell them what she planned to wear, but Kate remained mute for a moment. She had several gowns, but there was one she hadn't yet worn. It was of deep blue velvet, trimmed with the pelt of a red fox. The fiery color of the fur brought out the auburn highlights in her hair, and the deep blue accented her eyes and pale skin. The gown was the finest thing she owned, and suddenly she couldn't wait to wear it, just to see the admiration in Guy's eyes.

"I have just the thing," Kate finally said. She felt a telltale flush creeping up her cheeks and thought that Hugh would see right through her, but he barely glanced in her direction. His attention seemed focused on Eleanor this evening. She did look lovely, in a gown of deep brown velvet. Her creamy breasts swelled above the bodice and her fair hair, uncovered since she was at home and in the presence of family, glowed in the candlelight. She was still a beautiful woman, one who'd be even lovelier if she had the love of a good man.

"Guy, I wager Stanwyck's celebration will be nothing compared to the festivities you attended at court," Hugh said, pouring Guy more wine. "Tell us about Westminster, brother. What's the mood like at the palace this Christmas season?"

Guy forced a smile and went on to describe the entertainments planned by the king and his new queen, making the ladies gasp with delight. "But that's nothing compared to what the king has planned for his lady's coronation, which is to take place in May," Guy continued. "The preparations have already begun, and it will be the most splendid celebration London has ever seen. The king will see to that."

Hugh nodded. "He would, given the manner of his marriage."

"What do you mean, Hugh?" Eleanor asked. She was always a little slow on the uptake, and needed things explained to her.

"Well, His Royal Highness married in secret," Hugh replied patiently. "Not only did he take a bride who's beneath him, but he denied his subjects a royal wedding. You can't imagine the pageantry and expense that goes into celebrating a union between two royal houses, Eleanor. And had the king married a princess, the wedding would have been a sight to behold."

"Oh, I see," Eleanor replied, nodding vigorously. "I would so love to see the coronation," she went on, directing a pleading look at Hugh.

Hugh looked momentarily taken aback, but then smiled at Eleanor, his eyes twinkling with the kind of excitement Kate hadn't seen since they were newly married. "Well, why not? Perhaps we can undertake a trip to London for the festivities. What say you, Adam? It will be an education for you, boy, if my lord Stanwyck can spare you from his service for a fortnight."

"Oh, yes, please," Adam begged, so excited at the prospect that he actually ran toward Hugh and threw his arms around his uncle's neck.

Hugh, who was always reserved with his affection in company, seemed gratified by the attention and hugged his nephew back, then winked at him. "I'll give you something to tell the other boys about," he promised, smiling broadly.

"I think the Earl of Stanwyck will be attending the coronation, as will most nobles in the land. He might take Adam along as part of his own retinue," Guy pointed out.

"Even better," Hugh replied with a chuckle. "Less expense for me. Ordering new gowns and suits of clothes for us will come dear enough, not to mention accommodation in the capital. Every innkeeper will hike up the rate, keen to make a profit off the occasion. Perhaps I overestimated my willingness to undertake this journey," he mused.

"Hugh, please," Eleanor breathed, her eyes pleading with him to reconsider. "It'll be such fun."

"I'll have a think on it, my dear," Hugh promised, blessing her with an indulgent smile. "Perhaps we don't all need to attend." He hadn't singled anyone out, but Kate thought he might be referring to her. He meant to punish her, and this would be one way to do it.

"We'll all go," Guy said, his narrowed gaze daring Hugh to contradict him. "I'll shoulder part of the expense if you find it too crippling, Hugh."

"I was only joking," Hugh replied with forced joviality. "We'll all go. Ah, let's eat," he said, rubbing his hands as Joan brought out a platter of sliced beef accompanied by buttered peas prepared with bits of salted pork, and mashed turnips. Alf came tottering behind her with two fresh loaves of manchet bread and another flagon of wine.

The rest of the meal passed in pleasant discussion of their possible trip to London. Kate didn't say much, but the idea of going to London for the coronation appealed to her. It would be nice to see the capital, and perhaps she'd even get a glimpse of her father and his new wife. She knew that was unlikely, given the number of people that would be thronging the streets on Coronation Day, but perhaps Guy would know where her father would be and direct her there.

The thought of seeing her father soured Kate's stomach. Deep down, she knew if he saw her, he'd either ignore her or curse her outright. She was dead to him, but unlike his sons, who had died an honorable death, she was a traitor and a disappointment.

Kate sighed and accepted more wine. She didn't much like the taste, but at least it might help her fall asleep. She feared being alone with Hugh after the way he'd treated her that morning, and hoped he'd be inebriated enough to pass out as soon as his head hit the pillow.

Supper lasted several hours, but finally, the last spoon of syllabub was consumed and the final drop of wine had been drunk. Everyone rose from the table, eager for their beds. Hugh had been in good spirits all day, but that didn't mean his mood wouldn't sour as soon as the door to their chamber closed behind him. Kate waited for him to join her, but Hugh turned to Guy instead.

"I'd like to speak to you alone for a few minutes," he said. "Alf, bring us more wine."

Guy didn't look eager to talk, but he inclined his head in agreement and bid the ladies and Adam goodnight. Kate trudged up the stairs after Eleanor, glad to have been spared an awkward interlude with Hugh as they prepared for bed. At least she'd get to go to bed in peace, something that didn't happen often.

Chapter 58

Guy was tired after several days spent in the saddle and would have liked nothing more than to retire, but Hugh was starved for news and eager to hear all the details Guy had left out for the benefit of the ladies. He added two thick logs to the fire and offered Guy more wine.

"Not for me," Guy replied, and watched as Hugh drank a cup of wine in one long swallow. His brother was imbibing a lot more than he used to, whether due to boredom or unhappiness he couldn't quite tell.

"How are things at court?" Hugh demanded as he poured himself more wine. "The truth now, and not the pretty, glossy picture of life at the palace you painted for the women."

"Tense. Warwick is furious about the king's marriage and doesn't care who knows it. Words like 'witchcraft' and 'sorcery' are being bandied about," Guy added.

"In relation to whom?"

"Queen Elizabeth and her mother, Jacquetta of Luxembourg, the newly minted Countess Rivers."

"Is there anything in it?" Hugh asked.

"Who knows? I wouldn't want to get on their bad side, I'll readily admit that. I'd be hard pressed to believe the rumors of our queen, but her mother is a different matter. That woman is either as clever as Warwick or has the ear of the devil himself. Ever since she came to court the king has been handing out titles and lands to the Woodvilles like sweets to children at a fair. Jacquetta's husband has been created Earl Rivers, and she's using their newly acquired status to marry off her children, of whom there are many, into the greatest noble houses loyal to York. The king is supporting these unions, and in doing so is creating a solid base of support among the queen's family, ousting Warwick and diminishing his power."

"I can't imagine that my lord Warwick is taking that lightly."

"He isn't. He made the king, and he can unmake him, at least in his own estimation." Guy had heard Warwick express that particular sentiment several times before leaving his service, and hoped the words were more bluster than threat. After a period of uprisings and rebellions, the country was finally settling into Edward's reign, and deposing him would destabilize the fragile peace so recently achieved.

"So, what do you think is the price of his loyalty to the king?" Hugh asked. He seemed remarkably sober, given how much wine he'd consumed throughout supper and afterward.

"He's set on having his daughters marry the king's brothers and become royal duchesses," Guy explained. "That would bring them one step closer to the throne, and should Edward fall…"

"The throne would pass to George Plantagenet, the Duke of Clarence, and his wife Isabel Neville would become queen," Hugh finished for him. "How likely is that to happen?"

"Edward is not Henry. He leads his army in battle, and is as likely to die on the battlefield as any man."

Hugh shook his head in disgust. "The Duke of Clarence has no business being king. He's ruthless, conniving, and utterly devoid of compassion."

Guy tried to mask his chuckle behind a well-timed cough. Hugh had just described himself, but clearly, he didn't think a man with those qualities should ever be in power. Guy happened to agree. Seeing Kate and Eleanor after his prolonged absence had proved a shock. Kate looked worn and frightened, and Eleanor, although lovely as ever, drooped like a wilted flower, desperate for attention and affection. The only woman who appeared to be thriving at Castle de Rosel was Nurse, who was as autocratic as ever, ordering Kate and Eleanor about as if she were the lady of the house. Guy was in no doubt that Nurse wielded more power over

Hugh than either his wife or his sister-in-law and did much to influence his decisions, particularly when it came to Eleanor.

Preventing Eleanor from remarrying kept Hugh firmly in control of family finances and allegiances, and he wouldn't do anything to jeopardize his position. Adam was only eight, which left Hugh in charge of the estate until Adam was knighted at twenty-two. Much could happen over the course of fourteen years, and if anything happened to Adam during that time, Hugh would inherit the title and estate he so coveted.

"I agree with you there, Hugh, but if His Majesty continues to antagonize Warwick there's a very good chance Warwick will take matters into his own hands and commit treason."

Hugh leaned back in his chair, his eyes narrowed and his head tilted to the side as he considered the implications of Warwick's possible rebellion. No doubt he was trying to assess how such a turn of events would affect the country and his own personal situation. If Warwick managed to depose the king and take the throne for himself, Hugh would find himself distant kin to the king of England, an enviable position even for someone who stood to gain little by the association. "It's only treason if you lose," he mused, watching Guy to gauge his stance. "Should such a thing come to pass, our loyalties would come into question. Whose standard would you ride out under?"

"Warwick's been good to me, but if he took up arms against the king he'd be condemning all those who answered his call to death. My loyalty is to the House of York," Guy said. "I'll not be switching allegiances every time the wind blows in a different direction."

"You've changed, brother," Hugh said with an indulgent smile. "I'd not have thought it of you to become so politically savvy. Or maybe I've just grown more complacent, cooling my heels here in the frozen north and keeping my nose clean."

"We live in dangerous times, Hugh, and any misstep, no matter how innocent, can cost you not only your life, but everything you hold dear. Just look at what happened to the Duke of Somerset."

Hugh laughed uproariously. "Somerset hardly made an innocent misstep. The man was as wily as a fox and changed allegiances as often as he changed his hose."

"Nevertheless, his lands and titles are forfeit, and his head is no longer attached to his body. He'd made one misstep too many."

"Good thing we're not in line for the throne then," Hugh joked and slapped Guy on the shoulder. "Our beautiful new queen had better produce a son, and soon, or Edward's reign won't be secure."

"I heard she's already with child, if court gossip can be relied upon," Guy replied.

"Unlike my dear wife, who's as barren as winter rain," Hugh spat out bitterly.

"I'm sorry your hopes haven't been realized, Hugh, but surely there's still time," Guy replied carefully.

"She's not getting any younger, Guy, and if she hasn't conceived by now, chances are she won't in the future. I had such hopes for this marriage, but none of them came to fruition."

"Through no fault of Kate's," Guy argued.

"Well, it's certainly through no fault of my own," Hugh replied belligerently. "I've worked every angle, pursued every opportunity, and plowed that furrow often enough to plant at least one stalk of wheat, but nothing. I've no fortune, no title, and no son. My life has been an utter failure."

"Yes, I believe it has," Guy replied. He smiled to let Hugh know that he was agreeing with him in jest. "Go to bed, Hugh. You've grown too maudlin to tolerate any longer. I'm for my bed."

"Goodnight, Guy. I always feel better after talking to you," Hugh said, wrapping his arm about Guy's shoulder in a gesture of affection.

"Glad I could help. Now, off with you."

Hugh stumbled off to bed, leaving Guy to ponder his brother's assessment of his situation. Guy supposed Hugh wasn't all wrong, but in his eyes, Hugh was the luckiest man alive, just by virtue of having Kate.

Chapter 59

August 2014

London, England

Gabe held the sword reverently before stowing it in its lockable case. He could see the faraway look in Quinn's eyes and envied her ability to see into the past. He would have liked to see what she'd seen with her previous cases, but this one was special. The people whose lives Quinn could step into at will were his ancestors, his family.

She had been keeping him up to date on what she saw, from the point of view of both Kate and Guy, but if Gabe were to be honest, it was Guy he was most interested in, as well as Adam. He wished Quinn had something of Adam's, especially something that might have belonged to him once he reached adulthood. She hadn't asked to see Gabe's family tree, preferring to witness events as they played out, and he respected her wishes but drove her to distraction with questions, desperate to be a part of this foray into the past.

"Tell me about Guy," Gabe pleaded as he settled in next to Quinn on the bed. "Did his return from London upset the household?"

"Not greatly, no. Hugh was very happy to see his brother, and Nurse practically swooned with joy. Guy had changed, though," Quinn mused, her mind still in the fifteenth century and her gaze fixed on some distant point beyond the window.

"In what way?"

"When I first saw him, he was more innocent, more trusting. He followed the lead of his brothers, taking it as gospel that they knew best. William was something of a hero to him, but he also looked up to and trusted Hugh. Being away from Hugh, and from home, had matured him, and opened his eyes to the hidden motives of powerful men. He'd become disillusioned with Warwick, and with the whole struggle to win and keep the throne. He saw these men for who they were: selfish, power-hungry, and unapologetic. They'd sacrifice anything and everyone to attain their heart's desires, and Guy was beginning to understand that Warwick would not rest until one of his daughters attained the throne," Quinn explained.

"And Kate? How was he toward Kate?" Gabe asked. "Was he still in love with her, or had his youthful passion burned out?"

"I think Guy was a one-woman man," Quinn replied. "He loved Kate, and whereas before he'd never entertained the thought of pursuing her, that resolve crumbled as his loyalty to Hugh waned. Guy was angry with his brother, and wished to punish him for being unkind to Kate. I believe a confrontation is in the making, and it might turn ugly."

"You think Hugh murdered Kate?" Gabe asked. "Colin said he discovered no signs of violence."

"It's quite possible that Kate died of natural causes. Many people did. She might have fallen ill, but I can't imagine the relationship between Hugh and Guy didn't undergo some kind of major transformation around the time of her death."

"How I wish I could see them for myself," Gabe said wistfully. "Tell me about Adam."

"Adam was a clever boy, and more ambitious than anyone gave him credit for. He was tired of being coddled by his mother and ordered about by Nurse and was anxious to join the earl's household and be treated as a person in his own right."

"It must have been quite an education to go from such a claustrophobic environment to living in a castle that housed dozens of people."

"Hundreds," Quinn corrected him. "The Earl of Stanwyck was a powerful man and retained dozens of servants and grooms along with pages, squires, and hangers-on."

"Hangers-on?"

"Distant kin who hoped to benefit by their association with the earl. There were several teenage girls who'd been sent to the earl's household by their parents in the hopes of contracting beneficial marriages. A few of them were married off to Stanwyck's knights. Do you know anything about Adam as an adult?"

"He was a shrewd man, by all accounts, and only political when it suited his interests."

"Adam would have been a young man at the time of the Battle of Bosworth. Whom did he support?" Quinn asked.

"He was Richard's man, through and through. The de Rosels switched allegiances only once, when they believed the Lancastrian cause was lost. They remained loyal to the House of York until the bitter end."

"Can't say I blame them. I never did care much for the way Henry Tudor seized the crown, or the way he treated Richard's body after the battle. Richard was an anointed king, after all, and deserved some measure of respect. Tossing him naked over a horse and hacking at him as if he were a side of beef was unbecoming of a man who wished to be king," Quinn said scornfully.

Gabe laughed at her expression of displeasure. "You said it yourself; they were all selfish, power-hungry, and unapologetic. Henry Tudor wanted to humiliate Richard and discredit the House of York, and he'd accomplished that, although I don't think he ever felt safe on his throne. He was keenly aware of how fragile his reign was, at least in its infancy."

"I never did like that period in history, or the Civil War," Quinn said. "I always wanted to believe the British are more civilized than that, but in the end, they just slaughtered each other en masse to satisfy the ambitions of a few bloodthirsty men."

"Isn't that the basic definition of history?" Gabe asked.

"No, it's the basic definition of military history. That's why I prefer to focus on the women. They were the true backbone of civilization, and the ones who picked up the pieces when it all went tragically wrong."

"Spoken like a true feminist," Gabe replied with a chuckle. "And I love you for it." He planted a kiss on Quinn's nose, and then his lips moved downward, capturing her mouth in a tender kiss. She returned his kiss with unabashed ardor and slid lower on the bed, pulling Gabe down with her.

"Ooh," she said, her hand going to her belly.

"What is it?"

"The heir apparent is protesting this unexpected turn of events," Quinn explained as her belly vibrated from another kick. She reached for Gabe. "He's just going to have to deal with it."

"Strict mums are so sexy," Gabe growled as he began to unbutton her top, the baby momentarily forgotten despite its displeasure. Quinn might be more distracted and occasionally forgetful, but the pregnancy was wreaking havoc on her hormones, kicking her libido into overdrive. She'd been like a tuning fork the past few weeks, vibrating with desire, which he was only too happy to satisfy in whatever way she liked.

Chapter 60

Christmas Day 1464

Berwick-upon-Tweed, Northumberland

The celebration at Stanwyck Hall exceeded expectations. The earl had much to celebrate and wished to share his joy with his retainers. He'd become a grandfather just two weeks before Christmas and decided to use the annual feast as an opportunity to introduce the world to his grandson, Edward, named after the Yorkist king. The earl's son, Robert Ambrose, glowed with pride when he brought the baby to the great hall. The child looked contented enough, swaddled in blankets and furs to keep him warm, but the boy's mother hovered behind her husband, looking fretful as though she feared the child would catch a chill in the drafty hall.

Watching from her table, Kate could understand the mother's anxiety. Babies were so fragile, especially during the winter months. Any sniffle could turn into an ague and carry the child off within days. The mother was hardly more than a child herself, fifteen if she was a day. She had barely recovered from the birth, but the pride in her eyes when she smiled at her son was unmistakable and Kate felt a pang of envy, which quickly turned to shame as Hugh chose that moment to comment.

"Wed nine months, and a boy already in the cradle," Hugh growled under his breath. "A wedding night babe is a blessing on the family."

Guy turned to Hugh, a small smile playing about his lips. "Speaks of the prowess of the father, I should think," he said. "The Ambroses are a virile lot."

"That they are," Hugh agreed, probably too drunk to perceive the slight to his manhood. "It's now up to you, Guy."

"What is up to me?"

"You must marry and have sons, or our line will die out should Adam not live long enough to sire an heir."

Eleanor blanched at Hugh's words, her eyes growing round. Hugh had given voice to her worst fear, and possibly his own greatest hope.

"Adam will grow into a fine man and have many sons," Guy reassured Eleanor. "Don't listen to Hugh; he's too deep in his cups to talk sense."

Eleanor nodded, but her eyes darted around the hall, as though searching for Adam, who'd been seated at the end of the long trestle table on the opposite side of the hall with other children his age. Adam's seat was unoccupied, as were several others at that end. The boys were at the front of the hall, watching the jugglers, who'd begun their performance after the earl's grandson was taken back to his bedchamber. There were several girls as well, but they seemed more interested in the boys than the entertainment. Some of the girls were betrothed as early as eight years old, and the boys who were cheering on the jugglers and applauding the mummers might well have been their future lords.

"I do hope they finish soon," Guy said as he watched the jugglers. "I've a mind to dance, and I hope you ladies will partner me." Guy smiled at Kate and Eleanor. They had enjoyed the food, which was plentiful and exquisitely prepared, but what really made the feast special for Kate and Eleanor was the entertainment. The earl's minstrels had taken turns, singing romantic ballads about chivalrous knights and reciting poems of bravery in battle. They were positioned next to the earl's table, occasionally taking requests from him and his lady and keeping to tunes that didn't result in indigestion for their lord. Once the meal ended, they would collect their instruments and move into the adjacent chamber, where there would be dancing into the small hours of the morning.

"Of course, Guy," Eleanor replied politely. She didn't look in the mood to dance, but she'd never openly admit to being unhappy in public.

"And you, Kate?"

"If my husband has no objection," Kate replied demurely.

"It's all right with me," Hugh said, reaching for the pitcher of mead. "I've no love of dancing." *Nor love of your wife*, Kate thought bitterly.

"It's settled, then. First Eleanor, then Kate," Guy observed with more enthusiasm than was strictly necessary.

If he wanted to cheer them up, Kate thought it would take more than a dance or two to lift the pall Hugh had cast on their spirits—but she was wrong.

She hadn't danced in ages, and once the music began in earnest, she could barely keep her feet from tapping in time to the merry tunes. She waited patiently while Guy danced with Eleanor, then allowed him to escort her to the dance floor.

There were at least a dozen couples, all flushed from the warmth of the fire and the effects of the wine. Hugh was nowhere to be seen, which added to Kate's enjoyment of the dance. She danced with joy, remembering the steps without any difficulty. Guy was easy to dance with, and his fingers were warm and gentle as he held her hand, turning her this way and that as the current of the music flowed over them. Kate laughed when Guy made a face at her after he'd been nearly knocked off his feet by a portly man who was too unsteady on his feet to be dancing.

"Your laugh is like the tinkle of carillons," Guy said, referring to the hand bells one of the minstrels was playing. "I can't recall the last time I heard you laugh," he added, his eyes growing more serious.

"Neither can I," Kate confessed. She was enjoying herself and the laughter had come naturally, taking her by surprise. It died on her lips when she spotted Hugh and Eleanor down the line of dancers.

Hugh hadn't danced with Kate since the first time they'd been invited to Stanwyck Hall for the Christmas Feast, but he was now partnering Eleanor, looking for all the world like he was enjoying the dancing. His gaze was firmly fixed on Eleanor, who seemed to have recovered from his earlier bout of cruelty and was smiling up at him. Hugh's grin transformed his face and reminded Kate that she'd thought him handsome once.

It would have been unseemly for her to keep dancing with Guy, so she accepted invitations from the Earl of Stanwyck and his sons, as well as several other knights in the earl's service. Guy partnered the duchess and then danced with Amelia Ambrose and several other ladies Kate didn't know. She tried to focus on her partners, but her gaze frequently strayed to Guy, who seemed to be enjoying himself. Before his spell at court, Guy would have danced with Kate and Eleanor and sat the rest of the dancing out, reluctant to dance with ladies who were unknown to him, but today he seemed remarkably at ease and conversed with his partners easily as he led them around the floor.

Kate plastered a smile on her face as Hugh took her by the arm to claim a dance. "I thought you had no wish to dance," she said.

"I changed my mind," Hugh replied lightly. He was leading Kate, but his gaze remained on Eleanor, who was two couples ahead of them, dancing with the earl. "She's still beautiful," Hugh said softly.

"Yes, she is."

"Will would have been proud of her. And his son."

Kate wasn't sure what had brought on Hugh's attack of sentimentality, but chose not to ask. She supposed he missed his brother, and having Guy back reminded him of other Christmases and other feasts.

"I was about Adam's age the first time I was permitted to attend the Christmas celebrations. I was enchanted. I watched Will dancing with Eleanor and thought they made a handsome couple. I envied him because I knew my father would arrange their betrothal shortly and Will's future would be taken care of."

"Do you wish your father had had a chance to arrange a marriage for you before he died?" Kate asked. Will had arranged a marriage for Hugh with Eleanor's sister, Kate recalled, but that had been years later, and the marriage had never actually taken place. Perhaps she wasn't the only one who wished things had been different.

"No, Kate. I wish my father had sired me first. My life would have been very different had I been the eldest."

"We don't get to choose the order in which we're born. That's God's will."

"I've grown tired of contending with God's will," Hugh said softly, so no one would overhear such heresy spewing from his lips. "I wish to make my own choices."

"Whatever do you mean, Hugh?"

He laughed, his eyes twinkling with amusement. "Never mind. I've grown maudlin with drink and lack of sleep. I think it's time we made our way back. The party is starting to break up."

Hugh was right. The number of dancers had dwindled to only a few couples and the earl and his duchess had retired for the night. Sleeping forms draped some of the benches, and the servers looked run off their feet as they began to clear away the flagons of wine and pitchers of mead. Many guests would remain at the castle and enjoy the earl's hospitality, but the de Rosels lived close enough that they had no need to impose on the earl's kindness. Hugh signaled to Guy, who bowed to his partner and joined them by the door.

"We're off home," Hugh announced. "Fetch our cloaks."

Guy didn't seem to mind being ordered about. He strode from the chamber and returned a short time later with their cloaks, which had been left in one of the anterooms intended for that purpose. Hugh draped Kate's cloak about her shoulders while Guy helped Eleanor, whose attention was fixed on Adam. The boy looked dead on his feet, but his cheeks were flushed with excitement and his lips frozen in a smile.

"Did you enjoy yourself?" Eleanor asked as she ruffled Adam's dark hair.

"Oh, yes, Mother. It was marvelous. I liked the mummers best. I can hardly wait to come to live at the castle."

"If you think life at the castle will be all feasts and entertainments, you should think again," Hugh said, bursting Adam's bubble of happiness.

"Won't it?" Adam whined.

"No, my boy. It will be hard work. You'll be training, learning, and making yourself useful to your lord."

Adam hung his head in disappointment. "Still better than being at home," he muttered, earning himself an angry look from Hugh and a wistful glance from his mother.

Chapter 61

It wasn't a long ride back to the keep, but it was a merry one. Hugh, having drunk way more than his fair share, began to sing, and Adam and Guy joined in, making the night come alive with the sound of their voices. Hugh and Guy had nice baritone voices, but it was Adam's pure, childish voice that brought tears to Kate's eyes. How she wished she had a son to love and cherish. Adam was so sweet, so kind. In a few years he would transition into manhood and lose the naïve trust he had in all those around him, but tonight, he was still a boy who'd enjoyed his first grown-up evening.

"Well, I'm for my bed," Eleanor announced as soon as they returned to the castle. "Adam, time to say goodnight."

Adam didn't need telling twice. He wasn't accustomed to staying up so late or partaking in as much wine as he'd enjoyed this night.

Hugh looked the worse for wear as well. The drink had finally caught up with him, despite the sobering effects of the December night, and he staggered off after mumbling something about having to attend the St. Stephen's Day service at church tomorrow, leaving Kate and Guy alone.

Kate was about to say goodnight when Guy bowed his head and pressed his fingers to his temples as he leaned against the wall for support. "Splitting headache," he explained. "Too much mead."

"I have some lavender oil that might help. I can rub it into your temples. Shall I get it?"

"If it's not too much trouble," Guy replied.

Kate retreated to her bedchamber to fetch the oil. Hugh was sprawled on the great bed, his snores echoing off the stone walls of the room and his chest quaking with every rumble. He was a deep sleeper, as a rule, but he'd consumed enough mead to fell an ox, and would probably sleep well into the next day before waking with a sore head. He'd be as enraged as a bear at a baiting, especially once he recalled that St. Stephen's Day was traditionally associated with the giving of alms and he would have to make a respectable donation to be distributed among the poor of the parish. Hugh didn't enjoy being charitable, nor did he honor the tradition of allowing the servants a day of leisure on December 26. Since most servants served their masters on Christmas, the lords allowed them a day of rest and an opportunity to spend time with their families the day after, but since Joan, Alf, and Jed had been left to their own devices on Christmas while the family went to Stanwyck Hall, Hugh felt that was reward enough. Only Walter was permitted a few days' leave to visit his family.

Kate found the vial of oil and slipped out of the room. The castle was quiet and dark, the flame from her candle the only pinprick of light in the impenetrable darkness of the spiral staircase. Guy was sitting on his bed when she came in. He'd removed his doublet and boots and was wearing only a shirt and breeches. His hair was tousled and his gaze clouded with pain and the effects of alcohol. Kate approached the bed and positioned herself between Guy's thighs, which were level with her waist. She dabbed a bit of oil on her fingertips and began to massage it into his temples, moving her fingers in slow, steady circles.

She thought he'd close his eyes, but instead he looked straight at her, his pupils dilated in the dim light of the room. He hadn't bothered to light any candles, but had started a fire. The hungry flames were already devouring the kindling and caressing the thicker logs as the fire began to take hold, gradually warming the room and making Kate feel pleasantly relaxed. She was usually rigid with tension at bedtime, unsure of what Hugh's mood would be like when he came to bed, but knowing that he was sound asleep on the floor below eased some of the strain in her neck and shoulders.

"Any better?" Kate's voice came out in a whisper, as if she were afraid to be overhead, but she needn't have bothered. Guy's bedchamber was the only occupied room on the upper floor, and with the dense silence of the slumbering keep and the howling of the wind outside, it was as if they were the only two people awake in the whole world, safe in their tower.

"Thank you," Guy said softly. He reached up and took hold of her wrists, his touch gentle on the sprain she'd suffered a week ago. He lowered her hands, but didn't release her. Instead he pulled her closer, bringing her face within an inch of his. Their eyes met, his full of longing, hers wide with panic. She knew she should pull away from him, cross to the other side of the room where she'd be safe, or better yet, wish him a good night, and return to her own bedchamber and her husband, but she wasn't about to do any of those things.

Perhaps it was the effect of the drink, or the ever-present desperation that gnawed at her insides, but Guy's nearness made her feel safe and loved. She hadn't even realized she'd leaned closer to him until his lips captured hers and his arm slid around her waist, pulling her against his chest. Guy's kiss wasn't tender or loving; it was demanding, hot, and full of desire. Kate had never been kissed like that, not even in the early days of her marriage when Hugh had still played at being a lover.

Kate leaned into Guy, allowing herself this moment of abandon. His kiss stripped away all reservations and doubts, leaving behind a need so powerful it frightened her. A bud of desire bloomed in her belly, and the throbbing and moistness between her legs caught her by surprise. This was unchartered territory, and she was lost in its magical terrain, desperate to learn its secrets.

Guy got to his feet and turned her around so her legs pressed against the bed. He pushed her down with a gentle but firm hand, letting her know there was no going back. The attraction between them had been simmering since the night they met, and after four years of frustrated desire it was about to boil over. Guy pushed up Kate's skirts, exposing her thighs and hips. She'd never willingly opened up to Hugh, but now she spread her legs, offering herself up to Guy like a shameless wanton.

She expected him to use his fingers as Hugh sometimes did when she wasn't ready for him, but Guy did something utterly unexpected. He sank to his knees and buried his face between her legs, tasting and exploring her so intimately it made her legs tremble. Her face felt flushed, and desire writhed in her belly and coiled like a snake as something unknown and primal built within her. She grabbed Guy by the hair, forcing him to stop.

"Now. Please," she begged. "I can't take any more."

Guy leaned over her. His eyes were hooded with desire and his lips tasted of her as he kissed her hard. He stifled her cry with his mouth as he slid inside her, claiming her with one hard thrust. Her delicate tissue stretched around him as he filled the void inside her, making her feel whole for the first time in her adult life. With Hugh, she always lay still, waiting for him to finish, but now she felt driven to lift her hips to meet Guy's, desperate to take him in deeper and deeper until he slammed against her womb with every thrust, the exquisite combination of pleasure and pain finally pushing her over the edge. Waves of unspeakable pleasure radiated from her core, pulsing around Guy's shaft as he reached his own climax.

Guy rested his forehead against hers, his eyes closed and his brow damp with perspiration. He remained inside her, their bodies joined as one.

"I love you, Kate," he whispered. "I've loved you since I woke to find you praying over me in that ruined chapel."

His eyes opened and searched hers, as though he needed to know she wasn't sorry. As Kate opened her mouth to reassure him, she realized she truly wasn't. She had no regrets. Not yet. She felt alive for the first time in years and the feeling was heady, and dangerous. She knew she should go to church tomorrow, confess, and do penance, but she wasn't repentant. No number of Hail Marys would put out the fire in her soul or erase Guy from her heart. Tomorrow, the harsh reality of her situation and the unbearable weight of her sin would reassert themselves, but tonight, she was free, and she was in love.

"You're mine now," Guy said as he rolled off her to take the strain off his right arm.

"I belong to Hugh. You know that," Kate replied. The words felt wrong in her mouth, like bitter fruit that hadn't ripened into something delicious, but this wasn't a truth she could spit out. This particular reality had to be swallowed, every day of her life.

"Not for much longer."

"What do you mean?"

"Will you leave him if I find a way for us to be together?" Guy demanded.

"I'm his wife."

"Will you leave him?" he asked again.

Kate hesitated.

For only a moment, Guy's eyes flashed with anger and hurt. "I won't share you with him. Say the word and I'll be gone by morning."

Kate reached out and cupped Guy's cheek, looking deep into the blue pools of his despair. "Don't go. Please," she whispered. "I can't go on without you. I don't know how. I hadn't realized how empty I felt with you gone, how broken. But what we've just done is a sin, in the eyes of God and man. We can't love each other openly."

"I would risk hell and damnation for even one more day with you," Guy said.

"Hugh would kill us both if he found out," Kate said, knowing it to be true.

"Aye, he would. But if I leave you again I'll be dead anyhow because I'd be leaving my heart here, and I can't survive without it."

Kate allowed Guy to pull her close and rested her cheek against his chest. He was so solid, and so warm. He held her against him, his limbs intertwined with hers, like two parts of one whole. The beating of his heart was like the steady beat of a drum—a drum calling a soldier to war, for Guy had just declared war on his brother.

Chapter 62

August 2014

London, England

The day of Emma's birthday party dawned sunny and bright. Emma was delighted since she had fretted that it would rain. She danced before the mirror as she tried on outfit after outfit, eager to choose just the right one. She'd picked out a frock last week, then changed her mind. She'd settled on another dress two days ago, then had gone back to the original outfit last night, but when she woke in the morning, she had doubts once again and proclaimed the chosen dress to be all wrong.

"You might want to wear trousers," Quinn pointed out. "It'll be cold on the ice. You can change into a dress after the ice skating if you like."

Emma considered this for a moment. "Okay. I'll wear jeans and my sparkly pink top with a matching headband, then change into the blue frock after the skating."

"That sounds like a wonderful idea." Quinn found the top in question and laid it out on the bed before rummaging in Emma's plastic accessory box for the right headband.

"Is Grandma Phoebe meeting us there?"

Phoebe had arrived the day before and was installed in a hotel close to St. Pancras Station. She'd stayed there with Graham a few years before when they came down to London to visit Gabe and liked it enough to return. Quinn wished they had a spare bedroom so Phoebe could have stayed with them. She would have thoroughly enjoyed Emma's fashion show and would have loved to do her hair. With only the one son, Phoebe felt like she'd missed out and bought Emma a new outfit every time something caught her eye.

"We will collect Grandma Phoebe on the way to the skating rink."

"What about Grandma Sylvia?"

Quinn hadn't wanted to invite Sylvia, given the way they'd parted a few weeks ago, but it would be too difficult to explain to Emma why Sylvia couldn't attend her party. The skating rink venue was only for the children, so it had been decided that a second birthday cake would be served after the party at the flat for Phoebe, Sylvia, Logan and Colin, Jill and Brian, and Brenda and Pete. Quinn wished her parents could have come, but to return to England only two months after they'd come for the wedding was too costly, so they'd send Emma a present instead. It was a beautiful dollhouse. Not the kind made of plastic, complete with clunky fixtures and pink shutters, but one crafted of real wood, with exquisite Victorian furniture and real fabric curtains at the windows.

There was a family to go with the house—a dainty lady in a crinoline dress, a gentleman in a top hat, and two adorable children wearing baby gowns and bonnets. Emma had been in raptures when the house arrived. Quinn secretly thought Emma would tire of the Victorian set-up within a week, but her parents had never asked for her input, purchasing a gift more appropriate for the history-loving child Quinn used to be at Emma's age rather than for a Disney-obsessed five-year-old.

"Grandma Sylvia will come to the skating rink with Jude and then come back here for cake," Quinn said. She hadn't wanted Sylvia to come to the rink, but Logan had mentioned that Jude and Bridget needed a ride and Sylvia had volunteered.

"Will Jude and Bridget come back to the flat too?" Emma always liked to be fully prepared for what was to come. Quinn supposed that given what had happened to her mother and grandmother, she liked to feel in control of the situation.

"I've invited them, but they haven't confirmed."

381

"That's just like Jude," Emma observed as she allowed Quinn to brush her hair and affix the headband.

"Is it?"

"He's noncommittal."

"And where did you learn that word?" Quinn chuckled at Emma's precociousness. Some days, she was five going on fifteen.

"I heard it from Miss Aubrey. She's seeing a bloke who's noncommittal."

"Do you know what that means?"

"It means he doesn't want to marry her," Emma explained as she adjusted the headband and gave her hair a dramatic flip. "He's playing the field."

"Who's playing the field?" Gabe asked as he stepped into the room. "Never mind. Don't tell me. I don't want to know. You look beautiful, darling. Are you ready?"

"Yes. Oh, I can't wait. This party will be bloody brilliant!" Emma exclaimed.

"I'll thank you not to say 'bloody'," Gabe admonished her. Both Quinn and Gabe were dismayed by some of the terms Emma had started using over the past few months.

"Fine. Sorry," Emma mumbled.

"The party will be amazing, and you'll be very pleased," Gabe said, sounding more like his father than a man in his thirties.

"Yeah, chuffed to bits. Let's go." Emma stomped from the room, leaving Quinn and Gabe to follow.

"I hope my mum is right and we're having a boy," Gabe muttered as they left the flat. "I don't think I can handle two of those, especially not during the teenage years. One teenage girl is more intimidating than a marauding horde."

"Coward!" Quinn nudged Gabe in the ribs.

"And not ashamed to admit it."

Once they arrived at the skating rink, Quinn waddled over to the row of seats nestled against the wall and settled in. Her belly had popped over the past few weeks, and her center of gravity had shifted, making her clumsy. She was glad she'd worn flats and maternity trousers with a gauzy top instead of a dress. She'd have been too uncomfortable in shoes, even flat ones. Her feet were puffy and her ankles double their normal size, but they were cleverly concealed by the flared trousers. Her outfit was somewhat trendy, so she didn't feel too dull and drab, but she was beginning to miss her old body and wondered if she'd ever go back to normal post-baby.

Emma's school friends were already beginning to arrive. Emma greeted them effusively, accepted the colorful boxes and gift bags, and directed them to the counter where they could collect their rented skates. Gabe stood quietly by like a bodyguard, allowing Emma to play hostess. Most of the parents elected not to stay since there was plenty of adult supervision and the children would be escorted from one activity to the next. Quinn looked around, then glanced at her watch. Jude and his friends should have been there by now. She hoped Jude wouldn't let her down. Emma was looking forward to amazing her guests with 'real' *Frozen* characters.

Quinn tensed as Sylvia slid into a seat next to her. "Jude's in the Gents' getting his prince on. He didn't fancy coming already dressed up. Wasn't up for the ribbing from his friends."

Quinn was about to reply when Jude, Bridget, and two of their friends took the ice, dressed as characters from the film. Emma's girlfriends nearly fainted with excitement, and even the boys looked pleased with two pretty princesses to admire. Jude's friend Olly, dressed as Olaf, was a big hit as well since he really got into character.

"It's wonderful to be five, isn't it?" Sylvia asked as she watched the children skate in a circle to the soundtrack from the film.

"Emma's known more loss in her five years than some people know in a lifetime."

"I know she has, and I'm glad she's enjoying this."

Jude skated past them and slowed down long enough to give them a dramatic bow.

"Cheeky," Sylvia said, smiling at her son.

"I think he's having fun too," Quinn replied, watching Jude as he executed an elaborate twirl.

Jude did seem to be enjoying himself. He took Emma by the hands and led her into the middle of the rink, engaging her in something resembling a waltz. Emma was unsteady on her feet, but Jude helped her maintain her balance as he pulled her along and spun her around. She was delighted.

Quinn scanned the premises, wondering where Gabe and Phoebe had got to. They'd gone to check on the pizza and to bring the cake to the restaurant so that all would be in readiness once the children finished skating, but they should have been back by now.

"I hope you're pleased with yourself," Sylvia suddenly said. Her pleasure at seeing Jude in costume had evaporated and she now looked sullen and wary.

"Pardon?"

"Rhys's gone off me. I can only assume I have you to thank for his change of heart. You just had to tell him, didn't you?" Bright spots of color appeared in her normally pale cheeks.

"Tell him what?"

"About the other baby. Quentin."

"He was there when I found out," Quinn snapped.

"Then why did he stop coming round?" Sylvia demanded.

"Perhaps you should ask him. It's nothing to do with me."

"Isn't it? He's as devoted to you as a puppy," Sylvia hissed.

"I hardly think that's an accurate description of our relationship." Quinn was becoming angry herself. Sylvia had no business putting her in the middle. Rhys was her boss, but he was also her friend, and a mentor of sorts. She could not and would not intercede on Sylvia's behalf, more so because she knew the real reason for Rhys's decision.

"Rhys dotes on you. No wonder he's angry on your behalf," Sylvia persisted.

"I'm not having this conversation," Quinn said and sprang to her feet. "Enjoy the party, Sylvia."

Quinn swung Emma's backpack over her shoulder and headed toward the restaurant in the hope of finding Gabe, more annoyed with herself than with Sylvia. Her birth mother knew how to push her buttons, and Quinn fell for her antics every time, completely abandoning her well-intentioned resolve not to engage and to adjust her expectations to run somewhat parallel to reality.

"Fancy a cup of tea?" Gabe asked as he met her halfway and enveloped her in a bear hug. "It's arctic in here."

"No, I'm all right. Emma will want to change into her dress now that they're getting off the ice."

"I can help her," Phoebe offered. "You just stay off your feet."

Quinn changed her mind about the tea and settled at one of the tables with Gabe, a steaming Styrofoam cup in front of her. She hoped Sylvia wouldn't attempt to join them. She'd had about enough of her drama for one afternoon. In fact, she regretted inviting Sylvia back to their place, but it was too late to take back the invitation. She only hoped that Sylvia might be astute enough to see that she wasn't wanted.

Quinn smiled and waved as the children trooped into the restaurant, flushed from the exercise and ready for their lunch. Emma was already wearing her party frock and her pretty pink flats. Phoebe had brushed Emma's hair and adjusted the headband. She looked so cool, butter wouldn't melt in her mouth.

"She looks so happy." Gabe's eyes glowed with love as he watched Emma. "I'm so glad we were able to do this for her."

"Me too. I never had parties like this when I was a girl. I'm kind of jealous."

"So am I. For my fifth birthday, all of mum's siblings descended on the house with their kids. We played outside, then came in for orange squash and cake. Mum had a row with her sister, and dad, who was foolish enough to get between them, took refuge in the library after getting told off in front of the other husbands. Mum and Dad didn't speak to each other for days."

"Did you at least get good presents?"

"I got some toys and books."

"Not a bad haul," Quinn replied, smiling. She liked to imagine Gabe as a little boy, and could very well guess where Emma got her precociousness.

The children finished their pizza, sang a hilariously off-key version of "Happy Birthday" and clapped as Emma blew out her birthday candles. They wolfed down the cake in record time before running off to the arcade, armed with stacks of tokens, which they'd burn through within minutes. Quinn nibbled on a piece of cake, pleased that the party had gone off without a hitch. This was the first birthday party she'd planned, and it had been important to get it right.

Before long, all the children had been collected by their parents, and the pile of gifts was loaded in the boot of Gabe's car.

Quinn tried to hide her annoyance when Sylvia sauntered over to her. Sylvia's smile was forced as she acknowledged Gabe, but her gaze grew hard and accusing when it slid back to Quinn.

"I think I'll skip the cake at your place. I do hope you understand. I'll drop Jude and Bridget at their flat. They have plans."

Quinn wasn't surprised that Sylvia begged off or that Jude and Bridget had decided not to come. It was a relief, actually.

"Thank you for coming, Sylvia. It meant a lot to Emma," Gabe said, polite as ever.

"I hope she likes her gift. I put a lot of thought into it."

"I'm sure she'll love it," Gabe replied when he realized Quinn wasn't about to and it was up to him to fill the awkward silence.

"I'll just say goodbye to Emma." Sylvia looked around. "Where is she?"

"She had a few tokens left and wanted to use them up. She'll be back soon."

A few moments later, Emma came bouncing toward them, beaming. She held a tiny multi-colored bear that she must have won.

"Did you enjoy your party?" Quinn asked as she handed Emma an antibacterial wipe for her hands.

"Oh, yes. It was smashing. Can we do this again next year?"

"Let's wait and see, shall we? Now, why don't you say goodbye to Grandma Sylvia? She's not coming back to the flat."

"Bye, Grandma Sylvia," Emma sang as she twirled around. She didn't appear too disappointed.

"Are you ready to go? Grandma Phoebe's already in the car." Gabe held out his hand to Emma.

"Okay," Emma replied. "Oh, look what I found, Daddy. It's a pretty sticker." Emma had extracted something from her pocket and held it out to Gabe.

"Give me that!" Gabe grabbed the sticker from Emma's hand and shoved it in his pocket.

"But I want it," Emma wailed.

"Where did you find it?" Gabe demanded. He took Emma by the shoulders, frightening her with his sudden change of mood.

"Over there." Emma pointed to the table where Jude had sat with his friends while the children enjoyed pizza and birthday cake.

"Gabe, what's wrong?" Quinn asked.

Gabe didn't reply. His eyes blazed with fury as he scanned the premises until his gaze alighted on Jude, who'd just stepped out of the Gents', his costume over his arm. "I'm going to kill him," Gabe exclaimed and took off, heading straight for Jude.

"Gabe!" Quinn didn't know if she should go after him or see to Emma, who appeared to be on the verge of tears.

Emma clung to Quinn, her eyes huge with shock. "What did Jude do?" she whimpered.

"I don't know, darling."

Quinn looked on in shocked silence as Gabe grabbed Jude and slammed him against the wall, knocking the wind out of him. She couldn't hear what was being said, but when Gabe punched Jude in the face and then belted him one in the stomach, Emma began to cry, burying her face in Quinn's side.

"Let go of him!" Sylvia bellowed, but Gabe ignored her. He held Jude pinned against the wall, his face mere inches from

388

the terrified young man as his fingers closed around Jude's windpipe.

"Gabe, stop!" Quinn cried.

The sound of her voice seemed to bring Gabe to his senses and he loosened the hold on Jude's throat, but remained uncomfortably close, blocking Jude's escape.

"What's your problem, man?" Jude's hand went to his bruised throat. "You're barking mad."

"Am I?' Gabe growled.

"I'm calling the police. This is assault!" Sylvia exclaimed as she fumbled in her handbag for her mobile.

"Go on. Call the police," Gabe retorted. "And when they get here, I'll just show them this." He pulled the sticker he'd confiscated from Emma from his pocket and held it up in front of Sylvia's face. "Do you know what this is, Sylvia?"

Sylvia clearly had no idea what Gabe was talking about, or why Jude suddenly looked scared out of his wits as he tried to inch further away from Gabe.

Gabe's hand shot out and caught hold of Jude's arm. "You're not going anywhere."

"Gabe, what is that?" Quinn asked. She peered at the image on the paper, but whatever it was, she couldn't see why Gabe was so upset.

"It's a heroin fold," Gabe replied, his voice very low so Emma wouldn't hear.

"Please don't call the coppers, Gabe. I'm sorry, man. I really am. Emma was never meant to find that. It must have fallen out of my pocket," Jude sputtered. He looked around wildly, but his friends had legged it, having probably sensed that things might get ugly and the police would be called.

"I don't want you anywhere near my child. Ever!" Gabe hissed as he shoved Jude against the wall for emphasis.

Jude didn't fight back. He stood stock-still until Gabe finally stepped aside, giving him a chance to escape. Jude took off at a run, heading for the nearest exit. Sylvia opened her mouth to say something, but Gabe turned on her.

"Don't! Just don't!"

"Why is Daddy cross with Jude? It's only a sticker. I didn't mean to take it," Emma whimpered.

"It's all right, darling. Let's get you in the car." Quinn grabbed Emma by the hand and pulled her toward the exit. She needed some air. A lava-like heat was spreading upward from her chest and her heart hammered frantically as she fought for breath. Her vision blurred, softening the edges of the walls and making the door difficult to make out. Everything seemed to be reduced to one pulsating point of darkness, the black hole zooming in and out and making Quinn sway with dizziness. The sunlight nearly blinded her when she finally managed to get outside and she squeezed her eyes shut, unable to bear the glare.

"Quinn! Quinn!"

Gabe's voice sounded as if it were coming from underwater. Quinn leaned against the building for support as blood roared in her ears and she was overcome by crippling vertigo. She would have fallen had Gabe not caught her in time and settled her in the front seat of the car, which was parked near the exit.

"I'm taking you to A&E."

"No, I want to go home," Quinn muttered. "I need to lie down. Please, Gabe. I can't bear to be poked and prodded just now. I just need to rest."

"Her blood pressure is through the roof," Phoebe said as she took Quinn's pulse. She found Quinn's blood-pressure medication in her bag and pushed a tablet between Quinn's lips

390

before holding a bottle of water to her mouth. "There now. You'll start to feel better in a few minutes. Gabe, let's go. Do as Quinn asks."

"Mum, I don't think…"

"Gabe, there's nothing they can do for her. She needs quiet."

Gabe seemed paralyzed by indecision, but complied with Phoebe's command and strapped Emma into her seat. "You're going to see the doctor first thing tomorrow," he said and Quinn nodded, too weak to reply.

Chapter 63

March 1465

Berwick-upon-Tweed, Northumberland

Kate kneeled on the prie-dieu, her hands clasped in front of her. Over the past few months her prayers had become more fervent, more desperate. She'd never imagined that a moment of weakness would tear her soul asunder, but reality had set in very quickly after that Christmas night. She spent nearly every waking moment torn between duty and love, and consumed with guilt for turning her back on her faith. She'd gone to church several times since Christmas, determined to confess her sin, but when she entered the confessional, the words simply wouldn't come. They stuck in her throat, mainly because she couldn't lie to God any more than she could lie to herself. She'd tried to keep away from Guy, to erase the memory of his lovemaking from her heart, but when night came, she waited for Hugh to fall asleep and then stealthily left their bedchamber, climbing the stairs in complete darkness, her bare feet stinging with cold, as she hurried to her lover's room.

Guy was always there, waiting for her. He caught her in his embrace and covered her face with kisses, his hands exploring her body in ways that had grown even more intimate since that first night. He knew every inch of her, and made a study of what merely pleased her and what set her alight, playing her the way a skilled musician played his instrument. Her body never felt as alive as when he touched it, and her heart had never been as full. But then morning came, and with it self-recrimination and shame. She was a sinner, an adulteress, and a liar. She had dishonored her husband and herself, and besmirched her wedding vows. Guy sympathized with her struggle, but although he did share some measure of guilt, his sin wasn't nearly as terrible as hers. Guy wasn't married. He hadn't promised to love, honor, and obey in front of God. Men took lovers all the time, but women were taught to be pure and obedient, their only duty to please their husbands and bear children.

And now God had seen fit to fill her womb at last, blessing her with the miracle she'd prayed for rather than punishing her for her transgression. This morning, she didn't beg for forgiveness. This morning she thanked the Lord and praised his name, but her soul was torn. The child in her belly was not her husband's; Hugh hadn't touched her in months. It was a life created during an act of love and devotion, a life that had never been meant to be. What was she to do?

The answer came to her like a whisper on the wind, simple and devious. She had to protect her baby at any cost. Hugh need never know. He'd been drunk on Christmas. He wouldn't remember if he lay with her or not. The idea made her cringe with shame, but what choice did she have? The baby was more important than any of them. It was innocent of any wrongdoing and she'd rather die than allow Hugh to cast doubt on its parentage.

Kate rested her forehead on her clasped hands. She longed to share the news with Guy, but couldn't bring herself to tell him just yet. To rejoice in their infidelity and the result of their sin seemed wrong, even if the outcome of their affair seemed to be sanctioned by heaven itself. Kate's hand went to her belly. It was still flat, but she hadn't bled since before Christmas. Her breasts were tender and swollen, and her belly had grown firm, as if her body had donned armor to protect the babe within. Normally, Hugh would notice these changes, but their relationship had changed since the day he hurt her. He seemed content to let her be, and Kate was grateful for the respite. She wasn't naïve enough to believe Hugh was celibate, but if he chose to lie with someone else, she didn't care, as long as he did nothing to endanger her babe.

Kate crossed herself and got to her feet. She was expected in the kitchen. Joan needed help, and there was solace to be found in hard work. There was bread to bake, fowl to pluck, pies to make, and laundry to do. Kate didn't volunteer to do the laundry, on account of the babe, but she gladly undertook the other tasks. Keeping busy allowed her to avoid both Hugh and Guy in the mornings, which made things easier. They were often out on the estate in the afternoon and liked to practice swordplay in the bailey after dinner. Kate only spent time in their company after sunset. They ate supper, then retired to the Lady chamber where Kate and Eleanor sewed or read and Hugh and Guy played dice or shared the latest news. As long as Kate remained aloof and kept her eyes on the sewing she could barely see, she was safe.

Chapter 64

August 2014

London, England

Quinn's eyes fluttered open when she heard the doorbell. It had to be teatime since the slanted rays of the late afternoon sun flooded the bedroom with a golden haze. She felt rested and comfortable, and calm. Dr. Malik had ordered complete bedrest for the remainder of the pregnancy, a protocol that would begin to chafe after a while, but for now, was exactly what Quinn needed. She'd spent the past few days in bed, and slipped into a peaceful sleep several times a day, giving in to her body's need for rest. Phoebe was now installed in Emma's room, and would remain in London for as long as she was needed. Quinn was grateful to her for looking after Emma at a time when she couldn't do it herself, and being there for Gabe, who was frantic with worry.

Quinn scooted up higher and leaned against the pillows as Gabe poked his head in the door. "You have a visitor. Are you up to it?"

As long as it's not Sylvia or Jude, Quinn thought, but was certain Gabe wouldn't have allowed them past the threshold. "Of course." She hoped it was Jill or Logan. They always made her feel lighter, and she enjoyed their company.

Rhys stepped into the room, looking fresh as a daisy despite the heat of the August afternoon. He held a plastic container in one hand and a bunch of daisies in the other. "I brought you some scones. Just baked them, in time for tea."

"I'll put the kettle on and put these in some water," Gabe said as he accepted the container and the daisies from Rhys and retreated toward the kitchen.

Rhys sat on the side of the bed and gave Quinn a searching look. "How are you?"

"I'm better now. I must remain on bedrest until the baby is born."

"So I heard. When's that, eight more weeks?"

"Thereabouts. I don't know how I'll manage. I'm so used to being active," Quinn complained.

"Use this time to catch up on all the books and films you've not had time to enjoy. You won't have much leisure time once the baby is born, especially once you come back to work."

"Is that why you're here?"

"No. I just wanted to see for myself that you're all right. And I see in your eyes that you're not as Zen as you pretend to be."

"I'm sad, Rhys, and so disappointed in both Sylvia and Jude. I can't begin to image what might have happened if Emma had ingested that heroin. She could have died."

"I know. It doesn't bear thinking about." Rhys reached out and took Quinn's hand in his in a gesture of support. "Quinn, may I venture to offer an opinion?"

Quinn smiled. She'd talked things through with Gabe and Jill, both of whom advised her to banish her newfound family from her life, but Quinn was eager to hear Rhys's point of view. He was further removed from the situation, and someone who saw events in a unique way, almost as if he were always looking through a camera lens and imagining what his audience would see when they viewed the footage. "Go on, then."

Rhys looked away from Quinn for a moment, staring through the window at the cloudless sky outside, his gaze thoughtful. He often wore that expression when marshalling his thoughts, especially when he needed to say something that might not be well received. At last, he looked back, his gaze burning with intensity.

"Quinn, you are not my daughter, but I wish you were. I felt a connection to you from the moment we first met. Of course, at the time, I mistook it for sexual attraction, but I no longer feel that way about you," he added with an embarrassed grin. "I often catch myself thinking, 'I have to tell Quinn about this,' or 'Quinn would really appreciate that.' You are a kindred spirit, a person who understands me better than anyone I know, even my own family. What I'm trying to say, in a very awkward and roundabout way, is that we can choose our own family. We don't have to limit ourselves to the people we're related to through an accident of birth. I know you had high hopes when you first discovered your parents and siblings, and all you wanted was to play Happy Families, but life's rarely that simple. The deepest wounds are often inflicted by those we love and trust, and you gave your love and trust, albeit unwittingly, before you truly understood the nature of these people."

"Are you saying my expectations were too high?"

"Perhaps, particularly where Sylvia is concerned. Quinn, Sylvia will never be the loving, supportive mother you want her to be. She loves her sons, but there's a part of her that she always holds in check, a part that no one can reach. Perhaps it's something to do with her upbringing, or the trauma she went through when you were born, but this is who she is and you must either accept her as she is or move on."

"And Jude?"

"Jude's problems are not about you. He's a young man who needs help, but will not ask for it until he's good and ready. I hope that moment comes before it's too late. He does care for you, in his own way, and he has a soft spot for Emma. He's devastated about what happened."

"How do you know?"

"Sylvia called me. She hoped I'd come round and offer her a shoulder to cry on, but I decided to come here instead."

"And while you're being Freudian and philosophical, can you also help me deal with what happened with Brett?" Quinn asked, smiling at Rhys.

"I think Brett would have gone through his whole life without incident, had you not come along."

"So it's my fault?" Quinn gaped at Rhys. She hadn't expected him to spout that particular theory.

"No, it isn't, but you took him unawares, and threatened to expose something that he needed to keep hidden in order to get on with his life. I'm not saying his feelings or views are right, but very few situations are ever truly black and white. He felt frightened and threatened by what you were about to do, and he reacted much as a cornered animal would—he lashed out, driven by a sense of self-preservation."

"Am I supposed to forgive him, then?"

"Whether you choose to forgive him or not is up to you, but don't allow what happened to destroy your relationship with your father. Gabe says that Seth's been calling and texting you."

"We've spoken recently," Quinn replied, suddenly ashamed of herself for avoiding Seth for as long as she had.

"Quinn, I think Seth wants to be your parent a lot more than Sylvia does, and he's tormented with guilt over what happened. Perhaps it's time you let him off the hook, as you let me off the hook."

"Rhys, can I tell you something?" Quinn asked, smiling into his eyes.

"What's that?"

"Sometimes, I wish you'd turned out to be my biological dad."

"Come here, kid." Rhys pulled Quinn into a bear hug. He smelled of aftershave and freshly baked scones, and for the first time since returning from New Orleans, Quinn felt completely at peace.

"Thanks, Rhys."

"Anytime. Now, how about that tea?"

"Bring it on."

They made small talk while they drank their tea and enjoyed Rhys's mouthwatering scones. Emma had three, and even Phoebe ate more than she normally would. Quinn was grateful to Rhys for not mentioning *Echoes from the Past*, especially in front of Gabe, who'd taken away the sword and the rosary, effectively closing the window into the lives of the de Rosel family. Everything was on hold until after the baby was born.

Chapter 65

September 2014

London, England

The day had been unusually warm for September. Even with all the windows open, Quinn was perspiring. She took a cool shower before going to bed, one of the few activities still permitted during her period of bedrest, but she was flushed and couldn't get to sleep. The lace trim of her silky nightie chafed her skin, and she longed for something comfortable and soft.

Quinn turned on the bedside lamp and swung her legs out of bed, determined to get a cotton T-shirt. Rummaging in her drawer, all she found were tops more suited for work, and she realized Gabe had forgotten to do the laundry. Household chores had been piling up since Phoebe returned to Northumberland once Emma started school and Gabe returned to the institute for the new term. He'd accepted the promotion and all talk of moving north had ceased for the time being, making Quinn a happy woman.

She shut the drawer and turned to Gabe's side of the bureau. He had a plethora of cotton T-shirts, which he wore year round. She pulled out one of her favorites, a lime-green V-neck that had no annoying tag to scratch her skin. The glow of amber at the back of the drawer caught her eye. She knew she shouldn't, but the urge was too strong, and Quinn reached for the plastic bag containing the rosary before she could talk herself out of it. Gabe hadn't bothered to hide it well, trusting her not to go looking for it, but she'd been cooped up in the house for the past month, and she was expiring of boredom.

My blood pressure is perfect, there's no protein in my urine, my ankles are as trim as a ballet dancer's, and I haven't had a headache in weeks, Quinn thought proudly. What harm could a brief glimpse into Kate's life do? It would be a welcome distraction, and hopefully, help her get to sleep. She listened carefully. The only sound in the flat was the low hum of the TV. Emma was fast asleep, and Gabe was watching a film in the other room. He'd had trouble sleeping lately, and often came to bed after Quinn was already asleep, climbing in beside her and resting a protective hand on her belly.

She climbed back into bed, turned off the lamp, and drew the rosary out of the bag. Kate's face instantly swam into view, her blue eyes wide with anxiety.

Chapter 66

April 1465

Berwick-upon-Tweed, Northumberland

Kate grabbed the basin just in time as her stomach emptied for the third time that morning. She set aside the basin, rinsed out her mouth, and reclined on her pillows, panting. The first few months of pregnancy had been surprisingly unremarkable, but over the past two weeks nausea and fatigue had become her constant companions. Awful smells that brought on a bout of sickness seemed to lurk around every corner, particularly in the kitchen, which to Kate smelled of raw meat and blood. She hadn't been able to stomach any solid foods, except for bread dipped in broth, and ale. A bout of vomiting was usually followed by fitful slumber as her body recovered.

Had it been only Hugh and Guy in the house, she might have been able to keep her secret a little longer, but it was impossible to hide a pregnancy from Joan's watchful glare, and the old nurse had finally confronted Kate only that morning.

"I may be many things, but a fool ain't one of them," Joan had bristled. "Who do ye think ye're fooling? 'Tis good news, this is. Why not tell yer husband?"

"I've been wrong before."

"Well, ye're not wrong now. Ye've been sick for near a fortnight now, and yer courses haven't come. Ye think I don't pay attention?"

"I'm sure you do."

"Oh, I'm pleased for ye, Kate. I really am. Hugh will be beside himself when he finds out. A baby, after all this time. I was beginning to think ye must be barren."

Not only did you think it, but you mentioned your suspicions to Hugh time and again, Kate had thought bitterly.

"How long will this awful nausea last?" she asked, desperate to change the subject.

Joan shrugged, rolling her ample shoulders. "Can't say with any certainty. Some women feel better by their fourth month. Others suffer till the babe is born. There's no telling. Ye need to eat lots of bread. It soaks up the bile. Here, have a slice. Fresh from the oven."

"I think I need to lie down," Kate muttered. She was so weak she could barely stand.

"Ye go on, then. I'll bring ye a cup of ale later on. Best thing for a pregnant woman."

Kate had trudged up the stairs to her bedchamber, her stomach twisting with more than nausea. It was only a matter of time before Joan let it slip that Kate was with child. She wasn't one to keep secrets. Kate supposed it was as good a time as any for everyone to find out. She'd have to face the consequences sooner or later; it might as well be today.

She was just drifting off when the scrape of the door opening roused her from her stupor. Hugh stood in the doorway, looking at her as if he were seeing her for the first time. Sunlight fell on his face, its merciless rays underlining the softened jowls and the puffiness beneath the eyes. Strands of silver had invaded his dark mane, congregating at the temples. Hugh was only one and thirty, but years of frustrated plans, heavy drinking, and lack of purpose had taken their toll.

He shut the door and advanced into the room, stopping at the foot of the bed. "Is it true? Are you really with child at last?"

Kate felt a twinge of panic as she studied his face. He didn't look angry, but her guilty conscience wouldn't let her believe that she might get away with the sin she'd committed against him.

403

"Yes, it's true," she finally replied. She sat up and scooted backward, huddling against the headboard as she held a pillow in front of her like a shield.

Hugh's face broke into a joyful grin. "Oh, Kate, what splendid news. The good Lord has seen fit to bless us with a child at last." He came closer and sat on the side of the bed, reaching for Kate's hand. He looked contrite, not an expression one normally associated with Hugh de Rosel. "Kate, I'm sorry, eh? I know I've been less than gallant these past few months."

These past few years, Kate amended silently.

"I was disappointed and I didn't handle it well. Please accept my apology. Is there anything I can do for you? Anything I can get you? Nurse says you've been fearful sick these past few weeks. Can I tempt you with a tasty morsel or a length of damask for a new gown?"

"Thank you, but I don't require anything at the moment. My only wish is for this ceaseless nausea to pass."

"Well, I can't help you there," Hugh replied. He raised her hand to his lips and kissed it, as he had done when they were first married. "I do love you, Kate. I want you to know that."

Kate acknowledged his declaration with a nod, but couldn't bring herself to return the sentiment. She didn't love him, and never would, even if he treated her with kindness and respect.

"Well, I'll leave you to rest." Hugh got to his feet and kissed her lightly on the brow. "Ironic that you should finally conceive now, seeing as how I've barely been around you these past few months. The Lord certainly works in mysterious ways." He gave her a bemused look before leaving the chamber and shutting the door behind him.

Kate breathed a sigh of relief. Hugh didn't know about her and Guy, not yet. Her brow broke out in a cold sweat as another bout of nausea assaulted her. She grabbed the basin and retched again, belatedly realizing that the illness might be caused more by anxiety than by the pregnancy. Now that Hugh knew about the baby, Guy would know too. When Kate hadn't gone to Guy's room several days in a row, she'd allowed him to assume she had her courses. It was dishonest of her, but she'd had her reasons. She needed time to think. She'd managed to talk him out of running away together. Carrying on with him under Hugh's nose was bad enough, but publicly dishonoring her husband was another matter altogether. She couldn't do that. That would be snatching happiness from the jaws of betrayal, and it wasn't the way she wanted to start her life with Guy. But once he found out about the baby, there was no telling how he might react.

Kate sank deeper into the pillows and closed her eyes. She'd remain in bed for the rest of the day. She knew she was being cowardly, but felt too ill to face Hugh's bloated, self-congratulatory grin, Eleanor's ill-disguised envy, or Guy's accusing stare.

Chapter 67

Kate covered her eyes with her arm as bright sunlight flooded the dim confines of the bed. Joan yanked aside the bed-hanging, glowering at Kate, her hands planted on her hips.

"Ye should get some air. It ain't doing ye any good, moldering in here. Come. I'll help ye dress."

Kate reluctantly got out of bed and stood like a tree stump while Joan pulled the skirt over her head and tied the laces, then stuffed her into her bodice and sleeves. "Lift yer leg," Joan ordered as she crouched next to Kate with a rolled-up stocking in her hands.

"I can do it myself," Kate protested.

"Oh, aye? Can ye? Could have fooled me. I've seen corpses livelier than ye. Come on. Finish dressing and come down. I have some fresh broth for ye. Ye look half-starved from all that puking."

"I'm hardly half-starved, but I would like something aside from bread. Might there be an egg?"

"I'll get ye an egg. Will do ye good. Do ye feel up to a bit of cheese?"

Kate shook her head. "No, not cheese."

"All right. I'll have some roast fowl for ye for dinner. Can ye stomach that?"

"I think so." Roasted fowl actually sounded appealing at the moment. She needed to eat something besides soggy bread. Joan was right; she was starved for solid food. She'd sell her soul for an apple, but there wouldn't be fresh apples until the autumn. Some jelly perhaps. She craved something sweet desperately.

"All right then, I'll see to it. Ask Eleanor to join ye for a walk. Ye shouldn't be traipsing about alone in yer condition."

Kate shook her head. She couldn't think of anything she desired less. After countless hours spent in each other's company, the two women had never developed a bond, and Kate frequently wondered if Eleanor even liked her. Kate hadn't left her bed since Joan heralded news of her pregnancy, and she wasn't looking forward to seeing the simmering resentment in Eleanor's eyes. As long as Kate failed to conceive, Eleanor could pity her and feel less disgruntled about her own situation, but now that Kate was pregnant, even that little bit of comfort would be denied her sister-in-law.

Kate finished her breakfast, donned her cloak, and stepped outside. The sky was a cloudless blue, and the trees were decked out in luscious shades of green, their branches bursting with life after months of wintery slumber. The river flowed in the distance, a speckled band of silver and gold that hugged the curve of the castle mound. Kate took a deep breath and set off toward the woods, lured by birdsong and the smell of pine resin. She felt well for the first time in weeks, and the realization added a spring to her step.

She rested her splayed hand on her belly. There, beneath her palm, she felt a tiny bump. It was invisible beneath the folds of her skirt, but it was there, testament to the life growing inside. Kate had no way of knowing exactly when she'd fallen pregnant, but if it happened on Christmas, the baby would come in late September. Joan had said that expectant women felt movement midway through the pregnancy. She was almost there, so perhaps soon, she'd feel signs of life.

Kate caught her breath in wonder. Over the past few years, time had lost its meaning. She'd had nothing to wait for, nothing to look forward to. But now, time was everything. She'd bided her time until Hugh fell asleep so she could go to Guy, and with every passing day she was closer to holding her baby in her arms. She would not give in to despair. Guy would keep their secret, for her sake, and for the sake of their child. He loved her. He wouldn't do anything to harm either of them.

Kate had been walking for about twenty minutes when she heard footsteps on the path behind her. The footsteps weren't stealthy; they sounded brisk, as if the walker were in a hurry. Kate peered in the direction she'd come, but trees obscured the section of the narrow path beyond the bend. She wasn't frightened. This was de Rosel land, so the passerby could only be a peasant, which was just fine as long as he wasn't a poacher.

Kate smiled when Guy appeared round the bend. His color was high and his eyes glinted with irritation as he approached her. "You could have told me," he began without preamble. "I had to hear it from Hugh, who is pleased as punch that you're finally breeding."

"Guy, I…"

"Is it mine?" Guy demanded, his eyes pinning her with their intensity. "Is the child mine?"

"Yes, it is."

"How can you be sure?"

"I'm sure because Hugh hasn't touched me since before Christmas. You'd know that if you ever asked."

Guy's face softened and he reached out and took Kate gently by the arms. "I couldn't, Kate. I couldn't bear the thought of him inside you, but I could hardly demand that you deny your husband. I had no right," he explained. He was making excuses, but Kate saw the leap of excitement in his eyes.

"Are you pleased?"

"Of course I'm pleased." Guy lowered his hands to her belly and cupped her tiny stomach. "How could I not have known?"

"It's wondrous," Kate breathed, putting her hands over his. "We'll finally be a family."

Guy's gaze slid away from hers, as he shook his head in disbelief. "Am I meant to just step aside and watch you live happily ever after with my brother?"

"Guy, Hugh is my husband. What would you have me do? I must protect this child, above all else. I will not have it disgraced before it's even born."

Guy took hold of Kate's hands, squeezing her fingers painfully in his agitation. "Kate, I want us to be a family. I want the chance to raise my child."

"That's impossible, and you know it."

"Nothing is impossible."

Kate snatched her hands out of Guy's grasp and took a step back. "Guy, the only way we can be together is if Hugh dies, and I won't wish that on him. Not ever."

"What, so you love him now? Did you lie with me just to get with child? And now that you have what you wished for, you'll just discard me?" Guy exclaimed. He looked like his whole world had just come crashing down, his eyes wide with shock and his hands trembling at his sides.

Kate reached up and cupped his cheek, smiling into his eyes. "Guy," she said softly, "it's you I love. It's always been you."

Her words worked their magic and Guy drew her to him, resting his chin on top of her head. "I can't bear it, Kate. I can't bear knowing I can never be with you or play a part in my child's life. I will always be Uncle Guy, never 'Father'."

"Guy, there's nothing we can do to change that."

"I *will* change it. I promise you, Kate. We will be a family—soon."

She pulled away from him and met his fierce gaze. "Guy de Rosel, hear me now, for what I have to say will not change. I will never be with you or allow you to raise our child if you lift a hand to your brother. Never. You and I have sinned against Hugh, and we will have to live with our actions and atone for our betrayal for the rest of our days, but I will not—I repeat—I will not live with Hugh's blood on my hands."

Guy stared at her in shock. "Who said anything about blood?"

"How else can we live together openly, as husband and wife?"

"I will speak to Hugh. I will explain things to him and ask him to step aside."

"Guy, divorce is not sanctioned by the Church. You know that. Even if Hugh came around in time and forfeited his conjugal rights, the child would still be his by law. As would I."

"There's annulment."

Kate stared at Guy. He was understandably upset, but what he was suggesting was lunacy. How could Kate and Hugh possibly get an annulment after five years of marriage and a child on the way? They could hardly claim non-consummation.

"Kate, there are many grounds for annulment: fraud, coercion, fear, misrepresentation. If we can get Hugh to admit he coerced you into marriage—which, let's be honest, he did—we have a case."

"Guy, this might come as a shock to you, but most young women are coerced into marriage, most often by their fathers. And they're all afraid and ignorant of what marriage truly entails, but if those were all grounds for an annulment, half the marriages in the kingdom would fall apart. I agreed to marry Hugh. I stood in front of the priest, of my own volition, and made my vows. I will not use church doctrine as a scapegoat for my sins."

Guy grabbed Kate by the arms and shook her. "Kate, be reasonable. It's our only chance."

Kate was about to reply when she saw a flash of rust amid the green of new foliage. Guy's head whipped around, just in time to see Joan emerging from the trees, her cheeks ruddy with exertion, her rust-colored skirt billowing in the breeze.

"There ye are. I was beginning to worry. Ye'd been gone a good while."

Guy instantly released Kate, but she wasn't sure how much of their altercation Joan had heard. Possibly nothing, but she must have seen that the discussion between Kate and Guy had been heated, and private.

Joan pinned Guy with a steely stare. "Guy, will ye escort Kate back to the keep, or shall she walk back with me?"

"You go back with Nurse, Kate. I'll be on my way." Guy gave the women a stiff bow and disappeared down the track, walking away from the castle and deeper into the woods. Kate had no idea where he might be going, but it didn't matter. She meekly followed Joan down the path, suddenly exhausted.

"Everything all right between ye two?" Joan asked as they rounded the bend.

"Guy didn't think I should be out alone, is all," Kate lied. Being deceitful didn't come easily to her, but there wasn't much choice. Going forward, deceit would be a way of life.

"And he's right. Ye should have asked Eleanor to accompany ye, as I suggested. I know ye two don't get on at times, but she's yer sister by marriage, so ye must help each other. She's not been herself since Adam left, or have ye not noticed? 'Brethren, if a man—or woman—',." Joan added, "'is overtaken in any trespass, ye who are spiritual restore such a one in a spirit of gentleness, considering yourself lest ye also be tempted. Bear one another's burdens, and so fulfill the law of Christ'."

"I'll ask her next time," Kate muttered, duly chastised. Joan didn't often quote the Scripture, but when she did, it found its mark, like an arrow to the heart.

411

They walked the rest of the way in silence, each lost in her own thoughts.

Chapter 68

Kate curled up on the window seat and rested her head against the cool stone of the wall, both physically tired and emotionally drained by the morning's events. The confrontation with Guy had been unexpected and eye opening. She'd foolishly assumed he would step aside and allow Hugh to raise his child, but she'd been woefully misguided. Guy was no longer the obedient younger sibling. He'd matured and seen more than his fair share of death. He loved her and was prepared to fight for her, even if that meant confronting Hugh and appealing to the Church. Guy would lay claim to his child, whether she agreed to it or not, believing that Hugh cared for him enough to forgive him and agree to his terms. Kate had her doubts. Hugh was not a man who would look kindly upon being cuckolded and deceived. He was prideful and possessed of a hot temper. He forgave easily enough, she'd grant him that, but this time, there was much to forgive.

Not for the first time, Kate wished she could talk matters over with her mother. Anne Dancy would have been shocked and possibly appalled by her daughter's behavior, but she would have offered practical advice, as she always had. Surely Kate wasn't the first woman to find herself in this position, and Hugh wouldn't be alone in mistakenly believing the child his wife carried was his. Unless Guy told him otherwise.

Kate angrily wiped away a tear that slid down her cheek. Until that moment, she hadn't permitted herself to imagine what life with Guy would be like. She'd indulged in romantic fantasies from time to time, but her imagination never strayed as far as marriage. To marry Guy and raise their child together was a dream of such shining brilliance that she didn't even dare entertain it. It could never be, and she would not allow her mind to wander down the dark, twisted alley that beckoned her to consider the only solution that would make the dream a reality. Never. She had made a vow before God and she would honor it, no matter what, and if something happened to Hugh, she's have no hand in it, and neither would Guy.

Kate heaved herself to her feet as a wave of nausea washed over her. She grabbed for the basin and was sick, expelling her dreams along with her dinner.

Chapter 69

Kate wasn't overly worried when she didn't see Guy for the remainder of the day, but when he hadn't put in an appearance by the following evening, she grew concerned. Had he gone for good, hurt and rejected by her refusal to entertain the idea of an annulment? She went into his room under the pretense of collecting linen in need of washing, but couldn't tell if he had taken anything with him. His sword was gone, but he'd been wearing it when she saw him last.

When Kate brought the dirty linen to the kitchen, Joan was shelling peas, her movements efficient and practiced. Walter sat at the table, enjoying a slice of buttered bread and a cup of ale. He made to rise when Kate walked in, but she motioned for him to remain seated.

"Good day, mistress," Water said as soon as he swallowed the bite he'd been chewing.

"Walter, have you seen Master Guy?" Kate tried to sound nonchalant, but her heart raced beneath her calm exterior.

"Not since the day before last," Walter replied. "He went off somewhere."

"I see."

"Were ye needing him for something?" Joan's hands stilled as she watched Kate with that knowing smirk.

"No. I just wondered, that's all."

"He'll come back when he's good and ready. That's Guy's way," Joan replied, oozing disapproval as her hands returned to her task.

"I'm sure he will."

Kate left the basket of linen and went back to her room. She just wanted to be alone, especially since the nausea was making itself known again and gnawing at her guts as it intensified. She was curled up in the window seat when there was a soft knock on the door.

"Come," Kate called, hoping it wasn't Joan. Some days the woman really grated on her.

It was Eleanor. She looked pale and sad, her golden hair hidden beneath a dun-colored veil that matched her plain, serviceable gown. "How do you fare, Kate?" she asked.

"I'm well. Thank you."

"Won't you join me in the Lady Chamber? It's rather quiet without you." Eleanor stood awkwardly in the doorway. She'd never actively sought out Kate's company, taking for granted that Kate would be there whenever she felt like talking to her. "I've started a new piece of embroidery. With Adam gone, there's much less mending to do," she added wistfully.

Kate had no desire to make small talk with Eleanor, but she felt sorry for the woman. Losing Adam was a big adjustment for her, even if she'd always known the separation would come. "I'm sure Adam is well," Kate offered as she hauled herself to her feet.

"I worry about him so. He's so young and vulnerable. What if he gets hurt or falls ill?"

"Eleanor, the earl is a kind man. He looks after his people. Adam will thrive under his tutelage. You'll see."

"I wouldn't expect you to understand, but you will," Eleanor replied spitefully. "Just wait until your child is torn from you, and it will be, be it a boy or a girl. And that's if both of you even survive the birth."

Kate blanched at Eleanor's words. Was Eleanor hoping she'd miscarry, or die in childbed? Did she dislike her that much, or was there some other reason for her venom? She knew Eleanor was unhappy. A widow was about as useful to society as a three-legged horse, unless she could be married off to forge an alliance with another family or expand the family's holdings, but since Hugh never sought another marriage for Eleanor, she was caught in a an unenviable position. Eleanor was still attractive enough to tempt a man, and fertile enough to bear children, but without the means of getting on with her life, she was left to fade away and turn to dust as time wove its spell and stripped her of her beauty and vitality. Whatever Eleanor's reasons, Kate couldn't bring herself to ignore the barb.

"You know, Eleanor, I feel unwell after all. I think I'll remain here for a spell, if you don't mind. Please shut the door on your way out."

Kate turned away, but not before she saw the flare of resentment in the other woman's eyes.

Kate remained in her chamber for the rest of the afternoon. At any other time, she would have become lonely and left her room to seek the companionship of other women, but at the moment, she didn't mind the solitude. She opened the window and allowed the gentle breeze to caress her face as she looked out over the verdant hills and mist-shrouded valleys. The Tweed flowed peacefully past, the river rippling and sparkling playfully as it wound into the distance. Kate wished she could get into a boat with Guy and float away to a place where no one knew them and they could choose their own destiny and live out their days in blissful anonymity.

A knock on the door startled Kate out of her reverie. Perhaps Eleanor had returned, either to demand that Kate join her or to apologize for her thoughtless comment. Or maybe it was Joan, coming to check on Kate and offer unsolicited advice, as she did more and more now that Kate was with child.

Instead, Guy came in and closed the door softly behind him before joining her at the window. "I've come back."

"I thought I'd driven you away," Kate replied, smiling foolishly. The sight of Guy restored her spirits and her heart soared with certainty that he still loved her.

"There was a bit of intelligence I needed to follow up on," Guy explained.

"What sort of intelligence? Is it to do with Warwick?"

"No, this venture was of a purely personal nature. At the Christmas feast, Amelia Ambrose's father made several comments about lecherous priests," he said. "Do you recall?"

Kate shrugged. "I didn't pay much attention to what he said. He's a bit of a zealot, isn't he? He sees sin everywhere."

"He does, but it got me thinking. So I went to Newcastle to do some digging."

"Guy, I don't follow."

"I spent several days visiting taverns, especially those close to the Cathedral Church of St. Nicholas, which happens to be the seat of the Bishop of Newcastle."

"What were you hoping to accomplish?"

"Bishop Bridewell is a well-respected member of the diocese. He's always taken a hard line on sin, particularly carnal sin, preaching eternal damnation, and threatening his parishioners with the fires of hell should they commit the slightest transgression. He doesn't believe in repentance or forgiveness, only punishment and the everlasting wrath of a vengeful God."

"Sounds like the type of clergyman we should avoid at all cost, given our history." Kate tried to make a joke, but her voice sounded small and frightened. She was utterly baffled by Guy's strange errand.

"I was hoping to learn something of the bishop, and I did. It would appear that the very pious Bishop Bridewell, a man of seventy who's devoted his life to the Church, regularly visits a certain woman at her lodgings, and arrives there *sans* his clerical robes."

"Who is she?" Kate asked, intrigued.

"She's his mistress, and has been for the past decade, during which time she bore the bishop three children. I've no doubt there were others before her. He's sired half the bastards in Newcastle."

"What's this to do with us?"

Guy shook his head and smiled at Kate's naiveté. "Kate, if Hugh agrees to an annulment, it'll be that much easier to obtain if we have a bishop who's willing to see it through. And what would make a geriatric bishop cooperate short of a threat to his livelihood and reputation?"

Kate stared at him. This wasn't the Guy she knew. This man was ruthless and calculating, ready to exploit someone's weakness for his own gain. This was also a man who loved her and was willing to go to any lengths to free her from her marriage to Hugh. What Guy had done was an act of devotion, and a declaration of love for her and their child. He would never blackmail someone for money or power, only for love.

"You're serious about this, aren't you?"

"Deadly. I won't leave you ever again, Kate."

Her eyes flew to the door as it opened to reveal Joan holding a basket of clean linen on her hip.

"Guy, I thought I saw ye sneaking about. Come to visit yer devoted sister-in-law, have ye?" Joan gave them both an acid stare before stowing the clean garments in the chest at the foot of the bed and departing.

"Do you think she overheard?" Kate said as the door closed behind Joan.

"Her hearing's not what it used to be. She's getting on in years," Guy observed. He dismissed Joan and returned to the earlier topic. "Kate, I need to know that you agree before I confront Hugh. No sense poking a hornet's nest and getting stung if you won't agree to go through with it."

Kate lowered her eyes, unable to bear the intensity of Guy's gaze. Annulling her marriage, which was legal and valid, went against everything she believed in, but it might be her only chance at happiness. She doubted Hugh would agree, but if he did, she and Guy could marry and be a family. They could live in love and understanding and raise their children together. They could be happy. Even thinking along those lines made Kate cringe with guilt. What right did she have to ask for happiness? And what would be the price of that happiness? Hugh would be humiliated and ridiculed, and Kate would have to live with her deceit for the rest of her days. The world might believe that the marriage hadn't been valid, but she'd know the truth. Was she ready to risk her soul for a future that might never be?

Kate's hand went to her belly. Deep inside, a little person slumbered, waiting to be born, oblivious to all the strife its very existence had caused. Guy would never have conceived of blackmailing a bishop of the Church if it weren't for Kate's pregnancy. Or perhaps he would. He wasn't a man to lurk in the shadows and pick crumbs from his brother's table. Guy was willing to fight for what he wanted, and he was daring her to be brave and honest and do the same.

"All right. I agree," Kate whispered, shocked by her own boldness. "When will you speak to Hugh?"

"Tonight."

"No, please. Not yet. I need a little time to come to terms with what we're about to do. Wait until after the Feast of Ascension."

Guy looked disappointed, but nodded in agreement. "All right. If that will make it easier for you."

Chapter 70

May 1465

Berwick-upon-Tweed, Northumberland

Kate trudged miserably up the stairs, stopping every few steps to catch her breath. She'd felt a little better the past few days, but the nausea had come back with a vengeance this afternoon, reminding her that she wasn't over the worst of the sickness yet. Joan had insisted she remain behind in bed and rest, for the child's sake, but Kate had wished to participate in the celebration. The Feast of Ascension was one of her favorite feast days as it was usually marked by picnics held on hilltops. It was traditional to eat some sort of fowl, to symbolize the flight of Jesus to the heavens, and whatever fruit was to hand. The fruit was blessed by the priest after the Memento of the Dead.

Bless, O Lord, these new fruits of the vine which Thou hast brought to maturity by the dew of heaven, by plentiful rains and by tranquil and favorable weather. Thou hast given us this fruit for our use that we may receive it with thanks in the name of our Lord, Jesus Christ.

The blessing referred more to grapes, but as grapes were hard to come by in Northumberland, they had to do with the oranges that Hugh had managed to procure for the occasion. There had been only three, and they'd had to share, but the few slivers of the juicy fruit were ambrosia. Kate had devoured her share, her body starved for nutrients after months of monotonous winter food. Perhaps it was the orange that brought on this infernal sickness again, or perhaps it was fear of what was to come. Guy meant to speak to Hugh this night, and demand that he release Kate from their marriage. He'd been simmering since returning from Newcastle, and if she didn't give him leave to act, his temper would boil over.

As Kate had sat on a blanket overlooking the swift-flowing river and the rolling hills beyond, she had tried to calm herself by recalling the feasts of her childhood, when she'd spent the day with her parents and brothers, enjoying the fine spring weather after months of snow and rain. She could hardly remember the church services, or the food her mother had Cook prepare for their feasts, but she remembered the mood of those picnics. She'd felt safe and happy, delighted by the carefree banter between her parents and the camaraderie of her brothers. How life had changed since those sunny days.

Kate finally reached her chamber, kicked off her shoes, and crawled into bed. The room was pleasantly cool, and the dim confines of the bed were a welcome change from the sunshine outside. She closed her eyes and rested her hand on her growing belly, willing the babe inside to make itself known. She'd felt it for the first time only about a week ago, a gentle flutter that came and went, hardly noticeable at first, but impossible to ignore once she'd realized what it must be. . It took a few minutes now, but eventually she felt a bump against her hand, like that of a kicking foot. Could it be a foot? Or an elbow?

Kate sighed miserably. This should have been a happy time, even with the persistent sickness, but the thought of what would happen in a few short hours left her insides lurching with fear. She wanted to be with Guy more than anything, to live in harmony and raise their child in love, but Hugh wouldn't take this lightly, nor would the Church. She and Guy had sinned, and now they wanted to legalize their sin and thwart the laws of God. It felt wrong. Kate tried to explain her fears to Guy when he'd followed her to the chapel that morning, but he brushed her reservations aside, determined to see this through.

"Don't you love me?" Guy had demanded when Kate broached the subject. "Don't you want to leave Hugh and be free to follow your heart for once in your life?"

"You know I do, but I'm frightened, Guy. Do you know anyone who's been granted an annulment?"

Guy looked at her for a moment, considering the question. "No, I don't."

"Guy, the Church will not release me from my vows, even if we publicly confess that the child I carry is not my husband's. We will be disgraced, humiliated, and punished for our misdeeds. I fear for our child. He'll be branded a bastard, a child of sin. And what of Hugh? He might not be the husband of my heart, but he is my husband before the law. Does your brother deserve to be dishonored before everyone he knows?"

"Hugh's not been a good husband to you," Guy had snapped.

"He's been no worse than most. Do you believe that every marriage in Christendom is based on love and mutual respect?"

"Kate, you asked me to wait until the Feast of Ascension and that is what I have done. Tonight, I will confront Hugh, unless you tell me not to, but if you do, know that I will leave and never return. The choice is yours. I won't force you, but neither will I live my life in secret, always skulking in the shadows and hiding from the truth."

The answer had sprung to her lips, urgent and filled with longing. "Don't go," she had whispered. "Please, don't go. I can't go on without you."

Drawing her close, he had pressed his lips to her forehead. "I'll never leave you, Kate, not even if you ask me to."

"We must get back before anyone misses us," Kate had said, pulling away from Guy. "I just heard Joan outside."

"After tonight we won't have to hide ever again. Everyone will know."

That's what I'm afraid of, Kate had thought as she'd watched Guy slip out of the chapel and walk away.

Chapter 71

Kate raised herself on her elbow and reached for the cup of ale someone had thoughtfully left by her bed. The slight movement brought on a new bout of nausea, but the ale helped settle her stomach. It was cool and bitter, more so than usual, but she hardly noticed. She was thirsty, so she drained the cup and lay back down, breathing deeply until the wave of sickness began to ebb. Perhaps it was the potency of the drink, but Kate felt pleasantly detached, her mind at peace for the first time in weeks. She began to drift, enjoying the sensation of weightlessness as her body relaxed into the mattress. Perhaps she'd sleep for a while.

She wasn't frightened at first. The twitches in her belly seemed insignificant, like the rumbling of distant thunder, and the shortness of breath and nausea had been her constant companions for several weeks. It wasn't until that first sharp pain that she began to worry, wondering if something might be truly wrong. She tried to sit up, desperate to pull apart the bed hangings and allow some light into the dim confines of the bed, but another pain sliced through her, forcing her back down and pinning her to the mattress. She rolled onto her side and brought her knees up to her chest, praying for the pain to stop, but it didn't. Waves of nausea and dizziness rolled over her as the spasms in her womb intensified, no longer rumbles of thunder, but sharp, jagged bolts of lightning. Her extremities began to go numb, as her vision blurred and her hearing faded out. She tried to call for help, but her cry was like the whimper of a newborn kitten.

"Dear God, please, no," she prayed as hot, sticky blood began to flow between her legs, her womb mercilessly forcing the baby out. Somewhere deep inside she'd known that this could never be. She owed God a debt and He'd come to collect, with interest. He wouldn't allow a sinner like her to taste such joy. God was vengeful, and He was cruel, and in her time of need He had forsaken her.

She began to tremble violently as her breath came in short gasps, no longer seeing the darkness of her curtained world. What she saw were the faces of those she'd loved, floating before her like wispy clouds before the moon.

As she lay in a pool of her own blood, and life drained from her battered body, she had one final thought:

I've been murdered.

Chapter 72

September 2014

London, England

Quinn dropped the rosary. The pain she'd experienced in her vision didn't fade away, but intensified, forcing her to curl up on the bed and hug her knees. Her womb was contracting, the skin growing taut with every spasm. Quinn tried to think calmly as she searched for a more comfortable position. She'd experienced mild Braxton Hicks contractions on and off since the second trimester, but Dr. Malik had assured her this was perfectly normal and not a prelude to a miscarriage. The contractions were more uncomfortable than painful, and usually went away after about a half hour. This pain was more intense, but she was also closer to her due date, so perhaps this was all par for the course.

Quinn climbed out of bed, hoping she might walk off the pain. She walked from one end of the bedroom to the other, kneading her lower back with her fists. After a few minutes, the contractions receded, and she breathed a sigh of relief. The baby wasn't due for another three weeks, so this was definitely too soon. Quinn returned to bed and rolled onto her side, the only position she could sleep in since lying on her back made it difficult to breathe, and hugged her pillow. She was wide awake, her mind still on Kate, her heart breaking for the other woman and the baby that would never be. Quinn had known Kate would never carry the baby to term, since Colin had seen no evidence of a birth in Kate's skeletal remains, but Kate's death still shocked and devastated her.

Quinn couldn't risk picking up the rosary again, not after what'd just happened, and wasn't even sure there was anything more to see. Kate's story was finished, at least from her perspective. In her last moments, Kate had believed she'd been murdered, but there was no proof that anyone wished her harm. Perhaps the severe illness she'd been experiencing for months had been hyperemesis gravidarum, a form of extreme morning sickness that affected a small percentage of expectant mothers, but it wasn't fatal and usually subsided as soon as the child was born. Or perhaps Kate's body hadn't been able to withstand the extreme stress of the situation. In the twenty-first century, it was simple enough to end a marriage and find happiness with someone else, but in Kate's time, divorce had been unheard of and annulment had been granted rarely and after lengthy deliberation and examination of the situation.

It wasn't until Henry VIII rid himself of Catherine of Aragon that the possibility of ending an unsatisfying marriage had become a reality, and even then, only for those few who were willing to go to war with the Church and risk eternal damnation. Kate had had every reason to be terrified, and reluctant to risk her child's future for an outcome that was in no way guaranteed. If the annulment was denied, which it most likely would be; at best, she might have been disgraced and locked away by Hugh for the rest of her days, or at worst, she might have been whipped through the streets as a harlot and an adulteress, or even put to death if she were accused of bewitching her brother-in-law. Guy's love and desire to be with Kate had blinded him to reality and given him false hope. Even if he had succeeded in bending Bishop Bridewell to his will, the bishop would not have had the power to singlehandedly dissolve the marriage, so a happy ending would most likely never have been in the cards.

Pain tore through Quinn's belly, leaving her breathless and driving Kate's plight from her mind. This was the here and now, and something was wrong. She sat bolt upright, wrapped her arms about her middle, and rocked back and forth to ease her suffering. The next pain came right on the heels of the first one and was just as sharp, almost as if it were inflicted by a knife. These were not Braxton Hicks contractions; this was something very different. Quinn considered walking again when the next stab sliced through her womb. She cried out as something sticky and hot began to trickle between her legs.

"Oh, dear God, please, no!" she cried, unwittingly echoing Kate's plea. "Gabe!" Quinn screamed, her voice hoarse with desperation.

Gabe was at her side within seconds, his eyes wide with fear. "What is it?"

"I need to go to the hospital. Something's wrong."

"Should I ring for an ambulance?"

"No. An ambulance will take me to the nearest hospital. I want to go to the London," Quinn wailed.

"Right." Gabe raced to the other room to wake Emma. Quinn followed him, walking slowly and holding on to the wall for support. She went to the bathroom and found blood on her knickers, but thankfully, she wasn't bleeding heavily. She put in a sanitary napkin and grabbed a pair of maternity jeans she'd left hanging on the hook behind the door. Pulling them on took some doing, but she gritted her teeth through the pain and got dressed. She couldn't go to the hospital in her underwear.

Emma was groggy with sleep as she took in her parents' disheveled state. "What's happening?" she muttered.

"It's all right, darling. We just have to take Quinn to A&E," Gabe explained as he lifted Emma out of her bed and wrapped a blanket around her.

"Is she hurt?"

"She's just experiencing some pains."

Gabe managed to hold Emma in his arms and support Quinn as they walked to the lift that'd take them to the underground parking garage. Quinn hunched over and pressed her forehead against the cool metal wall of the lift, willing it to move faster. The baby seemed much lower now, pressing down and creating unbearable pressure in her pelvic area. Gabe helped Quinn

428

into the car and strapped Emma into her seat before jumping into the driver's seat and starting the car.

"I want Mr. Rabbit. I forgot Mr. Rabbit!" Emma screeched.

"We can't go back for Mr. Rabbit. There's no time," Gabe replied as he tore out of the garage.

Emma cried softy in the back seat, upset about Mr. Rabbit and probably frightened by Quinn's moans, which were beginning to escalate into grunts. Emma clutched the blanket to her chest and used it to wipe her streaming eyes. "I want to go home," she whimpered.

"We'll go home just as soon as we get the all clear. Everything will be all right." Gabe sounded authoritative and calm, but Quinn knew he was terrified. His hand trembled as he changed gears. Emma howled louder.

Quinn let out a gasp of pain and doubled over. She was panting, and perspiration covered her brow. "Oh, Gabe, I'm bleeding badly. Hurry."

Gabe floored the gas pedal, tearing through nighttime London with a screech of tires. Quinn hoped that a traffic cop wasn't waiting around the corner. They couldn't afford to lose any time. She screamed as stab after excruciating stab slashed her uterus, and she felt the familiar flush spread from her chest to her face. Her heart was racing, and a pounding headache was building behind the eyes, nearly blinding her with its intensity.

Overwhelmed with pain and fear, Quinn began to cry. She sounded like a wounded animal, and Emma, spurred on by Quinn's fear, began to shriek like a banshee while tearing at the straps of her child seat and reaching for Quinn.

"Let me out!" she screamed. "I want my mum."

Hearing Emma call her 'mum' for the first time should have been a special moment for Quinn, but the fact that Emma's outburst was driven by her fear of losing Quinn made Quinn cry even harder. She was trapped in a cocoon of agony, her treacherous body hurting from brain to groin. She doubled over as blood soaked through her sanitary napkin and bloomed on the denim between her thighs.

Gabe exploded into the parking lot of the Royal London, parking as close to the A&E entrance as he dared. He grabbed Emma from the back seat and supported Quinn as he maneuvered her toward the door. Two young doctors were standing outside, sneaking a cigarette when they saw the trio approaching, and instantly sprang into action.

"Oh, my God. We need a gurney out here," one of the doctors roared into the open door as the other one reached for Quinn, steadying her.

Emma was thrashing and pushing Gabe away, demanding to be let down. She was screaming and crying, her eyes wild with fear.

"Darling, it will be all right. We're here now." Gabe tried to calm her, but Emma fought harder, screaming louder.

"It won't! It won't be all right! Stop lying to me!"

"I'll call for a social worker," one of the young doctors offered as they helped Quinn onto a gurney and began to wheel her through the A&E doors. "She might be able to help."

Gabe nodded and followed the doctors into the waiting area.

"Please, remain here, sir," a nurse instructed him as he made to follow Quinn. "Someone will come speak to you as soon as they are able," the nurse hollered over Emma's screams.

A young black woman with dark almond-shaped eyes and long braids came rushing down the corridor. She flashed her identification card at Gabe before turning to Emma. "Hello, Emma.

I'm Nina Daniels. Was that your mum that just came in?" she asked. Her voice was like warm honey and Emma stopped screaming for just a moment.

"Yes," she finally replied, her voice small and shaky.

"Well, you have nothing to be frightened of. This is the best hospital in London."

"Is it?" Emma asked through loud sniffling.

"Of course it is. That's why your dad brought her here. Now, what do you say you and I play a game while Daddy visits with Mum? She knows this is the very best hospital, but she's probably a little nervous anyway and would like to see a friendly face."

"Are the doctors not friendly?"

"Of course they are, but they have a job to do, and your dad's only job right now is to look after your mum."

"And me," Emma protested. "He has to look after me."

"What if I look after you?"

Emma shook her head. "I'm not coming with you. I want to see my mum."

"We don't have to play a game. We can take a walk to the cafeteria."

"It's the middle of the night," Emma pointed out.

"Hmm, you're right. The cafeteria is closed, but there is a vending machine just outside, and I happen to know that it has three different ice cream selections. I bet you like ice cream. I sure do."

Emma looked tempted.

431

"Darling, please get some ice cream with Ms. Daniels. She'll bring you right back after you're done," Gabe pleaded, desperate to get to Quinn.

"All right," Emma conceded. "But I'll never forgive you if anything happens to my mum," Emma threw over her shoulder. "It's all your fault."

"How's it my fault?" Gabe demanded, wounded by Emma's words.

"You put that baby in there. I know all about it. Aidan told me how it's done."

Emma walked off without a backward glance, leaving Gabe staring after her, shocked and terrified for Quinn. *Get hold of yourself, man*, he berated himself as he sprinted down the corridor toward the room where Quinn had been taken, despite the nurse's request that he remain in the waiting area. The young doctor from earlier was there, along with a middle-aged woman whose eyes were glued to the fetal monitor.

"What's happening?" Gabe's eyes flew to Quinn, who appeared much calmer than she'd been before. She was already hooked up to several machines, including a blood pressure monitor.

"Mr. Russell, I'm Dr. Young," the woman said. "I've paged Dr. Malik, but I'm afraid we can't afford to wait for her. Your wife has suffered a placental abruption. The fetus is in distress, and your wife's blood pressure is dangerously low. We're going to perform an emergency C-section as soon as Mrs. Russell is prepped and ready to go."

"Why did this happen? She was on bedrest." Gabe felt as if he'd just been punched in the gut. He'd expected Quinn's blood pressure to be high, not low, and given the concerned look on Dr. Young's face when she looked at the monitor, this could be a matter of life or death for the baby.

"It isn't anything your wife did, sir. The placental abruption was likely caused by the preeclampsia. It usually happens around twenty-five weeks of pregnancy, but in some cases, it occurs later. Now, I'm sorry to have to ask you to leave, but we must get on. The operating theater is ready for us."

Two hospital porters appeared at the door, ready to wheel Quinn away.

"Can my husband not stay with me during the surgery?" Quinn asked.

Dr. Young shook her head. "I'm sorry, Mrs. Russell, but under the circumstances, we feel it would be safer for both you and the baby if we performed the cesarean section under general anesthesia. Your husband will have to wait outside."

"But I'll miss my baby's first moments," Quinn argued.

"I know it's upsetting, but we can't take any risks with your wellbeing."

"I understand. Gabe." Quinn reached for Gabe's hand.

"I'll be there when you wake up. All will be well," Gabe said as he took her hand.

"Please comfort Emma. She's so scared."

"Don't worry about Emma. I'll see to her. I love you." Gabe's voice sounded watery. He was frightened, for both Quinn and the baby, but there was nothing he could do to change whatever was going to happen. He could only wait, which was sometimes the hardest thing to do. Dr. Young allowed them a moment to say goodbye, but he saw the urgency in her gaze. There was no time to waste.

"I love you." Quinn brushed her hand against Gabe's as the gurney began to move toward the door. "See you on the other side."

Chapter 73

Gabe watched with trepidation as Quinn was wheeled away from him. She looked so small and vulnerable on that hospital gurney. Her belly, which had grown huge within the past few weeks, rose beneath the white sheet like a snow-covered hill. Gabe looked after Quinn until the porters turned the corner, then retraced his steps to the waiting area. Emma was there with Ms. Daniels. Her face was tear-stained and she was clutching her blanket as if it were a life preserver.

"She changed her mind about the ice cream," the social worker explained. "She's too worried about her mum to eat."

"Thank you, Ms. Daniels," Gabe said as he reached for Emma, who practically jumped into his arms. She wrapped her arms around him and buried her face in his neck.

"I thought you left me," Emma sobbed.

"Left you? Why would I leave you? I only went to check on Quinn—eh, Mum."

"Where is she?"

"They took her into another room where they will take the baby out of her belly." Gabe thought that was the least-involved explanation. He didn't want to frighten Emma any more than she already was with words like 'surgery' and 'operating theater.'

"Will it be alive? Will Quinn? I don't want to lose her," Emma cried.

Gabe nodded thanks to Ms. Daniels, who was turning to leave. There was nothing more she could do since it was clear that Emma had the support she needed.

"Ask the nurses to page me if you have need of me," she said and walked away.

Gabe sat down in one of the plastic chairs and settled Emma on his lap. She looked like a human burrito, wrapped in her beige blanket. "Em, I know you're worried. I'm worried too, but Dr. Young said that everything will be all right, and we have to believe her. She's the expert in these matters. So, how about we find you a place to lay your head?"

Emma nodded miserably. "I'm tired, Daddy."

"I know, sweetheart. It's well past your bedtime. How about I give Logan a ring? Maybe he's on shift tonight. Shall I do that?"

"Yes. I like Logan." Emma's eyelids were beginning to flutter as she leaned against Gabe. "I'll be nice to the baby. I promise," Emma muttered as she fell into a deep sleep. Gabe rang Logan.

"I'll be there in two. Just sit tight. Gabe, it will be all right. Dr. Young is one of the best."

"I feel so helpless," Gabe confessed. "Poor Emma is terrified."

"Gabe, countless C-sections are performed at the London every single day. Fatalities are very, very rare. Quinn will be out of surgery before you know it."

"How long does it take to do a C-section?" Gabe asked. He should have asked Dr. Young, but he had been too overcome with emotion to think of practical matters.

"The procedure itself lasts only a few minutes. I bet it's already done. Quinn is probably on her way to the recovery area."

"I could use a bit of support, to be honest," Gabe confessed. He knew Logan was telling him the absolute truth, but having lost his father so recently, after being told that Graham was on the mend, left Gabe feeling a bit weepy and overwrought.

"And I'm here to support you," Logan said as he materialized in front of Gabe, mobile still in his hand. "Come, there's a nurse's lounge just down the corridor. Emma can sleep on the sofa. It's quiet and dark. Just what she needs right now. You look like you could use a kip yourself."

"I can't sleep."

"Have you ever meditated?" Logan asked as he led Gabe into the lounge. Thankfully, it was unoccupied.

"No. Not really my thing."

"I'll show you how. It's wonderful during times of stress. Colin got me into it. You game?"

"I think a horse-dose of tranquilizer would be more effective," Gabe quipped.

"It certainly would, but I'm not at liberty to dispense tranquilizers to friends and family. I can, however, offer you the next best thing."

"What would that be?"

"Tea. There's a kettle in here, and we even have fresh milk. Would you like a cup?"

"Please."

Logan busied himself with making tea while Gabe tucked the blanket around Emma to keep her warm. She was curled up like a shrimp, muttering in her sleep, her hand searching for Mr. Rabbit.

Logan set a mug of hot, sweet tea in front of Gabe and pulled out his mobile. "Nancy, love, can you text me as soon as Quinn Russell is in recovery? Thanks ever so much. In your debt."

"Thanks, Logan."

"No need to thank me, old boy. That's what brothers-in-law are for."

Gabe smiled and chose not to point out that brothers-in-law had been the bane of his existence for the past few months. He liked Logan and was glad Quinn had at least one decent sibling out of three.

Logan's phone vibrated only a few minutes later. "Right. Thanks, love. Gabe, Quinn's out of surgery. She's doing great. And you have a…" Logan looked fit to burst with the news.

"A what?" Gabe cried, suddenly desperate to know.

"You have a healthy son. Congratulations, man. Oh, gosh, I think I'm crying."

"That makes two of us," Gabe confessed as he sniffled away.

Chapter 74

Hearing was the first sense to reassert itself. Quinn could hear the beeping of monitors, the low murmur of voices coming from the nurses' station, and the squeaking of wheels on linoleum. She felt warm and snug, but her eyelids weighed a ton, as did her limbs. She's sleep for just a few minutes more, she decided, allowing herself to be reclaimed by the pleasant darkness.

"Time to wake up, sleepyhead." The voice was rich and deep with a slight Caribbean lilt. "Come on, darlin'." The nurse touched her hand gently. "I know you can hear me."

Quinn forced her eyes open. Thankfully, the overhead light was off, so the curtained cubicle was pleasantly dim. The nurse smiled kindly at her. She was an older woman with a face as round as the moon and almond-shaped eyes fringed with ridiculously thick lashes. "How you feelin', love?" she asked as she removed the oxygen tube from Quinn's nose and checked her vital signs.

"Groggy," Quinn croaked. Her voice sounded as if she hadn't used it in years.

"That's normal. You'll feel more alert in a few minutes."

Memory came flooding back and Quinn tried to sit up, suddenly anxious. "My baby. Where's my baby?"

"Don't you worry, love," the nurse crooned. "Baby is just fine and sleepin' peacefully in the nursery. Dr. Young will be by in a moment to talk to you, so you just hang on tight."

Not as if there was anything else Quinn could do. She was hooked up to an IV and a catheter, and her legs felt like something that had emerged from a jelly mold. "Where's my husband?"

"Your man knows people in high places, I'll tell you that," the nurse joked. "He's in the nurses' lounge with your little one. She's fast asleep, God bless her. She was worn out with worry for her mummy."

Quinn teared up at the nurse's words. Emma had been worried about her. The knowledge was strangely wonderful. "May I see them?"

"Of course, love. Just as soon as you get the all clear and get transferred to a room." The nurse handed her a container of apple juice. Quinn wasn't a big fan of apple juice, but at the moment it tasted like ambrosia. She was just sucking up the last drops when Dr. Young appeared beside her bed.

"Well, hello there, Mummy," Dr. Young said, smiling broadly. "You came through with flying colors, and the little one is doing great. An on-staff pediatrician examined him, and he's been given a clean bill of health. He's a tad small, but given that he arrived three weeks early, that's to be expected."

"He?"

"Yes, a beautiful baby boy."

"Phoebe Russell scores again," Quinn said with a chuckle.

"What's that?"

"Nothing. Can I see him?"

"Absolutely. I'll have Nurse Winnie bring him to you as soon as you're settled in your room."

"When can I go home?" Quinn asked.

"We are going to keep you and the baby for a couple of days, just to make sure you're both doing well. I should think you'll be going home by Tuesday." Dr. Young scribbled something in Quinn's chart and turned to the nurse. "Mrs. Russell is ready to be transferred, Winnie."

"Right. I'll call the porters." Winnie rushed off, leaving Quinn with Dr. Young.

"Well, congratulations, Quinn. I'll check on you in a little bit. And so will Dr. Malik. I believe she's already in the building."

A broad smile spread across Quinn's face as soon as Dr. Young left. A boy. A healthy, perfect baby boy. She couldn't wait to finally see him and hold him. Now that she knew the baby was a boy, she couldn't imagine him having been a girl. It was as if she'd known all along, just as Phoebe had, and Quinn's grandmother Rae, who'd made the same pronouncement. Quinn would have liked to be the first to tell Gabe the news, but she assumed Dr. Young had spoken to him immediately after the surgery, to put his mind at rest, about both her and the newborn baby.

Chapter 75

"Happy birthday," Gabe crooned as he sat next to Quinn and leaned down to kiss her.

"Is it?"

"It's past midnight, so it's September twenty-seventh. And we have a son."

"I know. Isn't it marvelous? Have you seen him?"

Gabe smiled guiltily. "Through the glass. He's adorable. And speak of the devil."

Nurse Winnie entered the room, wheeling a plastic bassinet. "Here we are, Mummy and Daddy," she announced.

Quinn's vision blurred with tears as Winnie carefully picked up the baby and placed him in her arms. He was tightly wrapped in a hospital blanket and a knitted cap covered his head, but Quinn could see downy strands of dark hair peeking from beneath. The baby opened his eyes. His dark-blue gaze was unfocused, but it seemed to Quinn that he was looking right at her. She held her breath as she beheld his little face. The baby wasn't red or wrinkly, since he hadn't been pushed through the birth canal. He was the perfect shade of pink, and his little mouth opened and closed as he turned his face toward Quinn.

"He's hungry," Winnie explained. "Will you be breastfeeding?"

"Yes."

"Then go on and put him to your breast. The milk won't fully come in until tomorrow or the day after, but there's enough colostrum to tide him over until then."

Quinn pulled down her hospital gown and put the baby to her breast. It took him a few moments to latch on, but once he did, he seemed to know exactly what to do.

"Enjoy your midnight snack, little one," Winnie said and walked away.

Gabe looked on with such reverence that Quinn couldn't help teasing him. "We're not the Madonna and Child, you know."

"You are to me. I was so worried," he confessed.

Quinn nodded in understanding. "Is Emma still sleeping in the nurses' lounge? And what did Winnie mean when she said you know people in high places?"

"I didn't want to wake her. I called Logan after they took you into the operating theater. He wasn't on shift, but he immediately came over. He took us into the lounge and commandeered the sofa for Emma. He is with her, in case she wakes up." Gabe smiled sadly. "God, Quinn, she really lost it. She was so frightened. I couldn't comfort her. She thought you were going to die, just like her mum."

Quinn pulled up her gown once the baby stopped nursing and fell asleep. His face looked like a tiny moon, round and serene. "Gabe, it will take years for Emma to come to terms with what happened. All we can do is be patient and understanding, and never belittle her fears. She has every right to be afraid. For a moment there, I was pretty terrified myself."

"So was I. May I hold him?" Gabe carefully accepted the baby and cradled him in his arms. A look of pure wonder spread across his face as he smiled down at his son. "He looks like me."

"That he does. That's two for you, none for me."

"Does this mean you're open to doing this again?"

"Not in this decade. Check back with me closer to 2020," Quinn joked.

"Don't think I won't. So what shall we name this little man?"

"Alex," they said in unison.

"Alexander Graham, after your dad," Quinn clarified. "What do you think of that?"

"Well, it worked out quite well for Alexander Graham Bell. Maybe he'll grow up to be an inventor."

"Stop projecting your own dreams onto him, Daddy. He's only an hour old." Quinn felt overwhelmed with love as she looked at the two of them, so natural together.

She was just about to say so when Logan walked into the room. He had Emma, who looked wide awake, by the hand.

"Are we just in time for the welcome party?" he asked. "Look, Em, it's your baby brother."

Emma inched closer to Gabe, but her expression wasn't one of wonder but extreme jealousy. She glanced at the baby, then turned to Quinn. "Will you love him more than you love me?"

"Of course not. Come here."

Quinn stretched out her arms and tried to turn onto her side, which hurt like the devil, but it was worth it. She was able to wrap her arms about Emma, who burrowed her face in Quinn's neck.

"Don't ever leave me, Mum. Not ever. I was so scared."

"I know you were, but everything is all right, and now we have Alex."

"Hmm."

"Would you like to hold him?"

"May I?" Emma asked, her eyes lighting up. "You'll let me?"

Gabe vacated the chair he'd been sitting in and invited Emma to sit down. "You get comfortable, and I will put the baby in your arms." Emma did as she was told and Gabe handed her the baby. He stood directly in front of her, so the baby wouldn't tumble to the floor should she let go.

"I'm Emma," she announced to the infant. "I'm your big sister. You're smaller than I thought you were going to be, but we'll feed you up," she said, echoing a phrase she'd heard Phoebe use. "You'll get big and strong, and then we'll play together. But you can't have Mr. Rabbit. Not ever. You'll have to get your own. Okay, I'm done."

Gabe took the baby and placed him in the bassinet. "I'm going to take Emma home and put her to bed. Besides, Mr. Rabbit must be frantic with worry. We'll be back first thing in the morning. Get some rest." He kissed Quinn and escorted Emma from the room.

"Does Sylvia know?" Quinn asked Logan as soon as Gabe and Emma had gone.

"Yes. She'd like to come and see you. Shall I tell her she may visit?"

Quinn was tempted to refuse, but nodded instead. "Alex is her grandson."

"Thanks, Quinn. That's kind. I know how angry you are with her, and with Jude. He's promised to start rehab. That episode with Emma really frightened him. He'd never have forgiven himself had anything happened to her."

"I'm glad he's ready to get help, but I don't think I want to see him anytime soon."

"Understandable."

"Have you heard anything about our sister? Today is her birthday too."

"No, I haven't. Dead silence."

Quinn didn't mean to cry, but dissolved into floods, partially because she was a hormonal minefield, and partially because her heart longed for a sister she'd never met. Somewhere out there, Quentin had turned thirty-one years old. What would her birthday celebration be like? Was she married? Did she have children? Did she know that she had siblings who were searching for her and had she decided not to reach out to them?

"We'll find her, Quinn. I know it."

"We must. I will never feel complete until I see her and speak to her."

Logan patted Quinn on the shoulder and left her to rest, but there was something she had to do before going to sleep. Gabe had left her mobile within reach, so she got hold of it and selected Seth's number. It'd be around 8:00 p.m. in New Orleans.

Seth answered on the first ring. "Quinn, I'm so glad you called. How are you, sweetheart? Any news?"

"I'm all right. The news is that you have a grandson. He was born at eleven twenty-three p.m. local time. His name is Alex."

Quinn gave Seth a moment to collect himself. The sharp intake of breath was followed by what could only be a joyful smile. "Oh, Quinn, that's wonderful news. Will you send me a picture?"

"Of course I will. But I expect you to come and see him for yourself. Soon."

"Try and stop me!" Seth exclaimed. He sounded jubilant at the thought of seeing his grandbaby, but then his tone turned anxious. "Quinn, any word on Quentin?"

"No, not yet. I sent the letter, but never heard anything back. I think we'll need to start searching for her on our own."

"Where do we begin?"

"I begin by recovering from a cesarean section, and you begin by scheduling a well-deserved holiday."

"You just let me know when you're ready, and I'll be on the next flight. I'm ready to help in whatever way is needed."

"Thank you."

"You don't need to thank me. You're my girl, and I love you. And I'll move mountains to find your sister. Now, it must be past midnight in London, and you need your rest. Kiss my grandson for me, and give my regards to Gabe and Emma. I look forward to seeing them."

"Talk soon." Quinn rang off. She had one more phone call to make. Her parents would be asleep, but they'd never forgive her if she didn't call them right away with the news. She rang her parents, then texted Jill and Phoebe.

She replaced the phone on the nightstand, tired and in pain, and happier than she'd ever been.

Chapter 76

November 2014
London, England

Quinn deftly changed Alex's nappy, stuffed him into an unbearably cute outfit, and put him down for a nap, hoping against hope that he would just drift off. Alex was a happy baby, but he still woke up hungry at least once during the night and craved the company of his parents round the clock. As though leaving him alone in his cot was paramount to abandoning him to die on the side of a mountain, he whimpered and cried until someone came back into the room. He didn't demand to be picked up, but he liked the presence of another person, particularly if that person was Quinn, because in her case, company also meant a snack. Perhaps she'd get a break once Seth arrived and Alex had one more adoring adult to manipulate.

Seth was coming in two weeks, just in time to treat them to an all-American Thanksgiving, something Quinn was looking forward to. She'd always thought it was a lovely holiday, and this year she had much to be grateful for. Seth had promised to cook the whole meal as long as Quinn stocked the fridge with the required ingredients, including raw cranberries. Lord only knew where she'd get those. Or yams. She'd leave that to Gabe. He'd always enjoyed a challenge. They'd invited Logan and Colin, Jill and Brian, and Pete and Brenda McGann for their upcoming feast. It'd be nice for Seth to meet their nearest and dearest, and feel welcomed into the fold. Quinn hoped Phoebe would come down as well to meet her fellow grandparent. She had more than twenty years on Seth, but Quinn thought they'd get on like a house on fire.

Alex glared at Quinn from between the bars of the cot, preparing to holler if she so much as considered leaving the room.

"Okay, you little rascal, perhaps a walk will lull you to sleep," Quinn said. She was tired, but fresh air would do her good, and besides, she had much to consider.

She dressed Alex for the outdoors, settled him in his pram, and headed out the door and toward the lift. Emma was at school, and Gabe at work, so she and the baby were on their own. The day outside was overcast, but not unpleasant. Falling leaves twirled in the air, landing at Quinn's feet as she walked down the street, enjoying the autumn chill. She used to hate this time of year, when everything began to shrivel up and die, but she'd learned to see the beauty in bare branches interlaced against the cool blue of the autumn sky, and enjoy the anticipation of the upcoming holiday season, since for the first time since her parents had retired to Spain she had a family to spend Christmas with.

Got you! Quinn thought gleefully as Alex's eyelids began to droop after nearly half an hour of walking. Perhaps now she could find a bench and sit down for a while. What a blessing mobile phones were for new mums. While Alex slept, Quinn was able to catch up on her correspondence, return calls, send texts, and even do some research. She'd been reading up on the Wars of the Roses, but still hadn't returned to the past to see what had happened after Kate's death.

Now that Alex was six weeks old and Quinn was almost fully healed from the cesarean section, it was time to return to work. Rhys was patiently—or more accurately, impatiently—waiting for her report, desperate to begin the casting process for the new episode. The series finale was already in production, being filmed on a sound stage in Wales that had been transported to the pre-Civil War South, and the first episode of *Echoes from the Past* was due to air in a few weeks. It was time to complete her presentation for this episode and move on to the next one, yet to be determined, though Rhys had said he had a few ideas in the works.

There was much to accomplish on a personal front as well. After much deliberation, Phoebe had decided to sell the manor house and move into a retirement community in Berwick. Her guilt at parting with her husband's ancestral home was diluted by the promise of being closer to her dear friend Cecily Preston-Jones and the lure of all the activities they could enjoy together. The retirement community offered a wide range of classes for seniors, which appealed to Phoebe, who'd never really pursued any hobbies besides looking after her husband. She'd always wanted to try pottery and was warming up to the idea of chair yoga. Gabe fully supported Phoebe's plan to sell, and had promised to do everything in his power to make the process easier for his mum.

"Once the house is sold and the death duties are paid, I will give what's left to you," Phoebe had promised. "With the proceeds from the sale of your own homes, you'll be able to afford a nice, spacious house in London for your growing family." Phoebe had been barely able to keep the smile off her face as she contemplated more grandchildren. "Your father would have wanted you to have the money," she'd explained, silencing Gabe's protests. "He left me comfortably provided for."

Quinn had to admit that the prospect of a house of their own thrilled her. Perhaps it would even have a garden where the children could play and she and Gabe could enjoy on fine days. They were terribly cramped in Gabe's flat, but Quinn's little chapel in Suffolk was even smaller, never having been intended to house a family. She'd be sorry to part with it, but now that she was married with two children, she no longer had any use for it. She hoped whoever bought it would get as much pleasure and solace from it as she had.

The wind picked up and the sky darkened, threatening rain. Quinn put away her mobile and sprang to her feet. It was time to return home. She set a brisk pace, hoping to outrun the downpour and actually made it into the foyer of the building just as fat, lazy raindrops began to plop onto the sidewalk. Tonight, once Alex was down for the night, she would ask Gabe for the sword and see what had transpired after Kate hemorrhaged to death. Quinn didn't relish witnessing Guy's heartbreak, but it was time to find out how this sad tale ended.

Chapter 77

May 1465

Berwick-upon-Tweed, Northumberland

Guy had retreated to his room after the picnic under the pretense of having a headache. He did have one, though it wasn't bad enough to shun the company of others. But making small talk with Eleanor and conversing with Hugh as if nothing out of the ordinary were about to occur was more than he could manage. He'd rehearsed his speech dozens of times, but every time he imagined confronting Hugh, his stomach muscles clenched and his conscience gnawed at his heart.

Choosing between duty and love was no easy thing, even if he'd known all along who the victor would be. Hugh would not take the news well, especially now that Kate was with child. Had they attempted to get an annulment before Kate conceived, Hugh might have been easier to convince since he'd then be free to marry again. A new wife meant a new opportunity to make his fortune and start a family. But now, Guy would have to tell Hugh the truth about the child, an insult Hugh would never forgive or forget. Hugh might even wish to resolve this conflict with swords, a fight to the death to preserve his honor. Guy wouldn't put it past him, and in truth, he might have been driven to do the same had Hugh cheated him of his wife and heir.

Guy sighed, filled with self-loathing. He should have left as soon as Hugh married Kate and stayed away indefinitely. He had no right to love his brother's wife, nor had he acted honorably when he allowed his love to cross the line between the emotional and the physical. Being with Kate was the most sublime thing he'd ever experienced, but it was also the most underhanded, reprehensible act of his life, and no amount of self-flagellation would ever atone for the injustice he'd done to Hugh. He'd talked Kate into his chosen course of action, but would she ever be happy, even if they managed to secure an annulment? Would she ever forgive herself for the dishonor she'd brought to Hugh and the de Rosel family, or would she blame Guy for bullying her into going against her vows, her faith, and her conscience? Lying with him had been bad enough, but openly telling the world that she'd been unfaithful to her husband, conceived a child with another man, and wished to be excused from her marriage vows because she wished to be with her lover was something else entirely. Perhaps he'd been wrong to push so hard. Kate was torn, and terrified of the consequences of their actions, and perhaps her continued sickness was a manifestation of her internal struggle.

Guy folded his arms behind his head and stared at the tester above him. The die had been cast and no amount of recrimination would alter the situation. If he wanted to live with Kate and be a father to his child—which he did, more than life itself—he had to confront Hugh.

Guy didn't immediately react to the screams that seemed to reverberate through the walls of the keep. Perhaps Eleanor had seen a rat. She'd never become used to the vile creatures, no matter how many of them she'd come across over the years. But the screaming got louder and was followed by the sound of running feet. Something was wrong. Guy sprang to his feet and sprinted through the door and down the stairs.

Everyone seemed to be crowded by Hugh and Kate's bedchamber. Eleanor was weeping in the doorway, and Alf, Jed, and Walter stood about in stunned silence, staring at something just beyond Eleanor's shoulder. Nurse was inside, her normally calm voice sounding hysterical and weepy. Guy pushed past Eleanor and exploded into the room, desperate to know what had happened, but he wasn't prepared for the sight that met his eyes.

Hugh was down on his knees, his arms wrapped about his middle, as if he were trying to hold himself together, his forehead pressed against the wooden bedframe. Guy couldn't see his face, but he could tell by the heaving of Hugh's shoulders that he was crying. Nurse stood next to him, her hand on his shoulder as she stared at the bed, keening. Guy advanced into the room, but the

451

urgency to discover what had happened had left him. His heart already knew what he would find, and he wanted to run, without stopping until he exhausted himself enough to fall into a dreamless sleep from which he'd never wake.

The bed hangings were partially closed, but once Guy stepped around the side of the bed, he could see clearly. Kate lay uncovered on the bed, her eyes wide open, staring at something just off to the left, her face frozen in a grimace of pain. Her skirts were bunched up, the fabric soaking up the dark red blood that pooled beneath her hips. A tiny baby lay between her legs, its nearly translucent skin covered in blood. Its eyes were closed and it was curled into itself, but beneath the slimy cord that tethered the child to Kate's body was the unmistakable stub that identified the child as being male.

The desperate sob that tore from Guy's chest forced Hugh to look up. He staggered to his feet and came toward Guy, catching him in a bear hug. "She's gone, brother. She's gone," he cried. "And so is my son."

"What happened?" Guy cried, his anguish there for anyone to behold. "I don't understand. She seemed fine at the picnic."

"She took her own life," Nurse replied. She held up a small brown vial. "This is oil of rue. Some use it to dislodge a babe from the womb, but a large dose is fatal. Perhaps she got the notion from Aileen, who'd used the same poison."

"But why?" Hugh cried, his voice hoarse with agony. "Why would she do that? She was so excited about the coming babe, so filled with hope for the future."

Guy grabbed for the basin just in time as his innards turned themselves inside out and he retched and retched, until he sank to the floor and curled into a ball on the cold stone. He knew why Kate had done it. She couldn't bear the weight of her guilt or the fear of what was about to happen. Taking her own life, which she'd see as the ultimate sin, had been preferable to what he was about to subject her to. He'd as good as killed her. He'd killed his love, and his baby. And Kate, as a final act of atonement, had become the instrument of her own punishment, since as a suicide she'd be forever condemned to hell, her remains denied proper burial.

Guy forced himself to his feet. He was eviscerated by grief, but he couldn't allow anyone to discover the truth. No one could know what he and Kate had meant to each other, or what they'd planned to do. Hugh was already devastated by his loss, and Guy would do anything to spare Kate further shame or judgement. The truth would die with him when the time came.

"Come," Guy said to Hugh as he wrapped an arm about his brother. "Come away."

Hugh looked at Guy, his eyes unseeing. He seemed utterly lost, as if he suddenly had no idea where he was or what had just happened.

"Come, Hugh," Guy urged him.

"Ye go on, pet," Nurse said to Hugh. "I'll see to Kate and the babe. Ye shouldn't see her like this. This shouldn't be yer last memory of her."

Hugh nodded and allowed Guy to steer him toward the door, but not before Guy watched Nurse slip the vial into her pocket. There was nothing odd in that—she wouldn't leave poison lying about—but the one thing he had noticed, even in his state of shock, was the writing on the bottle, the penmanship that of his late mother. The label was written in tiny letters, the ink faded after years of exposure to the light. Kate would never have been able to read that. Her sight was failing. Had she perhaps been seeking relief from her sickness and taken the wrong thing by mistake? Was there hope that she hadn't done this awful deed on purpose? The knowledge that she hadn't taken her own life wouldn't bring her back, but it would ease his heart. God would still take her into his embrace, as well as their son, and grant them life everlasting. Salvation would have meant everything to Kate.

Guy and Hugh spent the night in the parlor, drinking themselves into a stupor and talking about Kate. Neither one could bear to be alone yet. They were united in their loss, bound by grief. Hugh didn't understand the extent of Guy's loss, but he'd recognized that Guy bore great affection for his sister-in-law and leaned on him for support, knowing that Guy was likely the only person who could truly understand his grief. By the time the first rays of the sun sliced through the gloom of the parlor, a decision had been made, and a pact had been struck.

Kate would not be buried at a crossroads with a spike through her heart, as was the custom with suicides. They would bury her in the chapel in consecrated ground, in the place that had meant the most to her and where she'd found solace in life and would also find peace in death. No one would learn the truth of what had happened. No one. For if word got to Father Jonas, he might order to have Kate's remains exhumed and reburied as the Church demanded. She would be forever safe beneath the stone floor of the chapel, sleeping peacefully with her rosary in her hands.

By the time Hugh and Guy abandoned the parlor, Kate's body had been washed and wrapped in a shroud—one that Nurse had prepared for herself to be used when the time came. Kate's remains were laid out on the table, a thick candle burning at each end.

"Where's the child?" Hugh asked.

"In there, with her."

Hugh nodded. "Come, brother. Let's go dig a grave."

"Dig a grave?" Nurse asked, gaping at them.

"Kate's to be buried in the chapel," Hugh replied, his tone brooking no argument.

"But she's a suicide," Nurse protested. "It's a sin to keep it from the Church. And she died unshriven."

Hugh paled, his eyes boring into his old nurse. "Kate will be buried in consecrated ground with all the respect due to her. And if you ever breathe a word of what transpired to anyone, you will find yourself buried right next to her. Do you understand?" Hugh 'didn't raise his voice, but the depth of his threat was clear.

"Aye, do as ye will," Nurse conceded.

They held the funeral for Kate in the evening. The chapel was hardly large enough to accommodate all six of them, but they wanted to pay their respects to her. Hugh, Guy, and Eleanor stood closest to the grave, with Alf, Jed, and Walter bringing up the rear. The chapel was alight with candles, the tiny flames dancing in the draft from the ill-fitting window and casting eerie shadows onto the mourners. After Hugh did a reading from the Bible, Guy and Walter filled in the grave and replaced the stone slabs. There would be no mark on the stones, and no name or date etched into eternity. Kate would remain hidden forever, safe in her resting place.

After the funeral, they all retired to the hall where Nurse had laid a cold supper in honor of Kate's memory. Eleanor sat next to Hugh and spent the meal seeing to his every need. He hardly seemed to notice her ministrations, but Eleanor was patient. She'd had to be.

Guy waited until everyone had gone to sleep before returning to the chapel. He was exhausted, and his arms ached from digging the grave and lifting the heavy stone slabs, but there was one more thing he had to do, and he had to do it in secret. Guy removed his doublet, rolled up the sleeves of his shirt, and reached for a crowbar. He'd dig all night if he had to, but he'd lay his sword in Kate's hands before morning came. It was the most precious thing he owned, and he wished for Kate and his son to be buried with it. It was the only honor he could accord his loved ones, and he'd see it done. And once the new day dawned, he'd leave Castle de Rosel, maybe not for good, but for a time. He couldn't bear to remain in the place where he'd loved and lost so much.

As Guy left his childhood home the following morning, a spare sword he'd taken from the armory slapping against his hip, he suspected that Hugh would marry Eleanor within the year. The marriage would be based on lukewarm affection and mutual gain. Hugh would continue as lord of the manor until Adam was ready to take up the management of the estate, but would remain nominally in charge for the rest of his life, being Adam's stepfather. Hugh would be set for life, one way or another. And Eleanor was still young enough to bear children, so perhaps Hugh would become a father after all. He genuinely cared for Adam, or so Guy wanted to believe, but if the boy fell in battle or died of an illness, Hugh's child would become the next Baron de Rosel.

Guy knew he would never marry. Kate had been his great love, and he would honor her by remaining pure for the rest of his life, however long that might be. From this day on, he'd live by the sword, and hopefully, die by the sword, since his life had become a burden to him. He no longer had a reason for being, but didn't dare end it all in the hope that Kate's death was accidental and they might meet again in the afterlife.

Guy spurred on his horse, eager to get away from Castle de Rosel. He'd get to London after Ascension Sunday and offer his services to Warrick, if the earl was still there. Guy wasn't sure of anything at the moment, but there were two things he knew for a fact—the conflict between the houses of Lancaster and York was not over, and the Earl of Warrick would not be thwarted in his plans to see one of his daughters as the Queen of England, a dream that was no longer as accessible as it had been even a year ago since rumor had it that King Edward had refused Warwick's request for a betrothal between his brother Richard and Anne Neville. There would be another rebellion, and there would always be another battle. Guy's life might have some purpose yet, even if that purpose wasn't his own.

Chapter 78

November 2014
London, England

Just past noon, a steady rain fell outside the plate-glass window, the feeble light of the gloomy afternoon resembling dusk. Rhys removed his reading glasses and laid Quinn's report on his ultra-modern desk, his gaze thoughtful as he his eyes met hers. "This will not do. We don't know what really happened. Our viewers need closure."

"I don't know what really happened, Rhys. I'm not Miss Marple. I can't conveniently solve the crime by the final chapter and explain my reasoning for the benefit of those who missed the clues."

"I know that," Rhys replied irritably, "but we need to come up with an ending that will give us a ratings boost. What are your thoughts? Who'd want to murder Kate?"

"We don't know that she was murdered."

"She believed she was."

"Yes, she did."

"So let's theorize," Rhys suggested. "You go first."

Quinn leaned back in her chair and considered the possibilities. She'd analyzed all this before, but perhaps Rhys would find a new angle. "The only people who might have wished Kate harm would be Hugh and Eleanor. Hugh might have found out about the affair and realized the child wasn't his. This would be an easy way to get rid of both Kate and the child, and punish Guy in the process. With Kate gone, his pride would be salvaged and he could get on with his life, as we know he did."

"And Eleanor?"

"Eleanor was trapped. She was a woman, still in her mid-twenties, who, for all intents and purposes, had been buried alive. Hugh would never allow her to remarry, for fear of losing his home and the income he pilfered from Adam. Her only hope was to marry Hugh and regain the status of wife, rather than remain a widow for the rest of her days. With Hugh, she would still be close to her son and possibly have more children."

"Would she really kill Kate?"

"They say poison is a woman's weapon of choice. Perhaps she did."

"Doesn't seem likely though, does it? And what happened to the baby? There were no bones of an infant discovered with Kate's remains, were there?"

"No. Joan said the baby was buried with Kate, but there was no evidence to support that. Perhaps it was buried separately and the bones were too tiny to notice when we searched the surrounding area. We might have mistaken them for the bones of a bird or a mammal."

"Hmm."

"What's your theory?" Quinn asked. She could already see the gleam of creativity shining in Rhys's eyes.

"In the episode, Hugh, having recalled how effectively rue killed the unfortunate Aileen, will use the poison on Kate after learning of her infidelity. He wasn't overly pleased with the marriage to start with, and finding out that his wife and his brother were playing him for a fool would be enough to push him over the edge. Oh, he'd play the grieving husband, but he'd send Guy a clue that he was aware of what was going on under his nose, and allow him to wonder for the rest of his days whether Hugh had actually murdered Kate and the child or whether Kate died by accident."

"And how would Hugh do all that without actually confronting Guy and confessing to the murder?"

"The sword. A knight's sword was his most precious possession. By burying the sword with Kate, Hugh would be letting Guy know that he was aware of their connection, and that he was burying everything that was precious to Guy in one grave: his lover, his child, and his weapon. I think the viewers will love that. Very dramatic."

"And that's why you're so good at what you do. I have to get going," Quinn said, checking her watch. "I have a Thanksgiving dinner to prepare for. I'm in charge of cornbread and collard greens."

"You'll be getting a dual citizenship next," Rhys joked as he got up to walk Quinn out. "I'm glad things are going well with you and your father. How's Alex taken to him?"

"Like powdered sugar to a beignet."

Rhys laughed. "Enjoy your dinner, and don't get too comfortable. I have a new case to discuss with you."

"You have the subject for the next episode?"

"Indeed, I do, but I wouldn't want to ruin all this family fun. Ring me tomorrow. You're going to love this one," Rhys said with a merry twinkle in his eye.

"I take it there's no urgency?"

"Oh, this poor sod is not going anywhere."

Rhys kissed Quinn's cheek and gave her a wave as she got in the lift. Quinn leaned against the wall and smiled. Tomorrow, she'd find out what Rhys had in store for her, but tonight, she'd enjoy a dinner of unfamiliar delicacies with the people she loved best in the world. She had much to be thankful for.

Epilogue

Joan was the last to leave the chapel after Kate's burial. She was about to return to the kitchen—she had supper to serve—when her hand closed around the smooth glass of the vial she'd taken from Kate's bedside. Joan trudged up the stairs to the top floor and walked to the end of the silent corridor, where she entered what had been Marie de Rosel's solar. No one went in there anymore—no one save Joan.

A heavy wooden cabinet stood in the corner, a brass key protruding from the lock on its ornate door. Joan turned the key and took out a small polished chest. Inside were several vials, carefully labeled in Marie's elegant hand. Joan didn't know her letters, but she could identify the medicines by their smell. It'd taken her no more than three sniffs to locate the oil of rue. Marie had used the rue to treat a multitude of conditions, such as her frequent headaches, the occasional toothache, and even bouts of anxiety, but she'd never taken it during pregnancy; she'd known the risks. Joan replaced the vial in the chest and shut the lid. She closed the cabinet and sat down on the window seat to rest, hands folded in her lap. This spot had been Marie's favorite place to sit during the day since she could enjoy the breathtaking view from the tower while she sewed or read, or just dreamed. She'd been a dreamer, Marie, just like Guy.

Joan wasn't a dreamer; she was a realist. She knew she'd committed an unforgivable sin and was more than ready to accept her punishment when the time came. She'd given the rue to Kate, and then placed the vial by her bed just before she began to scream, having pretended to discover Kate's body. She'd killed Kate and the child, and she felt no remorse. Furthermore, she'd thrown the child's remains into the fire. It didn't deserve to be buried in consecrated ground. It'd never been born, and never been baptized. That child was a product of sin, an abomination in the

460

eyes of God, and it had no right to be buried with the same respect Joan's own children had received when she lost them.

She was guilty, but she couldn't stand idly by as that harlot tore her boys apart and destroyed the good name of the family Joan had served since she was a child. Oh, Marie had given birth to those boys, and not an easy labor among the three, but it was Joan who'd nursed them and loved them, and sat with them when their teeth came in or when they were ill. It was Joan who had held them to her breast and whispered soothing words when they fell and scraped their knees, and Joan who had comforted them when their parents died. It was also Joan who'd enveloped Guy in her love after Margaret died, and helped him become whole again. There was nothing she could have done to save William—he'd died bravely on the battlefield—but she'd be damned if she allowed that sinful woman to come between her remaining children.

Hugh and Guy would grieve for Kate, each in his own way, but then they would move on, the way men did. They would find other women to love, and have children to call their own, but most of all, they would still have each other, and there was no greater bond after that of mother and child than the bond between brothers. They were de Rosels, and they would survive.

Joan finally rose to her feet, ready to return to the kitchen. She had to clean out what remained of the child's bones before anyone noticed them in the ash bed and suspected they weren't the bones of a pheasant.

"I did it for our boys, Marie," she said to the ghost of the woman she'd once loved. "I did it for our children."

The End

Please look for The Unseen (Echoes from the Past Book 5) Coming Soon

Notes

I hope you've enjoyed this installment of the *Echoes from the Past* series. I've always been interested in the Wars of the Roses and it was fascinating for me to research the period and set my characters amid all that political and personal strife. And as you've learned, there are some interesting developments for Quinn as well.

And now, a brief word about book five. The Unseen delves into the Russian Revolution and my own family's background. Sadly, I don't come from royalty or even nobility, but one of the characters in the book is based on my grandfather, who was a very enterprising young man and published his own newspaper during his student days. He was the first writer in the family, and whatever creative talents I possess, I owe to him. I hope you enjoy the story.

If you'd like to receive updates about new releases and promotions, please join my mailing list by clicking the link bellow. You can also reach me through my website or email. I'm always thrilled to hear from you.

http://irinashapiroauthor.com/mailing-list-signup-form/
www.irinashapiroauthor.com
irina.shapiro@yahoo.com.

And lastly, if you've enjoyed the book, a review on Amazon or Goodreads would be much appreciated.

35506094R00269

Printed in Great Britain
by Amazon